THE SERPENT'S DEEP

THE SERPENT'S DEEP

CHRONICLES OF TAROTLAND

KILLIAN WOLF

ISBN:

Copyeditor: Sara Lawson - sarasbooks.com
Cover design: Logan Keys - coverofdarknessdesign.com
Conlanger: Christian Thalmann - twitter.com/thalmach
Map designer: Zentra Brice
Header designer: Etheric Designs - ethericales.com/etheric-designs
Formatter: Michael Davie - grimhousepub.com/plans-pricing

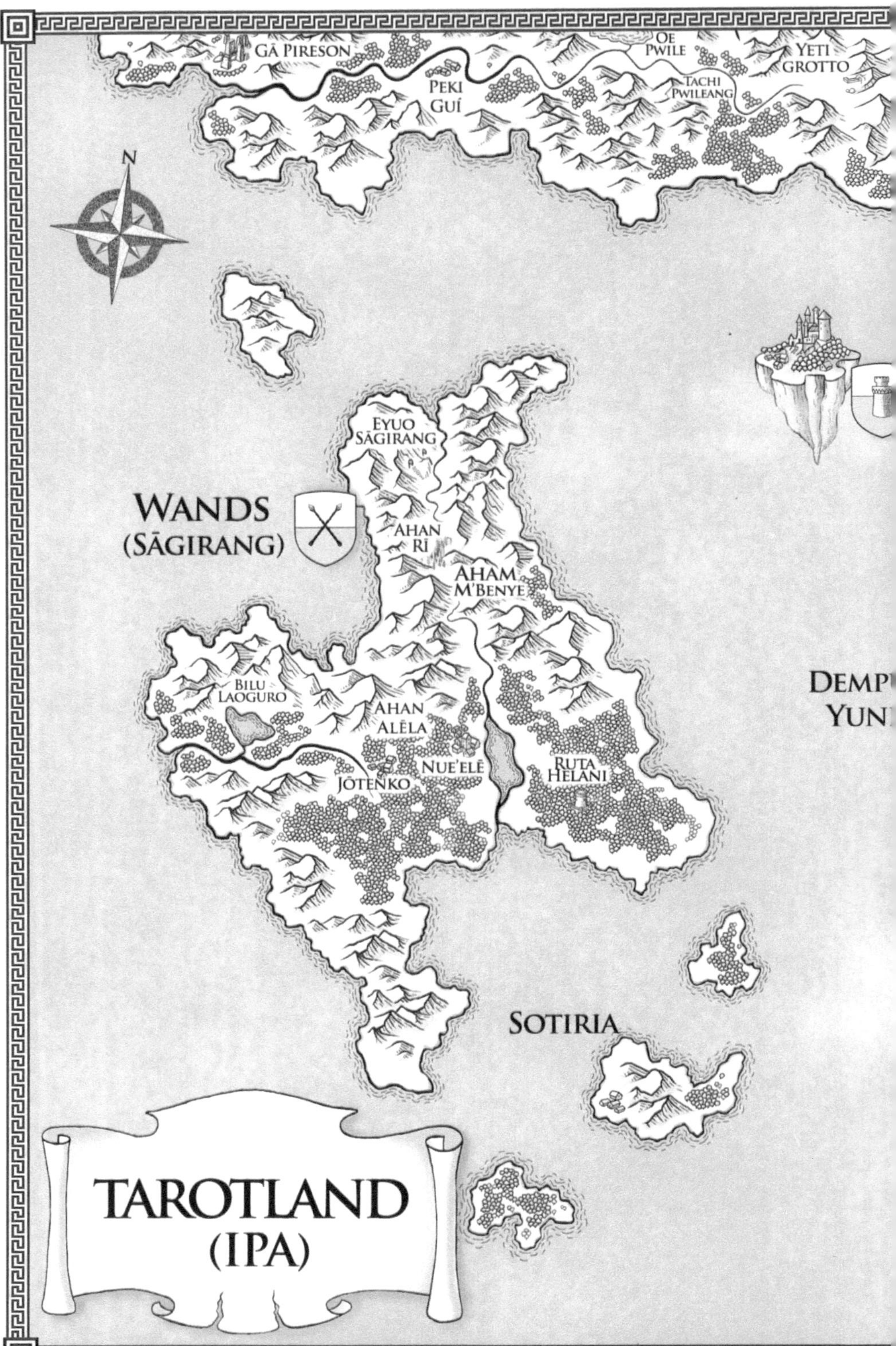

GĀ PIRESON
PEKI GUÍ
OE PWILE
TACHI PWILEANG
YETI GROTTO
N
EYUO SĀGIRANG
WANDS (SĀGIRANG)
AHAN RĪ
AHAM M'BENYE
BILU LAOGURO
AHAN ALĒLA
NUE'ELĒ
JŌTENKO
RUTA HELANI
DEMP
YUN
SOTIRIA
TAROTLAND (IPA)

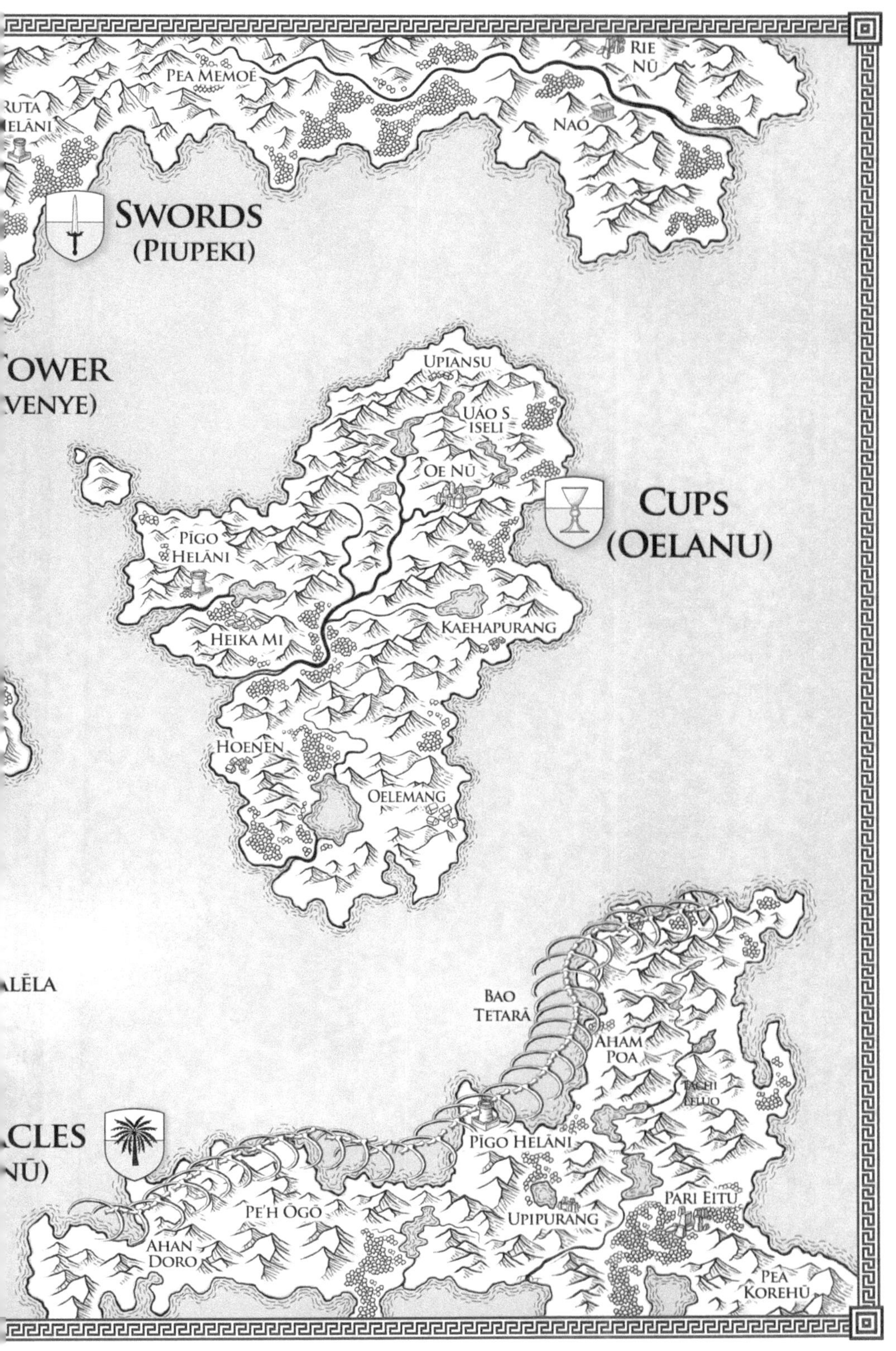

RIE NŪ
PEA MEMOÉ
RUTA
NAÓ
SWORDS
(PIUPEKI)
OWER
VENYE)
UPIANSU
UÁO S ISELI
OE NŪ
CUPS
(OELANU)
PĪGO HELĀNI
KAEHAPURANG
HEIKA MI
HOENEN
OELEMANG
LĒLA
BAO TETARĀ
AHAM POA
CLES
NŪ)
PĪGO HELĀNI
PARI EITU
PE'H ŌGŌ
UPIPURANG
AHAN DORO
PEA KOREHŪ

1

Every single person in this arena can drown in the Deep for all I care. Their cheering makes me sick. Betting on oumala animals to fight each other should be punishable by death, but instead, the Empress allows it.

Keep the people distracted with bloodshed while the rest of the world suffers by her hand.

My fingers trace the hilt of the dagger strapped to my thigh. The sooner we can get out of here, the sooner I can breathe again. Although, for as long as I've been doing this with the crew, I can never wash away the lingering stench of old blood mixed with ammonia.

The lanky guy with curly hair sitting in front of me roars. "*Diwe! Diwe! Diwe!*"

"The rabbit?" My features twist toward Harold who sits to my left. "It's so cute, though."

"You never got a chance to see one of those things attack back in Swords." Harold shifts from left to right, trying to see around the dude who keeps standing in front of him. "Jackass."

All his movement is making the frost fall from his blond hair onto my legs. I wipe it away. Poor guy was cured from the undead curse, but still has the curse of the frost giants. He's slowly being frozen from the inside out.

I squint at the bunny rabbit in the fighting cage. His white fur contrasts with his dark eyes. Cute and cuddly, he has no business being in a fight. The crowd cheers as the door slides open. A scrappy looking wolverine enters the ring. My grip tightens at the edge of my seat. "This can't be good. When's Kenjō coming out?"

Harold swallows. "Th-that should have been her. Something's wrong."

Shit.

The wolverine walks to the center of the ring, his eyes trained on the bunny. I don't know what kind of ouma this wolverine has but, whatever it is, a bunny isn't going to be any match for it. "So now we have the rabbit and the wolverine to save from the ring!" I whisper-shout.

Harold glances at the backdoor.

On the other side of the cage, Lāri's spiked pixie cut pokes up behind the Ipani in front of her. She stares at the fence door Kenjō should have come through with a worried expression on her face. She spots me staring at her, shrugs, and shakes her head.

"Alright, let's not panic," I tell him. "If something's truly wrong, AJ or Kae will give us a signal to move. I'm sure they just got held up." Panicking will only increase the risk of being found out, and fighting rings have recently been known to catch the whole place on ouma fire. If we burn, no amount of water will put us out. Everyone, including the animals will die. "They probably got held up with locking up the ouma fire wielding guard." Waiting until half our team locks up the guards and gives us the signal to move is how we've been infiltrating the fighting rings for the last six months.

"That's what I'm afraid of."

I frown at him and look back to the wolverine. The bunny hasn't made a move to flee, he's just sitting there unassuming, and wrinkling his nose. Doesn't he know how much danger he's in?

Harold stands. "I'll be back. Going to go check on them."

I shake my head. "You're gonna blow our cover."

The people behind us yell at him; Harold excuses himself and makes it to the steps. I stay in position, closest to the nearest exit. If they're just a little held up, the plan remains the same. If not, it won't take me long to sprint downstairs.

The wolverine leaps, his mouth gapes open and acid pours out of his raged teeth. I hold my mouth shut as the rabbit jumps back in time for the wolverine to land. Acid eats the floor right by the rabbit's feet.

No no no! Kenjō was supposed to be in the ring, not this wolverine. She was supposed to secure the oumala animal, while the crew in the back looses the other animals, and Kae secures the ouma fire guard. Harold and I were to hold back the crowd with Lāri. Even if I go down there, I can't open the cage by myself. I rip my gaze over to Lāri, who's up and moving swiftly down the stairs.

Oh no. Something *must* be wrong then.

The rabbit's eyes emulate a purple glow. His legs elongate, and his hair stands on end as his head arches back. His mouth widens at an abnormal width, showcasing growing piranha-like teeth. At an impossible speed, the rabbit lunges for the wolverine.

The crowd stands, blocking my view. Their shouts are amplified in the stadium. One of the guys in front of me starts smacking his buddy on the shoulder repeatedly as he laughs and points. I get up and squirm my way past people on my row, squeezing against the stairs.

My stomach sinks when I get a good view of the stage. The bunny sits in the middle of what no longer looks like a wolverine, but blood, guts, and fur. The bunny's white coat is tainted in red as it chews.

Harold wasn't kidding. Oumala rabbits are beasts.

Poor wolverine. We weren't supposed to let another animal die here today.

A voice amplifies from the speakers. "All bets will be collected at the end. Give a howl for the Piupeki diwe, and welcome its newest challenger. A natural predator for rabbits, it slithered its way from Oleanu. Let's all cheer for the oumala *siseli!*"

"Oy!" someone shouts at me. "Sit down!"

I ignore them. Lāri disappeared into the crowd, and I still haven't heard a signal from AJ or Kae. This is definitely weird.

The fence door rises, and I expect a snake to be thrown out onto the arena.

A double-roar freezes the audience instead as a jaguar jumps onto the platform, landing a foot next to the rabbit.

Kenjō.

Just then, a grappling hook shoots at the gate and pulls the metal apart. The cage fence crashes to the ground, and the audience screams as Tessa drags it back with her grapple gun. People jump out of the way, trying not get hit.

I guess we're improvising.

Quickly, I unlatch one of Kenjō's famous smoke bombs from my bandoleer and throw it far into the crowd. The glass shatters, releasing the blue fumes which in seconds will cause people to fall asleep at their feet. I sprint to the top of the stage, pulling away the remains of the metal cage. Kenjō shifts back to her human form.

"Are you okay?" I ask her.

She's out of breath. "Yes. You?"

"I'm fine. What took so long?"

She glances down at the rabbit and takes a step away from it. I do the same, quickly remembering this thing is a beast in disguise. Harold throws another smoke bomb to our side; he has a snake wrapped around his neck.

"The fire guard was expecting us." She pants. "We have to move."

I gape at her. "Where is he now?"

"Wounded. We had to let the animals out before I could come in."

I stare down at the bunny, still munching on wolverine meat, completely unconcerned about his surroundings. I guess he'll just leave at his own pace. All the other oumala animals should be long gone by now. Kenjō and I start to jump off the stage when fire surges against the walls.

"He must have gotten loose!" Kenjō yells.

Fumes rise as rows of seats start catching flame. She shifts to her jaguar form and I follow behind. A wooden pillar falls between us. I jump back, then spin around to face the rabbit. I need to get him to safety.

I squint through the flames and smoke for the crew but see no sign of anyone. Hopefully, they're all outside. I approach the bunny on the stage, but it backs away from me.

"Hey, little buddy. I just want to take you out of here."

The rabbit stares at me, his eyes give off a warning purple glow, but I don't back away. I wish I had a carrot or something to offer him. Or better yet, a piece of steak.

Another pillar crashes behind me, heating my backside. I'd better be quick.

"Come on little guy. We don't have time."

He opens his mouth, baring those piranha-like teeth. I pull my hand back. Sweat beads on my brow, and I start to cough into my shoulder. I lean close to the rabbit, and for only a second, I focus my intent, trying to make contact.

My ankle burns from the fumes. I slap my skin, the pain unyielding. That's going to scar. The fire is getting closer to the platform, and the rabbit is looks around, his ears pressed against his back. Upon closer look, I notice his eyes are blue. I've never seen one with blue eyes before.

"Don't be scared. Come with me." I close my eyes and try again, this time showing him a vision of me carrying him to safety. I have no idea if I'm just imaging stuff in my head—making no telepathic connection at all—or if this would actually work.

A magnetic force grabs my focus as he latches on. Connection made. I open my eyes and hold out my arms, hoping he gets the hint. The bunny jumps to my chest, and I wrap him close, turning to find a clear path out of here.

All the exits are blocked. I'll have to go the back way, but that involves going down the hall where the cages are kept. If it's blocked by fire, we're both dead.

But it looks like it's our only chance, so I move fast, stepping over pilings and seats. Fire blazes around us, but I don't lose sight of the hallway.

Once in, I make a run for it, ducking with my face low and holding the bunny close to my chest. The door at the end of the hall calls my name. I'm almost there.

A man steps out from one of the rooms holding a ball of fire in his right palm. The fire Ipani. His wide grin sends a shiver down my spine.

He's injured alright. He's missing his left arm, and blood drenches his torso, but the crazed look in his eyes says he wants revenge and taking me will suffice. I step back, reaching for a hū raku potion on my belt loop. Looking at his stature, I don't think a sleep bomb will bring this guy down, but poison gas just might.

Fire looms overhead and behind me, trapping us. "There's nowhere to run, little girl."

My hand moves across my belt feeling for a raku potion, but we only had enough left for me to have the one. I grasp my dagger and face him. "Come at me, you son of a bitch." He's injured. If it weren't for his fire ouma, I could probably take him. I would use magic to reach into his memories—pull something out that could harm him—but there isn't enough time.

The door behind him bursts open, but I can't see the figure through the smoke and flames. A metal arm grabs the fire Ipani's throat and shoves him against the wall so hard, the man goes through it. I blink a few times and make out Kae standing there, his body fully covered in metallic armadillo scales.

"Thanks," I say.

He grunts and leads the way out.

The rest of the crew is coughing on the ground.

AJ gapes at me and stands. "Are you out of your mind!"

Petting the bunny, I place him on the grass.

"Next time, leave the rabbit, Soren!" he yells.

Tears sting my eyes, but I hold them back. I stare at him square in the face. "No. I will not leave the rabbit. Too many animals died today, and the rabbit didn't even know what the hell was happening. He was defenseless!"

Harold hands me a canteen of water. "Yeah, but at the end of the day, you could've gotten killed. We can't save them all."

"Yes, we can!" I scream. "We can. And I'm not sorry for saving the rabbit." I turn to face Kaehante. "You didn't have to come back for me."

Kae stands there. He's breathing hard and his eyes are trained on me, but he's not saying a word.

Tessa turns her wheelchair to face me. "Why was it so important to you to save one rabbit?"

"Are you all kidding me right now? I thought saving the oumala animals was the point of all this!"

"Yes. But not at the expense of your life, Soren."

I squeeze my eyes shut and breathe. "It's—it's what Nkella would have done." I open my eyes again. Kenjō and Lāri are staring down at the ground.

"My cousin would not risk putting his crew in danger. You were reckless." Kaehante's words bite through the dense air.

My chest tightens. "Like I said, you didn't have to come back for me."

He turns his gaze away. My breathing is shallow. I stare back down at the bunny that's wiggling his nose.

Lāri hands me the potion to take off the ouma dampener. I'd almost forgotten about that. The rabbit probably won't let anyone else near him. I reach down and release a few drops from the small bottle onto his paw with the orange stripe. When the stripe disappears, the rabbit pulls me in, giving me a psychic nuzzle. I smile inwardly as he hops off into the woods. Saving his life might not matter that much to them, but it matters to this one bunny. He gets to live.

"Alright, let's all calm down," Tessa says. "Let's go home."

"Anyone have any ouma water?" Harold asks, scratching his head at the fire. A bit of frost falls from his hair.

"That's a negative," Tessa reverses her chair and readies herself for the hike home. "And we would need a whole lot."

"Forget ouma water," AJ says. "The ouma fire will be a nice little gift for the owners of the ring to take care of. Or the Arcana soldiers. Either one." He grins.

Kenjō places a gentle hand on Harold's shoulder as he stares at the burning building. "Oumala fire is a controlled flame, meant to burn in a specific range. It can't be put out by normal water, so there's really nothing we can do about it."

"I know. I'm just scared the fumes will reach higher and burn the trees and birds..." He lets her pull him away, but I stay a moment longer to stare at the flames. I rub my palm where it aches from tightening my grip so hard. I'm still stuck on what Kae told me. Nkella wouldn't risk putting his crew in danger. I was reckless.

Maybe he's right. But I still don't regret saving the rabbit. Taking down these rings and saving animals has kept me going these past six months. It's all we can do at the moment, and it gives us something honorable to do while Tetalla wages war on the Empress, and we're all stuck on our islands.

We head back through the woods to the Dempu Yuni beach.

"Why won't she use her Fate magic?" Kenjō's voice is just above a whisper. "She could have wrapped that guy in webs and stabbed him." Mumbling follows, and I slow my step to get away from their audible concern. I don't want to explain myself. I want to go back to who I was before magic and the Fates, to get away from anything that can cause more harm than good.

An owl hoots deep in the trees and diverts my attention.

AJ falls into step with me. "How are you feeling? You were in the fire longer than any of us."

"I'm okay," I say, still listening for the sounds of an owl's hoot, or the whispers of the wind among the trees.

After a few beats, he speaks again. "At least he's talking to you. That's an improvement, isn't it?"

I offer him a sheepish grin. "Yeah, even if it is to berate me."

"Just give it time, Soren. Kae will come around."

I scoff. "It's been six months, and honestly, AJ, I don't want him to forgive me." My throat clogs, but I still muster the words. "I don't deserve for any of you to forgive me."

He opens his mouth to speak but I yelp and fall into him as something prickly wraps around my leg. A corpse gapes with his only eye as a maggot wriggles out of the other socket. I kick to release my leg from his strong grip.

"Hold still," AJ whips out his gun. I cover my ears as he shoots it in the head three times. I manage to free myself from his grip after the last shot, shaking my legs and arms in disgust. No matter how many times the dead touch me, it always grosses me out.

"AJ, are you okay?" Lāri comes running back from the path, the crew behind her. "What happened?"

"Dead guy grabbed Soren again."

Her forehead wrinkles. "Don't stay behind, mei?"

We both nod and pick up our step. "Thanks," I tell AJ.

"We're crew. We have each other's backs. And as for what happened...it wasn't your fault. I don't believe it was, and deep down, neither does Kae."

I turn to keep walking, but he stops me.

"Hey, listen to me." His voice is soft when he says it, caring in every way. It only makes me feel more guilty. I stare at him and take a deep breath, cocking my head to the side. His shoulders drop. "Fine, we don't have to talk now, but this conversation isn't over."

"Okay." And that's all I say. I don't want to talk about it.

"We do need to find out why the dead keep grabbing you, though. What does Death want with you?"

"Beats me." I shrug, waiting for him to ask me if I've had any visions or dreams about Tetalla.

"You're sure you haven't—"

"I haven't."

He sighs. "Okay."

We walk in silence the rest of the way to the tree house. Nkella left it for his crew before I came and helped him save them from being a pile of bones under the sea. Because of what Nkella did, they're no longer cursed. They're all alive, and the rikorō was stripped away from my system. It was killing me, and his sacrifice saved me.

We reach the round three-story tree house, and I head straight to my room on the third floor. We've made some alterations since we moved in—with the Hermit's help. He likes to come around from time to time to bring us supplies. He never stays long because he enjoys his solitude, but I get the feeling he does enjoy our company. And I like having him around.

We now have a fully working kitchenette, sinks, bathrooms, and bedrooms. In the beginning, they continued sleeping in the *Gambit*, while I stayed in here. I didn't feel like staying in that tiny room right next to everyone, when...well, we weren't all on the best of terms.

Tessa would leave anytime Nkella came up; she never agreed with me about bringing my mom back from the dead, so she completely avoids the topic. And Kae still hates me.

I make it to the washroom I share with Lāri and Kenjō and start to clean myself up before they come up.

I would have gone home months ago, but Talia is still here. No matter how I'm feeling, I won't abandon her. And apparently, the crew won't abandon me either. Personally, I think they keep me around because I'm a Fate, and they believe I can put an end to this war between the Empress and Death.

I turn on the faucet and run my hands under the cold water, bringing it to my face. I don't know how to end a war between two powerful beings. The Empress and I nullify each other's powers, so all I can do is help the crew take down oumala fighting rings.

When I'm done washing up, I lean over the railing of the open floor hut, and stare at the crew sitting on the first floor. I plan on grabbing a plate of food to eat by myself on the beach, since lately, I don't like chatting with them during meals.

"Has anyone heard from Ntaoru?" Lāri asks before taking a sip of water. She has a plate full of lettuce and other vegetables.

"Not yet," Tessa says. "I'm sure she'll come around soon enough. You know how she is. She's dealing with things in her own way."

AJ takes a large plate of fish and takes a seat next to Tessa. I smile to see them eating. I'm glad they're no longer undead and can taste food. "I thought taking down fighting rings would be something she'd want to do."

Tessa shrugs. "She's finding herself. Give her time. She was under the Empress's control for a long time. I don't think she wants to be around fighting rings just yet."

"I know, just thought it would be cathartic for her to stop them," he says.

The candle-lit oil lamps that decorate the walls illuminate the steps as I make my way down to them. "We don't know what she's doing," I say, announcing myself as I reach the bottom steps. "Maybe she's saving animals but just doesn't want to be around me."

Kaehante turns his head to face the wall as I reach the bottom of the stairs. The others grow silent. I grab a plate of fish and walk outside. Kenjō and Harold glance at me and smile, but they're sitting pretty close and I don't want to be a third wheel.

Out by the *Gambit*, I sit with my feet touching the waves.

Seawater singes the burn on my ankle from earlier, and I stare down at it, letting the pain remind me of what I've done.

I stare at the water rising to my calves, trying to imagine the glistening scales that used to appear whenever salt water touched my skin. I remembered diving into the depths and feeling so free. No restrictions on where I could walk or where I could swim. The sight. The touch. The superior hearing.

Him.

The way he looked at me the first time we were both submerged underwater. Experiencing the beauty of underwater for the first time together, even if we were on a rescue mission. His thoughts. His heartbeat.

The feel of his lips. My yearning for his touch... Soon after it happened, I found myself needing him more than wanting to be awake. I remembered awakening from a dream of him screaming in the Deep, his emotions making me feel like I was really there. Feeling his torment with him. I'd still yearn for the nightmare over the reality of him being gone.

The waves crash against each other methodically under the moonlight. Sometimes even staring at the ocean hurts.

When Nkella's sacrifice cured me of the rikorō's poison, I also lost my mer-Ipani powers. Part of me feels guilty for wanting them back because they had belonged to someone whose life was taken in order to create the rikorō. But another part of me is jealous that Kenjō got to keep her jaguar ouma after Harold made his sacrifice so she wouldn't die.

I couldn't ask her to make me a new rikorō potion to let me keep the power. And besides, the rikorō Nkella and I had drunk was used up.

Kenjō still had the jaguar vial, so she was able to make more for herself. She had also perfected the concoction so it wouldn't kill her.

But she was bound from her ouma when she was a baby, so her new ouma is a semblance of who she was meant to be. At least, it allowed the Ipani who had been killed to live on within her.

It would be selfish of me to ask.

Except the only reason I wasn't born here was because the Empress killed my mom. I could have grown up here with ouma since my father was Ipani.

You may never get ouma on your own without rikorō.

I shake off the memory of Demitri's voice.

What does he know? Only now that I've had a taste of it, I can't help but imagine what my ouma would have been if I wasn't stripped of the life I would have had. Now that I've had a taste of it, I want more.

The mark on my arm rumbles, and the familiar pull of a vision coming through threatens to take me away. I glimpse Nkella's fierce eyes and shudder, shaking the vision away. Not now. I can't let myself get lost in the past. There's no point to it.

"Hey, birthday girl." AJ's voice cuts through the wind.

"It's not my birthday yet."

"One more day. Eighteen years old. How do you feel?"

I shrug. AJ takes a seat next to me.

"Can we talk about it?"

"AJ, please..."

"Soren," he sighs. "I miss the old crew dynamic. And you've already said you're staying—"

"Do you want me to leave?"

He gapes at me. "No. I want you to stay, I'm just saying, I think we're all ready to have you back."

"I haven't gone anywhere." I frown at him.

"You know what I mean. All of your sassy self." He gestures at my whole body, and I crack a smile.

"Not all of you."

He shrugs and stares out to sea. "Kae has always moved at a snail's pace. But none of us blame you for what happened. You have to know that."

I shake my head and stare out at the *Gambit* moving along with the crashing waves. "He trusted me."

"Kae?"

"Nkella." I breathe deeply. "I promised him I'd bring his sister back, so he helped me with my plan to bring my mom back. He ended up fixing my mess and brought his own sister back at the cost of his life. The crew doesn't deserve me. I don't blame Kae for not wanting me around, and I'm honestly surprised the others do."

"The thing is, Soren, Nkella was hardheaded as balls."

I chuckle. "Your point?"

"He sacrificed himself for all of us, not just you. He would have done it long before that if given the chance."

"But we were there because of me."

AJ gives me a pointed look. His long black hair wraps around his neck as he tugs at my arm so that I turn to fully face him. "You didn't make the rules of the Ace of Swords. He would have found out about it somehow—probably from Demitri at some point. I get that you failed to bring your mom back, and that mistake hurts like hell." I swallow at his words. "But Nkella's death doesn't fall on you. If you'd never come here, he would have eventually done the same to save us from the undead curse and to bring Ntaoru back from being Arcana." He grabs my arm. "So let that go."

My eyes start to swell, making my nose itch. I rub it and lean on AJ's shoulder. Nkella still wouldn't have been there if not for me, but I drop it. AJ's been trying hard to mend the crew and make sure I'm okay. He's like the best friend I never had. He's become the only person other than Talia that I can trust. I guess that does make him my best friend.

"We should get back. They're waiting on us to discuss where we're going next."

"Oh." I rub my nose and sit up. We've been lucky the last three animal fighting rings have been in Dempu Yuni so that we haven't had to camp or stay at any inns. Sometimes, we have Gari drop us off in Piupeki, or Wands. I must say, I've never thought taking down animal fighting rings would become a career. It's a far cry from working at a carnival, scamming people for their money with three-card monte tricks. This is more noble, even though it's against the Tower, since fighting oumala animals are completely legal. Sometimes we get hired by locals to take them down, but most of the time, we rob the guards of the event, and the hosts. And if I can, the attendees. Fuck them. Sick creeps.

We start to get up when the ground shakes below our feet. I hold onto AJ for balance, and he shields me with his arm as sand sprays our faces. Skeletal fingers claw out first—green skin hanging off phalanges—then the full arm. The head surfaces, and I grimace as its rotten flesh hangs off a cheekbone, covering a gaping hole. His eyes bulge out their sockets, and with a loud crack, his head snaps to face me.

I push AJ, urging him to walk, and he does so slowly, but I think he sees the same thing I do. There's something different about this one.

"I come to deliver a message from Death." His voice comes like a smokey whisper being carried by the wind.

"Uhh, Soren? Have they ever spoken to you before?"

"No."

We stare as the corpse rises to his feet. He wears a tattered vest, knee-high pants, and a torn tricorn hat. "I know who you are. You won't be able to resist me longer. I will find you."

2

Tessa and Kaehante argue with over each other in the open-air living room of the tree house as AJ tries to diffuse the argument. Oil lamps overhead hang along the spiral staircase, and I stare at the flickering flames of the candlelit room.

I know who you are. You won't be able to resist me longer. I will find you. Then his bones shattered to merge with the sand. What did he mean, he'll find me?

"Soren? Soren!"

I blink at AJ's face inches from mine. "Yeah?"

"Are you sure this has never happened before? The dead usually stay moaning in eternal torment. They don't just start having a conversation."

"No, this is the first time it's happened."

"Not even in a vision?"

I shake my head.

"Kh. She must be lying, daí?" Kaehante leans against the wall with his arms crossed in front of him, resembling his cousin even more in this moment. That stings. Six months ago, he would have backed me. Now he accuses me of lying and would trade me in to Tetalla in an instant.

I swallow. "Okay...I have been having visions, but not of that."

AJ slaps his sides and looks up at the ceiling. Kaehante scoffs.

"Why didn't you tell us?" AJ asks.

"Don't you trust us?" Tessa drives her chair closer to me, hurt and concern tinging her voice. Kenjō and Harold, who've been quietly sitting on the bottom step of the stairs exchange a glance.

"Because none of my visions were making sense. And I didn't lie. I haven't had visions of dead people talking to me."

"So what were your visions, hn?" Kaehante's eyes are accusing. I wish I could go back to Louisiana right now.

"They're..." I close my eyes for a moment and breathe out, "of Nkella. I think they're just dream-like memories. Nothing real."

Kaehante raises his brows, his features a little less hard, but he remains quiet.

"Philo visits me every few days," I continue. "She urges me to zoom into her pull, but I push her away." I pick at a loose thread at the end of my sleeve and twine it between my fingers. "My magic got people killed." Kenjō glances at me, and I avert my gaze. "Demitri was training me to be like the Empress, and historically, that's what a Fate would do —meddle and destroy people's lives. Me and Fate magic don't mix. Don't you understand?" I look to each of them. "It's best for everyone if I don't use my magic ever again. So forget about whatever visions are trying to get to me. Forget about what I could do, because I'm telling you—no, I promise you—the only thing that would become of me getting involved between the Empress and Tetalla is more death."

Silence befalls the room. I unwrap the loose thread from my finger, then start wrapping it again.

After a few beats, Lāri clears her throat. "I understand you, Soren. I think I speak for everyone when I say we should be celebrating rescuing those animals and planning the next rescue. But right now, it all feels kind of pointless. Like, we're ignoring the war literally outside our home."

The others nod in agreement.

"We can't force her, though," AJ says.

I scoff and raise my hands in the air. "I feel like you all think I can *actually* do something about the war. What do you all think I can do? I'm only a Past Fate, and the past has already happened. Do you want me to go to Danū and wrap webs around Tetalla? Do you think the Empress can't do that herself? I can't save the people from Danū either, guys. That's impossible for me or for all of us to do."

"You have the World Card, daí?" Kae lifts himself from the wall.

"Yes, of course I do," I pass my hands through my hair. "I retrieved it from Talia's memories the second I was able to. The Empress shouldn't have it. It was the least I could do to protect Asteria back home."

"Can you not use it to spy on Tetalla?" His eyes narrow at me.

I pinch the bridge of my nose. "Are you not hearing me? That would require me to use my powers. I can't get anyone else killed."

"If you don't do something, everyone in Danū will be killed." Wrinkles indent his forehead up to his bald head. He points a finger toward the ocean. "The Empress has brought her Arcana out from the middle of the sea to float all over Danū. Tetalla has his dead rising on land, and now," his voice lowers, "we know it's to search for you."

A chill runs down my spine. "So what would you have me do, Kae? Do you want me to give myself to Tetalla?"

"He was the leader of Danū. Maybe he wants you to defeat the Empress, daí?"

"Or he means to kill her," Lāri interjects. "Soren is also related to the Empress, and as far as he knows, the Empress is protecting her." She turns to me. "Didn't you say he blames the Empress for his lover's death? Maybe he wants revenge." The flickering candlelight makes shadows dance over her light Ipani stripes.

"I agree," AJ adds. "The way the dead guy spoke—*I will find you*—it didn't sound like he wanted to have a tea party."

"The sea is blocked anyway, there's no way into Danū, Kae." Kenjō's voice is soothing. "Taking down animal fights is the best we can do, and it's a good cause."

Kaehante turns to Kenjō. "Nkella gave his life for us. We should do something more meaningful."

"This *is* meaningful, Kae." Lāri says.

Tessa reverses her chair and drives toward the kitchen, her motor the only sound filling the silence.

"I don't want your people to suffer," I finally say to Kaehante. "I just don't know what I could do." He scoffs. "But I will take a look at the World Card. For you. If anything comes up, I will tell you."

He regards me for a second before finally nodding.

It's the least I can do for him. I'd be stupid to think I can just ignore Tetalla. But how does he even know about me?

"Any idea why Tetalla would be reaching out to Soren now?" Tessa drives back holding a pitcher of ginger and lavender tea and sets it down on the table.

Harold reaches for the pitcher and pours the drink into his wooden cup. "I've been thinking about that. We don't know that he hasn't been trying to reach out." He turns to me. "Maybe all those times the dead have grabbed at your ankles, it's been him trying to make contact."

"But why talk to her now?" AJ asks.

"Maybe because now he knows where she is," Harold says.

"Maybe because of curse day?" Kae suggests.

AJ perks up. "Oh, I'm so happy we don't have to worry about curse day anymore!" he shouts. "Can we celebrate it by baking a cake?" He stares into space like he just got an idea and gasps.

I quirk a brow. "AJ?"

He stares at me and smiles. I'm about to ask him what's wrong when he jumps up and starts gathering cups and dishes. Kae shakes his head.

"Wait." Harold starts. "You guys aren't cursed anymore, so what would Tetalla reaching Soren have to do with curse day?"

"Nothing at all," Tessa says shrugging.

But that doesn't make sense either. There's a connection somehow. Tetalla is getting his information from something or someone, just like I can reach into the past for information. "Is today curse day?"

"Tomorrow," Tessa says. "The seas always got fiercer on the days leading up to it. The Aō knew it was upon us. It was always a race to land to avoid the risk of our bones sinking to the ocean floor."

Right. I forgot curse day coincided with my birthday. "Tetalla was cursed with the Devil curse, like Nkella. This must have been the day he lost control."

"What would that have to do with you, though?" Harold asks.

I shrug. "More power? Nkella was always on the brink of losing control on curse day, but he was also stronger than ever."

Harold rubs his chin. "I think it's because he's Death. He must have known you were all undead at one point. And it probably isn't a secret that you know the Empress's one living descendant. If he controls the dead, it wouldn't surprise me if he could also see through them."

Kaehante's eyes widen. "He uses the dead as utwa. Spies."

"And today must have been a connection if he's losing control and making rash decisions." Harold sips his drink. How can he drink something cold, while freezing from the inside?

AJ and I exchange a grimace. "Using the dead to spy? I don't like the sound of that." AJ shudders. My stomach rolls.

Tessa holds her cheek in thought as we all contemplate quietly.

Harold slaps his thighs. "Welp, I need to do some rune practice before I go to sleep. So I'll see you all in the morning."

"Oh, yeah. How's that going by the way?" I ask.

"More than halfway done," he smiles, "thanks to Kenjō."

Kenjō blushes, and they both head upstairs.

Back in my room, I slip into my nightgown and sit at the edge of my bed. My room doesn't have a lot of decorations, but it does have a single bed with a comfortable enough makeshift mattress made out of sand and feathers. We all worked hard to make this into a home. Kaehante carved nightstands with a drawer for each room, and that's where I hide my few belongings.

Here goes nothing.

I open the drawer and pull out the World Card. Seeing into Tetalla's past won't help me right now—but this card, being a portal, can also show me the present moment anywhere in Ipa. If Kaehante wants me to be a spy, that's what I'll be.

I stare at the face of the card, admiring the gold details over the obsidian sea. I enact my mark as I've done countless times. I no longer have to try too hard. Within seconds, the waves start to move, and the serpent comes to life. A purple glare swipes across it.

"Show me Tetalla."

The image of the map of Ipa disappears. I hold my breath in anticipation of the living image of Death. Red clouds appear and disperse revealing the tarot illustration of the Devil instead. My insides twist. Yes, Tetalla also has the Devil curse, but he's Death. He became Death when he burned down the Tower to kill the Empress and burned Adara alive instead. He then went mad with the Devil curse, and the Aō made him King of the Deep because he took so many with him in his rage. "Show me Death in Danū *at this moment in time.*"

Black clouds overpower the red ones; lightning strikes between them. "Yes, that's it. Show me Death."

The clouds disperse to reveal a muscular man sitting on a black throne with jagged edges that rises over his head. He has a bored look on his face. His eyes snap to meet mine, and a cruel smile twists his face. I drop the card on the floor.

He *saw* me.

Wait. That's not possible. Get a hold of yourself, Soren.

Red clouds cover the image, and I bend to pick it up. The Devil replaces the image again.

I stick the World Card back in my drawer and shut it. I'll have to tell Kaehante that Tetalla is sitting on a throne like some pompous king, and that he has more power than we've bargained for. I swear he saw me looking into him. But how is that even possible?

And the Devil replacing the image was just my mind wanting to think about Nkella. That's all it was. It's all it could have been.

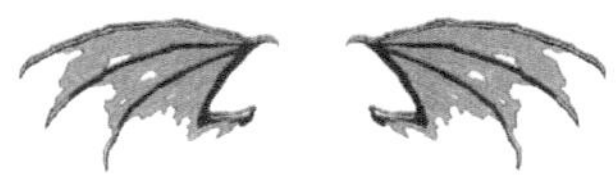

I'm swallowed by nightmares the moment I drift off to sleep.

"There is nowhere to run. Nowhere to hide." Kindness and terror seep from Tetalla's voice, soft yet commanding. I can sense his eons of experience leading armies into battle.

Wisps of shadows move around me. I glimpse a skeletal figure as he moves in the pitch black room. I reach for my dagger, but my wrist hits a cold metal bar.

"Where am I?" My throat cracks as I break my silence. "Let me go." He continues to move around me in the dark, until his warm breath caresses the back of my neck.

"We're the same, you and I. Both bringers of death."

"I don't bring death. It was a mistake to bring you back."

He guffaws. "Is that what you think I mean? Because you brought me back? I was never truly dead to begin with, that is not what the Death Card does."

I crane my neck to try and see him. "I know what it does. It exchanges one dead for another."

"It does not." His voice is deep and sinister. A skull stands before me now and I swallow a gasp. "It engulfs Death's power. Whoever is given the title and whoever it takes is meant to be the new Death. But," he draws back, "it appears you were rejected, and the job still belongs to me." I swallow. The skull speaks close to my face, and I inch back.

"Are you saying I was supposed to take your place as Death?"

His skeletal appearance fades away, now showing his Ipani face. His features are stronger than Nkella's, but something about him is similar. His cheekbones. His eyes. Tetalla smiles and raises the back of his hand to brush against my cheek. I wince at his touch.

"You look like her."

"Like who?"

"My Aovate."

He means Adara. I look away from him, and he takes his hand back.

"What do you plan to do with me?" I ask.

He chuckles. "Nothing tonight. This is your dream." A sly smile slides on his face. "Rest assured, *uoko yani*, I will find you, and when I do, I will never let you go."

3

FIERCE, DARK EYES WITH FLICKERING CRIMSON SPECS startle me awake.

I gasp, then I realize I'm in my bed. Light trickles in, and I yawn when something furry and white with two blue eyes stares at me from on top of my chest.

The bunny wiggles his nose, and I still.

"What are you doing here?" I slowly move my hands over his fur, cautious not to scare him. I once made a connection with a goat, but she never came to find me. Nkella told me it was cruel to make a connection with an animal and then leave. Maybe oumala rabbits are different. I always figured Iéle came back to Nkella because wolves are pack animals and trackers.

I never thought of a rabbit being able to track a human.

"What is it you want, little buddy? Are you hungry?"

The image of him gulping down that wolverine like a piranha comes to mind. "Yeah, I'm not sure I can help you with that." Carefully, I sit up and let the rabbit stay on the bed while I get dressed. He lets me pick him up to carry him downstairs. "Alright, little buddy, I don't know if or how you can understand me, but please don't bite any of my friends."

A psychic nudge comes from him like a magnetic pull, akin to when Philo does it, except no images follow. I'm content with that.

AJ is already running around the kitchen like a mad man, and Kenjō and Harold are sitting at the table. They glance up and wave sleepily. The smell of something delicious baking in the oven smothers my senses.

Holding the bunny to my chest, I pull a chair from the table with my leg and take a seat. "Where're Tessa and Kae?"

"Left with Lāri to get supplies." Harold yawns into his hand, a cold cloud leaving his mouth.

Kenjō has her arms wrapped around him, presumably to keep him warm with her jaguar warmth. Her eyes light up when she sees what I'm holding. "Is that the diwe you saved from the fighting ring?"

I'm about to answer her when the bunny hops from my arms and lands on the table. Harold jumps up from his seat, and I suppress a laugh. "I had to make a connection with him to save him," I tell her. "I guess he found me."

"Come on. We're about to eat here." Harold steps back. "And those things are mean as hell!"

My lips form a smirk. "Scared of a little bunny, Harold?"

"Little bunny? You did see that thing eat an entire wolverine, right? One of them nearly ate me back on Swords."

Kenjō laughs.

"Relax. I told him not to eat any of my friends."

Harold quirks a brow. "Oh, okay, guess it'll be alright then." He rolls his eyes.

"Are you going to name him?" Kenjō asks.

"How about Hannibal Lecter?" Harold says.

Kenjō stares at him with a confused look on her face. "Who?" She extends her hand to the bunny, and he seems okay with her being there, so she pets him.

"I miss watching movies," Harold says melodramatically.

I give him an apologetic smile. "I hadn't thought about what to name him. I wasn't expecting him to come back."

AJ walks in from the kitchenette and places a bowl of fruit on the table. The rabbit's giant needle-like fangs come out and nearly take AJ's hand off as he gulps down a whole orange from the bowl. AJ lets out a high-pitched scream.

I grab his hands to make sure he still has all his fingers. "Are you alright?"

AJ pants in place, his eyes wide and glued to the bunny.

"I'm so sorry. He's hungry," I tell him.

Harold's already halfway to the door. "I thought the rabbits here were carnivores."

"Koj. They'll eat anything." Kenjō picks the bunny up and flips him on his back. "Also, it is a girl diwe. Just so you know."

"Lordy. If you're going to keep her, teach her some manners, okay? I'm going back into the kitchen where it's safe."

"Sorry, AJ." I take the bunny from Kenjō. "Back home, they don't have giant teeth and aren't as fast. And they mostly eat vegetables." The bunny stares up at me from my chest, and I gaze into her big blue eyes. "Sapphire."

"Seriously?" Harold deadpans.

I bore into him. "What? She has blue eyes. Sapphire is a great name. Better than Hannibal."

"It's your rabbit. Call her what you want." He runs his hand through his hair, shaking out some ice from his roots.

"I will."

The door opens and Kae walks inside holding a barrel of food. Tessa follows holding a smaller barrel of what I assume are ingredients for raku potions. Lāri comes through last and shuts the door, balancing colored fabrics draped over her left shoulder. Kae squints at me, then at Sapphire, before walking to the kitchenette.

With all this gushing over my new familiar, I almost forgot about my promise to Kae last night. Then I had that strange dream, which... I'm no longer convinced it was a dream. It felt too real.

I follow Kae into the kitchen. He's added a wall as a separator, but it only reaches the second floor. His back is turned to me as he packs meat into the freezer.

"Kae?"

He turns to stare at me.

"Something happened last night when I checked the World Card."

His brows raise, but he waits for me to continue. I tell him how it changed from showing Nkella's Devil Card to showing me Tetalla sitting on his throne. And how Tetalla looked at me. Then I tell him about my dream.

"Hnn." He rubs his chin. "Have you told the others?"

"Not yet. We've been distracted with the bunny."

He stares down at Sapphire and lifts a finger to pet her. Sapphire unhinges her jaw, and I gasp, stepping back. In a loud pop, she disappears. Kae retracts his hand quickly.

"Sorry. Think she was just startled."

Kae stares at me with a perplexed look on his face.

"She'll be back. I think."

I spend the rest of the day picking firewood on my own.

AJ and Lāri seemed busy, and Harold and Kenjō went off so that Harold could keep making his runes. Tessa and Kae wanted to make bombs, but I needed space away from them.

Today is my birthday. And while no one has said anything, I'm not bothered by it, because I asked them not to. I don't care about my birthday. Today was meant to be different. I was supposed to be moving into an apartment in Louisiana with Talia, or, at least, providing a safe place for Talia to come if she needed to. Instead, I somehow led her down the rabbit hole to live with the Queen of Hearts, except this one is worse. The Empress has somehow brainwashed Talia into believing this is the best home for her, and that being the Hierophant is everything she's ever wanted out of life, no matter what I've said to try and change her mind. She also still believes we're all meant to be a family, even though I told her the Empress killed my mother.

And for that, I don't feel like talking to her either. But part of me fears she's under a spell, and I won't leave her here. My parents are dead. My dad wasn't my real dad, and he never cared about me, giving me away to the foster system.

And Nkella is... He's gone. So to me, there's nothing to celebrate. I just want today to be over. Not to mention that today is curse day.

The image of Tetalla staring at me fills my mind.

You look just like her.

What is he planning?

Something resurfaces in my memory. He said he'd been alive in the Deep. This whole time? It must have been hundreds of years. How was that possible? I know Ipani can live for a long time, but...isn't the Deep like hell? That makes no sense. How could he stay alive in the afterlife?

"Leave some firewood for the rest of us!"

I spin around and a wide smile spreads on my face. "Hermit!" I put the basket down and run toward him.

"Happy birthday!"

My stomach sinks. "Oh." I come to a stop but keep the smile on my face. "Thanks."

"Don't look so disappointed. I've brought you a gift."

"Thank you. I'm just not feeling great about my birthday is all. I told the crew I didn't want to celebrate."

A slight smile forms at his lips. "I'll tell you a secret because I think I'll be doing you a service. Your crew is only pretending to abide by your request. I knew of your request, but I ignored it. Anyhoo." He reaches into his satchel and takes out a rectangular object covered in layers of brown and black paper and tied with a piece of tweed. "This is for you."

I take it, still stuck on his words that my crew is pretending. It did smell really good in the kitchen this morning, but AJ is always baking stuff. It smelled like...

Oh my god. He didn't.

"Well, aren't you going to open it?"

I blink. "Sorry!" I uncover the tweed and start unraveling the paper to find a red leather-bound book with a gold insignia of a spiderweb on the front. My heart flutters. "Hermit...this is..." I flip through the handmade pages of a journal. "This is beautiful. Thank you." I give him a hug.

"I thought you could use one of your own. And if you noticed the insignia, I want you to know I chose to burn that on there on purpose."

I quirk a brow at him.

"You can't run from who you are. And the webs suit you."

"I've never minded spiders." I smile at him and hold the journal to my heart. "Thank you."

"I also brought you and Harold more of the translation potion because I figured you'd need it. Shall we go for a walk along the coast?" He gives me his elbow, and I take it.

We walk to the shoreline right outside of our small woods. The salty sea breeze whips my hair over my face as we walk side by side on the sand toward the *Gambit*. I have the basket of firewood in my arms with the journal on top.

"How is it coming with your new mark?" he asks. Always straight to business. I respect that.

I glance at my Fool's *O*. "Nothing's changed."

"Has it not?" he raises a brow at me.

"Well, the dead have started to talk to me. And I had a strange dream of Death last night."

He stops in his tracks. "And nothing has changed?"

I chuckle.

"When you say a dream of death..."

"It was of Tetalla."

His brows raise. "Do tell."

I relay the whole story. He doesn't interrupt. By the time we reach the ship, he has a strange look of contemplation on his face. "I didn't know someone could be alive in the Deep," I finally say.

"And what do you think that means?"

"I-I don't know." He stares at me expectantly, like he wants me to dig deeper. "I honestly don't know what it means."

"What do you want it to mean?"

My nose starts to itch, and I can feel the tears threatening to come out.

He nods. I shake my head.

"It's stupid. That kind of hope is stupid." I shake my head harder. "I saw him bleeding out. He cut himself open. He's dead."

A few beats of silence pass between us, but then he speaks. "A spider who builds the web is subject for another spider to come and steal it."

I blink at him. "What does that have to do with Nkella?"

"What I mean is, sometimes even the Fates lack insight outside of their reality. No matter how much they think they control."

My muscles tense as I regard what he just said. "That much is evident with the Empress—hell, with all the three of them. But I still don't know why you're telling me this." I bite my tongue, aware that I may have just sounded snappy and rude.

"Don't expect reality to be a dead end, even if the Deep is the dimension for the dead. The only way in is to die. But expect the unexpected." He smiles. "Come on, let's get you back."

Back at the tree hut, the Hermit converses with the crew while I climb to my room.

Sapphire is asleep on my bed, and I stare at her. I guess she's found her place with me and knows which room is mine. I set the journal on my nightstand next to a tank I keep for Philo for whenever she feels like hanging out. It's part of my dumpster-dive collection of items—to make sure I don't change the future—with me reaching into the past to grab stuff I need.

It's an open-air tank since there's no use holding her in anyway, but at least, it's somewhere she can feel at home. I've pushed her away so many times, I think she's just out with Asteria these days.

Funny. I could actually use her help now.

I reach into my drawer for my small collection of magical tarot cards. I currently only have the World Card and the Ace of Swords since the Death Card disappeared the day I used it. I guess it reappeared for Tetalla when he arrived. I choose the World Card and shut the drawer.

I lie back, my head next to Sapphire. She wiggles her little nose. "Don't eat my face," I tell her, giving her the side-eye. But I know she won't. Once you make a bond with an oumala animal, they won't hurt you—they'll even protect you. I stare at the World Card, not sure what I'm doing with it.

I take a deep breath and let it out slowly. "Show me Nkella."

The World Card starts to change. It shows me the Devil Card—a devil wearing a pirate's hat standing on top of the *Gambit*—but it doesn't show me a live image. I don't think it can...because, he's gone.

I sigh and drop my hand.

Or it doesn't show me a live image because it can't. Maybe it doesn't reach the Deep.

I hear the crew chatting downstairs about the next fighting ring we're going to break apart. I stroke Sapphire's fur a few times and decide it's time to go down.

The smell of sweet bread from the kitchen grows stronger and my stomach rumbles. AJ's eyes light up as I make my way down. I smile back, pretending to not know anything about the cake he's obviously baking for my birthday. I glance at the Hermit, and he winks with a knowing smile. He knows I won't tell them he told me.

"So...there's a fighting ring happening in my home island, off the coast of Wands," AJ starts.

"I'm not going to go to this one, AJ." Kae declares. The rest of us exchange surprised looks.

Tessa appears just as shocked as the rest of us, so he's clearly either kept this to himself or just made up his mind right now. "Oh?"

Kae's shoulders drop, but his hand forms a fist. "I've decided to go to Danū. My people need me, and I cannot continue to do nothing."

AJ gapes at him as I make my way to a seat. "This is the worst time to go to Danū. Even worse than before, Kae. They say dark red clouds are looming over the island, residual from Tetalla coming from the Deep."

"Which is why I must go. My people cannot take anymore defeat, and if Death brought the dead..."

"You think maybe your wife is there too?" I ask.

He glances at me. Wetness touches his eyes, but he holds it in.

"I understand," I say. "If there were any possibility at all to save someone I love, you know I'd take it in a heartbeat."

His lips thin.

"No way!" AJ shoots up off his seat. "I'm not at all okay with this. The Empress has Arcana everywhere, and it's been under siege forever. It's too dangerous, and you're going to get yourself killed. How will you even get there by yourself?"

A knock resounds through the open doorframe. Ntaoru stands there with loose black, wavy hair, shouldering a bag.

"Did I come at the wrong time? I heard yelling."

"Ntaoru! Where have you been?" AJ spins around, then looks over his shoulder at Kae. "We'll talk about this later."

"Come in, come in." Tessa reverses her chair. "We were about to discuss where to go next."

"Do you want to join us in taking down some fighting rings?" AJ asks her.

My breath stills. Ntaoru left us shortly after Nkella brought her back. She didn't want to be around us. I figured she didn't want a reminder of him. And I get that she doesn't want to be around me. I'm sure she hates me, and I don't blame her. She passes me a look, her eyes fierce for the moment she glares at me. Words unspoken lingering between us. Those eyes. Nkella used to look at me with those eyes.

Ntaoru's face is stern. "I'll respectfully decline. I'm not ready yet...to do that. I've only come because a certain drakon told me to. He speaks in riddles. I wanted to make sure you all were safe..." She pauses. "But it seems everything is fine."

"Gari is here?" AJ asks.

My eyes widen, and I bolt toward the door. I'd rather not be in here right now, and I'd like to see Gari. Ntaoru moves out of the way so I can leave.

Gari sways in the air, his purple and blue fur floating as if he's swimming in water. "Gari! What's the occasion?"

"It's your birthday, is it not?"

My cheeks flush. "Oh Gari...you didn't...bring Ntaoru all the way over here just for that, did you?"

Gari flips onto his back, while his head remains facing me. "No."

"Okay, good."

"I brought her because AJ asked me to."

That sneaky pirate. I hold my head.

Gari unravels his tail and hands me what looks like a dead mouse tied with a purple bow. "I brought you a present." He purrs.

I inhale sharply. "Oh Gari...you shouldn't have."

"Surprise." His jester grin spreads from fin to fin as his body wiggles. He drops the mouse into my hands.

I resist the urge to grimace as I quickly but respectfully drop the mouse down by my feet. I've had enough surprises for one day.

Two loud whistling sounds come from the sky. They sound like air-strike sirens, but I know the sound too well. The Empress's Arcana army. Apparently, my birthday surprises aren't over yet.

I step to the side, Gari wrapping his tail around me, as the Arcana land five feet away. A gust of smoke clouds part to reveal their pearly white expressionless mask...and Talia.

She stands straight and bold. All her past shyness is gone from her face, but her eyes light up when she sees me.

"Soren!" She runs at me, but I take a step back, my eyes trained on the Arcana.

"Don't worry, they're just here to keep me safe."

"From my crew?"

"No." She deadpans. "From the war? From all the other bad stuff around here."

"The war is in Danū and the seas near it. Not here."

Her shoulders drop. "I don't want to argue."

"Why are you here, Talia?" As much as it pains me to be this short with her, I can't forgive her for taking the Empress's side against me. She knew nothing about her and just trusted her with open arms.

"It's your birthday."

"I didn't realize your new mommy allowed you out." I glance at the soldiers. "But I guess she doesn't, not really."

"Look, I just wanted to come and say happy birthday. Aletha also sends her regards."

My brows raise. "Her regards?" I guffaw. "Nice language, Talia. She's really shaping you up to be like her." I walk around her and poke at her black fabric. "What? No lace?" Gari snickers behind me. She's wearing all-black leather leggings and a top with a diamond cut neckline that has a tail to cover just over her rear. It's sleek and agile and looks really good on her, if I'm being honest. I walk all the way around her to stand in front of her. A silver necklace of a spiderweb hangs from her neck. "I thought you hated spiders."

"It took me a while, but the ones in the Tower are nice. And kind of cute."

"Yeah, jumping spiders are cute. And these are pretty." I quickly school my face as I realize I'm letting my guard down again.

"Soren, please. Can't we just talk?"

"We have nothing more to talk about."

I take a quick glance at the crew. They're now outside, glaring at the Arcana soldiers being there.

"You're living with the Empress. The woman who killed my mother. And babies. Can't forget that."

"I know." She lowers her voice and looks back at the Arcana. "I made a mistake about that. I didn't know she had done that—"

"And now?"

Her mouth opens. I raise a brow and cross my arms. "She told me she never could have known it was your mother. It was the past and your mother was a threat. She said she would take it all back if she could. Whatever she's done was a long time ago, and she had her reasons. You know, she could really use our help with the Ace of Swords."

I roll my eyes. "Just go."

"Soren, you don't understand what's at stake here."

I laugh again. "And what do you know? You don't even belong here, Talia."

"Yes, I do. I do belong here. There's nothing for me back home. And Soren, you don't even want to go home. You were obsessed with this place, remember? Would you have ever gone back?"

My heart sinks. "This is why you're still here, isn't it? Because you think I don't want to go home?"

She shakes her head. "No, I like it here. Aletha's teaching me magic. What would I do back in Louisiana?"

My brows raise. "Wow. Magic, huh? And you're on a first-name basis. Good job. Okay, thank you for gracing me with your presence. You can go now."

AJ steps up beside me. "Aw, come on, Soren. She's your sister. Let her stay..."

I gape at him, then at the crew. They all stare back at me and Talia's pleading eyes.

I rub at my eyes. "Fine."

Talia gives me a hug, but I only offer her a half hug, still not knowing how I can ever forgive her.

"Great! Everyone inside for cake." AJ turns to face Gari. "You're going to have to shrink in size a little bit there, buddy."

We enjoy a blueberry and lemon cake with fluffy frosting, decorated with blueberries and purple raspberries. Despite telling him that I didn't want any attention on my birthday and having him completely ignore my wishes, I can't help but feel appreciative of AJ.

Harold takes something out of his pocket and hands it to me. "Here, I got you something." Cold fog escapes his lips, but I pretend not to notice.

"What is it?" I stare at a rectangular terrible wrap job done with banana leaves and begin to unravel it. "I thought I was going to get away with a quiet birthday without anyone noticing, and here I am with a room full of surprises."

"I thought you might want a little laugh, so I found you some of that stuff that lets you talk to plants mixed with the giddy laughter potion in the form of a cookie."

I stare at him and laugh. "Oh my god, Harold, you didn't." The last time I ate this, it didn't end well. But this time will be different, and I do need the laugh. "Thank you."

He smiles. "Happy birthday."

4

I WASTE NO TIME BEFORE EATING THE COOKIE. I SIT WITH MY back against a tree at the edge of the woods, the ocean still in my line of sight, and the sun setting behind me. Best of both worlds. Although, I'm hoping the tree won't mind when this stuff starts to work and doesn't tell me to buzz off. Harold did tell me he had the most interesting conversation with an oak last time; apparently, they're very welcoming.

Wind rustles the leaves of the trees, the cool breeze relaxing me as I wait for the cookie to work. The foliage in Dempu Yuni is similar to Wands. At night, blue lightning bugs illuminate the tree branches in these parts of the woods. I stare at a clover next to my hand and wait for a tiny face to poke out of it...hoping that this time, they won't be angry and shout at me.

Nothing yet.

I think it worked faster last time. Maybe this one wasn't a strong cookie?

Standing up, I decide to go for a stroll when the world tilts on its axis. I topple sideways. The ground moves beneath me as I struggle to hold in the cake I ate.

Okay, I think it's d-definitely working now. My knees grow weak, and I stumble against a tree, gripping its bark in an attempt to keep myself steady. Pressure tightens at my temples and my vision blurs just a little.

My breathing deepens; this isn't the light and fluffy feeling from last time. Instead, I feel...heavy. A burden presses down on my shoulders, and I can't pinpoint what it is. Or why it's happening. When I think I'm stable enough, I let go of the tree and take a few steps. A red hue has taken over the woods.

Something isn't right.

I should be laughing and talking to the flowers right now, not feeling like I'm about to fall.

And the guilt. The overwhelming guilt.

"Sooo-wenn."

My back straightens. The hair on my arms stand on end.

"Sooooowwweeennnn."

"Who said that?" I stare down at the plants, and then the trees, trying to make out any faces.

"Sowen." The voice is crisper now. A woman's voice. I spin around and scream.

A woman stands five feet away from me, her mouth an endless black hole as she calls my name. Her skin is burnt. Red embers spin around her as rivers of lava spill over her face, down to her neck, down her body. My knees buckle, but I force myself to take the first step.

She takes a step toward me, and I take two stable steps back. Her body vibrates as she stumbles forward, trying to reach me.

And I run.

I trip over a fallen log and use my hands and knees to push myself off the ground. Glancing behind me, I start to run faster as she moves toward me at an impossible vibrating speed.

"Sowwwen..." She reaches out to me with her hand.

Nope.

I raise my knees up to my chest and run through the woods, no longer caring which direction I'm going.

"Heeii allyyy."

"Nope. Don't care." I sprint through the trees, branches scratching my arms and legs. I run through them.

My face smacks into something hot, and I fall on my rear with a hard, painful thud. The burning woman stands before me, her crumbling finger spilling ashes as she points to me.

"Heee allyy."

I back up. "Who are you? What do you want with me?"

"Sowen."

"Are you trying to say my name?"

Ashes fall off her face as she nods. The red hues behind her make her look like she's glowing.

"How do you know me?" I climb to my feet and stare at her. A burning woman who knows me? Here? My mark buzzes, and I'm pulled into a past memory. The Empress is standing in front of Soanalo as she commands Ntaoru to burn her alive.

I come back from the vision and squint. It can't be. "Soanalo? Is that you?"

"Soren." Her voice is clearer. Ashes start to fall from her face to slowly reveal smooth skin. "He's alive."

"Who?"

"Nkella. He's here in the Deep. He's alive."

My breath catches, and I forget how to speak. How can that be possible?

"The E-Empress—" her voice comes in and out as her body flickers. "No match for..."

"What? What are you trying to say? Tell me about Nkella!"

"For Death."

Confusion swarms me. I try to piece together what she's trying to say. Nkella is alive. The Empress. No match... "The Empress is no match for Death?" Goosebumps spill over my arms and legs. Soanalo hated the Empress. She'd killed Soanalo in cold blood. But why would Soanalo be concerned over her not being a match for Tetalla?

"Only a Devil can defeat a Devil..."

She flickers in and out, and her voice grows farther away. "Soanalo?"

Her body disappears.

"You must be careful. Don't let Death touch you."

I gasp and jump back as she reappears right in front of my nose.

This can't be real. I'm hallucinating. It's another dream. "You're not real."

Her eyes widen as she turns, gaping at something behind her. "Soren, I have to go, but please listen to me. Do not take more itachi. It isn't safe. If I saw you, Death can too. He sees through the eyes of the dead." Her neck cracks as she again stares to the side. "Run."

"What?"

"Run, Soren. You must leave."

"How can I speak to Nkella?"

Soanalo stares off into the distance. The ashes start to fall on her again, making her skin crumble.

"Soanalo!"

She stares at me.

"How can I see Nkella?"

"You can't. He's lost. The Devil has him now. Forever. Gone."

"But you said he's alive!"

"He's alive...the only way to see him is...come to the Deep."

"To go to the Deep? But that's..."

She snaps her gaze back at me, her dark hollow eyes and mouth stretching to an abnormal width. "RUN!"

Her body crumbles to the ground in a pile of ash. The ground starts to rumble beneath my feet. Bones rise from the soil, skeletal hands reaching for me, clawing at my legs. I scream as one grips my ankle, and I fall.

I hear my name being called in the distance as I fight my way off the ground, kicking at the rising skeletons. A blast hits my side, and I'm momentarily blinded until I feel something furry nudge me.

"Hold on, Soren."

"Gari?"

"And me." Harold's voice comes from beside me. He takes my arm and helps me climb on top of Gari's back. I grip the drakon's hair as he swoops above the trees and flies us back to the tree hut. My heart is still thudding in my chest. I'm not sure what I just experienced was real, but it certainly wasn't a nice talking-plant inducing hallucination.

Gari lands, and I jump off to run inside. "What did you give me, Harold?" The red hue from the cookie still lingers over my line of sight.

"What do you mean?" He walks in after me. Gari, now shrunken in size, floats over our heads into the living space. The whole crew stares at us with surprised looks plastered on their faces.

"Maybe it was a bad idea for you to go off on your own when Death is trying to track you?" AJ says.

I pause. He's right. What I saw wasn't real. It was probably a cruel ploy to give up my location. A distraction. I'm such an idiot.

But why would she tell me to run?

"Soren? Are you alright?" Tessa asks.

"I don't think the ouma ipononchi you gave me was what you thought."

Gari floats in front of me. "Can I see it?"

I hold out the rest of the cookie. He takes it with the tip of his tail and sniffs it. "Nope." His nose twitches as he shakes his head. "It has trace amounts of itachi. Very dangerous."

A gasp escapes me, and I glance at Harold. "That's the poison that killed my mother."

Harold's face pales. "But I got it from you, Gari! I don't even know where to get itachi!" The crew exchange confused and concerned stares.

I take a deep breath. "I wasn't accusing you of doing it intentionally...but how come it didn't kill me?" The last time I drank it, it almost trapped me in my mind forever.

Kenjō steps up beside Harold and holds onto his arm. Her voice lowers. "Trace amounts may not kill you. They'll give you a different effect. Like the ability to see the dead."

Memories of Nkella reaching into my own mind to save me resurfaces, stirring my emotions. If he hadn't taken some of the poison to reach me, I would have died. He must have only taken a trace amount —just enough to reach me. This plant has the ability to blend reality with the spirit world, while it steals your soul. I rest my head on my hand.

"Could it have been switched?" Harold screws up his face, white frost falling from his lashes. "Who's gotten close enough to me to do that?"

I shake my head.

"It doesn't matter." AJ pours water into a pitcher and sets it down on the table. "What matters is you're alright. Drink all of this to get it out of your system. What happened?"

Harold grabs a cup and passes it to me. I take it from his freezing hands, averting my gaze from his blue fingernails. "When I got to her, there were dead everywhere trying to grab her."

I stare at the floor. I'm not going to mention Soanalo appearing to me and telling me what she did. The last thing I want to do is give them hope Nkella is alive when it was probably just a crazy hallucination. "Sorry, guys. I think I'm going to go lie down."

AJ nods, but I don't make eye contact with anyone else.

"Take the pitcher with you."

I do as he says and head upstairs.

The last of the water slips down my throat, and I think the effects have worn off. At least, there's no red hue in my room. It wasn't a very big cookie, and I didn't eat all of it. I don't have the energy to worry about who could have switched Harold's gift. The dead are literally everywhere, and Tetalla uses them. It could have been switched literally anywhere, at any time.

I'm going to have to be extra careful and watch my back.

Nkella is alive. Go to the Deep.

Allowing myself to believe that is a recipe for broken dreams. For the crew as well for myself.

That would mean that the World Card was showing me the Devil Card on purpose, and not simply it's what I wanted to see. And that the reason I see his eyes in my sleep...isn't because of trauma.

Maybe they're not images haunting me. Maybe they're visions of him. Of him *in the Deep*. My pulse quickens. If that's true...if he's alive...

No. I can't allow myself to have false hope. Not again. Not like I did, wanting to bring my mom back. I can't. A tear rolls off my cheek.

And there's no way into the Deep or the World Card would show it.

False hope. That's all it is.

The Empress is no match for Death.

What was Soanalo trying to say?

Sapphire inches over to me, so I turn to pet her. She drops her ears down and her eyes close slightly, showing her enjoyment. "What am I supposed to do here?"

My mark buzzes, and a vision carries me out of the room. It happens fast.

Nkella stands on a pile of rubble, his hands are on his head and blood stains are on his torn shirt. A red hue casts a deep red shade all around. His eyes glow a bright red, and his screams shatter my eardrums.

And I'm back. My heart is beating in my chest, and Sapphire's eyes are wide and staring at me.

"That was a vision." I swallow hard when I realize I spoke out loud. I don't want the others to ask me what's going on. I can't tell them. Not yet.

That had to be the past. It couldn't be anywhere else. But the red hue... Is there anywhere else we get a red hue in Ipa? There was a red hue when Soanalo showed up too.

I suck in a breath and sit up. Sapphire startles. Could that have been a past memory inside the Deep? It had to be.

I've never had memories of the Deep before. Not even the World Card takes me there. It's a dimension within this one. No other portals open in there...unless you die.

I pull the World Card out of the drawer. What am I supposed to do? Who can I believe? Soanalo? Tetalla? My strange vision?

Purple clouds emerge on the face of the card, and I narrow my eyes. I didn't mean to ask a real question. I'm not even sure what I intended to do with the card. Maybe I knew it would show me the plain tarot image of the Devil if I asked again.

The clouds dissipate to show the Empress walking in her corridors. What the hell am I supposed to do with this? I gasp. Believe *her*?

Would she know if Nkella is alive?

I hold my breath. I can't tell the crew where I'm going, but I have to find out the truth.

If she really knows...

If there's any chance Nkella really is alive...and if there's a way into the Deep to bring him back. Without undoing the consequence of his sacrifice. I have to know.

I would do anything for the ones I love.

I drop the card onto the floor, and a portal opens in my room. It's time to pay the Empress a visit.

Spears point at me from all sides the moment I step through the portal onto the throne room's black and white checkered floor. I hide the World Card in my back pocket. She'll have to search me if she wants it.

"Stand down."

The Arcana soldiers lift their spears and stand at attention. I wink at them, giving a smug smirk as I dust off my shoulder.

"Soren?" Talia's voice echoes through the large room and she comes running toward me. I embrace her as if we hadn't just seen each other last night for my birthday. Her smile turns into a frown as she reads the expression on my face. "Are you okay?"

"Finally come to accept my proposal, have you?" The Empress's orotund voice makes me cringe inside. I rip my gaze from Talia to the Empress's broad shouldered stature. Her black military-esque suit is decorated with black spiderwebs from her shoulders down to the tight cape that reaches her calves. Her eyes stare at me from behind her gold expressionless mask. "Or have you decided you could be an asset in defeating Death? I assume you aren't here to be a family."

"Definitely not." I walk toward her, my heels echoing on the floor. My eyes are peeled for her spiders, but I doubt she'll try to trap me right now. It would be counterproductive. "Talia, don't you get tired of staring at a mask all day?"

"Soren—" She cautions me but the Empress laughs.

"No, seriously, why don't you just take it off? We all know you were burned in a fire."

She stops laughing. "Rude as always. What is it you want? I expect it isn't to return the World Card I let you take."

This makes me stop.

"Did you think I'd let you get away with stealing it from your sister's memories? My dear, I let her see the World Card because I knew you'd go probing."

Talia gasps.

"I told you, dear," she tells Talia. "Soren will use just about anyone for her gains."

I ball my fist. "I took it because you shouldn't have that kind of power."

"Do not sass me, girl. You took it to keep me from finding my sister." Her voice bounces off the walls. She takes a breath. "I knew you wouldn't leave, not without Talia, and you have nothing to go back to. No, no. You're here to stay," she sings that last word. I can feel the smile stretching from behind her mask.

This is why she lured Talia here, all to make sure I'd never leave. And Talia fell for it. It takes everything in me to remain calm as I make my way over to her throne.

"You can try to convince her to leave if you like, but it would be a pity. She's mastering the ancient Greek art of divination quite well. I can teach you, too, if you'd like."

My blood begins to boil. "Just stop talking." Her eyes widen, and she clenches her fist, but before she can reply to me, I continue. "You killed my mother, and I will never forgive you for that. I've come on different business."

Her fingers tap the arm of her chair. "Make it quick. I'm in the middle of a war."

"You're no match for Death."

"Have you come to tell me you're joining Tetalla?"

"No. I mean, I had a vision." I run through what happened, careful to leave out specific key details. Like how Tetalla has been trying to reach me.

She stands at the foot of her throne. "They said only a Devil can defeat a Devil. Yes." She holds a finger to the chin of her mask. "I suspected this."

"Do you think Nkella could be alive?"

"Without a doubt. Tetalla survived the Deep all these years, and he had enacted the Devil's curse as well. The captain being alive does not surprise me in the slightest."

All the blood must drain from my face, because I feel faint.

"But we cannot be certain. And it would be no use to me if he were alive here and trying to kill me. He'd sooner join forces with Tetalla. They are both, after all, from the same island of Pentacles."

My heart is thudding so loudly in my ear I can barely make out her words. Nkella could be alive. "Is there a way into the Deep without dying?"

"Are you mad? Did you not hear me? Why would I help you to bring someone back who wants me dead? Who never respected my authority, nor thanked me for saving him and raising him as my own child?"

Talia whimpers behind me.

I clench my jaw, ignoring the Empress's ignorant remarks about Nkella. "What if I could convince him not to kill you?"

She chuckles. "You give yourself too much credit. His hatred toward me runs deep within his veins, not to mention, if he truly is alive in the Deep, the only reason would be that his Devil curse healed his knife wound and is keeping him alive. There's no coming back from that."

My chest tightens.

But I did bring him back once. He hadn't completely lost himself yet, but it worked. I couldn't live with myself knowing he's alive down there...forever. "I have to try."

She scoffs. "And why would he listen to you and not join Tetalla's war against me?"

"Because Tetalla is after me, and he won't like it."

It was so silent, I could have heard a pin drop.

"Death is after you." She stands. "Is that what you said?"

"You heard me. He's come to me in my dreams and in visions. The dead grab for me. He even sent me a message saying he will find me."

"So that's his plan," she whispers mainly to herself. "To have you on his side. Clever."

"Creepy."

"Yes, indeed. It's important for you to know, Soren, he won't attempt a peace treaty with you in order to take me down. He wants every single human on Ipa dead. And after he's finished, he won't take kindly to you either. He's for the Ipani species only, and no other. Do you understand?"

I normally wouldn't believe her...but the World Card had showed me the Empress when I asked who I should believe. And what she said makes sense. I've looked into Adara's past. Tetalla killed random people when he was upset. He won't go easy on anyone.

My throat dries, and I nod.

"So you propose to bring back your captain to defeat Tetalla. And then what? Turn on me?"

I lift my chin. "One problem at a time. But you're no match for Death. How is the war going anyway? How many of your people and Ipani have you turned into your soldiers? How many are dying on Danū? When do you think it'll spread to the rest of the islands? The dead are already—"

"Enough!"

My muscles tense.

"The Deep—being below waters—is governed by intuition and our higher sense of consciousness."

I blink, suddenly feeling like I'm speaking to Asteria. As sisters, I guess they have some things in common.

"Therefore, the way into the Deep will be by the use of the Ace of Cups over at my ally island."

"In Cups? That's your ally island?" I smirk. I wonder what Lāri would have to say about that.

"Yes, the kings there support me, which is why there is no strife against me. The other islands can learn a thing or two from Cups."

Sure, *that's* why Tessa and Lāri escaped. I bite back a chuckle. As always, this bitch is delusional. "What will I have to do with it?"

"It will have instructions. I'll send notice for the kings to give you entrance into the island, and you'll be granted safe passage. But heed my warning: this has never been done before. I cannot tell you if it will work. That would require Asteria's ability. And I cannot tell you how to make it work. One of the kings holds the mark of the high priestess and will be able to help you—but not without his price. Will you be willing to pay it?"

"Yes."

"I would do it myself, but in the case of the Aces, I can't touch them. You have Asteria to thank for that."

I sure do, and I'm thankful for it. Asteria made sure she could never obtain the power of the Aces. After a beat, she speaks again.

"Very well then. Once I'm informed that you obtained the Ace of Cups, I will temporarily allow portals to open in order for you to complete this quest. Bring back the captain and return to my Tower. If I find you've gone somewhere else instead, I'll have both your heads. Is that clear?"

"Crystal."

"Good. Go back and prepare yourself. I understand you'll be needing your crew to get to Cups, and since you have a ship, I'll send down flags to hoist. It was, after all, one of *my* ships, but the captain's alterations make it easier to travel to different lands, so I'll allow it."

"Why would I need the ship?" I wasn't actually planning on taking the crew.

"How else would you expect to get into the Deep? The Cup itself won't transport you, I can tell you that much."

"Oh."

"Oh, and dear girl, don't take too long in the Deep. You don't have a Devil curse to protect you, so whatever you do, it will have an expiration date. Make sure you have a plan before you go sinking down there. Don't use their transparency magic either. That takes you into the Aō realm, or a segment of it. Tetalla will be able to see you far more clearly that way."

Searching her eyes, I regard her words. If this doesn't work, it's her against Tetalla, and he's growing stronger by the minute. She needs this to work as much as I do. "Off you go now. No time to waste."

I turn to leave, but she clears her throat.

"Aren't you forgetting something?"

I quirk a brow, and she gives me a pointed look. Oh. I clear my throat as well. "Thank you, Empress, for giving me and the crew safe passage and for allowing me to undertake this mission."

"*If* you succeed, Fateland will be thanking you. And then, I hope you'll consider taking a seat next to me as a Fate. I meant what I said before, I don't want you as my enemy, Soren. I want peace. I really do."

"If that were true, you wouldn't be forcing people into your Arcana. You'd be inspiring them to fight for Ipa, to fight *with* you."

She raises her chin.

I take out the World Card to make my exit. I turn to Talia. "I love you. Try to stay out of trouble."

Her eyes are glossy; she knows I might not come back, but there's nothing she can do about it. After all this is over, I'm finding a way to send her home for good. I point the card's face toward the side of a wall to open a portal back into my room, giving the Empress one last look before I go. "By the way, the *Gambit* was never your ship. Nkella stole it back from you. It belonged to his parents."

She says nothing as she watches me leave through the portal.

5

It's been one agonizing long night or morning or whatever. Last night was my birthday, but I didn't sleep—I immediately ate the cookie Harold gave me. And then everything went downhill from there.

Given that the Empress and Talia were both awake and the sun is out, it must now be mid-morning, which means the crew is due to wake up soon, and I still haven't slept.

I'll take a nap later. I've wasted enough time—a whole six months have passed since Nkella has been trapped in the Deep. I won't let another minute go by without doing something about it. Sapphire wakes to my pacing and exits the room with a loud pop into the Aō. My stomach twists into about ten different knots, just thinking about what it could have been like for Nkella in the Deep this whole time.

Could this have been what Philo was trying to tell me whenever she'd tried to get me to use my powers?

I'm such an idiot.

I still don't know how I was able to see into the Deep without Nkella being here. How was I able to see into his memory?

A thud comes from one of the rooms. They're awake.

Here goes nothing.

I walk out my door, but no one else is out of their rooms yet. Tiptoeing downstairs, I decide to knock on Kae's door. He opens it, his brows furrowing when he sees me.

"Can we talk?" I whisper. He opens it wider for me to walk in. I close the door behind me, and surprise flickers over his features. I don't usually walk into his bedroom. He stands in front of his bed staring at me expectantly, saying nothing. His clothes and weapons are laid out—he's packing. "I just got back from visiting the Empress. I used the World Card."

"Daí?" His eyes narrow. "What for?"

"You're going to want to sit down for this." Confusion marks his forehead, but he takes a seat at the edge of his bed, and I stand in front of him. "I didn't tell you everything that happened last night." A muscle tenses in his jaw, but I continue talking before he can say anything. "The reason I didn't was because I had just eaten a cookie and I didn't know if what I was experiencing was real. But then, when I went up to my room, I had a vision which made a lot of things that have been happening make sense."

This makes him relax a bit. He listens intently to me telling him everything from the World Card showing me the plain Devil Card (which he already knew about), to the real vision I had of Nkella in the Deep, to my visit to the Empress's Tower. And now, I explain the plan for me to go to the Deep and bring our captain back.

I don't think I've ever seen Kaehante's jaw drop so close to the floor.

"This is madness," he finally says. My stomach sinks.

"You don't believe me?" My voice cracks.

He lets out a half chuckle, which sounded more like nerves than anything else. "I believe you, Soren. I believe you. But it's still madness."

"I have to go get him, Kae. He would do the same—"

A scream comes from outside the tree house. "Lordy! What the hell—"

My eyes widen. Kaehante and I bolt outside and run out through the wooded path to find AJ at the foot of the beach. Psychic Arcana soldiers with their white pearly masks surround the *Gambit*.

"They're seizing our ship!" AJ runs at them, but Kae tackles him to the ground. "What the—Get off me, you big oaf!"

"AJ, it's fine." I run to him and Kae while the Empress's Tower flag is hoisted over the *Gambit*'s flag with the skull and horns. I don't like it. And I know the crew won't either, but this is what has to be done.

AJ squirms from under Kae, and he looks from him to me. "I can shoot them down." He grabs his gun.

"Koj. Let it be, AJ," Kae tells him.

AJ's features twist, and he stares at me.

"Let them do their job," I press. "Let's go inside and talk."

He gapes at me. "What's going on?"

The sound of Tessa's chair greets us as Kae lets AJ up. "What's happening out here?" she asks.

"Inside, Tessa," Kae tells her. Her surprised look twists my stomach.

"Are they taking our ship?"

"No, they're not," I say. "We all have to talk."

Inside, AJ calls a crew meeting. To my surprise, Ntaoru is still here. Apparently, she slept in Tessa's room. She rubs her eyes as she walks into the kitchenette where Harold is already brewing coffee. The aroma of the dark roast smothers my senses. I've never been a coffee fan, and we didn't even know the beans grew on this island, but the Hermit is a forager and taught Harold how to supplement his old addiction. Thanks to them, I'm now addicted too.

Kaehante and I stand at the center of the living area as I explain everything I'd just explained to Kaehante. The looks of horror, hope, and fear blend across the tree hut. After I finish the whole story, I'm met with weary faces.

"Why didn't you tell someone you were going to the Tower? She could have kept you prisoner." Tessa's voice is filled with concern. Maybe she doesn't blame me for Nkella's decision to make his sacrifice.

"I just wanted to be sure before I said anything. I was afraid of giving everyone hope that Nkella could be alive only to let you all down. Again."

"Again?" Tessa sounds surprised. "I never blamed you, Soren. I hope you know that."

AJ smiles back at me. "I've been trying to tell her."

I avert my eyes. Ntaoru is sitting in the back, her dark eyes narrowed and fixed on me.

"My brother trusted you?"

My heart aches. I nod weakly. "Eventually, he did. And then I let him down."

"I don't know if you did or not, daí? I do know he would do anything for his crew. If there's even the tiniest chance his curse is keeping him alive in the Deep, then we're wasting time." She stands and my heart skips a beat. "What are we waiting for? Let's move. Everyone pack."

AJ jumps. "I'll get the food ready."

"I'll pack for the both of us, mei?" Lāri gives him a quick kiss on his lips before taking a dash upstairs.

Tessa calls behind her as she drives toward her room. "I'll get the bombs and potions. Kae, do we need to go to town?"

"I'm already packed since I was going to leave for Danū. I can go to town while you get your things ready."

"Someone, let the Hermit know we're leaving," AJ calls. Tessa answers that she's on it.

My eyes skim the room. This is really happening. We're going to Oleanu—Cups—to meet the kings who have the Ace of Cups card. Then we're off to the Deep. My eyes fall on Harold and Kenjō sitting on the floor. They glance up at me.

He rubs the frost at the edge of his eyes. This isn't Harold's quest.

"What are you guys going to do?" I ask softly, bending down to their eye level.

Harold and Kenjō exchange a glance.

"I haven't mastered all of my runes yet, but I have them all made. I just need to bond with each of them, which I can do anywhere. As ready as I am to leave, I can't without being able to open a portal out of here —which as you know, the Empress has me blocked. You can't open a portal to Jötunheim with the World Card, right?"

I shake my head, but a smile spreads on my face. "Only to earth. But the Empress *is* allowing me to open a portal in order to travel to the Deep."

Harold's brow perks up, and Kenjō's eyes widen.

"Which means she's temporarily allowing portals to open once I have the Ace of Cups."

"So I'm no longer blocked from leaving?" Harold's face blanks as he stares into space. I move my hand in front of his face, and he cuts his gaze back to me.

"Sorry, I just—so much is happening all at once. I'll finally get to leave this place and continue my quest. I was starting to think I was going to be stuck here forever."

I wince and glimpse Kenjō frowning. She moves a loose strand of hair from her face. Her lips morph into a fake smile, cat eyes flashing as she places a hand on his arm. I don't think he meant it the way it came out. Staying here means he'd die when his heart freezes over. But no one has wanted to breach that subject since there's nothing we could do about it.

Until now.

"You have four of your runes mastered," Kenjō says. "You need them all to open the portal, á?"

"I'll need to work on my runes while on the ship," he says. His tone indicates that he's completely unaware of what she must be feeling. "Also"—he smiles—"I care about the crew, and I owe Nkella for doing what he did. Without him, I'd still have the undead curse. But if I don't move fast, my own curse will kill me." Frost forms under his eyes, and he rubs it away. Kenjō rubs his back.

"How long do you have?"

"There's no telling. Kenjō is in danger on the water though. If her mother finds her—"

"But I also want to help," Kenjō cuts in. "So we're both going with you to make sure you travel safely."

"Are you sure?" I ask, looking at both of them.

Harold digs into his jacket and pulls out the leather pouch that holds his runes. "Are you kidding? What better way to practice my magic than with actual battles?"

I scoff. "Hoping we won't have any. We're traveling with the Empress's sails, and Oleanu will be expecting us."

"That doesn't mean other pirates won't come after one of her ships," Kenjō says.

My stomach twists at the thought. "That would be such a waste of time."

Harold smiles at me. "We've got this. And when you find Nkella—and I know you will—let him know we helped get you down there."

When we're ready to go and head back outside, the Arcana are gone, and the ship's flag has changed to gold with the Tower's emblem. I'm carrying a sack full of my things: two pairs of pants, four shirts I've acquired since being here, my bandoleer, and the two Tarot cards in my possession.

Tessa locks the door behind us and covers the tree hut with an invisibility potion. It probably won't last the entire time we're gone, but the Hermit will come around from time to time to add more and to tend to the garden. We make our way to the shore to board the *Gambit* when an Arcana soldier emerges at the edge of the woods.

Talia straightens as she lets go of the soldier. Her once loose bouncy curls are tied into a tight bun. I cringe. I don't know how she can obediently cling to these agentless beings behind their masks. They're almost like ghosts. Or robots. Following orders. They can't remember who they were before.

She wrinkles her face, and I change the disgusted expression I'm sure I'm wearing. "Everything okay?" she asks.

"Yep. Just leaving." The Arcana soldier stares at me through hollow eyes, and I clear my throat. "What's that?" Talia's holding a piece of neatly folded fabric, which she holds up.

"The Empress said you should all wear these so that it looks legit."

I scoff. "Did she use the word 'legit'?"

Talia rolls her eyes. "No. Here." She stuffs the garments into my hands, and I can't prevent the sardonic expression from rising to my face. "Does she really think the crew is going to wear uniforms from the Tower?"

"Over my dead body," Tessa mutters under her breath as she drives past us in her wheelchair.

I almost die laughing. "Yeah, thanks but, hard pass."

Talia shrugs. "Wear them, don't wear them. But if you want a disguise to get you out of any trouble, you might want to wear them."

I run a finger through the fabrics and stop at one that's lacy. If I didn't know any better, this one would be mine. Tucking the clothes under my arm, I shoulder my sack and head toward the shore. "Thanks. I'll see you as soon as I can."

"Promise me, you won't die."

I stop and gape at her. "Come on, Talia."

She takes a few steps forward. "Look, I know you're still really mad at me, and I think I messed up big, but...just promise me."

"I promise." She runs up and hugs me. I hug her back, clutching the sack in one hand. Letting go, I stare at her. "Are you sure you're safe with her?"

She nods. "She can be mean and tough sometimes, but I am learning a lot. And she has guards on me all the time."

That's probably to make sure I don't take her away with the World Card. "I don't understand you sometimes, Talia, but...it's your choice. You'll have to show me what she's taught you when I get back."

"I will."

"Ntaoru!" AJ yells from inside the ship. "Do you want us to wait for you to check the ship?" He stares down at me when I reach the foot of the gangway. "Hey, Soren, what are those?"

I'm about to crack a joke about our uniforms when Ntaoru steps up behind me. "Why would I want you to wait to check the ship, daí? Check the ship. Why is it not being checked? Kh."

My face pales, and I quickly walk up the gangway. I'm not sure I can get used to being this close to Ntaoru. After we left Swords, she went off on her own instead of joining us on our missions. She wanted time to find herself, to listen to her own thoughts. After everything she went through, well...I'd probably want the same thing. And with what happened to her brother, we'd be a constant reminder that he's gone because of me. I understand not wanting to be around the sadness, but now that she's back, I'm getting these weird butterflies every time she's around me.

Not the flirty kind. The kind that makes me feel weary and uneasy. She's Nkella's sister, and I want her to like me, but I know she should hate me. She's tall, strong, beautiful. Perfect in so many ways. As agile and skilled as her brother. She was meant to be the captain of this ship and rule Danū before she was taken by the Empress.

She has a regal yet military nature about her, different from Nkella in some ways, but just like him in so many others. I can't explain how I feel around her. Like I'm close to him, but so far from him at the same time. I can see him in her, but I can also see that she's not him.

And thinking of how she must feel about me makes me want to hurl.

She narrows her eyes as she catches me staring at her, and my cheeks flush.

"I just thought you would want to be here to witness it." AJ interrupts our silent staring contest. "You know, since you haven't been here and might not trust our abilities."

Ntaoru walks past me and leans toward AJ. "I trust you, daí?"

AJ nods and smiles. "Thanks, Cap."

But Ntaoru is already making her way down to the next level. His eyes fall to mine. "What were you saying about those?" He motions with his nose toward the garments in my hands.

"AJ, help me with one of these." Kae kicks a barrel to the edge of the gangway, while simultaneously carrying one on each shoulder. AJ runs down to collect the barrel at Kae's feet, when Harold jumps down to help him.

Kae glances at Harold. "No chickens this time?"

Harold scowls. "Didn't bother."

Kae furrows his brows. "What's on the menu, then?"

"Oi! No one is eating any birds!" Lāri calls from above, and I can't help laughing.

"He's joking, love. Kae knows what's on the menu because he helped pack these barrels. We'll have fresh fish and meat until it's gone, then it's dehydrated bits, which I'll get started on..."

His voice fades. I stand here admiring my crew. It's not quite like old times, but it still feels like home. Despite the dire danger we're headed toward, I can't help but feel a semblance of...happiness. Until I remember what I have to do, and then I'm back to being anxious.

I take a deep breath. We can do this.

"Captain." Kae plants the two barrels down near the steps as Ntaoru walks back up. "Is there a specific way you want things arranged?"

Ntaoru's face blanks as she slowly turns to stare at Kae. "What did you say?"

Kae starts to repeat himself. Tessa drives her chair toward Ntaoru, followed by Kenjō.

"Captain, we set up my lab to make raku potions, but we'll need to have some on the ready soon."

"I'll set up the gunpowder as well," Kae agrees.

"Everybody, shut up." Ntaoru says. Her voice is almost too low to hear, but I hear it. It sounds raspy, like she's about to explode. I stare at her, awestruck. The crew members exchange glances.

"Is something wrong?" Lāri asks.

Ntaoru holds the bridge of her nose and shakes her head. "Ko ko ko *koj*. We need to talk. I am not captain."

AJ lets out an exaggerated gasp, and Lāri smacks his elbow.

"I cannot be your captain. I have spent the better of two years under the Empress's guise. You think Nkella was out of control with his curse? Imagine me. Every time I close my eyes, I see myself killing an Ipani under her control. I was unable to stop myself. I've killed people I grew up with and love..." Her voice shakes. "I find myself staring into space as things happen around me. I am not fit to lead any of you, nor do I want to. I look forward to performing basic daily tasks and finding my brother. Nothing more." She crosses her arms, and I don't miss how her fists are balled up under them.

AJ fidgets with his bandana in his hands, his hair covering his face. "I thought—well, I saw your new mark earlier."

Ntaoru stares at her arm and gasps.

"You hadn't seen it?" AJ asks.

"It must have just appeared." She further inspects it, passing her fingers over what looks like a wheel of a ship. I don't remember Nkella having that mark. Her eyes find mine, and I shrink back.

"Soren has it too."

"What?" I stare down at my arms. The one on my right still displays the Fate's web. I know that one won't change. But the one on my left is...I suck in a tiny gasp. "She's right." A ship's wheel has replaced my Fool's *O*. My brows furrow. "Wait...this isn't what you think it is."

Harold stands to inspect our marks. A soft "ohh" escapes his lips. Our eyes lock.

"The Wheel of Fortune," we say in unison.

"What's this mean, daí?" Ntaoru asks, still grasping her arm.

AJ screams as he pulls up his sleeve and stares at his forearm. "I have it too!"

"Do we all have it?" I ask as the crew pulls up their sleeves to check their arms. Each of them has the Wheel of Fortune mark.

"This is the first time I've seen this mark," Tessa says. "Maybe it's not too late to find the hermit and ask."

Even the Fates lack insight outside of their reality. No matter how much they think they control.

Kaehante studies it intently. "All of us having this mark cannot be good, daí?"

"Wheel of Fortune? Sounds like it means good luck and fortune?" AJ gives us a lopsided grin.

I clear my throat. "It *can* mean that," I say carefully, recalling what the hermit had told me, "but it also means that things may happen outside of our control. Fate is at work." I remember it from Asteria's teachings, although, I didn't fully understand it then.

"What else is new? The Fates always control what we cannot," Ntaoru spits out. I'm not sure if any of her vehemence was directed at me. "Why do we all have it? Daí?"

I shake my head. "I wish I knew."

"Let's figure this out later, okay?" AJ says. "We don't know what the mark does yet. Right now, we need to decide who will be our captain."

They all look between each other.

"Someone needs to captain the ship," Tessa declares.

"Why not you?" Kae asks. Tessa widens her eyes and shakes her head.

"I did that once, remember?"

I let them talk among themselves as I stare at my new mark. The Wheel of Fortune in the *Rider-Waite* card deck is colorful, showing many possibilities. This one has a natural tone of a ship's steering wheel —I'm guessing, to show the many ways a ship can turn. How fast the seas can change. A change in course. I have a sinking feeling this mark is a warning—not one that brings us special power.

"I remember. We lost track of the route because you instructed everyone to do completely different tasks," AJ says to Tessa.

"And I only took control because Nkella had gotten captured. I never want to be captain again. I'll stick to my job as a tinkerer and making raku potions." She looks at Kae.

"Nuh-uh," AJ scowls. "Kae, I love you, but we need you to be the master gunner. If you're in charge, that leaves me to do your job, and I don't do well staring at gunpowder all day. I'll lose my mind down there —I much prefer the kitchen. Besides, you're not commanding enough."

Kae grunts.

"Sorry, you're not. But we love you for it, buddy."

"Hn." Kae turns to Ntaoru. "Nkella is my cousin and your brother, Nto." She squeezes her eyes shut and looks away. "We're in this together. It should be one of us to captain the *Gambit*. We all have trauma to work through. Hn? Nkella managed."

I nod in agreement.

Everyone's eyes skim the deck, passing over Harold and Kenjō. I guess Lāri was also skipped over since she'd been kidnapped and doesn't have enough experience in all ship departments.

"Shall we vote then?" I ask.

Ntaoru turns to me and narrows her eyes. I return her gaze.

Lifting her chin, she steps toward me. "You returned ouma to the crew?" My brows furrow, and everyone stares at us.

"To all the Ipani with the Ace of Wands, yeah...even though it didn't go as I had hoped but—"

"And you are owner of the sword and the cards...and you directly oppose the Empress."

It wasn't a question. "I guess so. I never wanted to but—"

"And you, Soren, you care about my brother, daí? You've stayed with the crew even though your home is somewhere else."

"They're my family now. Home is where my crew is." I give them a sheepish smile. AJ widens his eyes and stares at Ntaoru.

"You are the Past Fate, the only one we know who can defeat the Empress when this is all over. The one who sees visions of my brother being alive. One of those he loved enough to sacrifice himself for." My stomach turns. "Daí?"

My cheeks redden. Tessa and Lāri both gasp.

"You were cunning enough to be granted safe passage to Oleanu. You convinced the Empress that Nkella can defeat Death." She now looks to her left and right to glance at the crew. "And you are powerful."

I sigh deeply. "I'm not so sure about that."

"You know how to rig?"

I squeeze the clothes in my arms. "Yes. Kae taught me."

"You know cannons?"

"Kae taught me that too."

"You know where everything goes?"

"I've cooked and cleaned, so yeah, I guess you can say that." I scratch the back of my head. "But I think Kae would make a better captain."

"Kaehante is a knight of Danū and the first mate—he doubles as the master-at-arms. I am the quartermaster and will be at your side every step of the way. We train you." She points at Kae. "If he's captain and dies, we have to scramble. But if you die, we still have Kaehante."

"That doesn't make me feel any better." I hear Harold chuckle from the stairs behind Tessa.

"Kae?" I glance at him. There's no way he'd vote for me to be captain.

"That's logical," he answers. "If this ship gets stopped, you have the Empress's mark to prove we're sailing under her command. You being captain does make the most sense."

"Do you know how to steer the ship?" Ntaoru asks. My cheeks heat. "Nkella taught me once, but...have you all lost your minds?"

"I'll be honest, Soren." AJ stares at me. "I wouldn't have expected this, but—"

"Kaehante and Ntaoru are right." Tessa finishes for him. "For more reasons than one. You learned that Nkella is still alive, so if not for you, we wouldn't be going on this voyage. This is your journey. As much as we all want to go and bring our captain back, this quest is yours. You should be captain."

"But I'm not from here. I don't have a map. I don't even know how *to follow* a map!"

"We'll teach you," AJ says. "You know how to do most things on this ship. If any oumala animal comes scoping us from an enemy ship, they'll know who the real captain is. We can't just have you pretend. You're the one with the power on this mission, being a Past Fate and all, so I'm seconding what Tessa just said. You have more direction than any map because you can see what's going on in Nkella's past—in the Deep. It has to be you."

Ntaoru rights herself. "I vote Soren as standing captain of the *Devil's Gambit* until we bring my brother back from the Deep. All in favor, say 'Aye.'"

The saliva drains from my mouth as I stare at the crew, shaking my head. To my disbelief, AJ, Tessa, and Lāri all say, "aye," followed by Kae, and then Harold and Kenjō.

Ntaoru steps closer. "The crew has cast their vote. We hereby name you Captain Soren of the *Devil's Gambit*."

I CANNOT BELIEVE THE ONE PERSON WHO I THOUGHT HATED me the most just voted me captain of the ship.

My lips dry, and I remember my mouth is hanging open.

"Those look like Tower colors," AJ says. "What are they?"

"Oh." I look down at the stack of clothes I'm still holding. "Oh, these!" I chuckle nervously. "The Empress sent these down with Talia for us to wear."

"I told her, 'Over my dead body,'" Tessa crosses her arms.

"Yeah," I tossed the pile from hand to hand. "I told her there was no way any of us would want to wear them."

"But?" AJ raises his brows, and I sigh.

"But...what you guys just said about being convincing if we get stopped...well, we don't want to look like a bunch of pirates masquerading under the Tower's colors to other ships."

Kae and Ntaoru both share a look as the rest of the crew quiets. Ntaoru is the first to step forward to look through the garments, but the others quickly follow. I stare at them, awestruck, as they start pulling the clothes from my hand to inspect them.

I'll be honest, I expected a little more pushback, but even Tessa seems to be on board. They each grab an outfit, and I hold onto the one with the silvery webs. "I don't expect us to be wearing them at all times," I add, "but keep them close just in case."

"Right then. Shall we unpack?" Tessa reverses her chair with the clothes draped over her thighs. "The sooner we get to sorting out the ship, the sooner we can set sail."

I pick up my sack of belongings and head downstairs, only to be gripped by my shoulder. I stifle a breath as Ntaoru dangles a set of keys attached to a leather cord in her hand.

"Where are you going, daſ?"

"My room."

She smiles and shakes her head. "Not with us."

I blink at her. "Where am I supposed to sleep?"

"These are from Kae, so keep them close." She drops the keys in my hands and motions to the captain's quarters. "You're the captain now. There's a reason the captain's bedroom overlooks the ocean."

I chew on my cheek. "We don't have to follow all the rules, right? I'd rather be with all of you."

"If we do not follow all—or at least come close to the rules, we allow for grave mistakes. You need your eyes up on top." She points to both my eyes with two fingers.

She's really by the book, isn't she? "I just don't think I can sleep in there. Too many...memories."

"Sleep outside the room in a hammock then." She pushes past me and heads down the ramp. I stand there staring at the back of her head. Biting my lip, I climb up to the captain's quarters. My chest grows heavy with each step. Memories flood my vision. Sneaking into his room to steal back the World Card. Him catching me. His closeness. His lean body. His tattoos. His gaze.

That night at the wheel.

My cheeks burn.

Standing in front of the door, I grip the key. Then I stick it into the keyhole. I turn it until the door opens and put the leather cord over my head, tucking the key under my shirt. Stepping inside, the damp musky air of an unused room assaults my senses. The room is dark and the windows covered; only a little light comes through the thick beige curtains. The bedsheets are neatly folded. The crew came in and cleaned after we rescued the ship on Piupeki. Some things are missing from Demitri's gang looting. Nkella's bow and arrow. His weapons. That still ties an angry knot in my gut.

But other things, like his carved animals, are still on his desk. His clothes and other items are here because they couldn't find the key for the drawers. I guess they didn't care to break it. They had other things in mind when Demitri took the ship.

I set down my sack on the small table to my left, and open one of the glass windows to let in the ocean breeze. That's better. Maybe Ntaoru is right. They voted me captain, so I need to start acting like one. If this is the smartest place for me to be, then this is where I'm going to be.

I tie my hair up in a ponytail and begin to put my things away. It's still his. He'll get it back. But until then, I'm borrowing it.

"Keep the wheel straight. That's it." The boat rocks a little to the right, and Kae straightens it for me. "Keep it here."

While I'm doing my best to keep the wheel steady, the rest of the crew pulls on the ropes to raise the sails, and the ship starts to sail backward. I hold my breath the entire time. I can't imagine it was like this when Nkella stole the ship. Did he know how to sail before climbing aboard? Or did he just figure it out?

"Turn the wheel all the way, you have plenty of room. If this were in a berth, there would be no room for error, but this is good practice. Now move the wheel the other way." I do as he tells me, and the ship starts to straighten out toward the open sea. This isn't so hard.

"Usually, you would have studied the map and known where to go. But we know we're headed east, daí? Which is on the other side of the island, so we have to go north first, then make a right."

"How long will it take to reach Oleanu?"

"One week. We traveled much farther to get here from the ruins in Piupeki. It'll be a straight shot once we make that right turn, but we'll have to sail through the *harao*, the saltwater valleys, to *Oe Nu*. We'll study the map later, daí? Keep the wheel steady." He corrects my hands; I'd accidentally let them drift down while he was talking. The wind hits my face as we sail north, and my body is tense.

"Relax your arms."

I take a deep breath and try to relax.

The boat hits a hard wave, and I gasp, grabbing the wheel harder. Kaehante chuckles.

AJ climbs up the steps. "We're on water, Soren. The ship is going to jump sometimes—it's normal." I give him a tight smile. "Sails are ready, and I have the potion." He waves an orange bottle. Kaehante takes it from AJ and hands it to me.

"I remember where this goes," I say. I insert the bottle below the wheel where there's an hourglass-shaped hole, careful not to break the glass.

"This one is only for speed. But we have one for speed and transparency to use in an emergency. It is already under your seat." I look where he's pointing and find a built-in wooden compartment I hadn't seen before. "We only have one, so we use it if we're under attack, daí?"

I nod. "I know. Besides, the Empress said transparency will make it easier for Tetalla to find me."

"Hopefully, it will not be needed. When you're ready, turn the potion clockwise to go. To slow down, inch it to the left."

"Got it."

He nods at me. "Give it a turn."

I turn it to the right and the ship zooms forward. AJ buckles low to the ground, grabbing the rail. Lāri is thrown out of her crow's nest, and my heart leaps from my throat. Shifted to a bird, she flies behind us.

"Pay attention." Kae's voice booms. "Turn it to the left."

I snap my gaze straight ahead. The crew yells profanities over the flapping of the sails, but the wind and waves crash over their voices. I reach down to the potion bottle and turn it to the left. The ship halts, and a wave lifts the stern high, sending me hard against the wheel. AJ almost flies off the stairs. Kaehante reaches down and fixes the bottle to an easy speed.

My chest is panting hard, and I wince apologetically. AJ holds his mouth and stomach. "I'll leave you to it," he muffles as he runs down the steps.

Ntaoru walks up the steps with a sarcastic grin smeared across her face as she looks at me. "Learning is going well, I see?"

"Sorry."

"I don't have a weak stomach. And I'm confident that you'll learn. Steering a ship isn't so hard. It just takes practice." She slaps Kae on the shoulder. "You won't be alone either, daí? We'll swap places but one of us will be with you the entire time."

That makes me feel better. Then again, maybe she's only saying that because she really doesn't want to be captain.

"Now try again, slowly this time," she tells me.

Turning the bottle to the right, one notch at a time, the ship gains a little speed. Kae instructs me to turn it a bit farther since we want to make good time, and I start to get a feel for how far and fast this ship will go with each turn of the potion. We don't want to go too fast either because one, it's faster than any of us can handle—faster than any captain can handle while maintaining control of the ship, and two, we don't want to run out of sailing potion and have to do this manually the rest of the way. That's a good way to turn a one week voyage into two.

I steer for about two hours with Kaehante sitting beside me, giving me instructions and catching the wheel if I start to lose control of the current. It's a big ship, and I'd never realized how much the sails will carry us, even with the potion. At lunchtime, we slow the potion down and lower the sails. We're still going, and the ouma is keeping us straight on our path, but I keep staring at the sails as I scarf down my food.

"It's not a waste of time to rest and replenish," Kenjō tells me. She's been watching me eat.

"I know, but I'm trying to get us there as fast as I can."

"It will take one week at this speed—that is making good time from our location. You're doing everything you can," Tessa adds.

I shrug and take a bite of fresh cooked fish with lime and herbs. There's even some mashed potato on the side. Ever since they've been free of the undead curse, AJ has been an excellent cook. Since we were unable to get supplies to last us for the entire journey, we have to eat all the fresh stuff first.

After we eat, Harold takes the wheel while Kaehante helps me study the map inside the captain's quarters. Luckily, Harold had been interested in steering for the last six months, so we can rely on him to take a few shifts. Ntaoru is enjoying her solitude, filling the cannonballs with gunpowder below deck while Kae is up here with me. The rest of the crew is off doing other tasks around the ship.

"So these are the harao?" I point to a crooked line inside of Oleanu.

He nods. "And this is the Prefect's Tower at its entrance. But with the Empress's safe passage, we shouldn't have any problem getting past."

I rub my cheeks and stare at the map. "How tight will it be, sailing through the harao?"

"This map isn't the greatest show of scale. It will be wide enough." He assures me. "But in any case, either I, Ntaoru, or AJ will be there to help."

My brows quirk and I stand, picking up the World Card from the desk. I lay it alongside the map, comparing the two. The map on the World Card is a tiny bit different; a large skeleton of a serpent runs along the edge of Danū outside the fortress walls. "What is this?" I show Kae the card, and he squints at the small image.

"Hn. Your World Card is more recent. That was put in place as a warning not to cross."

"I guess that makes sense since the cards are magic." But I wonder...I walk out of the captain's quarters, and Kaehante follows me. Wind smacks my face as I hold out the World Card. I picture the entrance to the harao of Oleanu that leads to the castle, then I picture the Prefect's Tower at the entrance and ask for a portal to open.

"Soren?" Kaehante stands next to me.

A purple light shoots out of the card, opening a portal right behind Harold at the wheel.

The portal is easily big enough for a person to walk through, but not an entire ship. Not to mention the portal would have to be far enough at sea for the ship to fit, and I'm afraid to throw the card down in the water. Who knows if it'll follow me as it usually does if there's no way for the ship to cross. I lower the card and the portal closes.

I glance at Kae. "I wanted to see something."

He rubs his chin. "Do you think there's a way for the ship to go through the portal?"

I sway as the ship rocks back and forth. "I hope I can figure that out, but I think the cards were only meant for individuals. And we need the ship to get to the Deep—the Empress confirmed it."

"Hn. Back to studying the map then." A sly smile spreads on his face. "Can you tell me how far we have to go before we have to make a right turn?"

I screw up my face. A test? "Umm...I know there's some multiplication involved."

"Let me show you. Then later, you'll learn to navigate at night."

I take a deep breath and rub my eyes. "Can AJ take the wheel so that Harold could make me some coffee?"

"You're captain." He squares his jaw. "Tell him to make us both coffee."

By sunset, we've reached the northern tip of Dempu Yuni, and I stare at the cloud formation growing thicker over Rutavenye, the floating Tower Island. I've spent so many mornings staring at the Tower, wondering what Talia was doing, and thinking over memories of the past I've witnessed, memories of Tetalla and Adara.

"Looks like rain." Harold walks up behind me with AJ.

Kaehante is asleep so he'll be rested up for the second night shift. I yawn into my shoulder. I'm looking forward to knocking out...considering I've been awake going on twenty-four hours now.

"Harold, what are the chances of that being a light shower and not a torrential thunderstorm?"

He raises an eyebrow, but his face is weary.

AJ smacks Harold on the back. "It'll be fine, and I'm taking over anyway, so scoot." I stand so AJ can take the wheel.

"Thanks, AJ."

Rain starts pattering on the hardwood just as the sun gets eaten by the horizon.

"Oh, Soren?"

I look back at AJ.

"Good job on your first day as captain." He winks.

I smile. "Thanks."

"Are you going to hang out?" Harold asks.

I stifle another yawn. "Not tonight. I need my sleep. Especially if I'm meant to be back at the wheel at first light."

"Sweet dreams then. We'll hold down the fort."

A cool breeze chills me as I step into the darkness of my borrowed room. The flicker of the lantern right outside the open window grants me enough light to search for matches to burn the candles. Once I do, the room comes alive with shadows candlelight dancing on the walls.

For some reason, this makes me miss him even more. The flickering flames bring me back to the specs of fire behind his eyes.

Hold on, Nkella. Your crew is coming to get you.

I bathe in the tiny tub and get ready for bed. When I walk out of the bathroom, two glowing purple eyes greet me from the top of my pillow.

This warms my heart. "Sapphire, I wondered if you'd find me." I climb on the bed and make myself comfortable, gently stroking Sapphire's back. Her soft purrs let me know she's comfortable, and I drift off to sleep.

It's a restless night of tossing and turning.

Nkella is tied to a post, and someone is overshadowing him. Blood drips down his chin from his nose, and his eyes are puffy. Someone punches him hard on the face. Then again. And again. I scream. I shout at whoever is hitting him to stop. He can't take it anymore. His eyes flicker red, but he's losing consciousness. I can feel him slipping away.

I can't see where I am. There's no red hue. Is this a memory of him in the Deep or sometime in his past?

I can't tell. Why can't I tell?

"Shh sh sh...uoko yani."

I'm pulled out of my dream. A weight presses down on me. I'm already forgetting the dream I was just in...why was I so upset?

I'm standing on a red sandy beach. The moon is out, but it's warm beneath my feet. And the waves are serenading...calm.

"Quiet your busy mind. So much fury. You remind me so much of her..."

Wait—that voice. "Who's there?" My voice comes out like a hoarse whisper.

"I can stare at you for eternity, and I would never tire, uoko yani."

Tetalla.

I can hear him like he's close, even feel his breath against my skin... but I can't see him. "Where are you?"

"Do you want to see me?"

"Yes." I spin around looking for the source of his voice. A strong wind blows between my hair, bringing with it the warm scent of sun and sandalwood. Then the sand starts to spin into the form of a man. At first, it's a hooded skull, but as the sand starts to solidify, his skin starts to form. Tetalla stands before me. Flesh and bone. He wears a black hooded robe, the muscular physique of his chest and abs peeking between the robe's opening. A longsword hangs from his belt over black pants.

I've seen him before in Adara's memories, but never this close. His handsome face stares at me, and I have to remind myself who he is. This is Death.

"Hello, uoko yani. I can feel you drifting on the ocean. Are you going somewhere?"

"You must have the wrong person. I'm not...Uwoko—what did you call me?"

A soft chuckle makes his shoulders rise, and a mischievous twinkle fills his eyes.

"How can you feel me drifting?" I ask, knowing I'm not going to like his answer.

"I can feel everyone's heartbeat. It's louder when their time is soon up. Yours is faint, but I can find you when you sleep. I can feel your heart beating between my fingers." As he reaches toward me, his fingers touch the corners of my mind, stirring my memories. I stretch my neck, trying to shake the feeling.

A dark and cynical laugh fills the air. His voice is smooth like velvet, tempting me to believe he couldn't just snap me in half or turn into the Devil I saw before he sent himself to the Deep. Before so many people died from his vengeful temper.

"What do you want with me?" I finally ask.

A wicked smile creeps over his face, and he takes a step closer. I hold my breath as he presses his face close to mine and smells my hair. I step back, but he laughs.

"Sleep now." He presses his finger to my forehead, and I drift again, deeper this time.

I don't know when it started, but someone is stroking my hair. It feels nice, so I lean into it. A soft moan escapes my mouth. Then I get a phantom image of a skeleton hand and jerk away.

Sure enough, a skeleton hand is on my pillow and stroking my hair.

I jump up, reaching for the dagger under my pillow, and stab at the hand until it disappears.

Sapphire hops and with a loud pop, she disappears into the Aō.

I sit up in a cold sweat, my heart beating hard in my chest. My eyes brim with tears, but I wipe them away.

Wind howls, and I step out of bed to see who's steering the ship.

AJ. It's not too late then.

Turning back to my bed, I hear a pop from the dark corner behind the door. Expecting to see Sapphire, I stop at the sight of two bright red eyes.

A wolf steps into the dim candlelight, and my knees buckle. "Iéle?" I whisper.

She walks slowly toward me with her head low. Carefully inching my way backward, I let myself fall against the bed, scared of what she'll do since Nkella isn't here. The wolf never liked me.

She whimpers at my feet, laying her head on my thigh. I hold my breath, staring wide-eyed at her. She whimpers again, and this time I slowly bring my hand to the top of her head to gently stroke her fur.

My heart breaks.

I wonder if she heard noises coming from Nkella's room and came to see if it was him. She must miss him so much.

Iéle left after Nkella died. Or we thought she did.

"Don't worry, Iéle, we're going to find him and bring him back." I feel a gentle tug of ouma, as if she wants to bond, but only a little. Still, it's enough to tell me she's willing to communicate for the time being. A truce.

"I can live with that."

Climbing onto the bed, I hope to get some real sleep this time. Iéle climbs on top, too, and I don't dare tell her to sleep on the floor. She makes herself comfortable at the foot of the bed, and I fall asleep feeling a little safer. Although, I'm also a little sorry that Sapphire probably left because she felt the wolf nearby.

7

Iéle is gone when I wake up.

I turn over in the sheets, the gravity of my pillow not letting me go.

Then I jerk up. Kaehante's at the wheel—I need to relieve him of duty. Scrambling to my feet, I pull half the covers onto the floor with me. It takes about fifteen minutes to get myself dressed, face washed, and teeth brushed. The sun hasn't risen yet but my first watch of the day is first light. The good thing is the wheel is only a few feet away from the captain's quarters.

"Good morning, Kae," I greet him as I briskly step down to the quarterdeck. He wipes his face and yawns. A mist covers the sea, and the morning dew is thick, cold, and humid. I buckle my coat to the top of my throat.

"Do you think you can handle the ship in this mist?" he asks as he stands. He's looking rough; he must not have slept all that much yesterday.

"I'll be fine."

He squints at me. "I can stay until the sun comes up."

Staring out into the horizon, I point at the sun already peeking out. "The sun is coming up, Kae. I got this. Go rest." I give him a gentle shove, and he grunts.

"I cleaned the bottom floors instead of sleeping yesterday," he says. "They were covered in soot and gunpowder. One of the barrels spilled and Ntaoru needed a hand."

I have no idea why he's explaining himself to me. My eyes widen.

"Oh!" Right, because I'm technically in charge. "Umm...are we out of gunpowder? Do you know how it spilled?"

"It wasn't secured. Ship jumped..." I gasp. That was because of me. Yesterday, I caused the ship to jump. I wince. "We have enough," he says. "But you're still learning, daí? If you want, I can help you steer your shift..."

"No, go to sleep."

He raises his brows, probably unsure if he should leave me here alone while the crew is sleeping for another two hours.

"I'll be fine. There's a lot of work to do later. Go sleep. That's an order."

A smirk curls at the edge of his lip as he gives me a side-eye. "Scream if you need me."

"I'll send Iéle."

He does a double take, not knowing if I'm joking. I half am, because she left and I can't exactly communicate with her, but thinking of her makes me smile. "She's not here now but she visited me last night. Hopefully, she'll stick around."

His brows rise to the top of his bald head. "We'll talk later." He walks down the steps and calls out, "Keep it steady."

"Always."

The ship's masts block my view of the Tower that is now behind us as we sail southwest, straight to Oleanu. The sea is calm. Everything is peaceful, and I'm alone with my thoughts. At this point, we have about six days at sea, which isn't as bad as other times we've sailed to an island, granted everything goes according to plan, but with the Empress's colors, we should be fine.

The Empress didn't spare a soldier or two to guard our ship, though, and that's been eating at the back of my mind. It just seems like something she'd do to keep tabs on her investment. Unless she can't spare any. I suppose they're all guarding Danū, trying to keep Tetalla locked on the island. Although, I'm not sure what a guard or an army of guards could do to him. He's Death.

And being a warrior, he's tactical.

What's he waiting for?

He means to kill all humans.

I don't trust her. But since the World Card told me to trust her in that instance, I have to.

Most of the Arcana soldiers there are Ipani prisoners. It's hard to imagine what it looks like with all of them surrounding Danū—what the war looks like.

Rumor has it that she keeps making more soldiers. People are afraid to leave their homes for fear of being forced to become part of her agentless army. But she isn't only taking Ipani. That's how desperate she is.

The ship rocks as the mist starts to disperse, and the sun rises higher. Pink and orange hues make the water look like a painting.

An hour passes, and I'm itching for some coffee.

I remember that Nkella spent a lot of time steering the ship and studying the map. And giving Iéle orders—communicating with her about the secrets of other ships and islands. I don't have that type of communication, but I wish I did. I haven't seen Philo in ages, but she never gave messages to others for me. We didn't get a chance to tell Gari where we were headed, but maybe I can send word to him somehow.

A rain cloud forms overhead, bringing in strong winds followed by the heavy pattering of rain. I grab the wheel with both hands, keeping it steady, but the ship rocks to the right. Where did this come from? It was a beautiful morning!

The rainfall increases until large pieces of hail start hitting the wood. I grasp the wheel more tightly, but as the waves grow larger, the ship starts tilting to the right. I pull on the wheel to the left, but that only makes the ship tilt toward the wave and cause a giant surge of water to engulf us.

I lose vision in the deluge and gasp for air. Another wave carries the ship forward, and we land with a hard thud, causing several things behind me to fall and shatter. I fly over the wheel and land on my side. I quickly run back to the wheel, when another wave crashes against me, pushing me toward the bow.

Lightning illuminates the deck followed by a loud thunderclap. Jerking myself forward, I sprint back to the quarterdeck and grab the wheel. Nerves break goosebumps in my skin. If I can't get this under control, we're going to capsize, and we're all going to drown. I need help, but I can't let go of the wheel to wake them all up.

A loud clapping noise makes me spin around. I know that sound. That's not the sound of lightning. That's the sound of...

The cone of a cyclone stares us down mere feet in front of the *Gambit*.

My heart stops. It takes everything in me to force myself into action. I grab the wheel and turn it all the way to the right. We need to gain speed and get the hell out of dodge.

"Captain!" Ntaoru's voice comes somewhere in the distance. A large wave crashes over my head, and I struggle to steady the spinning wheel. Ntaoru shoves me out of the way and turns the speed up. The force of the ship now racing out of harm's way pitches me back against the captain's quarters. "This is no storm," she yells.

I scramble to my feet and run to help her. From the corner of my eyes, I see the masts being hoisted upward and AJ swinging on a rope. Kae and Lāri's voices shout over the loud winds and rain. Ntaoru steadies the wheel. We're aiming away from where we should be heading, but right now, we need to get as far as we can from the cyclone. Heavy winds threaten the masts.

I sprint down to the main deck to see what I can do to get us out of danger. Harold is helping Kenjō up. Barrels are rolling to the bottom deck. The ship catches a wave and capers to the right, causing one of the barrels to empty out whatever's inside. Afraid it could be gunpowder, I decide to go lift the barrel when green lightning illuminates inside the cyclone. I fixate on the color. Green.

I run back to the wheel. "What do you mean this isn't a storm?" I ask Ntaoru.

"Look at the color of the winds," she yells.

My web mark pulses, and I grab onto the rail of the ship so I can zone into it. Just for a second.

Something is amiss, and I need to figure out what it is. As I focus on the storm, I get a sense of someone's past. Emotions. I search deeper, trying to make out a vision, but it's hazy. I can't identify a face without a direction of where or what I'm supposed to be searching. Focus, Soren.

Then, my mind is inside someone's memories. The day is clear, not a cloud above. I'm standing on a ship, only it isn't me. I have dark skin with Ipani stripes, and I create a tiny whirling tornado on the deck, by twirling my finger from where I stand. A chuckle escapes my foreign lips as a bundle of grenades falls from someone's arms. A sandwhip slaps me in the face. My tornado spins itself out. I turn a hardened glare to Mūhī and see Bronte standing right next to him.

A sharp gasp hurts my throat. I'm back on the *Gambit*. "It's Bronte's crew!" I shout.

"Who?" Ntaoru shouts back. She's never met Bronte. Grabbing the spyglass from beside the wheel, I jump down from the quarterdeck and shout at the crew to grab weapons. I find Kenjō and alert her that it's her mother with a cyclone Ipani.

Kenjō's eyes widen in fear. "She's come for me."

Harold pushes her down the ramp. "Go hide, Kenjō. We're not letting her take you."

Tessa and Kae load cannons, while AJ and Lāri grab raku potions and their pistols.

Kae lights a match, but I yell at him to hold fire. We can't just shoot aimlessly in the cyclone's direction until we catch sight of the ship.

"Are you sure there's a ship out there?" Tessa asks.

"Yes!" The *Gambit* catches another wave, I cut my gaze to Ntaoru who is struggling with the steering. "Steer toward the cyclone!"

She gapes at me.

"Do it!"

Ntaoru steers us to the left, back the way we should be going. And now we're headed for a collision with the cyclone. Winds pick up, growing fiercer, and I run to the bow and grab onto one of the ropes, pulling myself up for a better look. Wind blows my hair back. They're not going to kill us. She wants Kenjō alive. This is an attempt to make us back down. A bluff.

And boy, only god knows how good I am at a bluff.

"Captain?" Kae shouts.

Without looking in his direction, I make a fist to let him know not to shoot yet. The hail grows thicker, and a piece of ice cuts my skin. "Let's go, bitch," I mutter, looking through the spyglass.

A bomb explodes, and I jerk against the rail, catching myself so I don't fall overboard. I crane my neck to look at Kae.

"Did you fire?"

"Koj. That wasn't us."

"Are we hit?" I jump down and run to the rail between Tessa and Kae. Harold simultaneously sprints to another cannon.

"That came from behind us!"

"There's another ship, Captain!" Ntaoru shouts. I jump up to the quarterdeck and look through the spyglass. Away from the cyclone, three ships are headed straight toward us, and with their black sails, they don't look like they're here to save us from Bronte's crew. I couldn't have misread my vision, could I?

A cannon from the first ship fires toward the cyclone.

They're not Bronte's ships.

Another bomb is thrown, but this time it hits us. The *Gambit* jolts to the side. "Fire!" I yell at Kaehante, as I jump back to the main deck. "Three more ships have joined. Fire!" I turn to Ntaoru "Get us out of here."

"There's nowhere to go!" she yells back.

She's right. We're surrounded by enemy ships. Three behind us, and one in front. My fingers twitch as I make a sudden decision and run to Ntaoru's side. I reach for the box under the chair and take out the transparency potion. "Hold the ship still as I take off speed for a second."

"They won't see us, but they can still hit us, daí?"

My heart pants in my chest. Rain rolls down my face. "Then you'd better get ready to make a sharp turn so they miss us. Are you ready?"

She nods once. "Ready, Captain."

I pull out the potion, and the ship comes to a sudden halt, causing the crew to slide toward the bow while I change bottles, then quickly ramp up the speed. A purple film sweeps the ship, masking us from sight. Ntaoru pulls us into a sharp turn as cannon fire hits the water right behind the stern. Close one.

"This won't stop them, but at least now we have some advantage," Ntaoru confirms.

Ice shatters down on the ship as the storm grows heavier. The waves grow bigger as the cyclone makes a beeline for the three ships. Ntaoru crashes into me. We both slide against the far end of the quarterdeck. Bombs explode. Between the sounds of the storm and the blasts, I lose track of the crew. Grabbing Ntaoru's hand, I help her up. The ship is a *disk'o coaster*, and I can barely keep my balance.

"Go help the crew," I tell her as I run to take the wheel.

Despite the ice and cold winds raining down on us, I'm met with a warm breeze, carrying with it a hot desert scent. "Smart girl to use transparency."

Tetalla. I wipe the water from my eyes so I can see and hold onto the wheel.

"But weren't you aware I can see you better in the Aō?" His dark chuckle makes my insides tighten. I can't deal with this right now.

Cannonballs shoot toward the cyclone as it closes in on us. Green lightning strikes down on one of the ships, and I gape as the ship catches fire—green flames.

A cannonball comes from the direction of one of the other ships and hits us. I hug the wheel to keep from getting thrown. The crew shouts, but I can't hear what they're saying.

"I can feel your death coming, uoko yani."

"Captain!" Kaehante hangs from the rail of the steps. "Do we fire back?"

I blank. "Um. Y-yes! Fire!"

"Careful," Tetalla's voice feels like he's right behind me. "They'll know exactly where you are if you do."

"Wait!" I shout. Kae pauses. What am I thinking. They hit us. They already know where we are. "Never mind! Fire!"

"Use your Fate magic, daí?" Tetalla says.

"W-wha— There's nothing I can do here." I don't even know why I'm talking to him.

"Submit to me, and you will be spared," he says. A phantom claw touches my neck, and I shiver violently.

"Submit to me..."

"Never!"

Three bombs fire from the *Gambit* and hit the ship closest to us.

The cyclone moves closer to them—it's faster now—and cuts right through both the ships. I gape as both ships are sliced in half as easily as a pair of scissors cuts through a piece of paper. Like they're nothing. The cyclone has been on the water too long, it's gained too much speed. How is that Ipani doing it? How is Bronte's ship under there?

A sense of dread sinks to the pit of my stomach.

The cyclone turns sharply and is now headed straight for us. What if Bronte is no longer on her ship? What if we're being chased because we're disguised as one of the Empress's ships, and these are pirates with a vengeance?

"Uoko yani." Tetalla's voice sounds urgent. "If you die, you will not be able to defeat the Empress. Submit to me now so I can spare your life."

"Never." I take off the transparency, and the ship almost flips over as I struggle to change it for the other.

"Captain!?" I hear the crew calling but I'll have to explain later. If there is a later.

Harold climbs up the steps and reaches a hand toward me. I grab it and pull him up.

"What are you doing?" I ask him.

"I needed to be closer."

"Closer to what?" I shout over the storm.

He extends his hand, and I stare at him, no longer feeling Tetalla's reach over me.

"Harold, what are you doing?" The ship sways to the right, and I grab the wheel. Harold's eyes turn white as icicles cloud over his eyelids. He mutters something I can't hear, and a bright blue line appears between me and the cyclone. My eyes widen as the cyclone moves back. "Wait— What's happening?"

He mutters the word again; it sounds like he's saying *"Isa."*

Another rune disappears into the cyclone. This time, the cone visibly shrinks. The winds also cease, and the hail and rain slow to a stop.

"Isa." He says the word with gumption, and the cyclone completely dissipates to reveal the *Ghost of the Sea*. And it's covered in frost.

I was right, it is Bronte's ship. Despite them almost killing us, a wave of relief washes over me. She wants Kenjō, and there isn't a doubt in my mind she won't kill us all to get her daughter, but at least, we don't have to deal with another crazy captain. Bronte killed all three of them for us.

A laughing breath escapes me, and I grab Harold's arm. "Harold, you did it."

Sunlight breaks through the clouds as relief washes over me.

He holds his chest and uses me for support.

"Dude, that was awesome!" His breathing intensifies, and I hold him up. "Harold? Are you okay?"

He squeezes his eyes tightly but nods. "Fine. Just cold." He rubs his eyes. Flakes of ice fall from his cheeks. His curse is getting worse.

"Go get warm. I've got this."

"I have to check on Kenjō."

Nodding, I let him go. He passes Ntaoru as she walks up the steps to the quarterdeck.

"Hey, Harold," I call after him. He looks back at me. "I'm glad you're getting your power back." He smiles and walks off.

"Daſ?" Ntaoru's eyes are wide as she stares at the back of his head.

"He's a magician from my world." I try to find the words that would make sense to her. "The Empress broke his magic, so he's had to remake it and relearn everything before he can leave."

She nods in understanding and stares out at the *Ghost* that's now much too close for comfort. I lean over the wheel and shout to Tessa and Kae, "Be ready."

"Aye, Captain." They say. AJ and Lāri walk up behind them and glance in my direction. We share a nod. Everyone is alive and accounted for.

The *Ghost of the Sea* sails closer. This time I stand on the rail, holding a rope. "Don't come any closer or we'll shoot."

"Prepare to be boarded, *Gambit.*" Bronte's voice comes from her ship.

"Do that, and we will shoot you down." Now I'm bluffing, I'm not going to kill Kenjō's mom. But I might start killing off her crew one by one.

A small cyclone starts spinning from the water.

"Kae, get ready," I say.

Bronte steps onto the cyclone and it carries her toward us. Well, I'll be damned. I was not expecting that.

"Ntaoru, lend me your gun." She quickly does what I ask. With one hand, I look through my spyglass to find the cyclone Ipani. Hurricanes leveled Louisiana in the past; it isn't beneath me to kill someone for causing one. There he is.

He's standing on their rail, his hands displayed in front of him as he causes the cyclone to spin. I can see Mūhī standing next to him, arms crossed as he stares at us. I point the gun at cyclone Ipani's head and take a breath. Then I pull the trigger.

I miss, but it's enough to set him off course and drop his ouma. Bronte crashes into the water.

Ntaoru starts laughing.

Mūhī spots me. One of his sand whips comes flying my way. I point the gun again and shoot at cyclone guy. This time I don't miss, and he plummets off the ship. Mūhī's face pales. He turns and gives directions to two others. Blood pools in the sea where he fell.

"Make another move and we will bomb you," I call. "I'm not playing around." I turn to Lāri. "Help Bronte onto the ship."

"Captain?" Lāri quirks a brow at me. Tessa's face is pale behind her.

"She's still Kenjō's mother. Let's see what she wants."

Eight months ago, I never would have killed someone in cold blood like I just did. But Nkella taught me that sometimes it's necessary. And I learned the hard way that he was right. Right now, it's kill or be killed. Bronte and her crew traffic Ipani for their ouma and they send oumala animals to fight. I'm not making bargains with any of them.

AJ and Kae throw down a raft so that Bronte can grab onto it, then pull her up.

"Tessa, Ntaoru, keep your eyes on the ship," I demand. "Any of them make a move, loose a cannonball."

"I think we voted well, daí?" Ntaoru winks at me.

I don't know where this sudden surge of command came from, but I hope I can hold it up.

Bronte coughs up water as soon as she's dropped to the main deck. I bend down to see her face.

"Was all that necessary? The cyclone? I mean, really?"

She stares up at me through the wet hair plastered over her eyes. "I wanted to make sure you knew we meant business."

"Oh, and how'd that work out for you?"

She spits water in my face. I cringe and wipe it off.

"You're disgusting. Get her up."

Kaehante and AJ stand her up from her shoulders. She squirms and reaches for her knife, so Kaehante yanks her by her hair. She shouts. I step forward, placing my face close to hers like Nkella used to do to me.

"Here's what's going to happen," I say. "You're going to tell your crew to stand down."

She laughs.

"Do it, or I'll have Tessa fire a cannon."

Bronte hesitates but then gives me a weak nod. Kae turns her around to face her ship and she waves a signal in the air—the command to stand down.

"Good. Now, what the hell do you want?"

"I want my daughter."

"And a friendly hello wouldn't have been enough? She's not a prisoner. If she doesn't want to go with you, I can't do anything about it."

"Why do you have Empress's colors, á?"

"Oh, this?" I motion my finger in a circle referencing the ship. "It's a disguise."

Her eyes narrow. "Why?"

"What's it to you?"

"I have a right to know what my daughter is up to. One of my utwa saw her on this ship. At first, I didn't know it was the *Gambit*. I thought she was a prisoner."

That makes more sense. "But then you saw it was me, and you still fought."

"We saved you from the fleet who tried to take down your ship."

AJ shakes his head. "Yeah, but you didn't stop there, did you?"

"How do I know I can trust a Helāni, á?" She stretches her neck to ask AJ. "She has the Empress's mark. And my daughter. I didn't know what was going on."

I exchange a look with the crew. They don't say anything, and I appreciate it. I did just kill one of her crewmates. But he almost killed us, and he had a sadistic look in his eye.

"If I let you go, are you going to try to kill me?"

"Koj."

"You better not be lying. I have no interest in hurting my friend's mother. Do you understand?"

She nods.

I give Kae a reassuring nod to let her go. She grabs her head from where he was holding her hair.

"Where is Kenjō?"

I shrug. "She doesn't want to come up."

A pained look crosses her face. "You killed one of mine, you must pay."

"He tried to kill us. I did what I had to." My answers are short, but I'm curious as to what she's going to do now that Kae has let her go.

A cannon fires, and I look past Bronte at two vultures flying toward our ship. I shake my head. Bronte takes out a knife and holds it to my neck, stepping back with me clutched under her arm.

Damnit.

The vultures land on the ship and quickly shift to their Ipani forms. AJ, Kae, and Tessa pull guns on the two birds and Bronte.

"Call Kenjō." Her breath is cold in my ear. She's shivering.

I sigh. "This isn't necessary. Let's talk about this."

One of the Ipani onboard falls to his knees, and smoke starts sizzling off his skin and ears. I move my eyes to stare at Ntaoru.

"She will burn each of your crew from the inside out," I say. "Let me go."

Armadillo shields form over Kaehante's arms, and I grin.

"I don't care how many of your crew board my ship—"

"You think you're the only ones with ouma?" She whistles, and a few more Ipani jump overboard. I expect they're making their way to us. I grind my teeth. I don't have time for this; the longer this takes, the longer it'll take us to reach Oleanu. I slide my hand into my belt and pull out my dagger, quickly pressing it against Bronte's skin, inside her shirt.

"I will gut you here and now. Again, I don't want to kill my friend's mother. But I will."

"I think you won't."

"*Ama.*" Kenjō walks up to the main deck with Harold following behind her. "Let my captain go."

"Your captain? You follow a Helāni now, á?"

"I follow her because she's going to put a stop to this war. And you are wasting our time."

Bronte holds the knife tighter to my neck, cutting my skin. I meet her the same way over her stomach. "How is she going to do that? Right now, the Empress is killing innocents to become her Arcana. She's no longer taking criminals. Another Helāni will only lead you to slaughter."

Kenjō and I share a glance.

"More and more Ipani and humans are disappearing from villages as the Empress's army grows. We have utwa circling Danū. They tell us the Arcana soldiers go there and disappear. Death takes them to form his own army, and the Empress cannot do anything about it. Please, Kenjō. I need my daughter by my side during all this."

This makes my stomach turn, and I loosen my dagger on Bronte's stomach. I do understand why Bronte is so desperate to take her daughter. I quickly hold the blade up against her skin again, not letting myself let my guard down.

"She's not like the Empress, Ama. Let her go. She's on our side."

Bronte stares at me, and I smile back. The other vulture Ipani falls to his knees, and the swimmers who jumped their ship are now climbing aboard ours.

"Apparently, your mom wants a massacre."

She lets me go. "I trust my daughter. Explain yourself."

I stretch my neck and dust myself off. "I don't have to explain anything."

The truth is that I'm afraid to speak of the plan out loud since Tetalla knows my whereabouts. I don't know if he's close or if I lost him when I got us out of transparency.

"Kenjō, grab your things. You're leaving with me."

Kenjō winces and looks at us apologetically. "It is for the best,

Soren." She reaches for Harold's hand. "If I don't go with her, she won't stop."

"Actually"—I take out Ntaoru's gun I had attached to my bandolier earlier—"if you don't leave without Kenjō and leave us the hell alone, we'll kill off your crew a lot quicker. It'll be a battle, but we'll take as many as we can. If you care about anyone on your crew, leave now, quietly." I aim the gun at the wet Ipani who just climbed aboard. He puts his hands up.

I glance back at Bronte. "I don't want to do this, so don't make me." Lowering my voice, I inch closer to her. "For reasons I can't disclose due to people in the Aō listening in, we are on a mission to save Danū and the rest of Ipa. Kenjō is safest with us, and the Empress knows we're her only hope. She won't take Kenjō for her army so long as she's with us."

Bronte narrows her eyes at me and holds me in place for a few moments as she studies my eyes and features, then finally puts her knife away.

"Thank you." I back away, but my eyes are still on her.

Kenjō walks up to her mom.

"Why do you not want to come with me?" Bronte's usually unwavering voice struggles to maintain its composure.

"I am sorry, Ama. I cannot trust you after Demitri. My entire life has been a lie. What I was doing, helping you with the rikorō...it was wrong."

"It was to save our kind."

"It was wrong, Ama. And I forever have to live with the guilt. I will not go with you. Maybe in the future. But for now, I need my time, è? Please, I ask you to respect that."

Bronte swallows. I don't know if it's the way her daughter is looking at her or that she's in shock and hurt, but she looks really small and fragile. She motions for her crew to leave the ship. It looks like Ntaoru didn't completely burn them alive, but they're going to be out of commission for a while.

Ntaoru and I hang out by the wheel as we watch Bronte board her ship and leave. I let out a huge sigh of relief and glance at the Wheel of Fortune mark on my left wrist. What matters beyond our control are going to come at us next?

8

THIS IS RIDICULOUS. I'M NOT CUT OUT TO BE A SHIP'S captain. Kaehante should take over. Holding my Alice in Wonderland playing cards, I absentmindedly practice my sleight of hand. It's been a hot minute since I've touched these cards, and despite not wanting to exercise my Past Fate power, they are currently the only thing keeping me from going insane.

The door creaks open, and Kae walks inside. "Captain?"

"Soren is fine."

He stands at the door, a perplexed look on his face.

"Seriously, just call me Soren."

He clears his throat. "The holes from the cannon fire have been remedied, and everything has been put away. All weapons are accounted for."

"Good. Thank you Kae."

"Is something the matter?"

I quickly glance at him and then back down at my cards. "Thinking about how I could have handled all that differently."

"Daf?"

"I almost capsized the ship, Kae. I shouldn't be captain." I stare at my Wheel of Fortune Card. "Our new shared mark might be making things worse, and I have too much anger to be in charge."

Kae shuts the door and takes a seat in front of me. "Or it's a warning. No matter who is captain, marks on any of the crew affect the ship. And Bronte almost capsized us, not you."

"I know. What I'm trying to say is I didn't have the immediate reflexes to know what to do when the weather started to change."

Kae chuckles. "And you think any of us do? We work together. Captain or not, you are not responsible for what you cannot control. You acted fast." He approaches me and squeezes my shoulder. "I was uncertain before, but I stand with Ntaoru in this decision. Without your power, we wouldn't have known it was Bronte."

"Yes, you would have. Iéle would have told Nkella."

"But he is not here. And Iéle does not bond easily. It's a special skill to do what Iéle does without having an oumala animal to report to you, daí?"

I stare at the wooden table.

"You have more than one familiar. And power. You'll make a great captain. You're already proving yourself."

"Thanks, Kae." I keep shuffling my cards. "But there's that other thing no one Is talking about."

He quiets. Something tells me he knows what I'm talking about. He looks down at the map on the table in front of us.

"We lost some time but we're back on course," I say, changing the subject.

"Captain..."

I glance up, not letting myself be annoyed that he ignored my request to use my name. I know how Kae likes to show his respect.

"Why did you do it?"

I swallow. "I've been asking myself the same thing, and I've been trying to justify it in my head. Back when you met me, I never would have thought to just shoot someone. I'd be trying to convince Nkella not to."

"So why did you?"

"I guess I did it because it's what Nkella would have done to protect all of you. I'm afraid of making the mistake of allowing someone dangerous to live only to later regret letting them go. A regret like that could only mean I failed as a captain."

"Nkella carried a lot of guilt."

"I know," I whisper.

"We stand by your decision. You should know that."

I quirk a brow. "We? Even Tessa? I saw her face when I took the shot."

He spreads his hands. "She was surprised. But she knows being in charge of a crew changes a person. And this mission means a lot to us all. She doesn't think differently of you."

I know that's a lie. There was a hint of fear in her eyes.

"It's not like she hasn't killed before, daí? She makes raku explosives." He laughs.

That's true. I shrug. Maybe I'm being paranoid.

"AJ is almost finished with supper. Let's slow the ship and have a meal. Hn?"

I meet his eyes and smile. "Sure."

He turns to leave. "Bring your cards."

"Oh, Kae?"

"Daí?"

"What does...owoku jani mean?"

He squints as if trying to understand me, then his brows raise. "Uoko yani?"

"Yeah, that's it. What's it mean?"

"It means...my viscous one. Why?"

My nose flares as I try to control my breathing. "Nothing. Heard it somewhere is all."

After we eat, we all sit around the main deck watching the nautilus dance of the Aō. Nkella had told me heading straight toward it meant we were traveling true north, and it's how I know we're headed east toward Oleanu. Lights shoot out from the swirls in every direction, and Kae points out how the lights change to different colors depending on which direction they're going. Those heading to Oleanu shift from purple to blue and green. So in case there's another storm, we move farther away from the nautilus, or the nautilus is covered by a cloud, I can still look for those colors and know we're headed in the right direction. The lights moving south turn yellow and red. That would mean we've made a wrong turn and are headed toward Danū.

AJ and Harold distribute wooden cups of rum. I let the warm vanilla and hickory swarm my senses, and then I have to look away. This scent reminds me of him. Whenever I'd smell it, I'd know he was near.

The crew chats while I briefly close my eyes, trying to connect to Nkella's past inside the Deep. If only I could see him.

My blood is filled with rage. I see red. Then darkness.

Blocked.

"So Kaehante," Ntaoru starts, and my eyes flutter open. "How do you feel being outnumbered by women on the *Gambit* now? Only you and Harold."

"Kh." Kae chuckles. "I'm not complaining."

AJ smacks Kae's shoulder. "Oi!"

Kae lifts a brow. "Do you consider yourself a man?"

AJ rubs his beard. "Neither? I feel comfortable as both or neither." Lāri kisses him on the cheek.

Ntaoru smiles at him and takes a sip of her drink.

"Harold," Tessa changes the subject. "I saw you use magic earlier. Well done. What was it called again?"

"Rune magic. Thanks. I'm trying to master the runes so I can open a portal."

"Are you close?"

He looks at Kenjō. "Getting there. Check this out." Harold stands and walks to pick up a lantern. He blows it out, and we all look at each other. He whispers something. A rune leaves his lips; it's red and looks like a "greater than sign." The moment it passes through the wick, the flame reignites.

"Harold, that's amazing!" Lāri says.

"That calls for more rum. Give me your cup." AJ tips the bottle into his cup and tops off the rest of ours.

"I couldn't have done it without Kenjō making me realize that...

sometimes we have to abandon what we've lost and start new." He smiles at her, and she blushes.

AJ sits back down, and Lāri grabs his hand, pulling him in close for a kiss.

I let myself sag against a barrel, then force my gaze to stare up at the sky.

"I'm afraid for my mother," Kenjō says. "She's lucky the Empress didn't find her and kill her right away."

As soon as the Empress learned Demitri was behind Alec's death, she'd appointed a new Sword's Prefect, and Bronte had gone on the run. Had Bronte not run, the Empress may have assumed Ipani were behind Alec's death and potentially started massacring Ipani to show what happens when a Prefect is killed.

Ntaoru says something in Ipani to Kaehante, and he whispers something back. My ears catch the word aovate, which I know means lover. My eyes shift between the two and I catch her glance my direction. Now my ears are burning.

Kaehante whispers back: *"Jalo kum a waoroang sa'y a chie."* My brows perk up. I recognize several words. Jalo means I, and waoroang means discovered. *"Movi pa a l'le'v eku pani, koru ko teteng ero en nupite pamoe."*

Kenjō's eyes lift, then she drops them to her cup. My cheeks heat. I've been here long enough to understand more than just a few words. I get the gist of what they're saying—they're talking about me and Nkella. Ntaoru's eyes are full of sadness. She throws back her drink, her eyes momentarily glancing at me again.

A smirk lifts the corner of my lips, and I clear my throat. "*Ko saora hevi*," I say out loud with amusement in my voice.

Kaehante gapes at me, but Ntaoru breaks into a fit of laughter.

"Soren!" Kenjō laughs. "Have you been learning Ipani?"

"I've picked up a bit while living here."

"What did you say just then?" Harold asks.

"I said, 'I don't kiss and tell.'"

Kenjō squeaks and slaps her mouth shut. AJ's laugh bellows over everyone else's.

I twist my lips. "Did I say it wrong?"

She shakes her head. "Don't worry. We'll go with that." Tears form in her eyes as she bites back a laugh.

"Whatever." I cross my arms, still smirking. "My pronunciation sucks, I know."

Kenjō narrows her eyes at Harold. "And why don't you learn, è?" I bite back a laugh.

He shrugs. "I know a few words. Ouma iponomchi means special cookie." Kenjō rolls her eyes, and the others laugh. "Maybe you should try to perfect the translation potion so that it translates both Imboe and Ipani," Harold suggests.

"Koj," she smirks. "It's better if you learn. In any case, the translation potion can translate any language, è? Ipani is the only language it doesn't work on because it's intertwined with the Aō, and the potion was intended to help us understand outsiders."

I stare at Kaehante. "What was the second thing you said?"

His cheeks turn maroon, and he glances at Ntaoru, then back at me. "He never gave himself fully...not to anyone."

Silence grows between us as I regard his words.

Lāri lifts AJ's hand. "When an Ipani fully takes another as their aovate, it's more than when two humans bond, mei?"

Harold quirks a brow. "What does that mean?"

I shake my head. "I don't follow that either."

Kenjō and Lāri exchange a glance. Kenjō looks at me. "Do you remember how you and Nkella bonded when you took the rikorō?"

"Yes." That's something I could never forget.

"It's similar. It's not quite as strong since with the rikorō you are still two different souls. An aovate bond unites both souls through the Aō." She looks at Lāri. "You two can describe it better."

Lāri's eyes soften whimsically as she leans her head back and stares at AJ. "AJ is human, mei? And it doesn't matter that only I am Ipani. We share a bond. It's not telepathy like you felt with the rikorō. It's even better. It's a closeness I've never felt before with anyone. When we are far apart, I still feel his emotions toward me, always. And I feel safe."

AJ brings Lāri's hand up to his lips and kisses it.

"We—Ipani—also have more control than a human does," Kenjō says, thankfully pulling everyone's attention to her.

"Not bound Ipani, mei?" Lāri says.

"Right," Kenjō agrees. "As long as we are not bound. But for example, I chose to not get pregnant when Harold and I had our special night."

My eyes widen, and I glance at Harold who is turning a bright red despite the dark night. AJ cracks up, and Tessa and Lāri start singing "ooo."

Harold chuckles, and with a forcibly deeper voice, he says, "Fascinating," then reaches for the rum bottle. AJ hands it to him. "So...giving yourself "fully"—that's more than just sex, right?"

Now Kenjō's cheeks turn a darker shade of pink. "Yes, Harold. It means more."

He nods and swishes his cup in a circular motion.

She clears her throat and cuts her gaze to me. "An Ipani would be able to control pregnancy for a human. But two Ipani together would need to both agree because they are united by the Aō."

I sit back and take a swig of my drink as I take in her explanation. It seems that if you're human—or cut off from the Aō—you don't get much choice if it's different than what an Ipani wants.

Not that any of this matters for me anyway.

At the corner of my eye, I glimpse Lāri and AJ staring into each other's eyes.

I take out my deck of cards. "Anyone want to learn to play a game called poker?"

Harold scoots forward. "Yes, let's change the subject. Poker sounds fun."

That night, sailing feels easier. I guess I've already hit the worst of it, or at least, I've gained some experience with the worst that can happen while being captain. I've endured a lot on this ship, with Nkella as captain. But this feels different. Even though they say we all rely on each other, and they'll be with me in the Deep, I feel more responsible.

Normally, I'd be going to bed with the rest of the crew, and whatever is happening in Nkella's room with Kae would be none of my business...or discussed with the crew later if it's important. I was never first in line and would just follow orders. I'd never even taken a turn steering the ship before.

Now, I'm the first to see a cyclone or an enemy ship. The first and last up so I can take care of the crew while they sleep.

Not to mention the impending doom I constantly feel. Tetalla has contacted me more than once and has asked me to submit to him, but I don't want anything to distract me from getting to Nkella. I'll deal with Tetalla after we come back from the Deep.

Tonight, I dream of Nkella again.

Blood comes from his eyes instead of tears as the Empress stands before him. Flickering speckles of light ignite his eyes whenever he feels rage then dim. He's trying so hard to keep it under control.

A soldier sends a striking slash with a whip behind him, and Nkella grunts.

"I'll ask one more time. How do I get in?"

"Even if I knew, I'd never tell you. This is why you took me. No other reason." A hint of hurt comes through his voice. The way he's looking at her, his eyes heavy. I know that look. That's the look of betrayal. "You stole my life from me, Helāni. Torture me all you want. I'll live through it and watch you suffer."

The Empress laughs and the scene fades. I reach for Nkella.

"That happened before his change." Tetalla's voice makes my hairs stand on end. I'm pulled away from my dream, but I continue to stare as the image shrinks until I can no longer see Nkella.

Darkness blankets my surroundings, but I get a whiff of warm desert spices.

"No," I finally answer. "I saw the flickering of his eyes. It had to be after he was cursed."

"Tell me, uoko yani, do you enjoy arguing with me as much as your fire excites me?"

I shiver. "I know what I saw."

"Perhaps your visions aren't reliable." His voice carries to my left, spinning me around, but all there is, is darkness. Like I'm standing in a black void, and can't see what I'm standing on.

"Where are you?"

"Why won't you submit? You could have died."

"That sounds like the last thing I'll ever do."

He laughs. "So much defiance. Such fierceness. You should consider my offer. It would be far better for you to come willingly, than for me to take you."

Take me? "Why do you want me so badly anyway? You're telling me Death really can't defeat the Empress without *me?*"

"I don't need you to defeat her. I need you so we can save Ipa."

"Or for me to help you kill all the Helāni descendants, right? You want me to help you kill all humans after we put an end to the Empress. Yeah, I know all about your plan. If you stalking me isn't creepy enough for me to never want to join you, you should know, I don't want to kill all my friends."

"Your friends can be spared."

"Yeah, I'll still pass. Besides, I'm kind of spoken for."

He guffaws. "Are you? I know your dead captain—he's too far gone. It is a lost cause, and you should abandon all hope of bringing him back. And he never promised himself to you as an aovate, hn?"

I clench my fists. "It doesn't matter. How did you come back from your curse?"

Another dark chuckle. "It isn't a curse. It's a blessing."

My stomach curls. He enjoys the killing. "Bet it makes you feel powerful."

Wind whips around me, and I grab onto my arms. My surroundings change and I'm suddenly standing on the main deck of the *Gambit*. It's the middle of the night; the waves are crashing rhythmically against the ship. In front of me, Tetalla comes into view a foot in front of me. He lifts his hand and brushes my cheek, but I jerk my face away.

He smiles. "Every time I see you, I get chills. I miss Adara so much. Even after so long."

I'm quiet for a long moment, then finally speak. "Answer me this."

His brow quirks. "Anything for you."

"Why was the Empress torturing him. She kept saying it was to give her access. Access to what?"

His smile fades, and he tilts his head. "Why would I reveal Danū secrets to a Helāni?"

"So much for 'anything for me,' huh? You want me to trust you, don't you?"

"Hn." He grins, showcasing the tips of his sharp canines and eyeing me up and down. "Inside the caverns of Danū, there is fire ouma."

"Like the type of fire some Ipani have?"

"Stronger. This fire can be harnessed and bottled and used for forging. She must have wanted it to burn the island down—or to use it for her own fortress... That is why she wanted the Danū prince so desperately, she thought he was the key to the fires of Pentacles." Sadness flickers through his eyes. "Knowing her, she wanted it for revenge."

"So she was torturing Nkella to take revenge because of what you did to her?"

He frowns. "In part, that is true. But whoever rules over the Danū fire also controls Ipa. Only a royal can gain access—she could never use it the way I can."

I regard his last words.

He holds my gaze inquisitively. "Why are you sailing to Oleanu? What is there that you are in such a hurry to get to, hn?" He lifts my chin. His grip tightens as I try to move my face away. Finally, he lets me go.

"I'm not telling you that."

The corner of his lips curves upward. "I will find out why, uoko yani. And you will submit to me."

"No, I won't. And I'm not viscous, and I'm not yours."

His eyes glint mischievously. He kisses his fingers and presses them to my cheek.

I wake to the sound of Iéle jumping on my bed and bolt upright. The bed is sitting on a snowy field—yet it's still warm. Sapphire hops away with a pop as she chases something in the bushes, then with a swirl, the captain's quarters come back into view.

Huh. Iéle distracted the rabbit with her hallucination ouma so she could jump up.

This time, Iéle lays down right next to me. I don't move as she rests her head on her paws facing me. I wonder if Tetalla left because he knew she was close...or if her presence chased my dream away.

Something stirs between us, and I can feel her inside my head, like she's probing my thoughts and memories, but not giving me any images in return. I want to pull away, but I don't. She still doesn't trust me fully, but I think she wants to. So I let her.

This time, when I drift back to sleep, I don't dream.

The next night, Iéle sits in the corner of the quarterdeck, her head tilted as she watches me steer the ship. I wonder how much she understands about what's happening after probing my mind last night.

"At least, the weather held up today," AJ says. He runs up the steps with a slab of meat and lays it down for Iéle. "Let's hope it stays this way this time, right?"

Tessa drives to the foot of the steps and smiles at the wolf. "Has she attempted to bond with you?" she asks.

I move my hair off my face. "As much as she allowed." I chuckle. "I'm just happy she isn't growling at me anymore, although I do wonder where Sapphire is and hope she's okay."

"I'm sure she's safe. Rabbits are carnivorous, as you are aware, but wolves will still win in a fight." She glances at AJ. "Don't spoil her too much, or she won't hunt."

"She's not going to stop hunting just because I fed her some meat."

Tessa is about to retort when a red bull runs across the sky and around the ship. AJ lets out a yelp, and Iéle growls as she stands and leans over the rail.

I squint at it. "What the hell is that?"

Harold laughs and walks to the center of the main deck. Kenjō follows behind him clapping and cheering him on. "That's *uruz*, my wild ox rune. Like it?"

I stare at the ox as it comes back around, red swirls trailing behind it as it disappears into nothing.

I blink a few times, and the ship catches a few waves.

"Watch it down there, mei?" Lāri calls from the crow's nest.

"Sorry!" I grab the wheel.

"It's my turn anyway." AJ pushes me aside. "Scoot."

"Thanks, AJ." I walk down the steps and pat Harold on the shoulder. "You're getting better! It's hard to believe you can do that back home too!"

Frost falls off his cheekbone as he nods happily. "That's nothing. Check these out." He goes from casting icicle blades and throwing them until they shatter, to summoning fire in his hands. Kaehante, Tessa, Ntaoru, and I gather around him and Kenjō as he puts on a rune show for us. Lāri and AJ watch from their posts.

Phantom fingers pass through my mind, and a shiver skirts up my spine. I sit up and hold my breath. My eyes narrow on the wooden floor.

Kaehante cuts his gaze to me. "Captain?"

I hold my finger to my lips. "Something's wrong," I whisper. Iéle starts to growl at my direction, but I know it's not at me.

Mist is rising from the sea. Quiet dread befalls the deck, and we stare as it rises over the rail and spills onto the floorboards.

"Chong Alēla is on the other side. We're not near it enough for the dead to rise," Tessa says.

The back of my neck prickles.

"Get your raku potions. Everyone, prepare for a fight," I tell them.

"Captain?" Tessa backs her wheelchair and stares at me, concern marking the lines of her face.

"It might just be mist. It might be an Ipani like the other day, or…it could be something worse."

Ntaoru grabs her gun and points it at the thick fog that's slowly coming toward us.

"Feel like sharing it with the class, Cap?" Harold says.

"Just be ready."

"Oi!" Kenjō's voice makes me jump. Lāri swoops down in eagle form and shifts right before landing on the wooden floor. She pushes Kenjō away from the fog almost touching her feet. A lantern lights up from the thick mist, except…it's not one of our lanterns. It's being held up by a skeleton hand.

"Everyone, come to the quarterdeck." I run to my room and snatch up the Ace of Swords. I don't know why I think this card is my best bet against the dead, but something tells me I'm right.

A gun isn't going to do, and the raku potions won't kill what's already dead. The sword glistens from inside the card as I reach in and pull it out. I stuff all the tarot cards I have inside my pocket, for fear of one of these dead coming in here and taking them.

"Soren. More are coming," Harold warns.

I open my door to see spirits flying above us and skeletons crawling over the walls. As they swarm the main deck, the crew huddles together.

"What do we do?" Lāri asks. "There are too many to fight."

"Don't let any of them touch you," I tell them. "A single touch can be fatal."

"As opposed to Chong Alēla? How do you know?"

"Because Tetalla has finally found me, and he intends on taking me against my will." I grab a raku potion and throw it onto the main deck.

9

The dead get blasted from the main deck by the bright orange light from a raku bomb. Bones shatter to the ground only to be called back to their counterparts.

"What do you mean take you by force?" AJ gapes at me.

"There's no time to explain!" I throw another bomb and cover my ears for the blast. I need a second to think.

We might be able to lose some of them by speeding the ship up. We might also break a few limbs of our own in the process.

Ntaoru takes her gun and shoots something behind me, I spin around to see a large skeleton taking in all of her blasts. I spin the sword in my hand and slice his skull right off, then kick his body hard, making it lose its grip on the rail and disappear into the dark waves.

Swarms of the dead climb aboard. A good handful of them wield swords. One looks like an old pirate who sunk down with his ship; half his face is covered in algae that doesn't mask a menacing sneer. Others come behind him. Dead men with half their flesh blue and green and gaping holes showing their skulls, wearing long coats and boots, dripping on the hardwood floor. Half of them hold swords, positioned to fight; others carry guns, although I'm not sure how they'd be loaded.

My crew starts to fire, but they walk through the blasts. I wield my sword and fight them off one by one as they come at us. Tessa is cornered. She shoots from her chair-cannon, but since the cannonballs go straight through them, they keep advancing and reach her as she runs out of ammo.

I decapitate one of them. Ntaoru pulls another off Tessa's back. In the corner of my eye, Kenjō gets thrown in her jaguar form to the main deck. Harold catches the one who threw her on fire with his rune magic.

Kae has run out of ammo and is fighting them off with his arms and fists covered by full armadillo shields.

My hands shake as I stare at my crew struggling to survive the masses of dead.

Something grabs me from behind. I bend over and flip him over my head. Another one catches hold of me; now I have two clinging onto me, squeezing my neck, and dragging me to the edge of the ship. A skeleton grabs my sword. It clatters to the floor.

I hear a loud popping noise and then a growl. My neck is released, which gives me enough flexibility to kick the skeleton in front of me. I glance at Iéle, her mouth snarling on the bony neck of the skeleton who'd had me only a moment ago. Another skeleton clutches her back, its claws making her whimper. I kick it off her. More swarms are climbing the ship.

A skeleton walks straight toward me, and I pick up my sword, wielding it in front of me. I can no longer see the crew, but I hear Ntaoru screaming something. I swing my sword, but to my surprise, the skeleton looks past me and misses. I chop off its head, and it rolls to the ground. I round on a dead man choking Ntaoru and stab him through his back. He releases her and stammers backward. Ntaoru gasps for air, her eyes wide and staring past me. I turn my head, but there's nothing there. Looking down, I gasp. I can see right through myself.

Iéle comes up behind me and nips my shirt. *"Are you doing this?"* I think at her while saying it out loud.

"Soren? Is that you?" Ntaoru gasps.

Iéle nudges me, zooming me into her. She's made me invisible. Her powers of illusion come in handy at the best of times. "Good girl. Can you make the whole crew invisible?"

A nuzzle from her connection and the dead lose sight of who they're fighting, making them step back.

"What's happening?" Harold calls from the main deck.

"Shh." I whisper out loud, unable to see him myself. "It's an illusion." I step to the side, hoping the dead will be unable to track where my voice is coming from. "Iéle made us all invisible." I walk toward the deck, keeping my eyes on all the skeletons looking around for us. "But they can still hear. Be careful."

A cold laugh makes my bones still, and I spot the tall skeleton with half his face covered in algae. He holds a long, curved saber and grins at me wickedly as he begins to walk in my direction. A flash of red in his eyes tells me that Tetalla's puppeteering that one; his devil curse is seeping through. Clutching my sword tightly, I hold my ground.

"That trick might work with them, but I can still feel your heartbeat, vicious one."

He's no longer speaking to me in Ipani. Not playing games anymore, I take it.

I throw my hand out, releasing my webbing for the first time in months. As it reaches him, he dissipates in a dark smog, my web landing on a skeleton behind him. The smog appears right in front of my face, and I stammer back.

A dark cold voice. "I told you I would find you."

Before I can say anything, he hooks his arm around my neck, and I let out a yell. With impeccable strength, I'm swung to the top of the rail and carried overboard, the Ace of Swords falling from my grasp. My life flashes before me as I hit the frigid water in the dead of night. A muffled scream escapes me underwater as I kick furiously, attempting to escape his clutches, but his strength is impenetrable.

Muffled cries escape my throat as he drags me deeper.

I stop trying to pull his arm away and grab for my Ace of Swords Card, hoping the sword went back in when I dropped it on the ship.

I reach into the card, blindly, hoping for something to come out, but I'm running out of breath. What happens if he drags me into the Deep this way? I'll die and won't be able to come back, that's what.

My chest is aching, and my eyes bulge. I can't hold my breath any longer.

Images of me swimming like a mermaid resurface. How I wish I could still do that.

But I can't.

Pressure weighs on me as Tetalla pulls me even deeper.

Dizziness overtakes me. I feel myself giving in to the dark and cold current.

Then I'm jolted backward. The movement makes me more alert, but I can't see what's happening.

Something's got a hold of the skeleton Tetalla is puppeteering. My last breath escaping me, I take hold of the sword in the card—I could cry from relief—and I plunge it to his neck, pulling as hard as I can, and decapitating the skull from its neck. I grip my sword just as someone rips me from its grasp. Looking up, my eyes widen at the light brown hair flowing in front of me. Tessa's eyes are huge as she urges me up and grabs me from under my shoulder.

She swims with such fierceness, her strength underwater carrying us both. I pass out before I reach the surface, and all I can feel are strong hands grabbing me and lifting me up.

After an unknown length of time, I wake in a fit of coughs. Tessa climbs on top her wheelchair as she pants for breath.

"Captain?" Kaehante looks down at me. He's dripping water over my forehead. He must have been the one to pull us up.

"He'll be back," I cough, forcing myself to sit.

Ntaoru drags a dead man's body overboard, and my eyes stop at Harold who's standing at the edge of the quarterdeck, facing us. He holds out a hand and in one large flash of red, a rune that looks like a stick figure of a tree flies from his tongue as he screams, "*Algiz.*"

The dead immobilize and fall to the floor. He does this a few more times until all the dead have stopped moving. The crew begins tossing the bones overboard.

A warm wind brushes past me, and I know he's back. I didn't kill him. The sword didn't kill him. Of course it didn't—it wasn't really him, just a dead person he was using to get to me. Tetalla is orchestrating all of this from Danū.

The dead start to board the ship again. This is going to keep happening until he takes me. But letting him take me makes me his forever, and I'm not going to submit damnit. Saving Nkella is my priority.

Harold keeps sending out his rune. There has to be something else I can do. What do I have available to me? Using the sword is no use if he's going to keep bringing more dead onto the ship.

The World Card.

I can open it to get us all to Cups. But leave the ship behind? The Empress was specific about me needing it to get to the Deep.

I can't leave the ship behind; I need to somehow make the portal big enough to go through it. Ntaoru shouts something at Lāri, and my gaze skips over to where they're fighting a pair of dead that have just climbed aboard. Harold tosses another rune at them, and bones shatter to the ground. It's only a matter of time before Tetalla comes back. I need to think of something quick.

I can't let him gain control of another dead person.

Control.

Out of our control isn't always a bad thing. It can mean actual fortune, can't it?

I bolt to the main deck and grab Ntaoru's shoulder. She spins around.

"Don't ask, just do, okay?"

Confusion flickers through her features, but she quickly nods.

"Give me your wrist with our mark." She does as I say, and I grab her hand, pulling her to the bow and looking out toward the sea. I turn to Kaehante and shout at him to leave the dead and take the wheel. "Be ready for high speed." With a deep breath, I pull out the World Card and mutter a little direction for good measure. "My fortune and her fortune combined to assist my will." And here's hoping I don't lose the card to the waves.

"Captain, what are we doing?" Concern hits her voice as more dead climb onto the ship to be swatted by the crew as Harold works his magic.

"Make sure that when this portal opens, no dead remain on the ship!" I shout to them, hoping they all heard me. I take a deep breath. Here goes nothing. Angling the card as if I'm throwing a fighting disc, I release it to the waves, and it spins, cutting through the wind. My frown hardens, hoping this works.

The card stops midair, and a portal opens in front of the ship, growing wider until it shows the Prefect's Tower on Oleanu in the distance.

"Kae! Now!"

"Full speed ahead!" he shouts.

Ntaoru and I collide, and we're flung back with the gust of speed.

My eyes are peeled open as we pass through the portal's barrier. I force myself to stand, then sprint to the quarterdeck, leaning over the rail to watch the stern of the ship leave the closing end of the portal. As if in slow motion, the card falls over my head and the portal closes. I catch it in my hand. My heart is beating hard. Spinning around, I stare at the crew, who are all getting their bearings.

"Is everyone alright?" I ask.

"You did it," Tessa says.

"Thanks to you, Tessa." I grab onto Kae's shoulder. "All of you."

"How did you know that would work?" Ntaoru asks, climbing the steps. I shake my head.

"I didn't. But that's the thing about the Wheel of Fortune: it's a wheel, so I took a chance. Figured if our mark has any power, if it's more than just a warning, we could put them together."

"Are they all gone?" Lāri asks, dusting herself off. "Where's AJ?"

A gagging sound comes from the main deck.

"AJ?" Lāri calls out.

My heart is still beating hard. We may have lost Tetalla for now, but he'll be back. I just hope it'll buy me some time.

Lāri screams from the foot of the ramp. The blood drains from my face as I see the shock on everyone's faces. Fear grips my heart. I'm afraid of what I'm about to see.

Lāri's voice moans, and my arms rip into goosebumps. I hold my breath. No. No, please, no.

I hurry down the steps, turn the corner to the ramp, and let myself fall against the wall. AJ lies next to a barrel with a sword sticking out from his chest. Blood pools out of him.

He has a smile on his face as Lāri strokes his hair. He tries to speak, as he reaches for her cheek.

"It's okay, my love. It's okay," he says.

Lāri shakes her head furiously, pressing her hands down on his wound. My gaze falls on the hilt of the sword. The curved saber of the skeleton Tetalla was puppeteering. He did this.

He killed him as a warning to me.

Tears stream down my face, and I run to his side, placing my hand on his wound. "AJ...no..." I turn back to the crew. Kae's face looks ghostly. "Isn't there anything we can do? Can't we save him?"

Kae walks over, a solemn expression on his face. "It is through his heart."

AJ whispers something inaudible, and we all inch closer. "What did you say, my love?" Lāri asks, tears stuck in her throat.

His eyes are glossy, and he smiles. "To think I hated the undead curse."

At that, my tears let loose. He coughs up blood a few times and Kae reaches down for the sword, but before he can touch it, AJ's eyes grow distant. He touches Lāri's cheek once more, then lets his face hang as the moaning from eternal torture fills the air.

10

Iéle howls.

Oleanu is visible in the distance, but the *Gambit* has been anchored and our sails are lowered.

None of us are ready to keep going. Despite Nkella's rescue mission weighing heavily on our shoulders, there's an emptiness in our hearts. One that could never be filled.

Hours have passed. It's night. The ship is lit with lanterns as we wrap AJ in sheets. We can't keep him on board, and Lāri says he would rather be at sea than buried on land. So we waited until nightfall to give him a proper pirate's funeral.

It is the stupid mistakes in life that will get you killed.

Why is that such a hard thing to learn? And why do Nkella's words always come when it's too late?

A sob escapes my throat, and I cover my face to keep the others from seeing me cry.

Tessa's chair fills the silence as she stops at my side. I see her and the others taking solemn seats around me. Lāri is still with AJ's body by the cannons.

Kaehante bends down to my level. "It's time."

I nod without lowering my hands. "After I find Nkella, I'm

returning home. I never got anyone killed back home. If I stay here, I'll only make things worse. I got my best friend killed." Pain bursts from my chest at my words.

"Daí? You did not." Kaehante says. I'll admit I'm a bit surprised he doesn't agree.

"Yes, I did."

"Soren..." Harold starts. "It was an accident."

"A stupid mistake because of my sudden move."

"If you hadn't done that, we'd all be dead," Tessa says. "We were outnumbered by Death. You did what you thought was best."

"My cousin carried the same sort of guilt, daí?" I can feel Kaehante leaning closer to my face, but I still don't look up. "Sometimes an accident is just an accident. It was beyond our control."

Removing my hands from my face, I stare at Kae. I have to tell him. "The sword that killed AJ was held by the skeleton that Tetalla was puppeteering. It was most likely a message for me—letting me know what will happen to me if I don't submit to him."

Kaehante shakes his head. "No. AJ died in battle," he says, giving me a poignant look. "This was Tetalla's doing and forever the war against the Empress. You may have brought him back, but he always meant to come back and kill all humans, daí? Nkella wouldn't want that."

I swallow hard. "Thanks for saying that."

"If you should hate anyone, hate Tetalla," Harold says.

My eyes narrow. "With everything in me." I don't even have words for the hatred I feel. I thought that type of hate ended with the Empress, but it's grown larger.

I stare at the Wheel of Fortune mark, and the others do the same. My gaze passes over everyone, Harold and Kenjō sitting crisscross in front of me, Kaehante just over my knee, Tessa on her wheelchair to my right, and Ntaoru next to Kae's left. This mark brings the worst of luck, nothing good ever comes from the Fates.

"No one will ever replace him," Ntaoru says, breaking the silence.

"AJ certainly was special," Tessa whispers, her voice heavy.

Kaehante is the first to look over at Lāri who is bent over AJ. None of us want to throw him overboard.

"We can't keep him here," Ntaoru says. His soft moans of eternal torment come from within the sheets. She looks to Kae. "You know what we must do."

Kae takes a deep breath as he stands and walks over to Lāri.

"No," Lāri cries. He tries to help her up, but she fights him, throwing a few punches until he wraps his arms around her.

"You'll see him again one day," he tells her.

She stands back as Kae and Harold carry AJ's body over the rail, holding him there. Lāri keeps her hands on the sheets, tears streaming down her cheeks.

"Be strong in the Deep, my love. Let your laughter carry in the wind and brighten the depths of despair. I will be with you once again." She leans down and kisses him over the sheets.

Each of the crew say their last words. I'm last. I walk over without much to say except, "I'm sorry." Even that comes out as an inaudible whisper. "You were my best friend in Ipa. And this is my fault." I swallow a painful bubble.

We all place our hands on him and gently push him into the thrashing waves. Kaehante, Lāri, and Ntaoru each light a cannon, releasing them one by one in AJ's name. Fires to the open sea.

Tonight, we'll all sleep on the main deck. At this point, none of us care if Tetalla comes. He'll find me in my sleep anyway. At least this way, we'll all be together and ready to fight.

But for now, we stare at the sky in silence.

I'll find him. I want to say it out loud, but I need to stop making promises I don't know if I can keep. I'll find him when I go to the Deep, though, I promise myself. I won't be able to bring him back—Nkella's curse is keeping him alive, and AJ is really dead—but I'll find him.

"Soren," Lāri breaks the silence, and my heart skips a beat. This is the first time she's spoken to me since it happened. I glance at her. "How did Tetalla find us?"

I swallow. "He's been using the dead to spy on me. When I turned on the transparency the other day, he had a good view of where we were, but he had to catch up to us since we were moving so fast. He isn't omniscient, but he has his ways."

Iéle whimpers by the side of the ship.

Lāri lies back down with her hands behind her head.

"Soren," Kenjō says. "What's going to happen when we get to the Deep and there are dead everywhere?"

"This is true," Tessa says. "Death is the ruler of the Deep."

"The Serpent is the ruler, daí?" Kae asks.

"I think the Serpent is the gateway. But yes," I say, confirming everyone's fears, "Tetalla will be able to see us at all times down there."

A few beats of silence pass within us. We're going to war, and everyone knows it. Retrieving Nkella from Tetalla's domain is going to be the hardest thing any of us have done.

"I know no one wants to sleep," Harold says, "but we should try and reach land in the morning. They're not expecting us for another two to three days at least, right?"

I nod. "And arriving in the middle of the night this far ahead of schedule might freak people out."

"What about Tetalla?" Harold asks.

"We left him a few days' journey behind. We should be fine for tonight."

"You only just got away, vicious one." Tetalla's voice makes me stir in my sleep. "Next time, I won't fail."

A deep hatred boils in my blood.

We're standing on a red sandy beach; I know he's taken me to Danū in my dream. I smile, knowing that if we're here and not on my ship, I was successful in making him lose sight of me.

"I know you're headed to Oleanu." A muscle in his cheek jumps. "There won't be many places to hide on land."

I raise my chin. "Even if you take me by force, you still need me to cooperate—to submit. And I never will."

"You'd be surprised how persuasive I can be when I have you here in front of me." The edge of his voice makes the back of my neck prickle.

His face is hardened, any hint of his amused tone gone. His hair rustles in the wind, and his eyes look hollow, his pupils so dilated I can barely see any white in his eyes. A forked black tongue slides out his mouth behind sharp teeth, reaching toward me like a snake, the shadow of his horns appearing on his head to disappear in the breeze, giving me a glimpse of his true devil form.

My feet want to take off at a sprint, but I know it's a dream. He can't grab me here. "You'll never take me."

"Do you think the survival of my island—of Ipa—is a game to me?" His voice is like sandpaper, that forked tongue of his slithering from his lips. "There are things more important than what you want. Heed my warning, vicious one. You have made things harder for yourself, and soon, you will beg me to take you."

A growl carries on the wind and grows louder. I stir awake to the darkness of the night. Iéle sits by my feet, her red eyes glaring at me. I pull my hand back, and her eyes go back to black. She whimpers and lays her head down.

"Thanks," I whisper. She's been pulling me out of these dreams since they started happening. I should probably stop referring to them as dreams; they're definitely happening.

I'm not sure there's a way to sever this connection he has with me. Especially when I don't know how it happened in the first place. I lay back down and let my eyes drift close, part of me wanting to stay awake, for fear of him returning. Sleep still claims me, and Tetalla doesn't return.

Seagulls mew above the horizon as the sun rises behind the island. Orange hues glisten in the calming ocean waves as we sail closer to land. I can see the pink sands of the beach. While I'd had a vision of my biological father and mother together on these beaches, I was never sure if the pink sands were real. But now, seeing them for myself, they take my breath away.

I hadn't thought of how I'd feel coming to Oleanu for the first time. This is the island my biological father, Sehu, was from—the island I would have been raised on. The place where my ouma—if I had any—would have been sourced from.

The *Gambit* feels empty; solemn silence lingers among us. I was used to being greeted with a breakfast cooked by AJ who would crack jokes as he set down plates.

This ship will never be the same again.

I fix the collar of my tight black suit coat with the intricate spiderweb design. Black on black. I hate that it comes from the Empress, but I'd be lying if I said I didn't look sleek. At least it's perfect for the weather, not too hot, but protects me from the cool draft coming in from the north. Plus it's flexible. I'll have no problems fighting in this. The crew also agreed to wear their uniforms from the tower. They all sport matching white and gold tunics with the Empress's emblem on the upper right shoulder and black pants.

"Tessa." She stares at me behind her wooden coffee cup. "I meant to thank you for saving me yesterday. I didn't know you were such an amazing swimmer."

She smiles. "I grew up here, along the harao of Oleanu. Swimming was the one thing I excelled at."

"Well, thank you."

"When I had the undead curse, being unable to swim was worse than not tasting food. Becoming bones whenever the water touched my skin..." She shivers. "I still get nightmares."

I frown. "I can't imagine."

"It was horrible." Harold wipes his face. "But we have Nkella to thank for breaking the curse." The crew grows quiet again.

"And we're getting him back," Tessa says, staring at me. I nod. Lāri turns away, and guilt sinks down to my gut.

I stare out to the island as we slowly approach. "Hoist the sails."

As much as it pains everyone to see the Empress's Tower on our ship, we know it's necessary. Residents of Oleanu don't agree with the island's politics—the kings' decision to call it Cups and abide by her legislations—but it keeps the island safe and as free as it can be...and away from any wars.

A few do decide to flee, Lāri and Tessa explained to me, because they're unable to stomach the hypocrisy. They care about Ipa and want to fight for it. But they also know their families are safest on the island.

The entrance of the harao is surrounded by floral willow trees with the bluest-green I've ever seen on leaves. Pink and white petals touch the waters, and the sound of falling water comes from within the forest. The Prefect's Tower is hidden within the trees, camouflaging itself from enemy ships. We proceed with caution as we near the edge. The structure is typical of other Prefect's Towers I've seen, octagonal in shape, tall, with a pointed tip on the top.

"State your business." A woman's voice comes from the direction of the tower. She's tall with short brown hair and a bow and quiver strapped to her back. She's wearing brown tights with a hip-high hooded green cloak, the Cups emblem of a chalice on a blue and green shield clasping her cloak together by her neck. Two Arcana soldiers with black robes and light blue metallic masks stand on either side behind her. Their masks have a greenish sheen, but the hollow dark eyes beneath the masks destroy any semblance of charm. These are agentless soldiers taken against their will, prisoners of the Empress, forced into her army.

I clear my throat. "The kings are expecting us."

"The kings have not alerted me of any visitors coming from the Tower by ship. I'll need proof of your flags and for you to state your business." I exchange a glance with the crew who all stand behind me.

"I suppose I can show you my mark, if our flag and clothes aren't enough." I try deepening my voice for effect but feel silly. "We're a couple days early, we had"—I probably shouldn't mention Tetalla trying to find me here—"some trouble, so I ended up using the World Card to get us here quicker."

The Prefect's brows rise at the mention of the World Card, and she darts a look to the Arcana soldiers. One of them disappears, presumably to the Tower to verify with the Empress that we are who we say we are.

"Dock your ship. I'll need to see your mark."

Kaehante docks the ship, and I prepare to walk down the gangway.

The Prefect meets me at the bottom, and I show her my spiderweb mark. This is the first time I willingly show my mark to a Prefect; it's also my first time dealing with a Prefect in official business. The Prefect raises a brow and purses her lips. I point a finger to a nearby spruce and shoot some webbing onto it.

"So that you can see my mark isn't painted on. I'm the *real deal.*" I grin.

My crew is silent, and I know what I just sounded like. AJ would have chuckled...

"Apologies." She straightens. "I have to do my due diligence."

"I understand." I hold out my hand. "I'm Soren."

She stares at my hand, and I bring it down, forgetting they have no idea what a handshake means.

"Follow the harao straight up, don't turn into any of the narrow neighborhoods. You'll see the castle when you reach Oe Nū. I'll send a raven to alert the kings of your visit."

"Are we going to have to watch our backs on the way there?"

She furrows her brows but ignores my question. "It won't take long to get there. Sail slowly, there are swimmers and children along these parts. I'll see you on your way out." She steps back and stares at the *Gambit* in a casual dismissal.

Peachy. I turn on my heel and head back up the gangway, then we're off to the castle of Cups.

11

Kaehante continues to slowly sail the ship at the lowest speed. I sit by the bow, leaning on my elbows. The rest of the crew sits nearby watching our surroundings.

"Tessa, Lāri, how does it feel to be back?" Kenjō asks them.

"Strange. I was afraid to speak in front of the Prefect," Tessa admits.

I squint at her. "Why?"

"We left, mei?" Lāri says. "Some might consider that treason to the crown."

My eyes widen. "You're not allowed to leave?"

Lāri shrugs and exchanges a glance with Tessa. "It's an unspoken rule."

"But the inhabitants of Cups have a lot of pride. Who knows how the kings will take it," Tessa adds.

Ntaoru scoffs. "Cups think they're better than everyone else. The Ipani from Oleanu know better." Her eyes drift off and I think I see wetness in them. I remember AJ telling me Ntaoru had a lover from Oleanu who lost his life due to the Empress.

I lean toward her. "When we get your brother back, the first thing we do is take that bitch down." My whisper is for her but loud enough for everyone to hear.

She glances at me, a sarcastic smile curves in her lips. "You're crazy if you think you can take her down, daí?"

"It's a promise I intend to keep this time. Nkella might be a match for Tetalla. But I'm a match for my great-great-times-a-hundred aunt." I chuckle, and she takes a deep breath.

"I'll hold you to it," she says.

After losing Nkella, I stopped caring about taking down the Empress, and even though right now I'm technically working with her, she knows it's for my own gain. I want Nkella back. Now that I know he's alive, I'll stop at nothing to get him back first. But that masked bitch is gone the moment I figure out how to kill her. With the Ace of Swords, it should be easy, but with the war on Tetalla, I'm not sure it's the wisest move right now. I need Nkella here first. Then I'll take Talia home. But one thing at a time. Thinking of all the things we need to do after saving Nkella gives me a headache.

I stare at the passing villages on the hillside. The water is calm and beautiful. Mer-Ipani jump from the pink sands and greenery into the water. Up ahead, a few mer-kids are playing a game with...are those oumala otters? Blue and green bioluminescent lights zip through the water, illuminating our path to the castle.

Waterfalls grow louder as we navigate father inland by way of the narrow river. Rivers and streams break off in dense branches leading to neighboring villages. I'm enamored by the beautiful flowering willow trees and multicolored foliage over pink sands and try to envision what the castle will look like—what it will be like to meet royalty. Children laugh and splash on the water beneath a waterfall and I can't help smiling. I try to imagine my father playing around here as a kid, and what it would have been like for me to grow up here.

Harold taps my arm, and I turn to see what he's pointing at. The castle turrets come into view as cascading willow branches brush the inside of the ship, shading us from the sun. Large spiraling shell-like towers glisten from the rising sun in a variety of pastel blues and pinks. Bridges covered in soft moss span from one tower to the other, and oval shaped windows and doors adorn the sides and lengths of the castle. I shut my mouth as soon as I realize it hangs open.

Kae walks to the bow and throws down the anchor. "We can't sail any farther," he says. He's right. We've reached a good stopping point—any farther and we'll hit pebbles.

"We'll need to walk the rest of the way. Will the ship be safe here?" My eyes skim the grounds and land on a group of armed men and women paddling toward us in three boats. Some are Ipani with scales glistening on their arms and subtly pointed ears.

"*Yorisi* Oleanu, welcome to Oleanu." One of them holds up her hand in greeting. "Leave your ship here. The kings are expecting you at their feast."

Kae scratches his chin and glances at us. "A feast?"

Lāri bows her head as she collects her belongings. Solemn expressions are plastered on all our faces. None of us were expecting this type of greeting, given the circumstances—especially being ahead of schedule.

Harold and Lāri lower the gangway, and we make our way down to the small paddle boats. We climb into the two of the boats, and Tessa gets into the third with a muscular Ipani man.

They paddle through the trees, where bioluminescent colors zip under the shallow waters, revealing multicolored glass-like pebbles underneath. Schools of fish swim in the crystal-clear water. I look down at my reflection and almost recoil. The black I'm wearing is a sharp contrast to all the bright and pastel colors of the island—I look like Morticia Adams with red hair.

When we reach the end of the river, we scramble out of the boats and walk over a moss-covered drawbridge toward the shell castle towering over us. It appears even taller up close.

We're led by the guards to a garden courtyard where a petite Ipani girl with straight brown hair wearing a white dress offers us all drinks in shell cups. I'm the last to take one as the crew eagerly drinks their fill.

I smile shyly and thank her. I'm not used to all this...elegance.

Elegant but natural. I love it. I can also feel myself sweating. Not from the humidity, but from the sudden realization that I'm about to meet royalty, and I'm afraid of saying the wrong thing. With the Empress, I was literally dropped inside her throne room with no idea what was going on. But now—I'm not sure why—I feel like I have to make a good impression. Although, it's not like they can stop me from taking the Ace of Cups; they'd be in direct violation of the Empress's orders. I walk up to Harold, taking a sip of the delicious pink wine.

"It's good, right?" he says. "It's cold and crisp but has a little kick."

"I wonder what it is."

Lāri turns to us and says, "It's *ranyo oeno*, an Oleanu delicacy from the pink salt mines north of the island." Her voice is monotone; I'm just relieved she's speaking.

"A salt wine?" Harold takes another sip and swishes it around in his mouth. "I can hardly taste the salt, it's so smooth and fruity."

"It is mixed with *baro*," Tessa chimes in.

I'm guessing that's some sort of fruit.

Two claps. "King Mayi of Cups will see you now." I spin around to see a man wearing Cups colors standing in the hall.

"Oh, Bilu, such formalities. You know it makes people feel uncomfortable, and I despise that." A tall man wearing a crown on his head, bright red lipstick, and a long flowing robe of gold and green approaches behind him. He places a manicured hand on the guard and tells him to go away. Then his eyes skim over all of us, stopping on me. He smiles a sharp toothy grin and steps forward. "You must be Soren."

"Hi—um, yes. That's me."

"The Empress has told me all about you." He places a hand on my back and starts walking us down the long open-air hall.

"She has?"

"No, she hasn't dear. Not really. The Empress and I don't talk." He chuckles. "But I *was* expecting you, albeit not so early. It doesn't matter, though. Lunch is almost ready. Come, come." He motions for the rest of the crew to follow, and we're led through the courtyard garden into another hall. "King Bako is at the luncheon gardens already. He can't wait to meet all of you. I thought with the weather being so nice today, why not eat out in the gardens, you know?" He shoots me a wide red smile, and I smile back, still unsure of what to make of this...or how to act.

I guess I was expecting a throne room.

"So, how was your journey?" His voice is soft and fluid. I'm not sure what I was expecting, but this certainly wasn't it. I think I was expecting someone more...authoritative; King Mayi is more like a warm aunt who I haven't seen in years.

"We had some trouble." I frown. "And...we lost someone very important to us, which is why we..."

He stops walking, widening his eyes as he stares at me and then the crew. "Oh... How awful." There's sincerity in his voice, and he quiets for a few beats while he regards us. "That's tragic. From what I've heard of the *Devil's Gambit*, the undead crew is a strong bonded family. It pains me terribly to hear you lost one of yours." His eyes stop on Lāri who is trying to hold back tears, fists at her side.

"Thank you. That's also why we're so early. I was forced to use magic that I'm not an expert in to get us out of there, but it got us here quicker. Wait—the *Gambit*? You knew?"

"That you're pirates in disguise as the Empress's ship? Oh honey, please, I know everything." He winks at me. I stare back at the crew, and their surprised looks match mine, especially Lāri and Tessa. I wonder how much of *everything* the King of Cups actually knows, and if it'll be a problem. "I'm not surprised you ran into trouble with the Empress's flags letting every pirate know you're there, but then again, other pirates wouldn't be your friends either."

The luncheon garden is a cobblestone courtyard with white tables and chairs. Wafts of gardenia and lavender hit me as I enter. Towers of food are displayed on each table. To the far right, a man with dark hair and a beard rests his chin on his hand. He perks up when he sees us, then stands.

"My king," he extends his hand.

"*My* king," King Mayi responds. "This is Soren and the rest of the *Devil's Gambit* crew, here to rescue the Devil from the Deep."

King Bako rests his eyes on me. He's quite slender, his high white collar covers his Ipani stripes, and there's an elegance about him that makes me feel underdressed. I'm now glad for my current outfit, even if it was given to me by the Empress. "And what an arduous task that will be." He leans forward. "Are you sure you're up for it?"

I swallow. "Whatever it is, we'll do it together."

"Well, let's feast first. We wanted you to feel welcome and let you know that we appreciate your journey. If it's true, the Prince of Danū is alive and can put Death away, then you're doing us all an enormous favor. While we eat, your rooms are being readied."

I quirk a brow and look at the crew.

Tessa tilts her head. "Rooms?"

The crew and I exchange worried glares, and I clear my throat. "I know we're early, but I'd like us to get started as soon as possible. The sooner you can give me the Ace of Cups Card, the sooner we can be on our way."

King Mayi licks his red lips and glances down, then back up at me. "Let's eat first, then you and I will take a walk in the gardens. Shall we?"

I swallow. Something isn't right. He's stalling.

King Mayi urges me to take a seat on the opposite side of his husband, and he takes his seat next to me. The crew is seated at a different table. I stare wearily in their direction.

Plates of green, blue, and pink berries covered in a light honey-like dressing and what I presume to be goat cheese sends a sweet aroma up my nose. In the center is what looks like steamed squash with the same sauce over it. A four-tier tower at the center of the table is covered with berries, unfamiliar fruits, and desserts sprinkled with powdered sugar and drizzled in...blueberry syrup? Considering everything that's just happened, the task ahead of us, and our destination, I'm not sure I have an appetite even for this.

I look back at the crew longingly. Ntaoru and I exchange a concerned glance, but I give her a reassuring nod. "Let's eat first. I'll get to the bottom of this."

I hate idle chit chat. I've never been one for small talk nor do I know how to navigate it well, but I'm literally having lunch with royalty. King Mayi has an appetite, which I respect. He also didn't make me feel like I was eating too fast. Despite my feeling that something is amiss, he makes me feel comfortable. I remind myself to keep my guard up.

I don't trust this.

King Bako doesn't stop staring at me, but all I can do is smile back. I want so badly to tell him to paint a portrait of me, but I bite my tongue. Royalty, Soren, they're royalty. Besides, I'm sure they've never seen anyone with hair this red, blah blah blah.

I take another sip of my drink.

"Do you like the rayo oeno?

"I love it. It's really delicious, thank you." I need to get them talking and cut the bullshit. "If you don't mind my asking..." They stare at me, and I consider my wording carefully. "How do you manage to keep Oleanu safe and so beautiful? You know, while the other islands are..." How do I put this?

"Suffering?" King Mayi finishes for me.

King Bako chuckles. "In turmoil? Grief? Dying? Hungry?"

My cheeks heat. "Sorry, I didn't mean to—"

King Mayi holds up a manicured hand. "No apologies necessary. We're not like the Empress—you can speak to us frankly." He sighs. "My family learned quickly we needed to rise above the regime."

Now this has my attention.

"We watched the other islands fight—Oleanu even fought for some time—but enough was enough. I'm not proud to say, I bent to her whims. But I did so carefully."

I take another bite of my squash.

"I *made* the cards keep me as king, my birthright. Otherwise, the throne would have been given to someone else, or just had the Prefects rule over it—you've seen how that goes."

I nod. "Trafficking. Corruption." Or they get killed, like poor Alec.

King Mayi points to my Wheel of Fortune mark, and his husband leans in to look. "Curious mark, but I bet you started out as the Fool. Everyone does." He smiles. "And now this one. What is your intuition telling you?"

"I don't know if my intuition is a good judge of character right now. It led to all this." I motion around with my finger.

"Why do you say that?" King Mayi asks. "What happened?"

I pause and swallow my food, unsure if I should say anything else, but the way he's looking at me tells me he knows more than meets the eye.

"What do you mean, you made the cards keep you as king? How?"

King Mayi laughs. "Right to business, aren't you? That's good. I like that, Soren." He lifts his sleeve and shows me his mark. The II of the high priestess. I stifle a gasp, remembering the Empress did mention one of the kings was the high priestess. "I watched the world carefully," he says. "I paid attention to what was happening. But my family has always been...in tune with our emotions, we may have a greater advantage with these waters than others in Ipa. I listen to what the Aō has to say. Unfortunately, it's a lost art for the majority of Ipani."

I regard his words.

"So tell me, are you certain you aren't a good judge of character? Or are you hearing in your head what you tell yourself. Listen harder."

I take a deep breath. "I wanted to bring my mother back. Instead...it took me, and brought back Tetalla. Then Nkella had to..." I swallow and look away. "And now another crew member has died."

"I get the feeling you were shortsighted with your quest."

I perk a brow. "What?"

"My intuition is telling me this, but you'll have to search within yourself."

"The power of the Past Fate isn't to change the past, but to learn from it. It's what someone wise told me." I don't want to mention Aletha, the Empress's sister. "I knew I shouldn't have tried to bring her back. All this was my fault."

He doesn't say anything, but stares with a caring smile, a smile that says he understands me. "We all make mistakes, Soren. Sometimes they end up hurting us and there's nothing we can do about it. But in this case we can do something, and we should. Never turn your back on a chance for transformation."

My eyes narrow. Why is he telling me all this?

"You know," he continues. "We don't say 'die' in Oleanu. We say 'change.'"

King Bako laughs. "Stop that nonsense," he says musingly. "It hasn't been that way since before the Empress."

"Fine, fine. If they're not sent to the Deep—if they die by natural causes, I mean."

Confused, I regard him. "I thought, before the Empress, Ipani lived for a very long time..."

"Well, yes, but if they choose to change, they will...eventually.

"Change into what?"

"It depends on the Ipani and their ouma. They can change into air, sea, perhaps lava."

The king rolls his eyes. "Such a romantic. Wouldn't it be the same as joining then? Not changing. Death is still death."

"Well, they'd have to change to join, wouldn't they?"

I quiet, not wanting to get involved in their bickering.

"Well," King Mayi blots his mouth eloquently and stands. "I believe it's time for our walk to the Ace of Cups. Shall we?"

King Bako stays seated and waves us off.

I follow King Mayi out of the courtyard, eyeing my crew as we walk past. They glance at me, and I give them a reassuring nod. We cross a white bridge overlooking a pond with oumala otters popping in and out of the Aō; they appear to be playing catch. I can't help but smile and wish I could play with them.

King Mayi gently takes my arm. "I wanted to tell you this away from everyone else," he starts. I stare at him. He looks like he's choosing his words cautiously. "I wanted to say that I know who you are—who you truly are."

I blink a few times. "I'm not sure what you mean..."

"Yes, I know you don't." He tilts his head. "We share blood, you and me."

My heart stops. I stop walking. So does he, his forehead crinkling.

"You see, your father was the bastard son of my father. I hate that word. Bastard. But by definition, he was what he was."

All the saliva dries from my mouth.

"So, you see... Despite what the Empress asks of us, I am less inclined to let you go on this dangerous mission."

My pulse starts to quicken. This is too much information all at once. If my father was his father's bastard son, then that makes him my... "Are you... Are you my uncle?"

He nods. "Your father was hidden away and adopted by the Danū royals, Prince Nkella's grandparents, when your father was a boy. We didn't grow up together, I didn't even know he existed until years later." He chuckles. "That's a story for another time. But you have every right to be here, and"—he takes my clammy hand in his—"you've been busy. You freed the Ipani from their binds, returning their ouma. You're special, Soren. The king and I believe you are the key to defeating her."

"Defeating her? I thought you were with her..."

"Oh dear, no. It's true what we were trying to tell you earlier—we just want to keep our people safe. But I'm tired of us being cowards. I know Ipani are leaving because they feel useless. We have family out there. But I can't risk the destruction of Oleanu either, don't you understand?"

I nod. "I do." I'm struck speechless.

He lets his hands drop, and we keep walking toward what looks like a mausoleum at the end of the garden. Water trickles down a small waterfall beside it, soothing the ambience.

"I learned about my father being from Oleanu, but I didn't know..."

"That he was a royal? Why else would the Danū royal family take him in?"

"I don't know. It's all so much..."

"There were wars between Ipani in the island long ago, the Empress was a different threat. Your grandmother pressed for your father's murder."

I gasp.

"She's dead."

I don't think my eyebrows will ever come down from my hairline.

We stand in front of the white mausoleum. "Is someone buried here?" I whisper. He laughs.

"This is where I keep the Ace of Cups."

"Oh."

"But first, I have a favor to ask of you. This is a dangerous task the Empress is sending you on. I understand why you want to go. And—" A deep breath. "I need something from you too."

"What?"

"First, listen carefully. The Ace of Cups will transform any liquid to its composite." He takes out a flask from a pouch he had hidden inside his robes. "This is water from the Deep. Pour it inside the Cup. The water will grant you, and anything else access to enter and stay inside the Deep for a period of time. To come back, do the same but with water from here. That's how you and Nkella will return. Are you with me so far?"

"I think so. I have to bring water from Ipa with me in a different flask. Do I have to drink the water?"

"That is correct. You will not be able to return without pouring the water from here into the Cup. And both of you must drink it, this is important.

"Now for my requests. The first is, the Ace of Cups stays when you come back. The people of Oleanu depend on it."

I quirk a brow at the word depend.

"There's a reason my family has always been so in tune with emotions," he continues, taking my silence as an invitation to elaborate. "And able to listen to the Aō. The Ace of Cups, when in harmony, is always filled and takes in the island's happiness, sharing it with all."

"And the other two favors?"

He holds my gaze. "Please keep away from the serpent. Most people don't know this, but tortured spirits stay in the waters because the serpent keeps them trapped. If he sees you alive, he'll make sure you don't return."

I screw up my face. "That's hardly a request. I'm not trying to get myself killed. I make it a goal to stay away from the serpent up here—I'm not hunting for it inside its home." I chuckle.

"Promise me, Soren, you will steer clear of the serpent. You will return."

"I promise. Was there something else?"

He frowns. "I care about Ipa. Deep within my bones, I do. And I'm tired of all the suffering. I'm tired of this island being seen as the Empress's allies, the cowards. But we cannot defeat her alone."

"So you want me to defeat her."

"I want your help, but I know no one single Fate can defeat her alone. And if the Empress truly is no match for Death who wants all humans dead, I'm going to need a bigger army to help fight for all of our survival. Nkella might be able to fight him off, but we don't know if he will be ready. And then there's the aftermath. This is bigger than me or you."

"I'm confused..."

"I need you to convince the Prince of Danū to take his throne. Once he does, the fires of Danū will listen and be his to command. We need to be allies."

My eyes widen. "You want me to tell Nkella he needs to become king?"

His voice deepens. "The survival of the islands depends on it."

I chuckle. "He'll never go for that. He hates to even be called prince."

"Something tells me you can convince him. Right now, Death is sitting on the throne, and on a whim, he can raise the fires and kill all humans. The only reason he hasn't done this already is that he knows the Empress will retaliate and kill all the Ipani. He has something up his sleeve, and it keeps me awake at night. You and Nkella are my secret weapon, Soren. Please tell me you'll do it."

"Let's get me there first. None of this will work if I can't bring Nkella back."

He nods. "Thank you. Now for the bad news."

"There's bad news?"

"You'll have to do this alone."

I blink a few times. "What do you mean?"

"The Ace of Cups only works for those who are alive. If Nkella's alive, he can come back. Your crew all suffered from the undead curse. Except Ntaoru, but she was an agentless soldier, and half her soul—"

"Was in the Deep." I squeeze my eyes shut.

"Taking them back will ensure they don't return."

"So I have to go alone." I shake my head. This just got so much harder. I haven't navigated the ship alone. Ever. And I'm not good at being captain, I'm too new. "I—"

A popping sound comes from my feet.

"Who is this?"

I gasp. "Sapphire, how did you find me?" Her eyes glow purple as she wiggles her nose.

"Well, if a rabbit is your familiar, maybe you'll have some company after all. Rabbits can travel through worlds, as can spiders." He points to my web, and I immediately think of Philo.

"What about wolves?" I can imagine Nkella's face if Iéle finds him in the Deep. Besides, as a hunting companion, she'd help me find him.

"Unfortunately, wolves do not travel well to other dimensions."

A rabbit and an absentee spider it is.

"Are you ready?"

"As ready as I'll ever be."

He opens the door to the white temple and points inside. The trickle of waterfalls along the perimeter greets me as I enter. An aroma of eucalyptus emanates from the fumes.

The Ace of Cups stands upright on a white podium.

On the card there's an inscription that transforms from Ancient Greek to English. It reads:

"Thee who walks more than one world may drink."

A glass chalice glistens from the face of the card. Blues and greens swirl in the background, and a purple glare swipes over it.

"So, it's not just anyone but any who walk more than one world. Nkella can drink because he's alive and has been there. But you say you've drank? To fulfill happiness?"

He nods. "This card can do a lot more than take you to physical places. It can take you to emotional ones too—it can fulfill wishes and help others."

"Have you been to another world?"

"Not exactly..."

"Then how come..."

He motions to his body, his makeup. "One can say I walk both worlds."

I smile in understanding. I pick up the card, reach in, and pull out the chalice.

12

By the time we walk back to the crew, my stomach is in knots. Sapphire is snug in my arms, and I pet her while we walk.

The kings of Cups are...my family. My biological father was a bastard son of the king. And I find this right before taking off to the underworld of a different dimension...right before learning I have to do this alone, with Sapphire as my only crewmate. I can't even keep the wolf by my side.

I chew my cheek. I am so devastatingly screwed. What if I get to the Deep and can't find Nkella? How do I know how to get around? All these questions were at the back of my mind before, but thought I could work it out with the crew. Now this feels impossible.

What if I do find him, and Tetalla is right...he's too far gone? All this would be for nothing, and Ipa would be doomed. My heart aches to even think about it. I don't want more innocent people to die, but it's more than that for me. I have to find him. *I need him too much.*

When we arrive back at the courtyard, the crew is chatting with King Bako, who is now at the center of their group, telling them a story. Sapphire starts to fidget, and I put her down on the ground.

King Bako stops talking as we approach, and the crew members turn in their seats to stare at me. I clench my fists.

"Soren, what happened?" Tessa is the first to notice the potentially hard expression on my face. I glance at King Mayi, and he gives me an apologetic smile.

I walk up to them and clear my throat. "The rules of the Card say the only ones who can drink from the chalice and cross to the Deep, have to be alive..."

"So what's the problem?" Lāri asks. "We're alive."

"That means no one could have been...dead. Or half-dead. And you were all under an undead curse, or had half their soul ripped out..." I glance at Ntaoru whose lips are parted. "If any of you go to the Deep, it will claim you completely, taking back what belongs to it." I stare at Kenjō, she's the only one of the crew who hasn't been under a curse, but I can't ask her to come with me.

Harold wipes the cold from his eyes and hair.

"Guys, I'm not ready." My heart starts to beat faster. "I don't think I can do this. How am I going to steer the ship alone? Let alone find our captain in an entire dimension?"

Tessa leans forward. "Soren, if anyone can do this, it's you. You fell from your land and found us. And you're a Fate—don't forget that."

"That's true," Harold agrees.

Tessa continues. "You're in control of your fate. Look what you did with that mark." She motions at my wheel of fortune mark. "You can say it was fate who brought you to us, to Nkella, but you *are* Fate. You can do this."

I shudder.

"She's right," Harold says. "You can find him because you see into his past."

I shake my head. "It only takes me so far."

"But you can see something," he argues. "Use it to your advantage. Follow the clues. Maybe you'll meet others and see into their pasts—maybe they've seen him. You can do this."

I nod, then glance at the kings.

"I have faith in you." King Mayi nods back.

"We all do." Kaehante adds. That means more to me than he could ever imagine.

Ntaoru's frown deepens, and I go to her.

"I'll do it. I'll bring him back."

She stares at me, her eyes as fierce as her razor-sharp cheekbones. "And I'll stay here and wait for your return."

Lāri stiffens. "I cannot wait for your return, Soren. I need to be doing something to keep my mind off of everything until you get back with our real captain." She cringes when she says that, but I don't react. "Maybe I'll go find Gari."

"I'll stay with Ntaoru," Kaehante says. "I don't want to risk missing my captain's return."

"Either of our captains," Tessa says. "And I'm staying too. If that's alright with you," she says to the kings.

"As we said before, your rooms have been prepared." King Mayi waves a hand toward the garden. "I would prefer it if all of you stay here as our guests. It will make things easier for their arrival. And there's plenty to do in Oleanu."

They mutter between themselves, and I clutch my necklace. As afraid as I am, I'm glad I'm the one doing this. Sitting here and waiting would drive me insane.

Harold clears his throat. "I need to say something." He turns to Kenjō. "I thought we'd have a little more time together." Everyone quiets. Ice forms at his lips, and he licks them. "I must go. I have all my runes, and I should be able to open a portal now." He stares at me. He's right; as soon as the king sends the Empress a message that I'm ready to enter the Deep, she'll lift the block to enter other worlds, and Harold will be free to go.

"Harold..." Kenjō stands and gives him a hug, but he pulls away from her. Her mouth parts, confusion on her face.

"Come with me," he tells her. Now all our mouths drop.

"E?"

His face lights up. "Come with me, Kenjō!" His voice rises an octave in his excitement. "Think about it, what else are you going to do? Go back to Piupeki? And do what? Have your mom chase you around? Or wait here with half the crew?"

She shakes her head and then laughs. "I'll go."

Oh wow.

He gapes at her. "Really? You're not joking? You'll come with me to Jötunheim?"

She laughs, tears at the corners of her eyes. "Will we come back?"

"After I beat my family's curse, I'll bring you back!"

"Kenjō." I go to her. "You do realize you are going to go to a different dimension, right? Things could go wrong, you might never come back, they might not have a translation potion there..."

Harold looks at me. "My ansuz rune can help her with that."

"Oh."

Kenjō gives me a hug. "Before meeting Harold, I never left my island. Harold has told me stories of the cold land he's going to, and I doubt it will be anything I'm not used to." She grabs his hand. "I want to go."

I pull out the Ace of Cups Card, and stare at the glistening chalice inside, the purple glare still swiping over it. "I should be off then. If I wait any longer, I'm afraid I'll lose my guts."

King Mayi calls for one of the green masked Arcana. He comes in with a swirl of droplets surrounding him, and quickly disappears again after being told to inform the Empress that I'm about to open the portal.

The kings join us in their little boats as we head off to the Gambit. We have a larger crowd than I'd expected because some of the guards want to see Harold use his strange magic to open a portal.

After Harold and Kenjō grab their coats and belongings inside the Gambit, I say goodbye to them first.

Kenjō squeezes my shoulders, and I feel the wetness of her tears on my skin. I squeeze her tightly. Without ever wanting to, I messed up her life after I killed Alec. It was Demitri's fault, but I still carry the guilt, and it's taken time to be able to look her in the eye.

"I hope to be like you someday, Kenjō," I tell her. "If I never see you again, I just wanted to tell you, thank you for not hating me."

She pulls away from me and smiles. I turn to Harold.

"It's been fun," he says. "Maybe sometime in the future we can grab a coffee at a Starbucks and act like normal people."

I laugh. "Go kick some Ice giant's ass."

"Frost giants," he grins at me. "We're both nervous for two entirely different reasons. Good luck, Soren, and be sure to bring our captain back." He glances at Kenjō. "I'll be back to bring her home, and I'll want to see both of you. Also, be sure to tell him I helped when you see him."

"Will do."

Harold holds out his hand and one by one, twenty-six runes form a giant circle. When the last one takes its place, the center opens into what looks like outer space—millions of stars in complete darkness—before a giant tree becomes visible. It grows and spins until a rainbow bridge connects to a platform. We all step back. Harold takes Kenjō's hand, and we wave them off as they walk into their portal.

The four remaining crew members turn to look at me. Watching Harold take the leap to go fight some giants in a Viking dimension gives me the courage I need. Sure, he has Kenjō by his side. But I got here alone and made it out just fine. I can do this.

The crew collects some of their necessities and helps me raise the sails. Kae reminds me which levers to pull so I can do this on my own. A hollow, sinking feeling fills my gut, and I dread it's going to be there permanently—or until I have Nkella with me. I give each of them a tight hug, not wanting to let go. Kae, Tessa, Lāri, and Ntaoru stand before me, worry hidden on their faces.

Everyone knows this is a crazy mission, and the truth is, I might not make it back. Nkella might really be gone forever. And then they'll be without us both.

Ntaoru is the last of the crew. She's not very touchy feely, but she grabs my arm, and brings me in close.

"I'll see you soon, daí? Bring my brother back in one piece."

"I will."

That leaves King Mayi who is standing by the gangway, patiently waiting for us to say our goodbyes. "Head south, and when the mists of the spirit waters start to rise, drink from the chalice."

"And turn the potion on the ship. Got it."

"Good fortune to you, Soren. When you get back, I would like to give you a proper tour. You are part of the royal family now."

I gulp. I have too many other things to worry about right now. But I smile and thank him all the same.

And with that, they step away from the gangway, leaving me to sail into the Deep.

With my heart planted in my throat, I sail out of Oleanu, alone. My nerves are on end, but I hum to keep from thinking about all the things that could go wrong. After a couple of tantalizing hours on the open sea, the mists start to rise, and the hairs of my legs and arms stand on end.

This is it.

I take the flask filled with water from the Deep, pour it into the chalice, lift the chalice to my lips, and drink.

13

At first, nothing happens. Then the empty chalice disappears back into its card. I hide it safely away in my bandoleer and go check on the potion-key under the wheel.

The candles on the main deck snuffs out, then the ones behind me. Finally, all the wicks on the ship go out.

There's a silence before a shake, and I hit the floor when the entire ship starts to spin uncontrollably.

The force of the spin presses me down against the wheel. Pulling my weight up, I gape at the wall of water rising high to surround the ship. It's not the ship that's spinning. The sea is spinning at a dizzying speed, swallowing me whole into a whirlpool. Grabbing on as tight as I can, my legs dangle, and I lose any sense of direction. My eyes are closed, and my lungs feel like they're about to burst open from holding my breath so suddenly underwater. It all happens so fast. The temperature drops rapidly, and goosebumps swarm my arms. And then, like the calm after a hurricane, everything stops. Water trickles down around me as crisp, stagnant air tells me I'm no longer underwater.

I open my eyes. A red hue is cast over the sea, but otherwise, everything looks...the same. I exhale a cloud in the chilling air and use the chair to help me stand. A low humming, like a sad song-turned moan emanates from somewhere. I step over the broken glass on the floor and check my bearings.

My eyes widen as I stare upward and gape.

Bodies.

Floating...but as if standing all around the sky.

I grab at my chest as I fall against the ship. Some of them are headless. Some are heads. And others float, standing, staring up, forever suspended in time. They cover the sky in lieu of clouds, and above them, ripples expand as if I'm underwater, except, I'm not. The Queen was right, this is a different dimension.

I'm somewhere under the ocean in a different dimension, in the Deep. And instead of a deep ocean blue, everything is red.

Red for blood.

"You're in my domain, vicious one." I startle, then my muscles tense. Tetalla's voice circles around me, spinning me around to try and find him. But he's not here, not that I can tell. A dark chuckle makes me realize I'm hearing him in my head. "If this was your way of hiding from me, you should have reconsidered your voyage."

I pull out the Ace of Swords Card, and reach inside, gripping the hilt tight.

"I can see you, vicious one. Your every move. Even when you're awake. Anywhere you go in my domain, I will know where you are."

I hold the sword up, darting my gaze from side to side. "You killed AJ," I croak. "Show yourself."

"Weep for your friends who die in battle, for his soul will see no rest. He was the first but won't be the last. Unless you submit to me."

My hands shake at the hilt of my sword, but I continue searching all around me for Tetalla.

"It's not I you have to worry about. Some of my inhabitants will be hungry for your blood and they will smell it in you. Why are you here, if you're not dead?"

My eyes widen, now searching for spirits. Was this actually stupid? My crew is at his mercy while I'm here...unless I submit to him. I need to find Nkella ASAP so we can get back to them, and he can take Tetalla down.

"Hnn... You must be searching for the newest Devil. This is hopeless, vicious one." A menacing chuckle permeates the air. "That is it, isn't it?"

I raise the sword higher, knowing he can come down here at any time.

With a commanding tone he tells me "I won't be able to help you if you die. Are you willing to be stuck in the Deep for eternity?"

I lower the sword just a little. "Why don't you come down here, then, if you're so worried about me?"

He guffaws. "Helāni witch, I have you where I want you. I have no intentions of letting you go. Go on your quest, and I will be waiting for you when you are finished."

"I bet you can't even come back here yourself." Taunting him is probably not the smartest idea I've had, but I had to test the waters. I wait for a response, but it doesn't come.

He's spent hundreds of years down here, so he's probably afraid to come back and be unable to return to the other dimension. Now that I've released him from the Deep and he's at war with the Empress, he's not going to let that go. I'm secondary to his needs. I have to focus on finding Nkella.

"Tetalla?"

No response means he's gone for now.

I lower the sword and let it go back into the card. The sea is so calm. No waves, not even a little breeze.

Finding Nkella in this vast world is going to be difficult. Glancing around, this place is identical to Ipa, only...red. And bloody, with bodies in the sky. No clouds. And...no floating island from what I can see. Maybe Rutavenye doesn't exist here.

Where do I even start? The serpent took him from Piupeki—would he still be there? Would it have taken him somewhere else? Would he have taken off to go somewhere else? That last idea seems most likely.

Before I do anything else, there's something I need to do. Taking a knee, I let myself rest on the floor and close my eyes.

AJ, where are you? I focus on moments after his death, trying to find his past here in the Deep. Where did he go after he died?

I wait and listen, letting my mind search for any places he could be.

My mark starts to rumble, and I zoom into the memory, but I'm met with darkness.

A sense of dread hits the pit of my stomach as I start to fall in a sea of nothingness. Despair. But not him. I can't see him, or feel him.

I open my eyes. Why couldn't I see him?

Could it be too soon? My shoulders rise and drop, and I wipe away my tears. I'll keep trying.

I try to reach Nkella too, yet I'm met with the same darkness, this time full of rage. I'm not surprised, I've been trying to reach him since I found out he was alive. Something is blocking me.

The next course of action would be to look at the map and decide where to go first. If I were Nkella, where would I go?

The tree hut he built in Dempu Yuni?

A wave makes the ship rock back and forth.

My stomach stirs at the possibility he's been at his old tree hut this whole time I've been there, but in a different dimension.

No. Knowing him, he'd have gone to Danū.

The ship rocks a little harder, and I grab onto the rail, narrowing my eyes. The waters have been calm this whole time, so why are there waves now? Is there a tide in the Deep?

Doubtful.

My grip tightens over the steering wheel as I catch a big wave, causing my stomach to roll. Something shoots from the water and flies up to the sky. My mouth hangs open as a serpent—*the* giant serpent, Apeiron—slithers through the air, up to the surface.

It can fly here? How the hell am I supposed to kill it if it can fly!?

I stare at Apeiron as his body grows smaller and finally disappears into the sea of bodies.

Then I startle at a chilling, high-pitched cry. A spirit flies toward me, its sharp teeth gnashing, its eyes hungry for blood. I swing my sword and slice it in half, making it disappear. I catch my breath. The moaning grows louder, and I find more spirits headed my way on the glowing red waters.

I lift my sword out of its card—no time to think as blood-drinking spirits start flying toward me. One lands on my back and sends me stumbling forward. Not what I was expect from something translucent. A sharp bite pierces my skin, and I cry out, hurling my body onto the ground to try and knock it off me. Another spirit flies into my hair, and I stumble back, careful not to drop the sword. More shrill cries come flying around me. I can't see them while my hair covers my face, but I try to pry the one spirit off me. How do these things still have teeth? I thought they were spirits!

Something latches onto it, and I'm released. Panting, I turn around to find Sapphire gulping down a fanged head. I've never been so thankful to see her.

More tormented moans, and I spin around fast. They're coming at me by the dozens. There's nowhere to run. I set sail on the ship, but they only come faster. Sapphire leaps in front of me and gulps down another spirit.

Good bunny.

Something grabs me, and I spin to see a woman with wet black hair plastered over hollowed eye sockets and sharp rotting teeth. I lift my sword and swing, but the sword drops out of my hand as the ship is hit.

When I turn to see what hit me, the woman claws at my throat with long black fingernails. More like her are climbing over the main deck. They're probably what hit the *Gambit*. I reach for the sword, and she pushes me down, while another one kicks the sword out of my reach.

They're cognitive.

Her grip tightens, and her teeth nip my skin, drawing blood.

Now another is on me, and flying spirits are closing in on my line of sight.

I'm surrounded, pinned down, and can't get up.

Sapphire jumps on her head, and her nasty black oozing guts spurt all over my face.

Unable to catch my breath, another one reaches at me from behind Sapphire, and I force myself up, ready to fight it off.

Shreds of rotting muscle tissue stick out of its translucent gray skin. Sharp teeth protrude from its moaning mouth as it claws its way to me. I swallow the bile threatening to come out.

Something whip-like wraps around its neck and drags him off the ship. I gasp as the spirit splashes away from sight.

I stumble back far enough to get my bearings and stand, grasping the sword.

Swinging behind me, I slice another spirit open. Sapphire, being the bottomless pit she is, continues gobbling them up one by one. Whatever took out that first spirit is still down there, and I don't want to find out what it is.

Two spirits back up from Sapphire, looking at her quizzically. Sapphire opens her mouth wide, and in one hurried pace, attacks one of their legs. Their eyes bulge, but Sapphire is too fast for them. I train my eyes on the second spirit who is now backing away from Sapphire, presumably not wanting to be next. With a swing of my sword, the blade cuts through his translucent torso, which disappears before he hits the floor.

A hauntingly sad cry comes from behind me, and I spin around.

He has no face and a gaping black hole with sharp ragged teeth for a mouth. His eyes and nose are covered in a thin film of skin, and he hovers on the deck, his long limbs twisted and convoluted as he comes for me. His bones snap as he walks.

I grip my sword. "I'm right here, ugly." He snaps his neck to look at me, and hisses, showing ugly black pointed teeth.

The whip coils around its neck, and he claws at it as he's pulled back. A soaking wet pirate wearing a long coat and wet boots covered in seaweed stands on the opposite end of the whip. His hat covers some of his features, but I can make out the snake tattoo on his face. It only takes seconds for me to recognize who had just boarded my ship.

Snakebite. Or...Nangraku, his actual name. My body tenses. Without bothering to glance at me, he pulls out his whip so fast he sends the beast flying over his shoulder and plummeting to the water. I back up, creating distance between me and the pirate who orchestrated my and Nkella's kidnapping.

The one who ordered one of his crew to do whatever he wanted with me.

The one Nkella slaughtered, massacring his whole ship before anything did happen to me. Nangraku snaps his attention to me, a frown deep on his face.

Out of all the dead to find me, why did it have to be him?

We stare at each other at a standstill.

"You can put your sword down. I'm not going to hurt you." He hooks his whip to his belt loop.

"What do you want?" I manage to find my words. "How did you know I was here?"

"I only knew these spirits eat fresh blood. They usually stay up on the mists." He points up. "I was curious about what would cause the swarm of them to be down this low." He smirks but displays no amusement. "Imagine my surprise when I saw the Devil captain's girl. How did you die?"

I chew my cheek and hold my ground.

Taking a few steps toward me, he sniffs the air. "Oh. You're not dead. That makes sense that the spirits were here then. How is this possible?"

I lift my chin. "I have my ways."

"Or who are you in search for?" His eyes narrow.

"How do you know I'm searching for anyone?"

"If you are here, fresh blood, then you are searching for someone you care about...like many of us. We search and search for lost loves." His smile widens. "I know who you are here for. Lost cause. You should go back." He turns to leave the ship.

"No. Wait!"

He pauses, looking down at his shoulder.

"Do you know where he is?"

He scoffs. "Everyone knows where the new Devil is. But you will not get anywhere near him. You won't make it."

"Please—"

"Please?" He turns to face me and takes a few steps closer. I step back, and grimace at the kelp merged over the tips of his pointy ears. "For months, I've searched for my aovate in these wretched waters—the one your captain killed in cold blood. I spent days after he blew up my crew—blew me up—searching for my head." He grabs onto his head and rips it straight off his neck for me to see.

I cover my mouth to prevent myself from hurling as he sticks it back on.

"Why should I help you?" he hisses. "Had I known it was you here, I would have let them suck you dry."

I swallow. I won't get anywhere with him by arguing. And really, I should try and find someone else I might know. Like Soanalo. She would help me. But the last time I saw her was in Dempu Yuni, and she died in Wands. Which means the dead here don't stay and haunt the same place forever. She could be anywhere.

It can't be a coincidence he's the one who found me, and he knows where Nkella is. I take a deep breath. I hate this.

"I don't want to work with you either," I tell him, "but for some strange reason, we've been brought together." I think of the Wheel of Fortune Card. "You know where my captain is, and—"

"And what? How do you think you can help me?"

"I'm a 'Helāni witch,' remember? I can find your aovate for you." I smirk and glance over his shoulder. When I don't see a ship, I walk to the edge and see a small boat with two paddles. "Also, I have a ship, and you don't."

He folds his arms in front of him. "I've searched these planes for months. How do I know you will have any greater success? I'd rather search for a hundred more years than sail with you." He turns to leave again. "All our marks are reversed here, Helāni bitch. Down here, luck and ouma do not exist."

I stare down at my mark. My spiderweb is the same, and the Wheel of Fortune doesn't have a reversal. "Maybe your mark is reversed. Mine aren't."

He pauses and turns back to me. I show him my marks, and he squints at them.

He shows me his mark of four chalices, the Four of Cups. And he's right, they're facing me, instead of him—reversed.

"How badly do you want your lover back?" I ask him. "You risked your life avenging his death. Are you really going to walk away from possibly your only chance at ever finding him?"

He squeezes his eyes shut and lets out a raspy grunt as he walks over to the rail and looks out. While he contemplates, I recall the moments before Nkella killed Nangraku's lover in the tavern. I zoom into that memory to get a clear view of his appearance. If only I could bring people back from my memories and not just objects. That would solve all our problems.

My mark pulses as I sense where in the Deep this man is. When I get a feel, like a web being tugged from my fingertips, I follow it. Whipping cold winds and snow surround me, and I have to squint through hail to see a man hanging upside down from a tree. The Hanged Man. His features are undeniably Nangraku's lover. I've found him.

"Helāni." Nangraku's voice pulls me back. His face is twisted in disgust as if he just caught me doing something gross. He hates everything my magic stands for. I get it. But a small smile tugs at my lips because now I know my magic still works here. Whatever the reason I can't reach AJ, or Nkella, it isn't because I can't use my magic. I'll just have to keep trying.

"Well?" I ask, placing a hand on my hip.

Nangraku pinches the bridge of his nose. "We'll work together." He looks around the ship. A howling spirit emerges through the wood, and Nangraku kills it with a snap of his whip. Chills crawl up my spine when the memory of the snake head at the tip of that same whip grabbed onto my legs. My jaw tenses. He stares at me.

"There are areas in Wands I have yet to search. We'll start there."

"No. We find my captain first."

He scoffs. "How do I know you'll keep your end of the bargain and not leave after you find him?"

"It's not so simple for me. He's not the only one I'm here to find. I won't leave."

He chuckles. "You're out of your mind." The howling grows louder as more spirits start to descend. "You are a magnet for the dead. This won't be easy."

"Let's get a move on then," I say. "What about your boat?"

"Leave it. There are others like it."

Inside the cabin, I bring out the map. "Can you tell me where we are? And where Nkella is?"

He points to the misted area where I drank from the chalice. "This is where we are." Then he points to a location in Danū. "And that is where your captain is."

A butterfly releases in my stomach. How did I know he'd be in Danū?

"I wouldn't be smiling so wide yet, Helāni. He's not easy to get to."

"My name is Soren. And how do you know he's there?"

"Everyone knows. When he arrived, he was dragged by the serpent to Danū. It was a spectacle for all to see."

"I actually thought the serpent was going to eat him," I admit.

"Yes. It was also curious to all who wander why he was not eaten."

Assuming the serpent would still eat someone with a devil curse, it must have been because of his sacrifice. The power of the sword.

"But you haven't actually...seen him, have you?"

He smirks. "I've seen him."

"And? Did he seem..." Alive? Okay? Completely gone?

"He is the new Devil of the Deep. He will most likely not recognize you."

An anchor lands in my stomach. "I will make him remember me."

He shakes his head. "But if you cannot, you still owe me my half of the deal."

I purse my lips but don't respond as I walk to the wheel, even though I intend on using the World Card. "Hoist the sails. We have to do this manually." The sailing potions won't work here, as they're made from ouma.

"Your map will be reversed here," he says. I quirk a brow.

"Danū on the map of Ipa will be southeast. Here is northwest."

"It doesn't matter, we're not using this map. Not exactly..."

His eyes narrow as I take out the World Card. A red sheen glares across the face of the card, the sign that the map on the card itself has physically changed. And sure enough, he's right. The map is in reverse.

After we hoist the sails, I sit back at the wheel.

"Hold onto something," I tell him.

His brows raise. "Helāni magic?"

"To Danū," I whisper at the card. Then I throw it toward the bow, this time knowing it will go where I want it to go, just like it did last time.

A red portal opens, and a fortified island sits at the other end. I slowly sail us through the opening. Cascades of howling screams appear just above us; I crane my neck to peer around the widened sails.

"They're coming," he says. "They're after the Helāni magic."

14

I SAIL THROUGH THE PORTAL AS FAST AS I CAN—ALTHOUGH not as fast as I expected. Sailing this boat manually is slow.

Nangraku jumps to the main deck and fights off spirits with his whip as they come. Sapphire lingers close by, hoping for a bite to eat.

Once we're on the other side, the card reappears in my hand, luckily leaving behind all the tortured ghosts I walk over to Sapphire and bend down to pet her. "Thank you for being here with me," I whisper to her. "I wonder sometimes how much you understand me and what's going on around you." She wiggles her nose at me. "Could you find AJ?"

Nangraku walks back up to the quarterdeck and Sapphire disappears. "If your Helāni magic attracts them—"

"I can't use it, I know." I stand to face him, disappointed that Sapphire left.

This is going to make things more challenging. "We'll have to get to Nkella the old-fashioned way."

He stands beside me at the wheel, his short hair pulled back behind his pointed ears, showcasing his snake tattoo on his face. It's tail wraps around his neck, which is also covered in bits of algae. I grimace. It feels weird being this close to him—standing near each other on the *Gambit*. Nkella would never approve of him being here...with me...on his ship.

A large fortress towers in front of us. My lips part. "Woah..." Cages with skeletons dangling their limbs are posted at a gated entrance.

"Everything in the Deep looks as it did before the Helāni came."

"What does that mean?" I ask.

"In the living world, Danū has a massive skeletal serpent wrapping around the island, in front of the fortress."

"Oh."

"Do you have anything to trade at the entrance gate when we get there?"

"I have gichang."

"That won't do here. They only take possessions. Something meaningful to you."

My breath hitches as I clutch my necklace, and I shake my head. Not if I can't use my magic.

He eyes me, frowning. Then he points to a shrouded area covered with dead trees. "Make a left. We'll have to sneak in."

"Sneak in? What'll happen if we get caught?"

"Torture."

I swallow. "I can't die here," I mutter.

"Then don't get caught, á?"

My frown deepens as I steer left. Nangraku directs me to a hidden spot he claims to have parked in while looking for his lost love.

"And you're sure they won't find the ship here?"

"The guards here are preoccupied, and it isn't necessary to chase the spirits here. But everyone wants something. Nothing is free."

We drop anchor and disembark from the *Gambit*. It's a long way up the fortress, and getting down on the other side is a whole other concern. Nangraku starts to climb a tree, and I follow suit.

"How come you're not a bloodthirsty, howling spirit?" I ask as I wait for him to climb onto the next branch.

"We all eventually become them."

"Everyone? I thought you stayed like you are for...eternity."

"We're never truly at rest." He climbs up to a higher branch and extends one hand to me. I don't take it, for fear of his dead hands not being strong enough to hold me up. "Because half of our souls are down here, and the other half is up there, we are always starving, needing, in pain. Eventually, we become mad. We lose our minds, and our primal needs take over."

He makes it to the top of the fortress and jumps down. I gasp, but he looks over from the other side. "Climb up. There's a platform."

Once we're at the top, I jump down onto what I can only describe as an open hallway. The other side of the fortress overlooks a vast plain of mountains, volcanoes, and red desert with palm trees. The trees have black leaves. I touch the coin around my neck. The black palm tree—the meaning of the word Mikiroro—is Nkella's lineage. It feels strange to be looking at them.

The clanging of steel against steel makes my teeth grind. Where is that coming from?

"Come on. We have a long way to go to Pari Eitu."

"Where?"

That's the name for the temple."

"Why is he there?"

He stares at me with a bored look on his face, and I can sense his sarcasm.

"Right. How would you know."

"Follow me," he says. I follow him into the dark corridors of this fortress, all the way down a stone stairway. Outside, the light is dimming to a deeper red. My guess is that it's nighttime in Ipa, and this is the reflection down below. "Stay away from the shadows."

He walks down the center of an open hallway with stone walls surrounding us and bridges connecting the fortress's towers and walls. "Won't we be seen like this?"

"It's fine. No one will question us now. No one cares. Guards or other dead are not who you should be worrying about. Just stay away from being seen entering or departing, and don't make any bargains if you have nothing to trade."

"So you mean, be careful of spirits?"

"And hungry monsters who lurk in the shadows." He gives me a toothy grin."

"Got it. How far is the walk to where we need to go?"

"A few days."

"Stop." He pauses to look at me. I reach into my pocket and take out the World Card.

"You will call all the dead and the *āngasoe*!" His voice dips at the last word he just said, and he actually looks scared.

"The what?"

"The guards are āngasoe."

"I thought you said not to worry about the guards."

"Because they won't be searching the dead, but if they detect you're not dead, then you should be worried, á?"

"It's worth the fight if it saves us days to get there! I don't have that long," I spit back. He squeezes his eyes shut and grabs his whip.

"Do it fast then."

I purse my lips. Regaining focus, I stare at the card. "Show me Nkel-la," I whisper. The card flickers to black.

Nangraku snickers. I scowl at him.

Fine. If it won't show me Nkella then... "What was the name of the place we're going?"

"Pari Eitu."

"Take us to Pari Eitu."

A red sheen swipes the card, and a portal opens to Pari Eitu. I glare at Nangraku, a smirk on my lips. His brows raise at the portal emanating an orangey glow. Inside the portal is a large structure. Loud clashes along with shouts and cheers come from it.

"Are you ready?"

"Are you? Because what you're about to see might change your mind about him."

I frown. "It won't."

He raises his brows as he gives me a pointed look. "As long as you hold up your end, á?"

"I won't let you down. Let's go."

His eyes narrow, and he motions for me to go ahead of him. He follows me as I step in front of a large temple.

A shrieking cry circles above us, and I slip the card into my bandoleer.

"This is a temple ruin now," he says, almost nostalgically. "Going inside is not going to be as easy as the fortress, á?"

"How do we get in?"

"It would be easier if you had something to give up." He stares at my necklace. Something tells me I'm going to be fighting a lot, because not using my magic here won't be easy.

A sigh escapes his lips, and he stares at the structure. "The āngasoe guard the entrance. They charge admission, and there's no easy way to sneak through. You don't want to get caught."

I draw my brows together. "Admission for what?"

"For the fights."

"Fights?"

"You're not going to enjoy what you are about to see, Helāni. But if you get caught, you're on your own."

It sounds like I run the risk of getting caught whether I use magic or not, so I'm going to take my chances. I take out my dagger. "Would this work?"

"Do you care about that dagger?"

My nose itches as I stare at it, my eyes threatening to tear. "It was the first weapon Nkella bought for me." But it's more than that. When the crew first rescued me, and Nkella thought I was a spy, he never allowed me a weapon to defend myself. By the time he bought me this dagger, he trusted me. What's more, he even defended me from a shopkeeper who'd called me names.

Nangraku regards me as I stare at the black hilt with red swirls.

"Then it'll do."

Clutching the hilt, I nod. If it'll be a way to get me closer to rescuing Nkella, I'll gladly give it up. Not that I wouldn't trade the necklace for him, it just...belonged to my mother, and this entrance isn't exactly a sure thing yet. However, if things go my way, I won't have to give up any of it.

"Trading valuables won't be a problem for us."

"Á?"

"Just watch."

He quirks a pointy brow over his tattoo as I smile and walk toward the entrance. He catches up with me and holds me back.

"If they can tell you're not dead, you're in trouble. Give me the dagger."

I hand it to him, unloosening my necklace and giving him that too. "So you can come in with me."

He takes my items, staring at the necklace quizzically after I had guarded it so fiercely. I follow him to the gate and almost lose my nerve when an actual minotaur steps from behind the stone walls.

I stagger back, my jaw dropping.

He's fifteen or twenty feet tall with huge, protruding muscles the size of truck tires. Large veins stick out from his neck, and he roars something at us. My knees shake.

Long, wide horns curve past the minotaur's broad shoulders. He has tusks under his nose. In his hand, he clutches a large bat and regards Nangraku as he cautiously offers our trade.

A minotaur. The āngasoe are...*minotaurs!*

The minotaur squints at the two objects, then at Nangraku, and he passes me a glare a few feet behind. I don't dare crack a smile for fear it'll give me away. The minotaur takes the items and moves to the side, letting us pass.

I walk quickly, with my head bowed down.

Dry heat hits me in the face the moment I join the crowd in an outdoor arena. Despite the red hue of the outside, it's darker in here, with orange and red lights stemming from the center surrounded by the dead.

"I hope you have more valuables where those came from. The longer you're here, the more you'll end up giving away."

"Don't worry about it," I reassure him as we quickly make our way deeper into the crowd. Glancing over my shoulder, I catch a view of the minotaur tossing my necklace and dagger on top of a pile of loot. He walks back to his post, and I close my eyes, reaching into my past only a few minutes ago.

The minotaur watches us leave and tosses my items to the loot. I reach in and grab them.

Nangraku elbows me in my arm, and I open my eyes.

"Taking a nap, Helāni?"

I open my hand and his eyes bulge.

"Told you not to worry about it. Perks of being Helāni." I wink.

Surprise crosses his features, and he stares back at the minotaur, then at me. "You take a lot of risk, Helāni."

I refasten my dagger and clasp my necklace back where it belongs as I gauge where we are. Hundreds of the dead stand billowing and shouting. I haven't gotten a good glimpse of what they're watching yet, too many people in front of me. "Where to now?"

He points to the arena, and I screw up my face trying to peer through the crowd.

A moat of fire surrounds a large circular dirt platform. I gape at what's piled up above the moat: minotaur heads by the hundreds, some burning, others with their eyes gaping wide at the audience.

The blood drains from my face.

Not because of the minotaur heads.

Two large draconic-looking beasts fight to the death. Heavy chains grip them around their waists as they snarl, punching each other until blood spurts from their faces. The one to the left is more bloodied and a bit smaller than the other. They both have wings resembling those of a bat, torn in some places, and pointed claws on each end. Horns curl on the tops of their heads; they have devilish tails with sharp ends and large claws on their hands and feet.

The smaller one starts to get pulverized by the larger beast, over and over again, and the crowd goes ballistic. They cheer, wanting blood and gore to be spilled.

The heavy chain snaps against the larger beast's back, forcing him off the smaller one. He turns his head and roars in the direction the chain is being pulled. A minotaur stands on a platform and roars, not far from the vicinity, but keeping his distance. By the looks of the decapitated minotaur heads outside the fire, this is a common occurrence.

The crowd becomes distant until all I can hear is the sound of my heartbeat. I shake my head and tear my eyes from the scene to stare at Nangraku.

"W-what—W-ho—What is this?"

"These are the Devils of Danū."

"I don't understand."

He points to the smaller beast lying bloodied on the floor. "That is your captain."

15

"No. That can't be him."

"It is."

I stare at the devils in the arena as a minotaur swoops down on a chain and probes the devil lying still with a hot iron stick. My gut clenches. It's hard to stop the tears from clogging my throat. "How can you be sure?"

"When he first got dragged here, he didn't look like that, but when he was recognized by the people from this island who he'd abandoned, they started to fight him.

We watched him transform. At first, it was a hazard to capture him, but when we die, we come back. Since there's so little risk, they finally managed it. The āngasoe have lost their heads many times but it's the island's only entertainment. Here, they only want blood."

The people he abandoned. When he left to try and save his sister, he made many enemies. The people revolted against the royals of Danū. I remember AJ telling me this. I stare at the devil as he's urged to stand. I try to catch the features of his face, but he doesn't look straight my way, and I'm too far up.

"How long has he been fighting like this? Do they get breaks?"

"It never ends."

Oh, God.

I walk closer to the edge of the fence and wrap my fingers around the metal. I stare down at him, then close my eyes, trying to reach his past. But I hit the same block as always. Darkness. Rage. And I'm pushed back.

It's the same as before. This is why I couldn't see him past a certain point after he entered the Deep. His curse won't allow it.

"It's time for you to hold up your end of the deal, Helāni," Nangraku demands from behind me. I open my eyes and gape at him. "You promised."

"Not yet."

His eyes cut daggers through me. "The deal was I get you here. Not that we get him out."

"I actually didn't agree to that."

"You evaded the question," he growls.

"Please—I will help you. You saw how easily I can retrieve an object from the past. Just help me get him out of here."

He scoffs, half turning to the crowd who look eager for the show to start again.

I grab his shoulder. "I need your help to get him out of here. All of Ipa is depending on it. Don't you want your people in Ipa to survive?"

"Why would I care about a home who discarded me, á?"

My heart pants in my chest. "Because…there've gotta still be people you care about up there."

"They're all dead. I only want my aovate."

"And I will help you find him. Please."

He hisses a sigh behind his teeth. "What do you suggest we do?"

I look back at the platform. This is far different than any oumala animal fighting ring the crew has taken down, but I'm not completely unfamiliar with ouma fire.

I'll just need to get through it. "I need a way onto that platform." I take out my World Card and flip it in my fingers. He eyes it, making a disapproving frown.

"Helāni, if you die here, don't think I won't force you to hold up my side of the bargain. And you're going to call all of the Deep if you use Helāni ouma here, á?"

"I won't die," I look over my shoulder. "And it'll be quick." The devil across from Nkella takes the metal rod away from the minotaur, slamming him close enough to pop his head off his shoulders. Blood sprays from the minotaur's neck, dousing the devil in blood as he pierces the torso with his sharp nails. I tear my eyes away before I lose what little food I've had.

"You're sure you want to go down there? What's your plan when you do?"

With an undead audience of this size, using my Fate magic is going to make me the target. Which means no World Card—not yet at least. But I'll use it to get us out of here and worry about the spirits later.

My fingers grip the metal fence behind me and sweat drips down my neck. I glance over my other shoulder at Nkella, who's still lying on the ground, blood pooling from his mouth. He's not getting up.

"You have no plan. This is madness."

"I just need to get to him."

He guffaws. "This is not some love story of myth where the beast will revert back when he sees his lost aovate, á? You are going to die."

I narrow my eyes at him. "After he killed you on your ship, he almost lost himself, but I—I was able to bring him back. I have to try."

He stiffens his bottom lip and regards me. Then with a hiss, he skims the roaring audience. "It won't be easy. It's not only your devil you have to worry about, but his competitor, and the āngasoe."

"I know," I mutter inaudibly. "How do the guards get down there?"

A minotaur jumps down a contraption tied to a metal zip line and lands on the platform. He immediately stuffs the hot end of the metal rod into the devil's mouth and falls back. I follow the metal zip line with my eyes to an open, upside-down *U*-shaped window on the top of the auditorium, where another minotaur watches.

"Okay," I spin back to Nangraku. "I'm going to need a decoy."

His upper lip curls, and he curses something inaudibly under his breath. "What do you need me to do?"

I grin and stare at the zip line.

Nkella is back on his feet, his tail flicking on the ground as he readies himself for the fight. The features of his face are almost unrecognizable. He's larger, that much is clear. Large horns curve down to the back of his head, and some kind of red sheen swipes across his face.

How much of him is still in there?

The crowd cheers as the minotaur shoots a fire ball into the air, and at once the chains holding the devils are loosened. They're still attached to the fence, but long enough for them to tear each other to shreds. I glance to my right where Nangraku has just finished climbing the beam of the stadium. He stands on a small platform leading to the minotaur's abode and stares down at me. I give him a nod, and he reciprocates. No one from the audience has noticed him. The minotaurs haven't either... yet. But I'm counting on them to notice him up there.

The minotaur on the platform starts to climb the beam and I make my way through the crowd.

Every time the crew and I took down an oumala animal fighting ring, we've counted the dumbest, most dangerous situations we've put ourselves in. This is *by far* the dumbest. When I get back, I'll have to tell AJ—

My heart sinks.

The minotaur reaches the top, and Nangraku's eyes bore into me. I refocus on my task. Extending my arm, a thick web soars from my wrist, cocooning the top of the minotaur's head, blinding him, and covering his horns. He lets go of the beam and crashes to the ground headfirst, but I don't let him go, as I wrap my webbing around his hands against his face. He doesn't move, and I think he may have knocked himself out, but I can't be too careful. More webbing pours out of me until his head is no longer visible. Some of the nearby spectators start yelling, and a few have eyes on me, confusion flickering their faces, but they're not my concern. They're prisoners of this place, and the minotaurs are the correctional officers.

A few of them spread out, giving me some space.

More of the dead roar behind me, shaking the fence, demanding blood. I refuse to look at the stadium right now. I can't get distracted.

A minotaur storms out of the hut, and the ground rumbles. Nangraku cracks his whip around the minotaur's leg, making him fall to the ground with a heavy bang that sends a ripple through the audience. As he falls, my webbing keeps him strapped in place with a flick of my wrist. I'm getting good at this.

Another runs out. We repeat the steps. Nangraku yells something to me over the screams and roars.

No more minotaurs. I give him a nod and wave for him to come down.

Nangraku grabs the zip line and swings himself down, landing right over the first guard lying unconscious on the ground.

"More will show, Helāni. You must be quick."

"I will." I turn to look at the stadium. The devils are at each other's throats; blood sprays from the neck of one. I need to get there now. I turn back to Nangraku. "Now, you have to go."

"Á?"

I whip out my World Card and hold it out. "He's been searching for you in Piupeki. That's why you haven't found him yet."

His eyes redden, and his voice cracks. "Why would he be searching for me?"

"Somehow, he knew you were here. Ask him yourself." A portal opens from the card, and a cold draft comes from it. Around us, the dead stop screaming, and eyes are on us. Inside the card, spirit-moans seep through.

Nangraku's eyes are weary as he gapes all around us. "Helāni..."

"Go." I shove him into the portal before he turns to face me."

"Engi."

I nod, knowing that means "thankful." He leaps into the portal, and I close it as quickly as I can.

Now I'm alone.

My heart races as I stare at the crowd. All eyes are on me. The minotaurs are still down, and as far as I can tell, there aren't any more coming. At least, not yet. The dead start advancing toward me; I take a step back.

Turning the World Card toward the stadium, I open another portal. I'll be where Nkella is fighting before any of them can reach me.

A circle of heat and smoke opens, and I step inside.

16

The audience of dead has multiplied. They're even shooting down from the sky, but I don't have time to deal with them now. I'll figure out how I'm going to deal with them after I've finished.

Not that I know how I'm planning on getting through this, let alone waking Nkella from his devil curse mid-fight. Getting onto the platform was as far as I'd planned.

Nkella's opponent leaps over my head. I duck as he lands behind me. He swings his gigantic arm in full force, striking Nkella so hard, he's sent flying against the fence. He lands with a thunderous crash that knocks me back down as I struggle to stand. Fire backlights him as he stands. I gape at the devil in front of me. He's a lot bigger in person, so much larger than Nkella.

Reaching into my pocket, I take out the Ace of Swords Card.

"Nkella," I yell, hoping he'll hear me. Hoping he'll recognize my voice even though I know he's far gone.

The larger devil snaps his attention, his eyes dilating and zeroing in on me. Quickly, I pull the sword from the card. He's on me faster than I could lift the blade.

I'm thrown against the fence so hard, I almost swallow my tongue. The sword drops out of my hand and into the fire behind me.

The devil breathes heavily over me, his veins popping out of his neck, fury emanating from his pores—as if insulted that I'm here on *his* floor.

I slide my back against the fence, the fire singing my skin. My eyes don't leave his, while I try to reach the hilt of my sword through the metal. He stares at me quizzically, probably trying to figure out who or what I am, and if I'd taste good barbecued or raw.

Fumes scorch my hand. My eyes swell as I nearly rip my arm out of my socket to reach the hilt. The devil's gaze falls to my movements, but before he does anything, Nkella tackles him. For a split second, I think he's recognized me and come to.

But no. He's still the same; he only took his chance once his opponent was distracted.

That does seem like him, but—focus Soren. Must. Reach. Sword.

My fingers grasp the hilt. I've got it.

I pull the sword from the flame, and my hand is blackened. I screech at the pain and bite down on my tongue.

Not seeing any other options, I pull out the Ace of Cups and pour a droplet of water over my hand. My shoulders ease as the pain subsides. The devils are still distracted in their fight. Ouma water cancels ouma fire.

I carefully grip the hilt as my long blade is now covered in ouma fire.

The crowd has become a never-ending chorus of noise. And since I used magic, the undead are gathering closer to the fence, some no longer caring about getting burned. One of them is caught in ouma fire but continues standing there, watching me. His screams merged with those of the audience.

The opponent has taken Nkella to the farthest point his chains reach, disabling his ability to move. He pounds on Nkella's face. Over and over. Nkella isn't even trying to move. His body is limp. And there's no minotaur to call the end.

"Stop!" I shout. With the sword in my right hand, I walk with determination and swing it against his back.

I hit steel. The sword vibrates in my arm, and I ricochet backward.

The wind is knocked out of me as I land on my back. Pains courses through my bones, but I force myself back up.

It didn't even hurt him. I stare at the sword still blazing with ouma fire.

How is this possible?

A sword that can defeat the Empress, but can't take down the Devil?

Is it because ouma fire won't hurt them?

The opponent blows fire in my direction. I roll to the side, dodging the flames. Time to think later. For now, I need to stay alive. Nkella frees himself from his opponent's grip and strikes him over the head, but the larger devil uses Nkella's force against him, grabbing the chains around his neck, and choking him from behind.

That's when I notice it.

Nkella's chains are attached to a metal collar around his neck, while his opponent is being held by his ankle. That isn't fair at all; no wonder he's struggling to fight back. His opponent grabs Nkella's chain and yanks him by the collar, dragging him down to the sand. Nkella grabs at his neck, his wings flapping hard behind him and causing winds to blow on my face.

If he had his ouma, he'd be able to blow his opponent up without even laying a finger on him. But none of the dead here has ouma. Nkella reaches for his opponent, but he's struggling. He visibly chokes. His arm starts to shake.

I scream out his name. Without the minotaurs controlling the fights, can he actually be killed in the Deep? If he's alive, then he could die here! His curse is the only reason he stays alive, but the opponent's curse appears stronger.

Harrowing cries grow louder, and I stare up at the darkening red sky. More and more dead are falling into the pit. The dead that were outside of the fence are now ablaze and making their way toward me.

I climb to my feet and run at the chains with the sword over my head. I have no idea if this is smart, but I swing down hard at Nkella's chains and...release him as it breaks with a powerful snap!

Nkella gasps for air and grips his opponent's arm. His wings lift him off the ground; his opponent is still attached from the ankle.

Something gurgles from behind me, and I spin around. A burning body stands a foot away, extending a burning hand toward me. I can't let that thing touch me. I swing my sword and slice his head clean off. More are coming, and I step back.

The opponent lands on the ground hard, and the stadium trembles. Nkella swoops down and lands on top of the devil's torso.

I swing my sword at the two burning dead approaching me.

"Seriously? I used magic like an hour ago. Go distract yourself with something else!"

But a hoard of them is coming. And I'm stuck at the center of this arena with Nkella still beating on his opponent even after being freed of his chain. I swing my sword again, killing more of them. The ones I had killed earlier, are already standing and reanimating.

Fire surges through the air, crisping the few dead before me. I take a blow to the chest so fast I don't know what hit me. I land on my back. Before I can stand, a devil is jumping down, pinning me in place. My heart pounds in my chest. I stare at the devil's face. I recognize his features, just barely—dark menacing eyes with lightning inside them. Red scales glimmer on his face in a deep red sheen. His pointed ears, curved horns, sharp teeth. A forked tongue slithers onto my face. I press my head back against the sand, wincing as hot breath sticks to my skin.

"Nkella," I rasp. "I know you're in there."

I'm no longer paying attention to the hoard of dead around us. From the corner of my eye, I think I can see the other devil eating some of them. But Nkella is still on me. He stares deeply into me. Confused?

"Nkella? Can you understand me?"

His eyes blink rapidly, but he grimaces. He brings up a clawed hand, metal stubs decorating his knuckles and continuing up his arm. I shudder and release a terrified gasp, expecting him to strike down.

His opponent roars, and Nkella snaps his attention back to him. He's eliminating the dead by the dozens, and soon, he'll be ready to resume their everlasting fight.

This was a terrible plan. I'm going to die here by his hands, and he won't even know it. Then no one will ever be able to save him...or me.

Nkella turns his attention back to me and makes a fist. I slowly bring my legs up to try and shimmy out from under him, but in one swift motion, he wraps his hand around my neck and squeezes. I gasp. I can't breathe. He narrows his eyes, tightening his grip.

This is it. He's going to kill me. I start to kick, tears blurring my vision.

A strangled cry leaves my lips. And he pauses.

His grip on my throat loosens and painful air rushes into my esophagus. I grab at my neck as the world tilts around me but before I can fall, he's caught me. I try to orient myself. Then his wings are flying us high over the stadium as he swings me over his back. I scream, grabbing onto his neck, terrified of what he's about to do.

His opponent flies at us but his chain pulls him back. His roars fill the stadium in a mixture of anger and torment as Nkella flies us higher above the arena. With me on his back.

17

I GRAB ON FOR DEAR LIFE, THANKFUL THAT MY WEBBING keeping me tied to his neck. I'm not sure if he forgot I was on his back, but he flings me off as we make a crash landing. I land with my heels over my head against a stone wall. With my chest tight, I scramble to catch my bearings in the darkness. His body blocks the only red light seeping in from...some sort of conical entrance. I stand upright in what appears to be a cave.

My hands grab rock behind me as I stumble backward, my gaze fixed on his enormous stature. A low gurgling sound like a continuous low thunder comes from somewhere outside of this cavern. It rumbles through the walls and beneath my feet.

The red dirt tells me we're still in Danū, not that the flight was long enough to be anywhere else.

Nkella's eyes emanate crimson as he fixes his gaze on me, holding me in place. His back-lit stature is menacing, his shoulders so much broader than they used to be. He towers over me, and I take a shuddering breath. His chest visibly heaves up and down. This close, I can see the tattoos and Ipani stripes over his large muscles; his horns are fully grown toward the back of his head. His skin is tough with metal decorations alongside his Ipani stripes, like they grew there on purpose.

A red glare swipes across his features, showing draconic scales. The lines on his face are deeper, like the rings of an oak tree.

He hasn't moved, which tells me he's considering what to do with me—and it's nothing good.

Remember he's changed. He's not himself.

His curse has taken over.

He's dangerous.

"Nkella?" I whisper.

Only the sound of our breathing and my beating heart fills the silence. We stay this way for what feels like an endless length of time. Finally, my leg is asleep, so I budge it just a crack to allow blood flow. He zeros in on my movement, and a growl reverberates from his lips. I stop moving.

"Nkella?" I repeat, this time a bit louder. He stares at me, and I let out a slow breath. "Nkella, it's me... Soren."

He stays silent. I'm not sure if he's able to speak. The red sky behind him is darkening into a shade of maroon.

"Don't you remember me?" I start inching to the side. He leaps at me, grabs my throat, and slams me back against the wall. A groan slips from my lips as air escapes my lungs.

His wings spread, blocking any light coming into the cave, so it's just me and him. I gasp in an aching breath. Wetness forms at the corner of my eyes as I squint through the darkness. The only thing lighting his face is glowing red eyes that haven't dimmed since we got to the cave. I grab his wrist and stare into his features, searching for the Nkella I know. His hand curls around my neck, allowing a tiny passageway to breathe, but I'm too scared to talk. My fingers involuntarily claw at his, trying to pry his grip from suffocating me. Small metal plates line the skin of his hands, running from his knuckles as far as I can reach. He stares hard at me as if he's trying to read my thoughts. I wish I could read his. I wish I could reach him like I could with the rikorō.

My eyes stop at the metal collar attached to the chain around his neck. Upon closer inspection, sharp points stick into his skin from inside of it. He squeezes my throat, drawing my attention away from the collar and forcing my face up as he comes up to my cheek. I sink my nails into his hand, trying to pull him away.

"It's me...Nk—it's...Ne...uro." A cough forces its way up my throat, and a tear falls down my cheek. "Ne...yuro...?" I try again, hoping his memories would come flooding back. His eyes narrow. Yes. Maybe he remembers. I try zooming into his mind, reaching for a memory of his that I can grab onto. There's a black void that I can only assume is his time in the Deep, a time he doesn't quite remember because he's not himself.

An image comes into focus. It's me. He's holding me, his head bowed. Sorrowful despair grips my chest, ripping it apart. His voice merges with my moaning cries. This is just before he makes his sacrifice, saving me from eternal torture. He doesn't deserve this.

A roar brings me back to the present. His hand pushes against my chest, his nails piercing my skin, lifting me. I start to kick, and shriek in pain

"C'mon, Nk...ella—-you...can...fight...this." It's getting harder to breathe.

He squeezes tighter. He doesn't like me saying that.

I'm flung into darkness and land hard on my arm. I think I heard a rib crack. Pain sears through my bones as I try to stand. Nkella leaps and lands in front of me, his roar making my ears shatter. I quickly sit up and hold my ribs, hoping they're not broken. I glance at the opening. He follows my gaze, quickly grabs a boulder, and stuffs it into the entrance, snuffing out the last remnants of light.

A small gasp escapes my lips. I can't believe this. We've come full circle. I started off as his gembella—his prisoner—and now I'm going to die as his prisoner.

His glowing red eyes snap back at me. I bring my knees up to my chest, slowly trying to lift myself with the help of the wall behind me. I take a staggering breath, grabbing my right side where my ribs hurt the most.

"You can fight this curse," I tell him. He growls, turns around, and starts pounding on the cavern wall. Rocks fall around us with each quaking blow he lands. I fall back to my knees, now covering my head. A huge rock falls in front of me, and I scream, scrambling to the side to get away. My wound aches, but I ignore it, trying to escape from the cavern rocks plummeting over my head.

He bangs on the walls harder and harder, and I slide to my left as several rocks fall to my right. A rock hits my knee, and I jump farther back.

"Nkella, stop, please... You can beat this. I know you're in there!"

One more punch, then he stops to look at me, opens his mouth, and lets out fire!

I dodge farther to my left. This time, I trip over uneven ground and fall. I fall backward down a hole and descend a slippery rock. A high-pitched yelp escapes me as I land-slide somewhere below the cavern.

Orange light burns behind me and lights up these new cavern walls. Nkella bellows from the other room as I dust myself off and slowly turn around.

Heat scorches behind me, and the gurgling sound from before is louder and more like the crushing of glass. I press against the cavern wall and gape at the cliff two feet in front of me. Beyond the cliff is a river of lava flowing through the tunnels. But that isn't what has my jaw unhinged. There are layers upon layers of open corridors with homes along the walls. At the farthest end left is a castle with sharp, jagged conical spires and large statues of men and women with horns on their heads.

Sweat drips from my brow and my tongue dries out. I snap my mouth shut.

I recall Kae telling me and Harold how large Danū is compared to what's shown on the map. Now I understand why.

It's an underground city.

A rock crumbles below my feet. It skids to the edge of the cliff, bouncing off the rocks all the way down to the lava. Pressing myself against the cavern wall, I shimmy to my right toward the larger area. An angry howl comes from above me, and I gulp.

Nkella comes plummeting through the same hole I came through. Did he cause himself to fall by beating up more of the wall, or did he jump through to find me? Who knows.

He lands on both feet with his fist against the gravel. He stares at me, his eyes burning bright. I back up just a little, keeping a close eye on that cliff.

A boulder crashes down on us. I drop to my knees, holding my hands up to cover my head, and shut my eyes. When I open them again, Nkella is tugging on his chain.

The boulder landed right on his chain, holding his neck in place. Despite his tremendous strength, something about that chain makes him powerless. He starts to punch the boulder, but it barely budges. I'm guess anything made from ouma fire is going to be null against him. I walk over.

"Maybe if you'd stop punching things and crash landing, you wouldn't find yourself in these situations." I cross my arms. He snarls at me, animalistically. I cringe and take a deep breath. "I don't care how much of an animal you've become. I know you can fight this." He lets out a huff and continues to punch the rock.

Webbing shoots from my fingertips as I aim it at his fists, wrapping around them as he tries to jump away. The chain keeps him held in place, but I don't want to take the chance at him getting freed quite yet.

His fists are tied together in a thick film of web...for now. I'll probably have to keep doing it. He stares down at his hands in disgust, looks back at me, and roars, showcasing sharp snarling teeth.

"Who's the gembella now, huh?"

I can't help myself.

He huffs.

Now, how to take that collar off. It's not like there'd be a key somewhere. Behind me, the sound of the flowing lava fills the space.

I have an idea.

I take out the Ace of Swords Card, reach in and pull out the sword. He stares at the glistening metal, fixating on the magical item. Ouma fire can't hurt him... "I can take off that collar."

He quirks a large brow. And now mine rises as well. I'm not sure if he can understand me, or if he's only reacting to my tone.

"But not yet." I stick the sword back in its card and stick it in my pocket. He roars at me, and I brace myself for the tremor. "First, I want you to listen to me. Listen to my voice."

He pants in place. Something like curiosity flashes across his features. Or it could be confusion.

"Can you understand me?"

He stays quiet.

Here's hoping something translates.

I take a step closer, and his gaze flicks down to my feet.

"Do you remember who I am?" I touch my chest and take out the necklace of Danū. He glances at it but moves his gaze back to mine. "Do you remember the crew?

Tessa? Kae? Ntaoru? AJ?"

He stays quiet, flicking his tail irritably as he stares at me.

"Please." My voice lowers. "Remember AJ."

His gaze fixates on the same spot by my feet.

"I came a long way to find you. Your crew...your family sacrificed a lot for me to find you, Nkella. I'm not leaving here without you. I *will* bring you back."

He roars and slams his web covered fists on the ground.

I step back, this time almost losing my footing. I gasp a sharp breath and stare at the lava.

Okay, for some reason, any time I mention the curse or him fighting it sets him off. I wipe the sweat from my face and neck and sit on my butt watching him as he punches the ground.

Finally, he calms down and stares back at me.

"I want to release you. I do." Keeping him chained up with that horrible collar on is cruel. But if I let him go, I'm not going to get anywhere with him. I have to reach his memories. I have to reach into his mind and make him remember. It's the only way to pull him out of this. The last time I did that, he immediately pulled away. I'd offer to make a deal, but I'm not sure how much he understands me.

My eyes wander around the abandoned city. A fiery glare catches my eye on the other side of him. I stand, and he alerts himself, watching my movements. I stick my hands up, then slowly make my way around. He doesn't reach out for me. He just watches.

Beautiful pictures come into view as I reach the wall.

Ipani scriptures dance in the lava light, alongside drawings of a family of devils holding a baby.

That makes no sense. How could devils function as a family?

The next drawing shows a toddler with Ipani stripes. He doesn't have a tail or horns. The next pictures are of the same child, a little older. Stubs have grown on his head.

Why would the empress curse a toddler with the Devil curse? What could he have done that was so bad? And how would he have devil parents? None of these drawings make sense.

Unless... A chill skitters up my spine, and I step closer to the drawings. They're...carvings. I move my fingers over them. The stone is long worn, down, ancient, maybe even more ancient than the Fates' presence in Ipa...

A cold draft comes from out of nowhere as the next photo is of a full-blown devil, akin to Nkella. The next one is of the same grown boy, but without the horns. He wears a crown on his head.

I rub my arms and scan the empty city around me.

Wait.

No.

I know for that the Empress has never been down here. That's what she wanted from him... Tetalla told me the Empress wanted Nkella to give her access to the fires of Danū.

Which means...

I gape at Nkella.

"It was never a curse?"

He's hitting his collar with his webbed fist when he stops to stare at me. Dizziness washes over me, and I lean against the pictographs. I don't understand how this could be possible.

It can't be. Adara, the youngest sister and the Past Fate who'd traveled through time with Asteria, had brought back the tarot from their future and shared it with the Empress. The Aō adapted their new magic, and that's why there are tarot marks...and the Devil curse.

I stare back at the pictographs. Unless these drawings really are older and the cards only granted him the Devil Card, because...because that's what he's always been. I trace the growing boy with the stumps on his head and glance back at Nkella.

"It's always been inside you, hasn't it?" I start walking toward him. His brows furrow, and he grimaces, getting ready to strike at me. Threatened.

"This whole time I wanted you to come back, to overcome your curse, to suppress it. You've been suppressing it when all it wanted was to thrive. Didn't it? Haven't you?" I lower my voice and I realize I'm not more than a foot away from him. Something in his features has shifted. He's softer now. Maybe he does understand me.

"I'm not sure I fully understand this, Nkella, or if I'm right about this. But I'm hoping we can figure it out together. Will you let me?" I crouch down to his level.

He sits with his fists against the sand, but he bows his head. I place my palm over his brow and close my eyes, zooming us both into his memories.

He's a baby being held by the Empress after she stole him from his family. After she murdered his parents. She teaches him to behave, scolding him when he touches her things. He's five years old. He starts to cry. She lifts him up and sits him beside her on her throne, holding him close. She dries his eyes. He leans into her. He loves her.

Fast forward. He's taken by a few Ipani people, my mom among them. He was asleep and screams when he sees them. The guards surround them, and a fight ensues. He speeds off to find the Empress, but my mom grabs him and takes off on a drakon. Moving forward, he's defiant. He hates his new captors. He wants his mom—he thinks the Empress is his mother.

A new scene. Now the Empress is here. He runs to her, but she doesn't take him back. In fact, she physically pushes him away.

"He's of no use to me now. I've found a better way to harness power through your bindings." A soldier grabs him. Nkella starts to scream in pain. He reaches for her, but the Empress doesn't budge. When the binding has stopped, he's on the floor. Confusion spreads over his little face. He hadn't come into his power yet. He doesn't know what happened or why it hurt so badly. But the look of betrayal in his face tears my heart apart.

"He's far more work than I'm cut out for." She looks down at him and waves her hand away. "Shoo. Go now and be with your degenerates."

Fast forward to the next scene.

The Empress tortures him, demanding ouma fire. A way into the caverns. A way to harness his birthright in order to seek revenge on Tetalla. I feel his pain. His fury. But I also feel hers. It's like mine. Hungry for revenge. Tetalla killed her sister. She killed my mom.

The next vision surfaces. We move in a wave through his life. And for some reason, mine. I feel Nkella with me watching my father give me up for adoption. Other scenes make me overcome by emotions.

We're on the Gambit.

He's lost a lot. Suffered a lot. So has the crew. So has all of Ipa. He struggles to maintain his composure and fight the devil inside, convinced it's the curse of the cards. But it never was a curse. The cards only show you who you are, what you're going through. Some have powers, but they don't curse you.

His next memory is of us on the Gambit. *His lips are on mine as I caress his body. The thrashing of the waves moves us together, and I want to hold on to this memory, but something pulls us apart.*

I open my eyes. Nkella's eyes are wide. They're no longer red, but black...his pupils dilated, his wings spread. His chest rises and falls with every heavy breath he takes, and he staggers backward. A hoarse cry escapes him. He grabs his horns, and arches back to look toward the top of the cave. Quickly, I take out the sword from its card. I dip the top of the blade in the nearest lava pit and walk toward him. He backs away from me, but I hold out my hand until he lets me get near him. His body is quivering as he drops to the ground. I have to move fast.

I'm gentle as I bring the tip of the blade to touch the collar; it releases instantly. Grabbing it quickly, I take it off him. Some blood seeps out of where it was cutting into him. I toss it aside, and he drops into my arms, his weight making me fall back. I don't move.

I caress his head as he lowers his face into my lap. His body starts to shift to normal size. His tail disappears into his pants, and the horns of his head fit into his skull. A painful moan leaves his lips, but he doesn't get up.

"It's okay. You can relax now. I've got you."

He groans and his eyes finally blink open. Tears fall down my cheeks as I stroke his hair.

"Hi." I say, a smile tugging at my lips.

He squints, staring up at me. For a few moments we stare at each other in silence. Confusion swarms his features, his beautiful dark and fierce eyes. His smooth skin on razor sharp cheekbones. He brings his hand up to my lips, and I hold it in place, planting a soft kiss on his fingers. "You... You brought me back," he whispers.

My heart clogs my throat, and I almost forget to speak. Tears stream off my chin, my vision is blurred, and I hold him tight. "I thought you were gone. You died."

At first, he doesn't move, but then his hand reaches to the back of my head and grasps my hair. He shudders, taking in a deep breath, but doesn't say anything.

I pull back. "What do you remember?"

"Everything."

My throat clogs again. "I'm so sorry, Nkella. I should have known to look for you sooner. All your torture...everything you went through here...it's all my fault."

"Don't cry, neyuro." Tears stream faster down my face. He does remember. "It's not your fault."

I nod defiantly. "It is. I shouldn't have used the Death Card."

"You wouldn't have known, daí? If I had a chance to save my sister like you thought to bring back your mother, I would have done." His eyes narrow, and he looks away, then he chuckles. "I did."

A nervous laugh escapes me. "Yes, you did. And she's okay. Ntaoru is okay."

His smile of relief washes over me, and I feel suddenly lighter. "I'm glad you're back."

"You didn't give up on me, neyuro."

"I could never."

He starts to get up, and I reluctantly let him go, despite my desire to keep holding him longer. The webs loosen from his normal-sized wrists as he walks, and he shakes them off.

"I remember..." His eyes drift off to the distance. "My whole life. My crew...I—This isn't a curse?" He looks down at his hands, the metal stumps now gone. His horns are also completely gone. He walks over to the pictographs on the wall, and I follow. He pauses at a scripture painted in a faded burgundy and passes his fingers over it. "*Daekente.*"

"What does that mean?"

"It means...the horned ones." He stares back at the markings. "It means...me."

"It's true then," I whisper. "This is who you are."

He stares at them for a while. "I remember you...us... He turns to me and suddenly his lips are on mine.

My breath catches. My hands press against his chest, at first from surprise, then I let myself lean into his kiss and wrap my arms around his neck. He comes in closer. My breathing quickens. I've missed this so much. I'd dream of him every night, wishing he was with me, waking up to remember he was gone. What I had done to make him do what he did.

His lips are hot. Powerful heat cocoons me in his warmth. But it isn't fierce. He slows, and I embrace every moment just as he does. He takes my bottom lip and softly nibbles, before pulling away.

My eyes flutter, and he smiles into me. His eyes are normal, calmer than I've ever seen them, but the smile he gives me is one I wasn't expecting. I've never seen him smile like that at anyone. He brushes my cheek, and we stand there for a minute longer.

There's so much I want to tell him. The words lodge in my throat, and every time I want to say them, I feel...strange. It feels right, but I've just never uttered them to anyone before, and even though he died for me, I still can't bring myself to say it. I should be able to...

"Nkella..."

He comes in and takes my lips again in one sensual kiss, and I almost forget what I was about to say. When he lets go, he stares at the lava of ouma fire and takes a few steps toward it.

"Soren...how did you get here?"

"Inside this cavern?"

"To the Deep." He steps toward me, his brows furrowed. "How, daí?"

I scratch at my temple. "It's a long story...in fact, we need to go."

"Neyuro...how did you get here?"

"I'm not dead." His body relaxes. "But...I did make a deal."

"Daí?"

"It doesn't matter now. What matters is I found you. And I can bring you back."

"What deal did you make, Soren?" His voice is serious.

I chew on my cheek. He's not going to let this go right now. "When I found out you were alive in the Deep, I made a deal with the Empress"

—his eyes widen—"to give me and the crew safe passage to Oleanu in order to use the Ace of Cups. I had to drink from the chalice in the card in order to cross over."

"In exchange for?"

"We go straight to her when we return."

He tilts his head, regarding my words.

"The only way I was able to convince her to do this for me…is because you—with your devil curse—are the only one able to go up against Tetalla. He has the curse as well…but now…"

"We discover it was never a curse." He looks down at his hands and studies his palms. His shoulders drop. "Soren, I don't know how to control this, daí?"

"But you will. You just did, and you can do it again."

He shakes his head. "I didn't want you to come down here for me. If you die here…" He squeezes his eyes. "I would have done this for nothing."

"I knew it was a risk when I did it."

"You need to go back. Without me."

My eyes widen. What did he just say?

He turns away and points to the castle. "This belonged to my parents." He's silent for a few moments before he turns back to me. "I need to release my people. They looked to me in Danū, and I turned my back on them. I cannot do the same again. I can't leave them to suffer."

I take a step toward him. "Then we'll do it together."

"Koj. This is my task. Mine, Soren. Not yours, it is too dangerous, daí? I don't even know if it's possible."

"It is—"

"And I must do it alone." His voice is raised just above a whisper, but he's determined.

My hands shake, and I ball them in an attempt to control myself. I raise my chin and take a deep breath. "You have no idea what I've been through to get here. I can handle a little more danger. Did you forget I saved your scaly ass from that even larger devil?" I cross my arms, struggling to keep my voice steady. "Or did those horns of yours grow through your brain? Because you're clearly not using it!"

"Kh." He smirks. "It is not that. You already know I cannot live with myself if you die."

A smile tugs at my lips, even in the grim state of things. I fight to keep my frown.

"Why did you come for me?" he asks.

"I just told you why."

"Was there another reason?" His eyes search mine.

"I—" My mouth dries. Just say it. Why can't I say it?

He licks his lips. "You have to let me go. The Empress's fight is her own."

"No—everyone's lives are at stake with Tetalla there."

"They're in trouble with her. With him. Ipa is always in trouble, daí? But I can help the ones who need me here."

My throat dries. I can't believe I'm hearing this. The world doesn't make sense if I came all this way, and he doesn't want to come back with me. Maybe he doesn't love me like I'd hoped.

I shake my head. "No."

He sighs and takes both my hands in his. "Yes."

It's getting hard to speak with my chest tightening. "But I don't want to leave without you. You're alive. You shouldn't be here."

He brings me in and kisses me on the forehead. "No, you should not be here. I made a deal with the sword. We cannot break it."

"Yes, we can! You served your time—"

"You will go back without me. And you will stay with the crew."

I fall into his arms and let him hold me tight. My tears wet his shoulders.

"Keep them safe for me, daí?" He places another gentle kiss on my head, and the sound of his voice tells me he's made up his mind. I'm going back on my own.

18

Rocks start to trickle down around us. Nkella pulls me into him as the walls and ground give off a violent shake. The heat emanating from the lava intensifies as it starts to rise.

I cling to him. "What's happening?"

Nkella pulls my arm. "We have to go."

"Is the volcano erupting?!"

The ground trembles again, and we make a run for it. He lifts me, helping me back up the slate I slid down. Rocks crumble from above as we climb up. I really wish I was wearing a helmet.

When we reach the boulder he'd jammed in front of the entrance to keep me trapped, he isn't strong enough to budge it. He leans his whole body into it and starts to push. I feel my way around the darkness to help when glowing red veins with draconic scales protrude from his arm. I suck in a gasp, readying to jump out of dodge, when the boulder budges. Half his body becomes devil-like as he pushes the boulder so hard, it fits through the opening.

Nkella breathes heavily. His eyes glow, and he begins to enlarge.

Oh no.

No no no. Not now. "Nkella! Nkella, come back! Please!"

I place my hand on his arm, and he roars at my face. I hold my ground and search for the very last conversation we had. As the cavern crumbles around us, his body shifts back to normal size. I take a deep breath, letting it out slowly.

Regret and fear cross his features. "Soren..."

"It's okay. Let's get out of here."

The tremors stops once we've walked far away from the cavern. We remain in silence for a few minutes, processing everything that just happened. Nkella's decision. He doesn't want to come back with me. It still feels surreal. I don't want to accept it. I can't accept it. He looks behind us, and I follow his gaze back at the cave. The dark maroon skies shield us from seeing the dead bodies that float on the surface. It feels like I'm in some sort of a dark whimsical land. I guess I am. I wonder if AJ is up there somewhere. Before I go, I'll find him.

I break the silence. "Who builds a castle inside a volcano anyway?"

"We don't feel the ouma fire like you do, Soren. That's why you must leave before you get hurt."

"I've dealt with ouma fire before."

"Kh."

"I have. After you—" I clear my throat. "The crew and I took down some animal fighting rings...and I got unpleasantly introduced to ouma fire."

A smile tugs at his lips, and he stops walking to look at me. "That brings me much pride. More than you know."

My cheeks heat. I break eye contact and search our surroundings.

"How will you get back?" he asks.

"Well, since I'm going back on my own...I need to find the *Gambit*, but—"

"The *Gambit* is here?"

"Of course. It's the only ship I could put the Ace of Cups waters in—"

Nkella's brows are furrowed, and his hand is on the back of his head. "Who steered my ship?"

"I did."

His eyes widen. "You? By yourself?"

"Yep."

He guffaws.

"What's so funny? How else would I get here? The cup could only take me."

He quiets, the surprise on his face replaced by something more serious moments later. He stares at me intensely.

"What is it? Why are you looking at me like that?"

He steps into me and brushes my face with the back of his hand. "My bayoa..."

I blink, recalling the first time he called me his bayoa—the Nautilus lights that guide him—and I can feel my cheeks heat.

"Just imagining you steering my ship..." A guttural sound comes from inside him and my breath hitches. He's about to lean down for a kiss when a high-pitched wail shatters our ears. A flash of red crosses his eyes as he steps away from me. I gape, then we both stare up to the skies searching for the source of those cries.

"That doesn't sound like the tortured," I say.

"Koj."

We spin around until we see it. A hooded figure with a swirl of darkness inside. It spins like a vortex, and it's pitch black, visible in the maroon sky but endless. It has a mer-tail as it swims through the air and lets out another wail.

"What the hell is that?"

Another joins it. Then a third. They pause when they see us and swoop down.

He yanks my arm. "Run."

I gasp and run as fast as my legs can carry me. The three hooded merfolk swoop down. One is right on my tail. It screeches behind me. I dodge to the side, and it follows me. Another flies in front of me, and I skid to the right. Nkella calls my name, and I reach for him. None are chasing him, though. They only seem interested in me.

Nkella grabs me from behind, swings me with an impossible strength, and carries me on his back. He runs faster, sprinting. I hope he doesn't shift into devil form right now.

Actually, that might not be a bad idea. If he can control it...

A harrowing wail fills my ears, and it's as if my soul is being pulled in different directions. I gape in horror at the pain within my bones.

Another screech makes me jolt, falling down to my knees.

"Soren!"

"Nkella...turn into the devil," I rasp.

He doesn't question me. My body is lifted as his form changes and grows ten times taller than his normal stature. I wrap my arms around him as tight as I can, and he strides longer and faster than before. The flying merfolk keep up, but this gives me enough time. Holding onto his neck with one hand, I reach into my bandoleer and pull out the World Card. I envision the *Gambit* and throw the card out in front of us.

"Don't freak out," I yell, hoping he understands me.

We enter the portal. The merfolk scream just before it closes. We walk onto the main deck, and I put the card away.

He sets me down, and slowly, his body shifts.

My chest pulsates wildly. "You controlled it," I say. "And by the way, did you notice my mad new skills?" I know, my timing is poor, but I had to rub it in somehow. He's not smiling.

"What the hell were those things?"

"Reapers."

"Reapers? Why were they chasing me?"

"Because you're alive."

"But so are you!"

"Yes, but they must know of my deal. You don't belong here, Soren. You must go now. Before they come back. Before you die here."

I grab my head. I can sense tortured souls coming in closer. Ugh. Just because I used the card. "They smell magic whenever it's used."

"Another reason—"

"I know." I hold my temples and then walk to my—the captain's room. After a few seconds, he follows me inside.

"What are you doing?"

"Giving you your hat."

"Daí?"

"I brought it back for you. Thought you might as well have it." I grab his captain's hat from the bedroom closet and hand it to him." He takes it and frowns. His eyes skim around the room, and I light a candle in the corner. My eyes fall on his muscular chest, his tattoos on full display. "You can put on a shirt, too, if you want." I clear my throat.

"Not that you have to." Not that I won't be able to focus on anything else if he doesn't...

Nkella quirks a brow and walks to his drawers, slowly opening each one and inspecting everything I left in there. It's just like he left it.

We're right outside the island's entrance. I can always get him back to the stadium if that's where he wants to go. I can't believe I'm about to help him get away from me, but I can't force him to come.

I mean...maybe I can. If I hit him hard enough on the head and drip the Cups' water down his throat...

He's quiet as he looks around. "You've been sleeping here?"

"Your sister convinced me it was the most convenient space for the captain. I guess because the wheel is right there, and the windows..."

"Captain?" He tweaks an eyebrow.

I give him a slanted smile. "It was the dumbest idea ever. But your sister voted me captain."

A soundless chuckle escapes him.

"I know it was crazy. And stupid. Bancha." I smirk.

"Koj. Ntaoru knew what she was doing. You made it here, daí? With your Helāni magic."

We remain in silence for a few beats more, listening to the sounds of tortured souls nearby. A few of them pass the ship, but when they don't sense any magic being used, they leave.

"You know...I promised so many people that I'd bring you back. He frowns, but I keep going. "Not only to defeat Tetalla, but...they love you. So much."

"I do too," he says quietly.

"The people who died for me to come—" My voice thickens.

"Died?"

My voice hitches.

"Who else died?" His voice darkens. I sniffle and look away. "Soren, who else is dead?"

I shudder, and his face pales. "One of our crew?"

I try to respond yet only silence escapes my breath.

"Who?" he bellows. I shake. He speeds toward me and takes my hand. When I look at him, a red glare sweeps his eyes, but his features display sadness. Concern. I step back. "Tell me who died, Soren."

"AJ," I whisper. I didn't want to hear myself saying it out loud.

His mouth gapes, and he drops my hand. He steps back and drops to the floor beside the bed, his face in his hands. Afraid that he might revert back to a devil, I hold my ground. But after a few seconds, I walk toward him.

"I'm so sorry...Nkella..."

He grabs my wrist and I gasp. He lets go but doesn't look up. I don't know what that means. Or what to do.

"How did it happen?" he says into his hands.

"It was Tetalla. A sob escapes from my throat. "He killed him."

Nkella's shoulders shake, and he lets out a hoarse cry. I wrap my arms around him, and he leans into me. Hearing him crying for one of our crew tears my heart to pieces. I want to take away his pain so badly, and I know I never can. I'll never be able to take away a sorrow like this. Ever. AJ is gone forever. Even after Nkella made his sacrifice, AJ still died.

"I'm sorry," I whisper into him.

He lowers his hands and lifts my chin, looking into my eyes. "It wasn't your fault, Soren."

"It was."

"Koj. Evil people govern this world. No matter my decisions or yours. You are not responsible when they make choices to harm the ones we love. You made sacrifices to find me. I made sacrifices to save you. AJ made a sacrifice for us both."

Tears fall down my cheeks, and he wipes them away. I understand what he's saying, but he doesn't know Tetalla was after me. It was still my fault.

"He's here?" He clears his throat.

"Yeah. He's here in the Deep somewhere. But he's not alive like you are. Even if we find him, he can never go back."

Nkella nods. "I know this."

"AJ wanted you to go back and defeat Tetalla. Everyone is waiting for our return. If you don't come back, AJ died in vain."

Nkella rubs his temples, then lifts his sad eyes to stare at the corner of the room. A few silent beats pass between us.

I've broken him.

"Nkella?"

He still doesn't look at me.

"Nkella...I don't want to beg but...I can't go back without you. I—" My throat clogs again. "The crew is waiting for you."

He stares at me, but his expression looks tired.

"What I'm trying to say is..." My fingers twist the bottom of my shirt. "I—I need you."

A flicker of surprise crosses his face as he searches mine. I fight to keep my breathing steady as I study his beautifully brutal face in the candlelight that dances over his features. He doesn't speak. We're both too sad and emotionally spent to say anything.

He bites the corner of his lip, an action I've never seen him do before. "You...need me?" He chuckles. I crinkle my forehead. "Of all the people I've met in my entire life, Soren, you're the only one who can calm the devil inside me. You and no other can bring me back from a place of no return. You are the light that guides me back. My bayoa. And now you have come to the Deep and have brought me back from having lost myself after thinking that was impossible. You are the light of my fire. My *roé yani*, I am the one in need of you."

A shuddering breath lets loose from my lips. I can't help it. I reach for his face, and he catches my hand, taking my fingers gently in his mouth and planting a soft kiss. On my knees, I crawl closer to him, and he lifts me up as I straddle his waist. I pass my thumb over his lips and his eyes momentarily close as he leans into my touch.

Tell him now. Just tell him.

I feel his hardness under my core and my breathing picks up. My hands wander up his chest. I've missed this so much. The feel of him.

He leans in to kiss me, and I close my eyes, but he grabs my hand and pulls away.

He releases a heavy sigh. "If we are to go, we must leave now. The longer you stay here, the closer to your death."

I part my lips; my heart flutters as I stare straight into his eyes. "Are you saying you're coming back with me?"

"Yes. I won't let AJ die in vain. Soon enough, I will meet my true death. Then I will return to meet my family."

I swallow. I don't like how that sounds. "You're not going up there to die. Ipani live for a long, long time, Nkella. And devils live for even longer. You're going back up there for good."

His eyes meet mine. "Neyuro." He chuckles softly. "You're an optimist. If I am to fight the King of the Deep, Death himself. Do you think I will survive?"

I sit up. "Yes. Absolutely. Of course, I believe that."

He shakes his head. "Such delusions, Neyuro."

"Delusions? I traveled to another dimension for you. Two, in fact, being that I'm from a different world than you."

He stares at me, and I brush his cheek with my thumb, studying his face as I talk.

"You can beat him," I say. "And...let's go release your people from their torment." Even though I have no idea how we're going to do that.

He blinks at me. "Kh. Did you not hear what I said? The longer you—"

"I don't need you to protect me, Nkella. I'm not the weak girl you met a year ago who couldn't hold a sword."

He scoffs, but before I can protest, he leans close to my ear, his breath tickling my skin, and whispers. "I don't protect you because I think you're weak. I protect you because you're important to me, Neyuro." Surprise flashes in his eyes, and he looks away.

I swallow and lick my lips. "I know. I'm part of your crew." I smile. "Besides, I have an advantage. I have magic."

His eyes lower. "Magic that attracts reapers and the dead. This sounds like a disadvantage."

"So we keep a low profile and use it only when we have to."

Nkella's eyes fall back to the side. "I know you don't need me to protect you, daí? But don't ignore what I said. I've seen you fight and use your magic. You take too many risks."

"So did you."

"I don't want you to take the same risks for me, neyuro."

"A little too late for that." I smile, placing my hands on his stomach, still keenly aware of me straddling him.

His hands caress my back, pushing me into him. I close my eyes, but he pulls away again.

"Nkella?"

His eyes glow as he sits alert, one ear twitching toward the window. Wrapping his arms around me, he gently pulls me off him and stands up. I follow him to the back of the room. The shadow of a reaper floats over the water. He holds a finger to his lips, and we wait for it to leave.

When it leaves, Nkella turns back to me, his fingers trailing down my arm. "We need to go."

"Right. Let's help your people. I don't know how, but we should at least try. I'm not bringing you back to the land of living to have you try to get back here so soon."

Something the king of Cups told me rings in my ear...something about the serpent. What was it?

"You really want to help me do this?" he asks, all seriousness in his voice.

"I wouldn't think of doing anything else."

His features soften and he gives me a longing look. "Neyuro..."

"And I think I have an idea."

"Daſ?" A sigh leaves his lips. "'Splain."

"I had to promise the king of Oleanu that I would steer clear of the serpent. It guards the surface and keeps the tortured spirits from escaping, and he said that if it catches me alive, it would make sure I never escape the Deep."

He scoffs. "That is at least one sensible promise you have made, neyuro."

I shove him playfully. "Don't you get it? The serpent guards the tortured..."

Surprise flashes in his eyes. "Kill the serpent, release my people."

"With the Ace of Swords."

A whisper of a smile dances on his face, but he quickly suppresses it. "Kh. Is there anything else I should know? Any more deals you've made?"

I slant a smile. "Oh, so many." Any hint of amusement has left his face, so I open a drawer. "What do you say to getting dressed, and then we go help your people and kick some serpent ass?"

19

Inside the walls of Danū, the faint sound of steel hitting steel reminds me of what I heard when I arrived with Nangraku. I watch as Nkella searches the area. His eyes are wide, more in awe than anything.

"It's been a long time since I've been inside the walls of Danū. It wasn't like this."

"I know. The Danū in the Deep stayed the same since before the siege."

"How do you know this?"

I was about to respond, but then thought the better of it. It's probably best not to mention me running into Nangraku while we're still here. "The king of Cups prepared me for where I was going."

He curls his lip. He probably doesn't think much of the Oleanu royals...like everyone else.

He's endured a lot, and I don't want to overwhelm him with upsetting information. He needs to know he's going to be fighting Tetalla, which is why the Empress aided me, but he doesn't need to know Tetalla has been after me. And spying on me. What would be the point? It'll piss him off, and we can't do anything about it now. Any unnecessary information can be discussed later when we're back.

The jagged points of the volcanic terrain decorate the view with swirls of red and black sand in the distance. Everything here is still. There isn't even any wind and it's a lot cooler than I'd expect an oasis to be. But I suspect it's because this isn't the real Danū. Only an echo of it here in the Deep.

"How do you think we'll find the serpent?" The last time I saw it was when it flew up to the surface. There's a lot of Deep to cover."

"We will have to bait it," he says.

"How?"

"This I don't know. It favors the living. Leaves the dead alone."

"So that leaves us as the bait. Why am I not surprised?"

"Because you're always making big promises."

I gape at the back of his head. "To save you!"

"Hn."

"How does that make sense? Just because I've made a lot of promises to people, doesn't mean I have to kill a serpent each time!"

He turns his head, quirking a brow. "Koj? What about promising the dead to come back to life?"

An anvil hits my gut. Okay, that one stings. And I have done that once or twice. Maybe three times, but the third one I promised is actually alive and walking with me. I promised Soanalo's family that I'd bring her back, but I didn't understand how the Aō worked back then. Her soul was half taken, and plants had grown over her, which was different than what I'd seen with the other spirits.

We walk in silence away from the fortress walls and toward the populated area of the island. Dark maroon blankets the night, spirits moan, and steel clangs faintly.

"I shouldn't have made promises to Soanalo's family, or to Kae about bringing back his wife. I just wanted to...to fix things. I never meant to make things harder for everyone...or you." I walk past him and head toward the noise, a darker shade of red outlining the silhouette of a volcanic mountain region.

Nkella grabs my arm and pulls me back; I arch my neck to stare at him.

"Neyuro, you were only trying to help them. I understand this now." I stare at him through the red darkness. His apology takes me by surprise. I study his features. I'm used to his witty comebacks and low blows, but I'd never expected him to apologize for one of those throws at me. I nod and give him a weak smile.

"You understand why I don't like making big promises, don't you?"

I blink at him. I think he's trying to figure out if I accept his apology. "I do."

Relief washes over his face. "When I said making promises to bring people back to life, Neyuro...I was talking about me."

"But you're not dead." Guilt resurfaces as he lifts his chin. He still thinks he's supposed to be here to help his people. This is a way for him to redeem himself after leaving his people to save his sister.

"You cannot always rule the fate of others. One day you will learn this." He walks past me, and I stand, staring at the back of his head as he puts distance between us.

"Did you forget?" I call after him.

"Daí?"

"I am the Past Fate. I can do what I want."

"Kh." He shakes his head. I catch up in time to see a smirk form on his lips.

Commotion comes from the nearby village Nangraku and I had avoided. Nkella and I exchange a curious glance and head over.

"It's strange to think of dead people living in villages here."

"It is natural to want to unite." His hand brushes mine as he urges me to quickly follow.

People scamper out of the village—the ones who aren't decapitated or trailing organs. Some have deep cuts on their wrists or purple along their necks. I suppose depending on the way people died and if they managed to retrieve their body parts—thinking about Nangraku—they'd have to learn how to survive here.

"Where is everybody going?" I glance behind me to find them running toward the walls. "Do you think the *Gambit* will be safe?"

"With Helāni magic? If they try to steal it, they will attract reapers."

"Good point." They wouldn't make it far.

"Release. Release. Release," is being repeated over and over between the sounds of metal hitting metal. Nkella arches a brow in that direction.

A roar of blazing fire courses through the sky, and screams fill the air. High over our heads, a devil soars with a chain dangling from his ankle. I gape. It's Nkella's opponent from the arena! The clang of steel stops, and the ground trembles beneath our feet. I grab Nkella's arm, and he holds me tight.

The devil flies toward the mountains as two minotaurs stomp from the arena, crushing anything in their way.

"How did he get loose?" I cry out over the sounds of screams and crashing.

"I don't know. But soon this village will be swarming with guards. We need to take cover."

The sound of clashing steel continues in the background, even louder than the people now running in terror.

The ground trembles. One stomp. Then another.

I grab my empty bandoleer out of habit alone, and I slide my hand to my Ace of Swords Card. Two minotaurs stomp through the village carrying clubs. They swing at anything that gets in their way, blundering what's left of broken buildings. Their long strides bring them closer; someone doesn't get away fast enough and is caught at the end of a club, their head being ripped right off their neck. The minotaur stomps on the body, unaware. Shrapnel flies at me, and I turn toward Nkella who wraps his arm around me, shielding me from debris. His wings spread behind him, sending out a sharp gust of wind. His eyes have turned blood red and are glowing. I gape at him as he shifts forms and his teeth grow longer, sharper. So do the nails that grip my shoulder and pull me behind him.

"Nkella?"

I stand behind his wings, ready to reach his memories if he starts to drift too far. Although, he pulled me behind him. I'm not sure if he's still conscious, or if it was an unconscious movement. Or if he just wanted me out of the way to get to the guards.

The minotaur to the left roars as he spots Nkella. He pulls out a chain from his back and starts to swing it. I take out my sword. We'd never make it if we ran. Even if he flew with me on his back, their reach would knock us to the ground. The minotaur swings his chain hard at

Nkella, but Nkella catches it, yanking it toward him. I jump back, my heart lodged in my throat.

Nkella rips the chain from the minotaur's grip and strikes back so hard, I duck for fear that it might hit me. The chain wraps around the minotaur's neck as he grabs for it but gets yanked down.

Screams burst around me as the minotaur plummets to the ground, causing dust and debris to explode into the air. The minotaur groans painfully.

Nkella tightens his grip of the chain, choking the minotaur. The other minotaur readies his club to strike at us. His giant stature towers over us. This wasn't our best plan. He can take us both out in one hit. I pull my sword from its card, the purple sheen coursing through the blade. This attracts the minotaur, and he trains his eyes on me. Nkella jerks the chain on the other one more time, finishing him off with a loud crack of the minotaur's neck bones, before he turns to face the other.

The last minotaur cocks his head back and sends out an alarming bellow as if blowing through a horn. The ground quakes as more minotaurs emerge from the arena, their towering statures and oversized horns aimed toward us as they run, giving us no time to escape.

A minotaur then takes his chain and swings it over Nkella. Nkella tries to catch it, but the blow is so hard, it wraps around his neck.

A scream leaves my lips, and I run to grab the chain, but Nkella pushes me back so hard, I fall to the ground. I quickly stand and pick up my sword, ready to aim it at the chain. The minotaur has him gripped tightly, and by the looks of it, he intends on holding him still so the others can take turns beating him. They may have lost one devil, but they caught another.

My devil.

Not on my watch, dick heads. I thrust forward and swing at the minotaur, slicing his leg. Black goo spurts out, and I cover his face in webbing. Then I turn and slice the chain open while he's distracted.

Another minotaur reaches us fast, his chain double wrapping around Nkella, but he gets an arm free and catches it.

I aim better this time and send a burst of webbing over the minotaur Nkella's fighting. Nkella rips the chain off, readying himself for a bigger fight against more of them. He shoots me a glance, and I swear I see a smirk in his appreciative eyes. I smirk back. We make a good team.

Then his eyes widen.

A haunting wail bursts my eardrums as sharp claws dig into my shoulders. I swing my sword back at the reaper, but she yanks it out of my hand and flies away with me in her clutches.

20

My feet kick furiously as I fight the reaper lifting me off the ground; my nails dig into her grimy arms as I reach behind me. I grimace as her hot breath hits my face every time she screeches. I'm not worried about having dropped the sword; I know it'll reappear back inside its card.

Nkella roars below me, and I know minotaurs have surrounded him. I have to get back to him. I can't let myself be taken away from here.

An arrow bolts past me, and a scream lodges in the back of my throat. My hair is in my face, I can't see who's attacking us or if that was meant for the reaper...or for me.

I suddenly remember I still have my dagger. I unlatch it from my belt and stab her hard, managing to hit her bare green stomach. As I pull my dagger back, I realize a little too late the mistake I've made.

We're too high off the ground, and the minotaurs are directly below us.

But with a sudden wail, she lets me fall.

I fall fast and am caught in a tight grip. Spinning around, I see Nkella's tattoos on his enlarged devil chest. I let out a sigh of relief as he sets me down, then ushers me to get on his back. I do as he says, cautious of his awareness while in his devil form.

All around, villagers are shooting arrows at the minotaurs. They won't do much damage, but it distracts them. Now on Nkella's back, I see an arrow stuck to his shoulder blade.

As he lifts us off the ground and flies toward the mountain range, I glance at the villagers left to fight off these giant guards. One is shooting from beside the blacksmith's building, but the bullets don't take them down. One of the minotaurs catches sight of us, and starts running, causing the ground to shake with each heavy stomp he takes.

"We're being followed!" I yell over the whooshing of Nkella's wings.

He flies higher, and I grip him tighter. The farther into the distance we go, the darker it gets, with only a slight red hue cast from the vast mountains.

We finally land, and he sets me down. We're on a mountain surrounded by a black river of lava, its orange cracks creating an amber glow around us. I'm afraid to move, the darkness over the edge gives the illusion that I might fall if I take a step.

Steam seeps into the cold air, an acrid stench of sulfur emanating from it. How hot the lava must be in comparison. It's still weird to me how the Deep is so cold, even though Danū is meant to be hot. Piupeki looked like a blizzard through the portal.

I stare at him. "Nkella? Are you okay?"

He breathes heavily, panting but staring at the ground. I walk over to his front and place my hand on his chin. He leans into my touch, his body gives off a soft tremble, and he starts to shift back.

His pointed ears poke through his hair, and he checks his torn shirt, which he now pulls off. I guess it wasn't worth putting one on.

"You'll get the hang of that, I'm sure."

Slowly, his eyes slide back to me. "Kh." A sharp incisor peeks from his smirk.

"You're getting good at controlling it." Pretty damn quickly too. He turns and grabs the arrow sticking out of him and yanks it out. I grimace. "Doesn't that hurt?"

"It had to come out."

"Let me see it." I walk over to his back, squinting to inspect it.

"I'm fine."

"You're not. It's an open wound. You're probably just pumped up with adrenaline right now. You'll feel it more later."

He huffs. "This is why I wanted you to go, Neyuro. You were almost killed by that reaper."

"And you would have been fighting the other devil for literally eternity if I hadn't showed up."

He squeezes his eyes shut. He knows I'm right.

"But you're not wrong about the reapers. I guess the power of the Ace of Swords attracted them, but I didn't see another choice. Good thing the villagers showed up when they did."

Would the reapers have made me drink water from the surface to make me leave? Or would they have killed me to even the score?

I dust some dirt from Nkella's wound, and he hisses, bringing his hand around to grip my wrist.

I inhale sharply. "Let me clean it off."

He lets go of me gently, his eyes softening as he turns his body to me. "We have no water. In time, I will heal."

I flick my gaze to his. "Right...I forgot your, uh—" I right myself, remembering it's not a curse. "You heal fast."

He gives me a brisk nod.

"So what now? Should we give it some time for the minotaurs to leave the area?"

"If they do leave. We should focus on trapping the serpent first."

I nod, then smile. His dark gaze is illuminated by the fiery lights around us. My eyes fall to his full lips, and he stares back at me. I swallow. His eyes soften. I part my lips, the tip of my tongue heavy with what I've been holding, but he peels his eyes away to check where we are.

Now that my eyes have adjusted more, I can see we're outside the mouth of the cave. Far in the distance is complete darkness, the endless seas of the Deep. It's still night as the bodies are not lit above us.

"It's peaceful up here," I say.

"There's not a soul for miles." His eyes return to mine.

A droplet of something hot burns my skin, and I gasp, raising my arm up to my face.

"Neyuro?" Worry fills his voice.

Another drop falls on my head. This time I cuss out loud.

"What's the matter?" He then jumps and smacks his shoulder.

Boiling hot rain starts to patter on the ground, steam rising as it hits the ashen gravel.

"Acid rain." He grabs my arm, and we run to the entrance of a cave. Bright acid rain illuminates the sky and sizzles as it joins the dark waters and volcanic streams surrounding us, heat finally making its way into the Deep.

"Looks like we're not going anywhere for a while." I pant.

"Hn." Sweat glistens on his chest as he stares out at the view.

I lift my hair up, attempt to cool myself in the warm breeze. He touches my skin. His fingers are warm to the touch, yet they send goosebumps rippling up my arm.

"You're hurt." He traces the injuries made by the reaper's claws, and I wince at the sharp pain. He hunches down and rips a part of his pants, then tugs me down to sit on the ground. He gently moves my hair out of the way and begins to dab my wounds with the dry cloth.

"But we have no water," I say in a sing-song whisper, giving him a half smile.

He quirks a brow. "I will still try to clean the wound, daí?"

"So I can't help you, but you can help me?" I chide.

"Quiet, Neyuro. I can heal. You cannot."

I chuckle but let him work. After a few moments of him dabbing the wound with the fabric, his hands trail a little farther down, softly tickling my skin. I close my eyes, leaning into his touch.

My chest tightens, and I have to cover my eyes to keep the tears from welling up.

"Neyuro?" His hand moves under my chin, urging me to show him my face, but I resist.

"What's the matter?"

"I thought you were dead." My voice comes out in a hoarse whisper. "I thought I would never see you again." And now he's here, cleaning my wound. I shudder. "I—"

He drops the cloth, and his fingers trace from my neck all the way down my back. I turn to look at him.

His gaze slams into me, sharp and burning, those dark fierce eyes of his holding me captive, and suddenly I'm back where we started.

"Hold her under the light," he had told the crew. Those eyes never stopped searching mine. Even when we resisted each other, he'd always looked for me.

I can feel my defenses crumbling. The wall I'd put over my heart is tumbling down, and even though I know how I feel about him, even though I came all the way down here to this hell, I always have an excuse for the things I do for him.

It's for the crew.

To defeat Tetalla.

But it's more than that. And I want so badly to tell him how I feel. But the moment I say it, I'm going to jinx myself. The moment I say it, it's all going to be taken away from me. Just like everyone else.

"What were you going to say?" he asks.

His hair is pressed flat against his head, and his ears stick out a little. His eyes are fierce with that brutally handsome stare of his. I reach up and trace the Ipani stripes on his neck, and a smirk threatens his lips.

My pulse quickens, and I kiss him.

He takes my head gently in his hands, and he kisses me back, his fingers twining with my hair, our beating hearts picking up the pace as we give into the want, the fury, the temptation we've been repressing since I brought him back down in that cave.

My hand caresses his warm chest, while he embraces me in his arms, bringing me up to his legs and holding me tightly as he kisses me savagely, his tongue exploring my mouth.

I straddle his hips, and his eyes blaze as I push him down to the volcanic ashes. Acid rains harder outside and I don't care. I press my lips to his, and he takes me in, kissing me so deep it's like he wants to devour my soul.

He tightens his grip around my torso. In one fast movement, he spins us around so he's the one on top. My breath escapes me, and I gape at him. He takes a fistful of the back of my hair, squeezing, lifting my face. He sucks on my neck, causing a moan to escape my lips. His moan responds to mine. My leg has a mind of its own and wraps around his waist, bringing him closer to press against my groin.

His gaze is an inferno as he stares into my eyes, I stare at him back, gasping for air, trying to calm my nerves.

A flash of the red glow emanates from his eyes. He pauses, pushing me back.

"What's wrong?" I ask.

He stands, wiping his face.

"You're not still pushing me away, are you?" He doesn't respond. "Nkella, answer me."

"I will not risk your life, Soren."

I walk up to him, and bring his arm down so he could look at me. "You can't hurt me. Not anymore."

His chest expands and contracts as he stares at me, considering my words. The fiery rain backlights his hair, but the orangey glow hasn't left his eyes.

"You proved you can control your devil power. And if you can't, I can bring you back. You don't even have your air ouma here. You can't hurt me, Nkella. I know you won't." I'm standing an inch from his chest.

His lips part only slightly, but his eyes remain serious as he stares at me from his lowered face. "If we do this, it's for real, daí? I am yours, and you are mine."

I pause for a moment to study his features. Intense and beautiful. And I know with every inch of me that this is what he wants, and what I want. "Yes," I breathe. I almost can't believe this is finally going to happen.

The way he looks at me—like I told him something he's been longing to hear—makes my stomach erupt in a flight of butterflies.

With one swift motion, he undoes his belt and rips it off him. My breath catches in my throat as he advances toward me, heat tingling down to my core. He sweeps me off my feet and gently lays me down on the ash; I stare up at him as he caresses my hair, and our lips crash against each other. He undoes his pants, and I hurry to take off my clothes, only leaving my shirt for his lips to yank over my head.

He catches my lips, and I get lost in the motions of him, and his mouth, taking me deeper and deeper into oblivion. My nails dig into his skin, and he groans with a deep appreciative sound.

"Soren," he rasps.

I can't even speak. I respond in shallow breaths.

"I can't—"

My eyes widen as his wings burst from his back.

"Control—"

"Don't stop. You *can* control—"

Horns on his head appears, growing to full length. My fingers wrap around one of them, and his head lifts, his eyes blazing a fiery red. His eyes roll to the back of his head as he continues to move deep inside me, in and out. My fingers trace his chest as he pulls up and I get a view of him, his wings spread across, blocking the cave's entrance.

I feel him growing bigger inside me, fear pulses in my veins. His chest gets bigger, and his thrusts get more rapid. I push against his chest. "Nkella..."

His eyes close, and he pants. My hand grips onto his wrist, but I don't think I need to go into his memories. Not yet. He breathes in and out. With each wave of his motion, his body normalizes, his horns and wings retracting back into his body.

And I'm filled to where I don't think I could be stretched anymore.

"You can--control it," I say in whispering rasps of air. He is controlling it.

His wings erupt from his back, and I gasp, but the sexiest smirk reaches his eyes as he lowers himself to my level. The warmth of his breath caresses my ear as he softly speaks.

"Pa chae."

"What?"

"Be my aovate."

"Yes." I inhale as he keeps thrusting inside me.

"Say it."

"I—"

"I want you to say it."

My chest pants. It's hard to speak. "I will be yours. Your—aovate."

"Forever. Say it."

"Forever."

His hands wrap around my back with him still inside me, and his wings spread out, rising us to the top of the cave. A yelp escapes me, but he's strong, so strong as he carries me up higher.

Despite us once being able to share our thoughts, I've never felt closer.

As his wings whoosh, keeping us afloat, he has me wrapped around him.

He thrusts his powerful wings, pressing me hard into the wall. His gaze fixates on mine, as if it's the only thing keeping him anchored to himself.

I reach and hold his cheek. "You've mastered this—both you and the devil now."

A devilish grin, and he responds by lifting my leg tighter around him. I slip him inside myself.

His eyes roll to the back of his head as he tilts his head back, and I moan into his mouth as he takes my lips.

He flies us higher against the wall, pressing me back, and he speeds his motions, calling my name. "Soren," he whispers. I arch my back, and he catches my neck in his sharp teeth, a groan escaping him as he thrusts faster and faster. My nails dig into his back at the base of his wings. He starts to shake as he thrusts until he releases inside me.

My heart pounds in my chest, a euphoric tingling sensation fills my body, and every nerve in my body tightens, taking me to the edge and threatening to explode. My legs tremble. "Nkella—" He thrusts again, and I moan, losing myself in him. Colors fill my vision as my orgasm lashes through me.

I'm still shaking. My nails are still dug deep into his skin, but he doesn't seem to mind. My center clenches around him, and he kisses me deeply as he gently pulls out of me and flies us down.

My legs are shaking, and my skin still feels incredibly sensitive. He pulls me close to him and whispers again, "Pa chae."

"I am." Tears sting the corner of my eyes. "I am your aovate. Yours forever."

He chuckles silently. "It means I love you. My neyuro."

I stare at him. The acid rain hasn't subsided, but the cave is too dark to reveal his features. He doesn't wait for my response, he reaches down and kisses me softly again, and together, we fall into a deep sleep.

We wake to a pinkish hue seeping in from the entrance of the cave. Nkella and I are both covered in ash, but he's still holding me. I try to gently move his arm so I can get up and find my clothes, but this wakes him, and he immediately pulls me closer. I can't help the smile spread on my lips.

"I told you, you could control it."

He smiles, and we stay this way for a while longer, neither of us wanting to move. If we move, it means this has to end. We'll have to get back to work. To fight a serpent. And join the tortured souls down below.

"Soren..." He breaks the silence, and I stare up at him. "Back when you were trying to bring me back from my devil self..."

I laugh. "Your devil self?"

"I cannot call it a curse anymore."

"I know. I've been wondering what to call it."

"I saw your memories too," he whispers.

"Yeah, I don't know why that happened. I guess because what you went through, and the betrayal you faced, it all hit close to home for me too."

"With your father?"

"You remember that?"

"I remember all of it."

I sigh and lie back against his arm. He cradles me closer, and I smile.

"We don't have to talk about it," he says.

"No, it's okay. Remember when we were on Bronte's ship, and I found out my father wasn't really my father...but Sehu was?"

He nods.

"My father didn't torture me, but I still feel the pain of my father giving me up. I was a burden he didn't want to have, and I do get it. It just stings, you know?"

He doesn't say anything, he just listens.

"Oh, and I found something else out. The king of Wands told me

Sehu was the bastard son of the king and queen of the time. Which makes me..."

His eyes widen and he raises himself to lean on his elbow. "A princess of Oleanu."

I laugh and slap his shoulder. "Okay, that's enough. This conversation has gone farther than I can handle."

He smiles but draws me close. "I never want you to feel that betrayal again, neyuro. He sits up, his face serious, so I sit up as well. "Soren..." He clears his throat. "I never asked you to be my aovate before, because I was busy trying to save my sister, and then busy fighting the empress, and then afraid I would mess up or die..." He chuckles. "I've accomplished all of those things, and you're still by my side."

My heart starts to beat rapidly.

"But there is no one else for me. I love you, Soren. I meant what I said last night. I want you as my aovate, together by my side. Forever."

My heart is stuffed in my throat, and I can't mutter the words, so I just reach for his face and rest my forehead against his, and I nod. The pink hues hitting my back are turning a bright red. "I think it's time we find the serpent and go back."

A smirk twists his features. "Just a little longer." He leans me back, and smiles a devilish grin as he starts to kiss me all over.

It would be rude of me to interrupt my captain as he works.

21

Sleeping in Nkella's arms was the safest I've ever felt, even though we were sleeping in a cave surrounded by ouma lava in the Serpent's Deep. I don't want this night to end. But inevitably, I fall back to sleep, and my dreams are not as pleasant.

I stand on the red beach as a swirl of sand spins to reveal Tetalla standing before me. His curls are pulled back away from his frowning face, and he's sporting a casual black tunic, Ipani stripes peeking from his clavicle.

"How are you enjoying my domain, my vicious one?"

I lift my chin. This is only a dream; he hasn't been able to take me from a dream. "It has it's quirks, but it's livable."

A sadistic smirk slides onto his face. "That can be arranged, if you like. You may have stayed alive, but the reapers will bring you back."

"Were you sending them after me?"

"Vicious one." He sounds surprised. "Did you think I didn't have dominion over all of the Deep?"

I resist the urge to roll my eyes. "What's the point in sending them if all I need to do to go back is drink from Ipa's water?" That I have, in the ship.

His eyes glint mischievously. "What did you think of my castle?"

My eyes narrow at his avoidance of my question. He also just told me he's been keeping a close watch on me. Just exactly how close is the question.

My cheeks burn, and I can feel myself blushing.

"It's quite dusty," he continues, "and it could use a maid. Perhaps one with a human girl's touch."

I fold my arms. I'm calling his bluff.

"Do not think for a moment, my viscous one, that you are in control here. I've allowed you on your little voyage down to my domain but I don't need the reapers to bring you back to the living lands.

I stare at him. Each time we speak, he says something different that leaves me with a new unsettling feeling. Every time I think I understand his motives, he changes them, and I'm sure it's by design. He's toying with me. Sending reapers to try and sabotage my plans. He can change his mind about anything, at any moment, and I don't like it. "Why would you want to keep me here?"

"I believe that once you understand my stance, you will agree to do what I say. Keeping you in Ipa was for your comfort and my convenience. But I don't need you here, I only need you alive."

"I guess I can't use my powers for you if I'm dead."

"I do enjoy your wit." But there's no amusement in his voice when he says this. He looks me up and down, a flash of fury crossing his eyes, which he disguises with a smile. "Have your fun. I'll be seeing you soon." The sands start to rise over his feet, and his smile grows wider. "Oh, and I think I like you covered in ash."

Before I can say anything back to him, he disappears behind swirls of sand. I startle awake.

Something skitters over my arm, and I blink a few times before recognizing the shards of red and black reflective glass of Philo's little body. I don't move, afraid to wake Nkella up, but I stare as she moves her little arms in an expressive gesture. "Where have you been?" I mouth.

Could my nightmare have attracted her?

A magnetic force pulls me into her, and I let it. "What are you trying to tell me, Philo? Is Asteria okay?"

Images of Talia flash from Philo's memories in a series of pictures.

Talia stares out the window of the Tower. The Empress shows up behind her and Talia jumps in fright. There's worry in my sister's features, fear in her eyes. Her fear emanates through from the vision.

Philo releases her hold on me. she lowers her arms and tilts her head to stare at me with those puppy-like eyes of a jumping spider. I swallow.

"She knew what she was getting herself into, Philo. So she's having a hard time with her lessons and doesn't want to be there anymore? Good. I can't do anything about it, especially not now."

Philo tilts her head in the other direction.

"Do me a favor. Tell Asteria where I am."

She shakes a leg at me, and I crinkle my nose. With one pop, she leaves. I lick my dry lips. Maybe I shouldn't have told her to go to Asteria, seeing how Philo shares information through pictures in thoughts, and...I look down at Nkella's arms wrapped around my breasts. What are the chances of Philo knowing that I meant to show her the Deep, and not literally where and how I am right this minute?

Oops.

Nkella stirs, and I turn to face his chest. He blinks his eyes at me.

"We fell asleep again."

"Hn."

"We should go."

"In such a hurry to fight?"

"In a hurry to get back to our crew...and my sister." Despite what I told Philo, I am very worried about Talia, but I've been trying my best to keep to my mission. One thing at a time.

This gets him up. "You're right."

Fully dressed, we emerge from the cave. Well, as dressed as he can be. It's going to be hard to concentrate with the memories of last night and this morning resurfacing in my mind. And with Nkella giving me his devilish glares.

I wish we didn't have a serpent to kill.

I just want to stay in bed with him all day. And night. Actually, a real bed would be nice.

We've dusted off as much of the ash as we possibly could, but we're practically covered in a permanent coat of gray as we step out into the reddish hues. I can't imagine how dirty and ridiculous I must look, but when Nkella looks at me, I don't feel ridiculous. He looks at me like he wants to stop what he's doing to devour me. It makes my stomach swim each time.

I can't believe he's my...aovate...forever...and we...

"Be careful, neyuro, daí? Do you want to fall down the mountain? Kh."

I open my mouth to speak, then snap it shut.

He gives me his hand, but I walk past him.

"I'm not falling down any mountain. And put a shirt on." Jeez.

"I will once we get back to the ship."

"Your pants stayed on at least. Maybe it's like ouma. When I ate the ouma iponochi, Gari taught me how to keep my clothes on."

"Hn." I glance at him, and he's fighting to hide a smile. My cheeks heat remembering that time on the ship when I tried to fix the sail. When the cookie wore off, I was completely naked.

I slap at his arm. "You were totally thinking about me being naked under Kae's coat, weren't you?"

"Kh. I had no thoughts about an utwa on my ship." A smirk threatens his lips. "Pay attention to what you are doing, daí? There are dead around us."

I take out my dagger. "I got this. And no magic tarot cards, just the dagger."

He grabs me by the waist and pulls me to him. My heart skips a beat, and he kisses my lips. My eyes flutter open. Here we are, on the way to kill a giant serpent, and neither of us can keep our hands to ourselves.

His eyes snap past me, and my brows furrow. Clutching the dagger, I turn to find the serpent slithering in the air above the village we were in last night. If Apeiron hunts whoever trespassed the Deep, it's only a matter of time before he comes after us.

"We must get there faster," he says.

"But how? If I use the World Card, it'll attract the reapers. If you fly us down there, the minotaurs will follow."

"Hn. We cannot take them all at once."

I look out toward the serpent's sinuous body. "How do we kill something that's hunting us, and not get killed?"

"Kh. Just like we always do at sea, daí?"

The real question is are Tetalla's reapers trying to get to me before the serpent does? If the Empress knows I'm here, why wouldn't she have called Apeiron off? Or could the serpent have switched to Tetalla's side when he was down here, and could Tetalla have the snake bring me to him?

The serpent disappears between the bodies dangling from the surface until we can't see him anymore.

"The only plan is to trap it," Nkella says.

"We can use me as bait."

Nkella guffaws. "If you think I will put you in danger, you think very poorly of me, neyuro."

"He's after me. It might be the only way."

"It can be after me too, daí? I am also alive here."

I press my lips together. No point in telling him about Tetalla's plans for me. I need him to focus. "So how do you propose we trap him?"

"Climb on my back." He starts to shift. "Let us see what that blacksmith has in his hut."

I grab onto his shoulders. "But what about the minotaurs?"

"I will glide close to the ground, and if we see one, we'll take cover." He's fully shifted.

"Nkella?"

He turns his head to his shoulder as I grip his back and wrap my legs around his torso.

"You realize you're talking while you're...shifted."

His brows rise, and in a single leap, he takes off. I grab on tight. We fly close to the ground. Once we've reached the height of the palms, we can no longer see the vast volcanic mountain ranges, and we stay out the guards' sight by taking cover among the trees. Outside the village walls, he sets me down and shifts back. I don't think I'll ever get used to seeing his wings disappear from behind him or his horns sink back into his skull. He's managed to keep his features, and parts of him from growing too large, or his tail from coming out. But I know what he could become if he wanted to.

"Each time I change, I try something different."

"Well, you're picking it up quickly. It seems all you had to do was accept who you are, and the devil in you would be easily controlled."

He picks up my hand, lifting it to his lips, and says, "What it took was you accepting me for the devil I am. How lucky am I that a devil like me should be favored by Fate." He kisses the back of my hand, his eyes locked on mine.

I'm about to open my mouth to speak when a magnetic force grows around us and I'm pushed into him. It's a strange sensation, one I've never felt before. As it courses through my body, I feel it coming from him. The love and protection he feels for me.

His eyes momentarily drift closed, and a warm smile tugs on his lips. "Do you feel this?"

"Y-yes. What is it?"

"The power of aovate. It is ouma, but ouma does not work here."

"Then how—"

"Shh...I'm not complaining." He's feeling it too...from me? A moment later, it disappears, and we let go of each other. My eyes flutter open to see him smiling back at me.

"Maybe it is because of your Fate power. We are more powerful together," he says.

"Yeah..." But my Fate power is its own different magic. Could his control over his Devil have opened something up? There aren't any reapers or dead after us, so it has to come from him. "Is that what it'll always feel like once we're back on the surface?"

"I don't know. I've never had an aovate before. Let's go."

Once we're inside the village, the earsplitting sounds of steelwork coming from the blacksmith is the most annoying noise around us—besides the tortured souls of course. I've somehow managed to tune those out until I remember they're there.

"Do we have anything to trade?" I ask, not wanting to summon the dead or reapers by using my magic to return items.

Nkella shakes his head, but we approach it anyway. The clanging of steel on steel makes my teeth hurt.

We reach the half-open stone structure with tools and weapons leaning against the wall. A man with his back to us hits a hammer hard against an anvil. My eyes skim the village. People are working on weapons, some making clothes, but no one is shopping. And there isn't any food since no one here eats. For the first time, I realize I'm not hungry, and it's been more than a day since my last meal in Oleanu. The water from the Deep suppresses any need.

"Free. Free. Free," the blacksmith mutters to himself between his strikes.

I exchange a glance with Nkella, and shrug.

A man sprints past us and stops at the blacksmith.

"Āngasoe!"

The blacksmith ignores him and carries on forging his weapons, chanting, "Free, free, free."

I gape at Nkella. I remember that's the Ipani word for minotaur. If the guards are coming, they must be searching for Nkella. "They must have seen you!" I whisper-shout.

He shrugs and says nonchalantly, "They are looking for *a* devil, daí?"

"They can't tell who you are?"

"They're not that smart." Nkella quirks a brow at the blacksmith and steps closer.

I relax my shoulders, and follow Nkella, despite the sound hurting my ears.

"Must free," the blacksmith repeats.

We search the stone hut, but I don't see anything big enough to trap a serpent. "We need something like a giant harpoon or a giant crossbow."

Nkella rubs his chin. "He only has a hammer and swords here."

"Maybe he can make us something?" Although that might take ages. I sigh.

More people run past, but the blacksmith keeps working and chanting.

Nkella leans into the hut. "Blacksmith, why are you not running with the rest of them?"

I stare at him, but his eyes bore into the blacksmith's back.

"Maybe he knows something we don't," he whispers to me.

The blacksmith lowers his hammer and spins around. Surprise crosses his face. "Did you say something to me?"

"I did," Nkella responds. "Why are you not running with the rest of the dead?"

More dead jump over debris and rocks as they sprint past us.

The man gapes at us. He's covered in sweat and soot, his clothes are ripped at the elbows and knees, and his skin is blackened with grease and ash. Only his dark eyes and white teeth stand out from the dirt. "Apologies." He clears his throat. "It's been a long time since I've been spoken to."

I screw up my face, and Nkella and I exchange another glance.

"I am crafting a weapon worthy of fighting the minotaurs."

"But there's a devil on the loose," Nkella responds.

"I fear no devil. Only the minotaurs who keep us prisoner." He picks up his hammer again. "If you'll excuse me, time is limited. I intend on freeing the devil from his binds." He continues hitting the sword and repeating, "Free. Free the devil."

"What do you know of the devils?" Nkella demands, surprise plastered across his face.

He stops again to answer, this time without turning around. "Only that one of them is the lost king of Danū. I intend to release him from his binds. Only then, will we be saved."

"The lost king of Danū?" Nkella's voice shakes. "Do you not mean the lost prince, daſ?"

Something in him just changed. I stare at him. "What? What is it?"

Nkella is now leaning closer, sparks from the friction of metal on metal flying toward his face. "Which king of Danū do you speak of? Would you remember the name? Blacksmith, answer me!"

The blacksmith arches his neck. "King Nkura Mikiroro."

Nkella takes a small step back, then raises his hand halfway to his mouth. "This whole time, I've been fighting my own father."

My jaw drops. "Oh, Nkella..."

"Did you say something?" The blacksmith turns around slowly.

"Blacksmith." Urgency fills his voice. "Let us join you. I too want to release the devil from his binds."

The blood drains from my face. I touch his shoulder. "Nkella," I whisper, not knowing how I could possibly tell him that this detour could get us both captured and killed by minotaurs or reapers or both.

That we really need to get on with trapping the serpent and leave. But how could I tell him that? If this is true, he's never going to leave knowing his father is trapped in his devil binds forever. My memory skips to the pictures on the cavern wall. This makes sense. Nkella stares down at me, concern in his eyes.

"Neyuro..."

I place my hand on his chest. "Of course we have to find your father. We'll kill the serpent after."

He doesn't say a word, but the look he gives me is all the thanks I need.

The blacksmith lets the blade fall to the floor, and he turns around slowly. He walks toward us, his eyes never leaving Nkella's. "Did I hear you correctly? Did you say...the king is..."

"My father." Nkella's voice is heavy. "My name is Nkella Mikiroro."

The blacksmith's jaw slackens. He stares from Nkella to me, and his eyes land on my necklace—the Danū royal coin. I quickly stick it back in my shirt, and the blacksmith averts his eyes to Nkella. "Then my service is to you. They call me Kaonī. I know my way around these parts. Let me be your guide."

Nkella chuckles, but I don't bother to ask what's funny. The ground rumbles with the heavy slow steps of the minotaurs making their way, and more people run.

"Great. I'm Soren. Is there somewhere we can go so we can come up with a plan? Preferably away from giants."

Kaonī squints at me. I'm not sure if he's offended by my being here or if he's staring at my red hair, but I don't really care. We have to go. He turns to grab the weapon he was crafting and starts hitting it again. I cringe, and glance at Nkella. The blacksmith stops and turns it in his hand to inspect it.

"It's ready." He stares at me. "Do you not like the sounds of steel, young maiden?"

"Not really, no."

"Well, you'd better get used to it. It is the sound of Danū, bringing about the forging by ouma fire. Our pride." He takes a wooden hilt and sticks it on the opposite end of his weapon. "And this hammer will take down any minotaur, serpent, or beast."

Nkella raises his chin, and a smile spreads across his face.

The minotaurs come closer. The dead villagers have started shooting their arrows at them. My fingers are twitching over the pocket that holds the Ace of Swords Card, but I know if I take it out now, the reapers will come. We can't afford to lose any more time. Kaonī sticks his hammer in his belt, and spins around to grab his bow and quill full of arrows.

"Follow me." He quickly walks out of his stone hut and leads us to a dead forest.

"Where are we going?" Nkella asks.

"I thought to walk in the direction I saw my king fly. But we will take refuge in an abandoned temple, *Upipurang*. There's a lake where we can get clean and think of a plan."

"You have strategy, Kaonī. How long have you been in the Deep?"

"I cannot remember. I had been in torment for many years until I decided one day that I would free the devil. And then he was set free, but not of his chains."

I exchange a glance with Nkella. "Are you saying the chains are keeping the king in devil form?"

"What else could be keeping him that way?" He huffs. "My king was the strongest. Helāni magic has done this to him."

"Koj." Nkella stops walking, and the blacksmith turns to face him.

"Nkella?" I turn to him. "Are you sure?"

"If we are going to do this, he has to know."

The blacksmith looks between us with his brows furrowed. "Know what?"

Nkella reveals his horns, then his wings snap open.

Kaonī's eyes widen. "You—?"

"It's not a curse. It's...who we are. My father is lost inside himself, perhaps the curse is that we become so easily consumed by our guilt and grief." He looks down at the sand. "We hide behind what we think gives us strength. He needs to regain control of who he is in order to come back."

Nkella had always thought this was a curse. But if his father knows this isn't a curse, then maybe he's stuck this way because of anger, regret, even grief. We know that devils protect themselves, and the longer he's stayed that way, the deeper he could be buried inside himself.

Kaonī swallows, but his eyes remain on Nkella. Then he looks at me, and relaxes, seeing how I'm not unnerved by Nkella's change. Nkella shifts back, and the blacksmith clears his throat. "How will we free him them? How will he gain control?"

"By remembering," I answer.

Kaonī takes a few steps back and scratches his head. Finally, he starts to laugh, and I gape at him.

"Umm... Kaonī?" I look at Nkella. "Are you still up for this?"

"Come. The minotaurs will come through here if we don't hurry. But this just got harder, daí?" He looks at Nkella. "How did you gain control? The legends say once a devil curse overtakes you, there's no coming back. But you...you seem to have full control."

Nkella looks at me. "I didn't do it alone."

22

The sun is never bright in the Deep, and red hues blanket the sea. I now realize that's because the blood of the bodies hanging on the surface have been dripping down to the waters for so many generations and reflecting to the top. The sands of Danū are red, so that's normal, but the water and sky shouldn't be red.

The minotaurs turned in a different direction, and we've made it to Upipurang. The three of us walk to a clear red lake. Kaonī bends down first, and cups a handful of water, bringing it to his face. The water doesn't clean much of the soot off his skin, but a little is better than nothing. Nkella and I aren't as dirty, but we haven't spent the last hundred years with soot and grease.

Nkella and I sit next to each other, a few feet from Kaonī, and scrub the ash off our faces. I help him with his back.

"Neyuro..." Nkella mutters. "This mission to save my father..." I can see the pain in his expression before he continues. "We do not need to do it."

"Why are you saying this?"

"I am slowing us down. For my own gain." He stares at the water.

"It's not for your own gain, Nkella. It's important to you, so it's important to me."

He turns to stare at me.

"It's not like you wouldn't go anyway." I chide, but I'm also serious. He would.

"Koj. I am not going anywhere without you. We pledged to each other. You are my aovate. Forever."

My lips twist to a smile, and I place my hand on his. "We're doing this."

Kaonī clears his throat, bringing our attention to him. "I'm sorry to interrupt." He walks up to us and takes a seat. "Maybe we should discuss the plan to bring back my king." A mud smear across his eyes makes him look like a raccoon, and there's more on his neck. I have to stop myself from smirking.

"I'll use myself as bait," Nkella says. My eyelids fly open, and I gape at him. "You will constrain him," he tells Kaonī. Then looks at me. "And when he's constrained, we will try to bring him back."

"How?" Kaonī asks.

"We will talk to him," Nkella says, still looking at me. I give him a reassuring nod. He's being careful not to mention who I am, or anything about Helāni magic. He's gotten a bad reputation for leaving his people, and the last thing we want is let this man know Nkella is meddling with a Fate. Who knows how he'd react.

"You will bring the king back from his devil curse by talking?"

"We told you it isn't a curse," Nkella repeats.

"This is madness." Kaonī stands. "I will be ready to break his chain."

"As you should anyway," Nkella responds.

"Wait." I stand too. "We're not using you as bait."

"Neyuro, my father is trained to want to fight another devil, daí? This is the best course of action."

"How will I constrain him?" Kaonī asks. I cross my arms, waiting for Nkella to come up with an answer.

"I'd like to know that as well," I say. Nkella looks at me, and then at my wrists. "Oh."

"I want to free my king, not be killed by him, daí?" Kaonī takes more water and rubs it over his eyes, causing the mud to drip down his face.

I take my dagger, slice a piece off the bottom of my pant leg, and hand it to him, tired of seeing him struggle. "How can you be killed by him? You're already dead."

He takes it from me and wipes his face. It's a little better at least. "Dying is still painful here. And I will be returned to where I first started. I might not remember you or my mission to free the king."

I swallow my gasp. Good to know. "You won't get killed. I promise." Nkella shoots me a stare. "I won't let the devil kill you, Kaonī." Nkella takes in a deep breath. I know, I'm making another promise, but this one I can keep.

Kaonī guffaws. "You have a lot of courage, Soren, but you should not make promises you don't know you can keep. It is a dangerous game, that. Take it from me, I would know."

"Daí?" Nkella stands after washing his hands and looks at him.

"You two are aovate, yes? I had one once. I made many promises to her. And, now I am here, unable to keep her safe." His voice falters, and we grow silent. "I don't remember much. It was long ago. But I remember that she was taken from me, and then...I don't remember the rest."

"Who took her?" I ask.

He shakes his head. "She was gone one morning." His voice sounds distant as he stares out toward the mountain ranges. "I searched and searched, but never found her. Then one day I awoke in the Deep but I don't remember how I got here." He returns his gaze to us. "My heart bleeds for you both to have lost your lives so young, but at least you are together."

I chew on my cheek and glance at Nkella.

"We should get going, daí?" Nkella says. "We have a lot of ground to cover."

The blacksmith looks at our surroundings. "We're not far from the castle entrance."

My heart skips a beat.

"I found myself near the entrance as well," Nkella passes me a smirk, "before I was brought back."

My heart starts pounding in my chest. The castle. Where Tetalla wants to keep me locked up forever. Sweat forms at the back of my neck.

"How did you bring him back?" Kaonī asks me, but I can hardly hear him over the sound of my beating heart.

"Soren? Are you alright?" he asks.

"Neyuro?"

I glance at Nkella. "Yes, sorry. I'm fine. Um...do we have to go back down through the cave to get to the castle entrance?"

Nkella shakes his head. "I don't know. We were there before. Why do you sound hesitant?"

"I'm not. I just want to mentally prepare myself for going is all."

His brows furrow. "Did you suddenly develop a fear of closed spaces, neyuro?"

I chuckle. "No. Maybe."

His eyes narrow.

"It is possible that he will go where he remembers." Kaonī rubs his chin. "And the castle was his home."

"Right." I clear my throat. "Let's get going then." I start walking but Nkella doesn't budge.

"Are you sure?"

I look back at him. "Yes."

I take the lead, walking toward the mountain ranges, not that I know exactly where to go, but at the moment, there's nowhere to go but straight ahead. The ground is an ashy gray hardpacked sand, with cracks going for miles to the volcanic mountains. I don't see another spot of lake or river anywhere around, although black leaf palm trees sway ever so slightly in the chilling breeze. The reddish hue lights our path, still never as bright as the sun.

Nkella and Kaonī walk behind me in silence. If I had the rikorō back in my system, I know I'd feel Nkella's worrying thoughts about me or his brooding feelings. I used to want to run from them, then for so long, I'd missed having them.

Now, having him close to me, I still wish I could feel those thoughts again, to know what he's thinking. The power of aovate was beyond words though...I can't wait to feel that again.

Something swooshes behind me, and I look back. Kaonī is tossing his hammer in the air and catching it.

"How did you two die?" Kaonī breaks the silence.

After a beat, Nkella responds. "It's a long story."

"We have a long journey." He catches his hammer again. "But I will keep silent if you don't want to talk about it."

"It is not you," Nkella sighs. "My death was complicated, daí? And my aovate came here because of me..."

This is going to be a very long walk if we have to lie and tiptoe around every single one of Kaonī's questions.

He catches his hammer, and this time holds onto it. "I am sorry for both of you. I understand now why it is complicated."

I feel bad for him. He lost his lover and doesn't even remember how he died. He's been here for who knows how long making weapons over and over.

I glance over my shoulder at him, and I have to look forward straight away to keep from grimacing. There's soot all over his face again, as if we hadn't just watched him clean it off. I look back at him; he brushes his hair back with his hand, dirt coming off it. It dawns on me that this must be part of his eternal torment. But being dirty? That's an odd form of punishment. I wonder what else might be going on inside his head.

He catches me looking at him, and I turn back around. He continues to throw his hammer, catching it melodically.

"I overheard you speaking about this journey slowing you down. It makes me wonder what else you have to do now that you have eternity together? Besides keeping safe from danger and guards." He chuckles.

Wow, he really doesn't like silence, does he?

Before Nkella can say anything, I answer. "We plan on killing the serpent and freeing the dead from their eternal torment."

Now I really wish I could hear Nkella's thoughts.

Kaonī makes a whistling sound behind me, and I hear him shuffle. "Is this true?"

"Yes," Nkella says. "It's the least I can do."

I turn back to Nkella. He's walking faster to catch up with me. He'd been quietly walking deep in thought. He takes my hand and kisses it. My cheeks heat, and I smile.

"I am truly in debt to you, my prince," Kaonī says. "And to you,

Soren. No one has tried to kill the serpent in the Deep. He is protected by Helāni magic and has been Tetalla's pet for a long time."

Tetalla's pet. I knew it.

Nkella quirks a brow. "Hn."

"He eats anything in his path and destroys villages by only passing by them."

Nkella stays quiet, and I know what he's thinking. It doesn't matter, though, I'm not letting him do this alone. And I will bring him back with me.

"If we survive freeing the king, I would like to aid you in your noble quest to kill the serpent. I would too like to be freed from my torment, and if I can do anything to help those in the Deep, there's nothing I would rather be doing."

I stare at Nkella blankly. He shrugs.

"I do not have anything to lose, daſ?" Kaonī says.

"Are you not afraid of the serpent killing you?" Nkella asks.

"I would gladly give my life again and again for a noble cause such as this."

"What about the Helāni magic?" I ask.

"It is not the Helāni magic I am afraid of. Nor ouma for that matter. It is who wields it that I fear, and a serpent has little mind to wield it, ko?"

My brows perk up at that.

"He talks almost as much as you, daſ?" A smirk crosses Nkella's features as he whispers to me, and I slap his arm. Kaonī continues to melodically toss his hammer in the air and catch it. He seems to be lost in his own world now, deep in his thoughts.

"It's funny he hasn't realized I wasn't dead," I whisper out of earshot. "You have that deal with the serpent, so maybe no one can tell. But when I first got here, I was attracting all sorts of beings, and one said I was alive." I'm careful not to mention Nangraku.

"It could have been your use of Helāni magic giving you away. Or perhaps the longer you are here, the more you smell of death."

"Lovely."

The ground starts to rumble under our feet, and my first thought is that the minotaurs are here. We stop in our tracks. Nkella holds me back in a protective stance, but I still take out my dagger. A flash of red crosses his eyes, and his horns protrude from his skull.

Kaonī already had his hammer in his hand, but now his back is against ours as he scopes out the distance.

The ground rumbles again.

"Where are they?" I say, mostly to myself. Silence falls over the grounds as we wait for the minotaurs to appear.

A skeletal claw rips from the ground and grabs my leg. "Oh!" I take my dagger and stab at it. It takes Nkella a moment to realize what's happening, but he stomps on the bones, and shoves me away from danger.

Then bodies begin to appear all around us. Some emerge from the ground, and others swoop down from the sky. We're surrounded. No. No no no.

Tetalla's chuckles swarm me in a cocoon of dead laughter. "*I told you, my vicious one. I can hear your heart beating, and you are in my domain. You are getting closer to your forever home, daí? I wanted to welcome you as my personal guest.*"

The dead aim toward Nkella and Kaonī.

"*There is nowhere for you to go. Submit.*"

"No!"

"*Submit.*"

"No!" I scream on the top of my lungs. "I will never submit to you!" Nkella's eyes glow red as he stares at me. I don't know if anyone else can hear Tetalla's voice, but I take out the Ace of Swords, despite it attracting more dead and reapers. Right now, I have no choice.

The sword extends out of the card, emanating its purple glare as I spin it in my hand and start splitting corpses in two, all around me. I don't stop. I keep stabbing, and slicing, my heart pumping in my veins, my breath staccato as I go. I see no one but me and the dead, coming to be spliced.

As they fall, they reanimate.

Tetalla's laughter bellows through the wind. He won't kill me, he said himself that he needs me alive. But he can kill Nkella, and I will not let that happen.

And that's when I realize how much danger we actually are in.

He can kill Nkella.

Take him away from me forever. For real this time. The only reason I can bring him back is that he's still alive. Tetalla knows this.

Nkella shifts to full on devil, and I relax a little. He heals, and so far, that has kept him alive down here. But if Nkella can kill Death because he has the strength of a devil to match him, then the same can be in reverse.

Nkella is swinging his arms, taking dozens out at a time, and Kaonī is smashing their heads with his hammer. He stops to look past me and points. I take a quick glance and see a new hoard of dead coming at us in rows. An army of the dead marching straight for us.

23

It looks like an earthquake erupting around us as fifteen-foot-high minotaurs start to run toward us, a cloud of sand forming around their feet.

The dead swarm the sky, and I swing my sword over my head, lobbing off a wailing head. A reaper screeches overhead.

"You cannot escape me. I will not stop asking you to submit to me."

Even though I can't see him, I feel his eyes on me with his voice following my every move. I refuse to respond and keep my focus on the reaper. Her mer-tail sways in the air, and her jaw elongates, showing jagged needle teeth. Her eyes are large, with tiny white pupils in their center. Her nose is nothing but two slits in her green pasty face. I swing my sword, and she swims backward in the air. She speeds to my face, and grips my chin with a fierce vengeance, her mouth opening wide. I expect her to scream her dreadful siren wail, but instead, a hoarse voice fills the air.

"Submit, Soren," she says with Tetalla's voice.

Her head is taken off by something hard and metallic. I gape as the hammer boomerangs back to Kaonī's hand. I blink at him, but he turns to Nkella who's busy fighting off more of the dead.

As I run to help, another reaper appears. This time, she heads for Nkella, and my heart stops. Clutching my sword, I race toward her and slide the blade into her torso. Her head spins one hundred and eighty degrees to stare at me; a high-pitched siren call emanates from her black lips. I stumble back but don't let go of my sword.

Nkella's eyes glow red as he grips the reaper between his hands and starts to rip her apart. Black goo and guts spray out of her, and I wince as I'm drenched in them.

A dead person walks beside me, and I swing to the right, beheading it in one stride, then I swing to the left.

I need time to think.

The last time I got away from Tetalla was on the ship. If I use the World Card, it'll attract more dead, but I'll be able to lose Tetalla for at least a little while. To give me enough time to think.

Kaonī throws his hammer at a reaper headed in our direction, and as it hits her, she lights on fire. She screams and flies higher. Kaonī catches the hammer when it returns back to him.

A deafening rip makes me pause. Shock paralyzes me as the ground opens beneath Kaonī and swallows him whole. His scream is muffled by the sinkhole caving in.

I reach for his hand to pull him out, when something grabs my hair. I spin around to fight off a large beast of a dead man, with shriveled purple and black skin sliding off his face. It takes all my strength to power through and swing my sword, but I catch sight of others behind him. We need to get out of here.

I yell at Nkella over the sounds of Kaonī's horrible cries, "I need a location!"

"Daí?" Behind the Beasty I'm fighting, he pulverizes a dead person with his fist .

I hit steel as Beasty takes out a spear and blocks me. "Somewhere to go!"

"The castle." He grabs Beasty's spear and punches his face as he rips the spear out of his dead hands.

While Nkella holds him, I stab Beasty's torso with my sword, finishing him off. "No. Anywhere but there." Beasty drops to the floor.

"The ship." Nkella spins to block a blow from the next dead attacker.

"Too far." Then we'll have to climb back inside the fortress walls and make our way on foot to avoid using my magic all over again. Swinging my sword in one final swipe, I slice the dead attacker's head clean off. "We can't lose any more time. Anywhere on the island."

"Then where?" he growls.

"I need a location. Now!"

"Our cave," he shouts. "Go to our cave."

I take out the World Card and open a portal. I grab Nkella and push him toward the hole that swallowed Kaonī.

As we fall, I grope the sand until I feel an arm. I assume it belongs to Kaonī, since Nkella is directly under me.

A moment later, we're toppling over each other in front of the cave. I grab at the ground, and it feels like my chest is going to explode. Kaonī falls to the ground as well, unintelligible sounds coming from his lips. His eyes are shut, and he's clutching his knees to his chest. I place my hand on his shoulder, and he yells. I snap my hand back and stare at Nkella.

Nkella's eyes flicker as his horns, wings, and tail withdraw into his body and his physique changes back to his normal self. Nkella holds out Kaonī's hammer but tucks it into his own belt instead. Probably good thinking at this point.

"Kaonī?" he says. "You're alive, daí?"

Kaonī still has his eyes closed. He's rocking himself, muttering something in Ipani. I try to place my hand on his knee, slowly. He stops talking.

"Hey. It's alright," I say. "We're fine."

Kaonī's breathing is hard, but he stops talking to himself. His eyes open slowly. He gasps and looks around.

I smile at him. "You're okay."

His shoulders slump, and he looks around for something. I glance at Nkella, and with a perked brow, he takes the hammer and sets it down beside Kaonī.

I stand and walk toward Nkella. "He's really freaked out."

"Hn." Nkella's eyes are narrowed. "Give him some time." He takes my arm and pulls me toward the cave. He stares at me, his brows furrowed, confusion sprawled on his face. I swallow. "Something tells me you know why the dead were being commanded. They were"—he stares down at the ground—"hypnotized."

I bite my lip.

"That reaper knew your name. Why?" His eyes search my face.

"There's something I still haven't told you..."

"Kh." His eyes roll. "Are you going to tell me now?"

I glance at Kaonī who quickly averts his gaze. He stands and walks away, leaving us alone. At least he finally stood up.

I take a deep breath and let it out slowly. His features harden. "You fighting Tetalla for Ipa isn't the only thing."

"What are you not telling me, neyuro?"

"He's been...following me. I don't know how, but he knows where I am whenever I sleep. He says he can hear my heartbeat. And he can control the dead...so as soon as he gets a whiff of where I am, he sends them. The reapers are also under his command, so if I use magic, I guess, that's a dead giveaway for him."

His brows knit together, a flare of red illuminates his eyes, like they used to when he looked at me. "What does he want with you?" He growls with his teeth showing.

"He needs my help to defeat the Empress—that much I know—but...it's more than that. He wants all humans dead. He wants things back to the way they were hundreds of years ago." I swallow. "He killed AJ." I have to stop myself before I can't speak again. "He wants me to use my magic to destroy what keeps the Empress in Ipa—the cards—but with it, he'll kill humans as well. And he—"

"Daí?"

"He says I look like Adara...the Empress's younger sister. I think he meant to kill me before he saw me—before he knew what my power was and why the Empress was fond of me. He likes to go into my dreams and talk to me." My hands shake. "I should have told you..."

Nkella's chest rises up and down, and his eyes are like lava. "Why didn't you?"

"I didn't want to worry you more. It's a lot...me coming down here.

Tasking you with having to fight Death. AJ. Everything. And...I didn't know how much you could handle given"—I motion to his body—"your changes. It's all so new."

He rushes toward me and grabs my hands. "Neyuro. Now more than ever I want to see him buried beneath my feet. I will not let him harm you."

"That's the thing. He says he needs me alive. He can't use my powers if I'm dead." I pull away and grab my hair, staring down at the sand. "Also, he's unpredictable. He changes his mind at a whim." I shake my head. "He's impossible to figure out."

"He's a warrior. He's playing us like a game."

I nod. "We're toys in a sandbox to him." A long moment of silence befalls us. Kaonī is still slowly pacing in front of the lava, giving us some space.

Nkella blinks, as if coming back from whenever his mind has drifted. "We do not have a lot of time to free my father. And kill the serpent."

I shake my head and mouth no. "But we'll do it."

He groans into his hand.

Kaonī glances at us and starts to walk back. Even after shaking all the new dirt off him, his face is black with soot.

I start to walk over to the blacksmith, but Nkella pulls me back to him. "Neyuro, we cannot keep secrets from each other, daí?"

My cheeks heat. "I know," I say above a whisper. "I'm sorry."

"Promise me. No more secrets."

Nangraku. The promise I made to King Mayi. I part my lips to speak, and his face turns serious.

"Is there something else?" he asks.

"Yes, but now is really not the time to talk about it. I promise I'll tell you everything you need to know when we're back. Just...trust me. Please."

Nkella lets out a sigh, but his shoulders drop. He brings me in by the waist and presses my body up against his. He stares down at me, his eyes on my lips, but he doesn't kiss me.

"You are the only person beside my sister and sometimes the crew"

—I let out a bubbled laugh—"that I have ever trusted as much as I do now."

I swallow. "Me too."

He brushes my lips with his, nibbling my bottom lip ever so slightly. Then he lets me go, and walks back out of the cave, leaving me breathless.

I take a second to get a hold of my composure. Kaonī's voice is weak when he speaks to Nkella.

"You really are a devil."

"Yes," Nkella says, "but I'm in full control now."

Outside the cave, I let myself fall to the floor in front of Kaonī. My muscles are sore and still trembling from the fight. He stares at me.

"And you...you have Helāni magic, daí?"

I wince. "You saw that, didn't you?"

He stares out at the mountain range and nods.

"I'm not like the Empress though," I tell him.

"I am not afraid of Helāni magic."

"I know. You said that already. I wanted to tell you anyway."

He squints. "In that case, you can restrain the devil. You don't need me."

"You know how to get us around, and that's a pretty awesome weapon you made. We know someone who would really think it's... *wicked.*" I chuckle to myself, and glance at Nkella. "Harold would love that hammer."

Nkella's lips curl into a tight smile. His arms are folded as he watches us talk, but I can tell his mind is elsewhere. He's probably contemplating how we're going to find his father.

"So what do we do?" I ask out loud.

Nkella sighs behind his teeth. "If Tetalla is after you, this makes things more difficult. He will only sabotage our plans."

"He'll sabotage our plans whether I'm here or back home."

"Back home?" Kaonī takes a sharp breath. "Where is...back home?"

"Oh." I give him a sheepish smile. "We're not really dead. The devil heals. He kind of made a deal to save me, which is why he's here. And when I found out he's alive, I came to bring him back. It's—"

"Complicated," Kaonī finishes my sentence. "I think I've heard enough."

"Sorry."

"Don't be. I'm glad you're both alive. But my prince is right. If Death is looking for you, this will make things more difficult."

I smile at Kaonī referring to Nkella as his prince. I mean, he's right, but normally Nkella doesn't like to be called that. I sneak a peek at Nkella, but he hasn't moved from his brooding. His eyes look distant.

"No magic," I say. "Whatever we do now, unless we need to escape from Tetalla again, I won't take out the Ace of Swords or the World Card. It attracts undead and reapers, and they're how Tetalla is tracking me while I'm awake."

"You cannot sleep either, neyuro, if he is visiting you in your dreams."

"Sleep is for the dead." I smirk at him. His eyes drift to me, and his brows furrow.

Kaonī gives me a blank stare. "I am not asleep."

"Never mind." Obviously my humor doesn't translate here. "I don't need to sleep. I'll sleep when we're out of the Deep."

"But he can still find you in Ipa," Nkella presses. Which is why I didn't want him worrying about all this now.

"We'll worry about that later—"

"Kh."

"For now, let's focus on how we're going to get your father. What will attract a devil's attention? You've already shifted more than once, and that doesn't seem to call him."

Nkella shakes his head. "I cannot sense another devil either."

"Does anything call to you when you're shifted?"

"Hn." He rubs chin. "Ouma fire. I feel it as if it's part of my bloodstream. I want to go to it. I think that's why I was kept inside the arena and didn't care to escape. Until there was a distraction with the minotaurs. And then you." Softness flicks through his features.

We sit in silence as we consider our options. Then, Kaonī gets up and starts walking around the edge of the cliff. Nkella follows his movements.

"We're surrounded by ouma fire here," the blacksmith acknowledges.

"Daí? So what?"

"What will attract him is the fire from the castle chambers, daí? The fire controlled by your father. *Your lineage.*" Kaonī's voice rises in excitement. "There are two different kinds of fire, and those who can control them. You know this, don't you?" he asks Nkella.

I blink a few times. I remember Kae telling me about the two fires. I've dealt with ouma fire before in the fighting rings because some Ipani are born with it. But that was never good enough for the Empress. She sought a special kind of fire that would listen to the royals —that would listen to Nkella. That's why she wanted to control him when he was young. It was the same fire that was able to burn and kill a Fate.

Nkella doesn't respond. He just stares at Kaonī. Nkella never wanted to acknowledge his royal background. If someone had tried to teach him about it, would he have shut them out? How much of his own lineage does he even know?

"How do we get to the royal fire?" I break the silence. My stomach turns. "Do we have to go down to the castle?"

"I don't think so," Kaonī answers for Nkella. "I cannot say how I know this, because I cannot remember." He pinches his brows together. "I think *you* can control any ouma fire, my prince. Tell it who you are, and it will become yours. Maybe if you control the ouma fire on this volcano, you can control the royal fire as well."

Nkella stares at him, his expression solid. He stands with his arms crossed in front of him. "I hope you will come to find out how you know this, Kaonī. This is new information, even for me."

Kaonī shrugs modestly. "Perhaps this knowledge comes with being a blacksmith," he says, rubbing his chin.

I flick my gaze to Nkella. "If you didn't grow up knowing the stories," I tell him, "it can't hurt to try it."

Nkella scoffs and walks to the far stream of ouma lava. He bends down, and sparks fly over him, so I keep my distance. I exchange a glance with Kaonī and shrug. Nkella laughs, shakes his head, and gets up to walk back.

"My ouma was that of the spirits of air, daí? It was my sister who controlled the volcanic ouma. The throne was never meant for me."

"You give up too easily." Kaonī climbs to his feet and shakes himself off, although the soot remains in place. "Any Ipani can be born with ouma fire. But every royal shall take control of it." He glances down at me. "Do you have your dagger?"

I pull it out of its sheath. "This?"

He reaches for it. I squint at him but let him have it. He hands it to Nkella, the hilt pointed toward him. Nkella gives it an inquisitive look and takes it.

"Why have you given me Soren's dagger?"

"I could be wrong, but you have nothing to lose. If it doesn't work, you will heal."

"Daí?"

"Try bleeding on the fire. Tell it you are from the Mikiroro bloodline."

I jump up. "Wait. He has to cut himself?"

"Kh." A smirk tugs at his lips as he tilts his head. "I can handle a little blood, my aovate, daí?"

A butterfly lets loose in my stomach.

Kaonī turns to me. "Fire responds to blood. The fire in Danū is like the fire in our veins."

"And if the devils ran Danū..." Nkella's voice trails.

I gasp. "You've always had fire inside of you..." It's in his eyes.

Nkella walks back to the stream of lava and bends down. I follow close behind him, ignoring the heat warming my face. He cuts his palm, and a few drops of his blood fall to the lava. We all stand there staring in silence.

His shoulders drop, and he turns toward us, ready to give up.

Something sparks suddenly, and I jump back. But then flames start to rise slowly, to my height, as if becoming an immense controlled flame. My eyes widen, and I move farther back, thinking the fire is going to pour out and cover us all. Nkella spins around and sees the wall of fire around us and pushes me behind him. But then, the flames turn dark, into a translucent black and purple color.

I gape at the change, slowly, the flames go from the fiery pits of orangey-red to a dark blackish-purple. The sky grows dark, but the air feels different. It's not the heat I'd expect, but a cooler, bearable warmth.

Kaonī erupts into a fit of laughter. Nkella's face is pale as he stares at the black flames along the lava pit. The streams have changed color as well. In the distance, we can still see the red lava. So it's only up here.

"You did it," Kaonī says. He chuckles with excitement.

Nkella breathes hard, his mouth slackening into a wide smile. He smacks Kaonī on the shoulder, and they both laugh. "How did you know?"

"I told you. I haven't a clue. But it worked."

"You are a genius."

Carefully watching my step, I walk around and stare at the dark flames. My muscles tense.

"Neyuro?" Nkella steps up beside me.

I stare at him. Concern fills his voice. I'm not jumping for joy. I'd promised King Mayi that I'd try to convince Nkella to take the throne. I'd had only agreed to try—I was in a hurry to get down to the Deep—but his request isn't something that's my decision to make. And Nkella never wanted to take up the throne.

But this...this confirms the king is right. Nkella needs to take the throne when we return. This proves that he can and he should. He can control the fires of Danū. The Empress will want him more than ever now, and she'll try to stop him taking the throne.

We're not even supposed to return to Cups; we're meant to head directly to the Tower to see her.

He's right about me making too many promises.

And what would that mean for us?

You are my aovate, Forever.

"Neyuro?" he says again.

I smile weakly at him. I don't know where I fit into any of that. I don't know how Ipani take up thrones or unite islands...or whatever. But one thing I do know. He's always going to be a pirate. And so am I.

Leading a kingdom? That range of responsibility is far beyond my comprehension. Not to mention, after all this, I do have to take Talia home. Somehow. I can't force her, but Philo showed me she doesn't want to be there anymore—

But...*it's his birthright.*

"Neyuro." He comes closer and grabs my arms. I shake my head. I'm spiraling.

"Sorry."

He lifts my chin and searches my eyes. "Where did you go?"

"Nowhere." I clear my throat. "So what now?"

"We wait."

Kaonī flips his hammer in the air. "We wait for the king to arrive. Then we set him free."

24

Nkella and I lie on the ground, staring at the black flames as we wait and hope this attracts his father.

"What if this attracts Tetalla?" I say out loud, then regret it. I don't want to bring up Death.

"It hasn't yet," Nkella responds. "But if it does. I'll be ready for him."

I study his features; he's stoic and confident, but there's so much he's not saying. He's taken control of his devil form. He's controlling ouma fire. And these things are suddenly coming easy to him. I wonder if he's concerned about it at all, or if it's just me. He'll make a formidable match against Death. I hope. I lean against him, and stare at my Fool's mark.

He lowers his head, and I lift my chin to meet his lips. His teeth brush gently on my skin, making my spine tingle.

"The only mark I care to have, roē yani, light of my flame, is the Lover's mark awaiting us once we return. We are bound as one."

"Do you think we haven't gotten it yet because we're still in the Deep?"

"My Devil mark is in reverse, and my Fool's mark has not changed," he says. "I do not think any marks will appear until we leave." He kisses me on the head.

I smile into his lips as he takes them again, kissing me deeply. Something in me stirs.

Kaonī comes back from walking around the flames and takes a seat beside Nkella. "What will you do when you get back?"

Nkella kisses my hand, a glint in his eye, and I sit back. "A war waits for us back home," Nkella says.

"Against Tetalla?"

"Yes. And then the Empress."

Kaonī grows quiet, and I glance at him.

"Do you remember the Empress?" I ask.

"Yes." He sighs. "I remember hating her. I know she's insane, daí? But I fear details have escaped me."

I rest my head on Nkella's arm as he strokes the inside of my forearm. It must be painful not to remember. I always made excuses for not going to see my mom because it would be painful to not be remembered by her, but I never stopped to wonder if she was in pain.

"Is it one war, or two separate ones?" Kaonī asks.

"It is us against them. Always." Nkella says. "Two wars for now, but really just one, daí?"

"It's never-ending."

"Yes."

"Kaonī?" I start. "How come your hammer has ouma? I thought ouma didn't work in the Deep."

"Ipani ouma does not. I forged it with Danū fire. That's why it comes back to me."

"How does the fire know to come back to you?"

"Hn." Nkella answers before he does. "It is more complicated than that. The steel you use is from Piupeki. It must have ouma steel." He tilts his head down to look at me. "Like the steel used to create the Ace of Swords. It's superior in strength because of the fire, but the steel will recognize its master. Piupeki and Danū were allies once. Before the siege." He turns to Kaonī. "How did you come across such metal here?"

"Loads of it has washed up on the shore."

"Hn." He passes a longing look to me, and I swallow. "Ouma does not work in the Deep for Ipani...but ouma of the land does."

"Elemental ouma," Kaonī adds.

Nkella whispers into my hair. "I think I figured out why we felt the power of aovate here."

"Why?"

"Perhaps because love is an element," he says. I consider that. It isn't true back home, but so much in Ipa is different. If love is an element here, it makes sense that it would seep into the Deep as well. "It would be a strange occurrence for this element to live in the Deep, daí? But we brought it."

I brush his cheek with my fingers, and he leans down and kisses them. My mind wanders to all the flowers and trees that thrive in the Aō. I never thought of them feeling love like we do. Love is an element that lives among the spirits of the Aō. I smile at the thought.

It's getting dark; the red hues have turned to a darkened maroon. A tremble on the ground makes us sit up.

I face Nkella. "Did you feel that?"

He holds a finger to his lips and stares out in the direction of the village.

Another tremble, but nothing in sight.

"Why would there be a minotaur?" It's not the undead, because we'd be feeling rumbles right below our feet, and it wouldn't take long for them to crawl up from the ground.

Another tremble; this one feels closer. We stand and ready ourselves. Had I known I wouldn't be able to use the Ace of Swords, I would have brought another weapon. Why am I never as prepared as I should be?

A burst of fire ignites the sky, the flame cascading down to the ashen ground. A devil soars through the sky, four horns curving back on his head. His pointed tail swings behind him. His eyes are set on us.

Two minotaurs run in pursuit of the devil. One wields a long chain that drags against the dirt, while the other bears a metal club. Nkura is either not bothered by them or too distracted by the black flames to care.

"What's the plan?" I ask.

"For now, nothing," Nkella says. "Let them come closer. And be ready." He turns and takes me by the arms, pulling me into him. My heart skips a beat at his sudden movements as he leans down and gives me a passionate kiss before he shifts.

Nkura flies over us, spreading his bat-torn wings, his gaze flicking between each of us before training on Nkella.

The minotaurs also come closer, but I leave them to Kaonī who's readying himself to throw his hammer. I keep my eyes glued to Nkura. I just need him to get a little closer so I can hold him in place with my webbing.

Nkura starts to descend, and the minotaurs pick up speed, now running toward him. Kaonī throws his hammer, and it hits one of them square in the chest, going through him. I steady myself as the minotaur plummets to the ground. His club flies out of reach. The hammer comes back around, and Kaonī grips it in his palm, readying himself to throw it at the other minotaur.

Nkura roars at Nkella as he swoops down. I throw my webbing, and it covers his torso. Nkura lets out a spit of flame, catching the web on fire. My eyes bulge as I watch it disintegrate. Nkura leaps at Nkella.

Nkella tackles him to the ground as they topple over each other in a fit of rough landings. More webbing spins out of my hands. It tangles him a bit but gets on Nkella as well. I wince. Out of the corner of my eye, I spot more minotaurs appearing, surrounding the fires, looking in.

Can they not cross royal fire?

The ground shakes violently. I drop down and grip the ash to keep from sliding into the lava, the fumes singing my arm. We don't need more dead rising. I squint through the gray dust as two large horns penetrate the ground. A giant minotaur's head emerges from the dust, but it's not actually emerging from underneath, it's...being built?

The minotaur is being formed from the ground.

Kaonī squares off with him, clutching his hammer. The rest of the minotaurs surround the fire. It seems they can't cross the flames.

I pick myself up and run to Nkella who's on the ground fighting his father. I send out another surge of webbing, keeping at it until he's completely covered in my thread. Nkella crawls from underneath him and pins Nkura onto his back.

Nkura groans as he struggles beneath Nkella's hold—hopefully, long enough for me to do this. I place my hand on his head, trying to ignore Kaonī and the minotaur fighting, trying to erase the noise and the stares from the minotaurs outside the fire. Nkella struggles to hold him down while I concentrate. I try making a connection. There's nothing but sound. An endless red sea fills his mind—years and years of pain and suffering. I can feel him fidgeting with Nkella as my hand struggles to stay on his head, but I have to keep searching. Somewhere in here is Nkella's father, and I'm going to find him.

The wind knocked from my lungs. I open my eyes and find myself catapulting in the air. I scream. Nkella jumps up, his wings taking flight as he calls my name and reaches for me, but Nkura lands a billowing blow and knocks him to his side.

I land hard on my back on the other side of the ouma fire, disoriented as I bounce on the hard surface. I dig my nails into the ground, trying to stop myself from plummeting off the cliff. Somehow, I grab onto a rock. My legs swing off the edge, and I swallow my scream as the ragged, rocky boulders pierce my vision from below. Quickly, I swing my left arm up and hold on for dear life, trying to fit my foot into any crevice I can find without looking down.

To the literal lava below.

I forget to breathe. A second ago I was searching someone's past, and a moment later I'm being flung in the air.

I can hear Nkella's screams as he tries to get to me, but he's still fighting Nkura at the same time.

A rock bounces down from above, and I wince as it skips past me.

Kaonī's head peeks over the edge of the cliff, and he reaches down to grab me.

His hand hangs a little too high; I'm too scared to let go, for fear I can't hold myself up with one arm. My knees tremble, as my foothold loosens.

"Give me your hand!"

I press my chest against the rock I'm holding onto, trying to push myself up. If I can just find something to lean my weight on, but it's hard at this angle. I feel myself slipping, and I shake my head furiously.

The rock I'm holding shifts, and a strangled cry escapes me. I'm going to fall. I'm going to die in the Deep.

It cracks again. this time I scream.

Kaonī screams. He leaps down and grabs my arm. "I've got you... *Diana*!"

Gooseflesh rips down my arms despite the heat from the lava below. He pulls me up with remarkable strength, and I quickly let go of the rock that plummets to the ground. He swings me up and I fall onto the flat surface.

I stare at him, my palms sweating. He pants as he stares back at me. Eyes wide. Confusion on his face.

"D-did you just call me Diana? Th-at was my mother's name."

25

Behind Kaonī, two more minotaurs rise from the ground.

Soot falls from his head as he reaches for his hammer. "Go help Nkella. I'll take care of the guards."

I shake away my bewilderment and confusion. For now.

Reluctantly, I rip my focus from Kaonī and run toward Nkella who's losing the fight against Nkura. Kaonī turns his attention to the minotaurs and starts fighting them off, but he won't be able to take them both on his own.

Aiming straight for Nkura's head this time, I thrust my webbing so hard, it almost blows me back off the mountain. It blinds him successfully. He backs away, grabbing the thick strands of webbing, which gives Nkella enough time to rush his stomach, pinning him on his back. I act fast, adding more webbing to his face, then holding down his arms.

I search again. Swimming into the depths of his mind, I call out his name. Then I see something, a man standing on top of a fortress. His gaze snaps to me, his eyes cruel and menacing. His lips curl into his sharp fangs, and he swiftly moves into an attack position, a sword over his head. I reel him in with webbing, even inside his mind.

His hand still grips the sword, but his eyes tell a different story as I dig deeper into his memories, drawing them out for him to see.

"Helāni berisi," he hisses.

"He's your son," I tell him. "You're fighting your son. You need to stop."

His eyes widen, and he drops the sword.

"Lies."

"No lies. Only the truth." I dig deeper to find Nkella as a baby, then I show him snippets of me and Nkella fighting Demitri, fighting the Empress, flashing images of the ship and the crew. Then I show him Ntaoru. His pupils are dilated when I draw back. "You have to trust me, okay?" My voice is shaky, but I try my hardest to stay calm.

I open my eyes, and a breath of relief escapes me. A man lies on the ground with his hands by his side. His wings begin to shrink into his back. Nkura takes a sharp breath as Nkella brushes the webbing off his face.

It worked.

I fall back on my shoulders. Nkella gives me an appreciative look and tries to pull his father up. Nkura has a distant and confused look on his face. He doesn't look at Nkella. His eyes are on the ground. He searches his surroundings. He's young. Only a few years older than Nkella is now. A clash of steel makes us both turn.

One minotaur lies face down on the ground, while Kaonī is going hand to hand with a minotaur's spear. In an attempt to keep the minotaur in place, I shoot webbing at him, giving Kaonī the chance to knock him out cold with his hammer, which causes the giant to land at our feet with a deep shaking thud.

Along the outside of the ring of ouma fire, the minotaurs duplicate, wielding their metal, trying to get inside. The fire has spread, trapping us in all directions. Flames reach the sky. It'll be hard to fly out of here without me or Kaonī being burned.

Nkura motions his hand toward the army of minotaurs outside the ouma fire. He pushes at the air, but nothing happens. Was he expecting his ouma to work? He lowers his hand and turns to Nkella.

"Son?" Nkura takes a few steps toward Nkella. "Nkella...my son?" His voice croaks as he gets closer and grabs his arms. Nkella stands still, his chin high. I can tell he's trying to stay strong. I've never seen him so shaken—and we've been through a lot. "Can you command it?" His voice is rushed, exasperated, but deep.

"Daí? Me? Command the guards?"

"Koj. The fire," he rasps.

Surprise washes over Nkella's face, and he shakes his head. His father extends his hand and pushes the flame. Nkella tries the same, but nothing happens.

Nkella and I exchange glares. I take out the World Card, and he purses his lips. "If he finds you, it will be worse, neyuro."

"You guys are going to have to fly us over the flames and out of here then," I tell him. Nkella stares at his dad. Nkura has been down here a lot longer than Nkella, trapped and lost in his devil form. Nkella's hesitation to flying us down is warranted. He fears losing his father again.

"I'll bring him back," I say.

"We have to fly down," Nkella agrees, staring at the cliff.

Kaonī is watching us—watching me. I glance at him but look away.

Diana.

That's something I'm going to have to deal with later.

Nkura nods, closes his eyes, and tries to shift back. Or at least, that's what I assume he's doing.

The swooshing sound of steel draws my eyes back to Kaonī. His eyes are wide and staring up at the sky. The hammer is back in his hand. We turn to see the serpent zooming toward us at a terrifying speed. I don't have a second to think. I have to kill it.

I take out the Ace of Swords Card, but before I reach in, the serpent sweeps down and sprays water over the ouma fire. The fire sizzles out, filling the air with steam. Then the serpent turns and snaps at Nkura. Nkella starts to shift, but his father grabs his arm.

"Do not shift. Not now."

Nkella's chest rises up and down as he stares between the serpent and the minotaurs that are ascending toward us at the same time.

"We will not outfly the serpent, daí?" Nkura yells.

He's right. The serpent is quicker, and this is his world. There's nowhere to go.

The serpent snaps at Nkura, but Kaonī rushes at him, and pushes his king out of the way. I cup my mouth, holding back a scream.

He throws the hammer at the serpent, but Apeiron dodges it, snapping his mouth at Kaonī. That was too close for comfort. I'm angling myself to strike at the serpent with the sword, when a minotaur appears right in front of Nkella.

Nkura shifts immediately, letting out a roar as he steps in front of his son, shoving him away. Nkella yells as the minotaur snatches a metal collar around Nkura's neck.

Nkura's wings burst out of his back and fly him backward, but the minotaur yanks at the chain and starts to run. The serpent has his eyes trained on the minotaur, then he ascends into the air and flies toward the village. Nkella runs after them, but he hasn't shifted.

I get why Nkura told him not to. If he shifted, he'd have been grabbed too. There's too many of them for us to fight. I run after Nkella and grab his arm. "We'll get him back."

He yells into the wind and falls to his knees. The minotaurs ignore us and march away in unison. We can no longer see Nkura as he disappears into the army of minotaurs and the sea of ash and dust rising as they march.

"They're headed back to the arena," Kaonī says behind us.

I place my hand on Nkella's shoulder. "We'll find him again. We have to strategize."

Nkella glances at me from the ground, his eyes filled with pain. I want to hug him. We had his father—we had him. But we failed. I hold his head to my stomach, and he clenches his fist over my shirt.

"What do we do now?" Kaonī asks. I stare at him. I need to confront him about what he called me. Later.

Nkella stands and wipes his face, his gaze searching the smoldering lava, no longer the dancing black flames. "He tried to control the fire."

"With practice, I'm sure you can too," I say to him.

His expression is stoic as he looks out toward the village where the minotaurs took Nkura. I take a deep, slow breath, and pull out the World Card. His gaze flicks back to me.

"We can get there quickly. I noticed that the serpent ignored us. If Apeiron was here for me or you, he would have tried to eat us, but he must have been searching for your dad. If we can relocate ourselves to where they took him, the serpent might be close by. We'll rescue your father, then go after the serpent."

A muscle in his jaw jumps. "There are too many guards. Too many dead. We need a plan."

"All we need to do is be inconspicuous," Kaonī says.

A smile slides on my face. "Now that I can do."

"The king won't be fighting without an opponent. They'll have locked him inside a dungeon. We need to get past the guard," Kaonī continues. "It will be too dark and dangerous to go now."

Nkella's face is grim, but he nods, letting out a sigh. "We'll rest and fight tomorrow." He looks at me. "I need to get you home, neyuro."

"*We* need to get home," I snap. "Don't give up hope." He reaches for me and brushes my arm gently.

"Yes. We. But we need to do it sooner, daí? You almost fell off the cliff earlier. I couldn't reach you..."

I swallow. "It wasn't your fault."

"And yet, the result would have been the same."

"Kaonī saved me." I glance over at his soot-covered face. He's staring at me with somber eyes. I get the sense I know what he's thinking about. "Nkella, what does Kaonī mean?"

"It means blacksmith," Nkella says. "It's fitting for him."

It's a nickname. My heart skips a beat.

I pull away from Nkella and walk to face Kaonī. Nkella's brows furrow, but he lets me go.

"You called me something earlier. Do you remember?"

He nods. The filth is making his face unrecognizable under the darkening red sky.

"Did you call me...Diana?"

"Diana," he whispers, his gaze growing distant.

"Daí?" Nkella steps up close to me.

I glance at him. "Is Diana a common name in Ipa...among Greek people?"

"I haven't heard of it," Nkella whispers back.

I take out my necklace, and Kaonī's eyes widen. He reaches for it, then stops midway to look at me, asking a silent question. I step forward and let him take it in his hands.

"This looks...so familiar."

"Who was Diana to you?" I ask.

"Diana..." He drops my necklace and looks away again. She was my aovate."

My pulse quickens, and tears brim in my eyes.

Kaonī stares at me, confusion all over his face. "Did you say...she's your mother?"

"Was."

His eyes widen, and I walk up to him. "May I?"

"She can bring your memories back, Kaonī," Nkella tells him. "I think you should let her."

Kaonī relaxes his shoulders and closes his eyes. I gently touch the sides of his temples, and dive into his past.

My mother gets up from where they were sleeping and sneaks away. I have the strongest urge to follow her, but I don't. I'm in his memory, not hers. When she leaves, Arcana soldiers emerge all around and grab him. Minutes later, he's thrown into a giant hole and buried alive.

His terrified screams echo in his memory.

She didn't even know he was gone.

It must have been when she went to make the deal with the Empress and was poisoned. This whole thing was orchestrated by her.

My mother was trying to save me—her unborn baby—and was poisoned with itachi instead. And my father was killed.

I go farther into his memories, but take a step back, letting them flood him. I don't want to witness everything. They happen so fast. I get whiffs of the sea breeze, and glimpses of them on the pink sandy beaches of Oleanu.

Then I pull away. I let go of him, my breath shaken and tears streaming down my cheeks.

"Sehu," he says. "My name is Sehu."

I nod and wipe the wetness from my cheeks.

He stares at me. "You... You're..."

I nod.

"Diana was with child, but..."

"She went back to my land, but the itachi took away her memory."

"Oh, Soren," Sehu says. He reaches for me but holds back. "You're my daughter..." His voice cracks. "And I wasn't there for you. All this time..." The dirt and grease is slowly disappearing from his face, hair, and arms. His face is beginning to resemble the face I'd seen in memories of him. He has an angular face with round cheeks and brown eyes. I can't believe I hadn't at least recognized his eyes.

"You look like her," he says.

I can't speak. I clench the bottom of my shirt in my fist and glance at Nkella who's looking at me, his eyes full of concern.

"Soren, I—" Sehu reaches for me again, and this time I hug him. He wraps his arms tightly around me, and I let myself cry in his arms. "I'm so sorry," he says into my hair.

"You didn't do anything wrong," I say into his arm. "It wasn't your fault."

"How did you end up in Ipa?" He pulls away.

A silent chuckle escapes my throat. "It's a long story."

"She is the Past Fate descendant." Nkella answers for me. "I believe —now—that she was fated to come."

"And you two found each other." He addresses Nkella. "She has to leave the Deep." His voice quickens. "You know this. She cannot stay here. If she dies here, she will be trapped forever."

"Try telling that to your daughter, daí? She makes her own choices."

Sehu sighs. "On a mission for justice. Just like your mother."

"Not exactly," I say. "I never cared that much about justice, but I did mess things up, so I'm here to take him back so we can fix it." I point to Nkella, smiling.

"Hn." Nkella looks at me, but he knows it was more that brought me to him.

Silence engulfs the space as Sehu and I stare at each other, disbelief washing over us. How strange that the blacksmith who happened to join us on our mission ends up being my father? I touch my Wheel of Fortune mark. Goosebumps ripple up my arm.

A brisk memory of walking on the beach with the Hermit resurfaces in my mind.

Don't expect reality to be a dead end. Expect the unexpected.

Did he know that I would come down here and meet my father?

Things out of my control are still governing my fate. But this one was good.

"Did your mother die in your land?" Sehu's voice interrupts my thoughts.

I nod. He wouldn't be able to find her here.

He clears his throat. "This was a lot to take in. It's been a long day."

Nkella takes his seat on the ground, and I follow suit, sitting next to him. "Let's make camp here and rest." Spirits sway in the distance. "It would be foolish to use Helāni magic now. We can wait until morning."

26

I'd never thought the dead needed their rest, but no one needs it more than the tortured souls of the Deep.

We sit awake, staring at the dark flames of a bonfire while Nkella practices controlling it. Sehu stares at the flickering purple lights, deep in thought. And I think about everything I've done to bring me to this moment, to be in this other dimensional version of hell, to find the man that lives in my dreams. *That* I could bring myself to understand. But meeting my biological father? Never in a million years would I have ever thought that possible.

Even after knowing this is the place of trapped spirits, even after witnessing ouma—real magic—and drakons, I still find myself in awe of this place. Despite all I've lost, and the dangers we've faced, and are about to face, I couldn't feel luckier.

The distant moans of the tortured souls serenade the night, not for being soothing, but for becoming familiar.

None of us get any sleep. I'm not sure Sehu actually can fall asleep. Nkella and I could use the rest, but neither of us can let ourselves drift away with the impending feeling of doom that can befall on us at any moment. Not to mention I'd rather not have Tetalla pay me a visit in my sleep tonight.

Although, if Sehu wasn't here, I'm sure we'd be finding different ways to pass the time.

There's so much I want to ask Sehu. We talked a little, but I don't know, I never thought I'd be speaking to my biological father. I don't even know where to start.

"Soren?" Sehu's voice is soft as he breaks the silence, yet it still startles me. "Can I ask you a question?"

"Of course."

He glances at Nkella who's still trying to command the fire with his hands, as his father tried to do. Sehu moves closer to me. "This is a hard question for me to ask."

I stay quiet, but I can't help staring at his features—his eyes, his skin—trying to find any resemblance to me. He has light Ipani stripes that only reach his clavicle. His hair is short and curly, but his lips are like mine. I always wondered why my mom's lips were thinner and I looked nothing like my dad. My cheekbones are his too.

"You said your mother lost her mind because of the itachi. It must have killed her when you were young."

Sitting up, I hold my knees to my chest. "She passed away last year." I bite my lower lip. "She was sent somewhere she could be looked after my whole life." St. Germain's Hospital.

His frown deepens. After a few moments he asks, "Who raised you, Soren?"

"It's complicated."

"Why?"

"Because...my dad—my mother's husband who I always thought was my father..." Sehu glances away. His eyes squeeze shut, and my gut clenches.

Nkella has stopped trying to command the flame, and I can feel his gaze.

"It's okay," Sehu looks back at me. "I want to hear this."

I lick my lips. "He gave me up. Sent me to live at a group home, which is like an orphanage." I don't know if they have orphanages in Ipa, but it's the only comparison I could think of.

"You lived as an orphan," he mutters, wincing. "I am so sorry, Soren."

"It wasn't your fault. You don't have to keep apologizing. I don't fault you for anything."

"I should have known Diana would try to make a deal with the Empress. I should have been awake to stop her. I should have fought harder when the Arcana showed up—" He takes a sharp breath and looks away.

I shrug. "It's the past. There's nothing we can do about it now."

He nods. "I know," he utters under his breath. "Tell me about you. Do you have ouma?"

I shake my head. "Did you? Or..." were you bound is what I wanted to ask.

"My ouma was with water. I could control the waves. If I wanted, I could make a person drown on dry land by moving the water in their body to their head. But I would never do that." I'm staring at him wide-eyed. This is the first time I've heard about ouma from someone so close to my blood. Something I might have had if I had been raised with the Aō. "I was never bound by the Empress. I hid."

"Do you miss it?"

"Yes, but only since remembering who I was. Before, I didn't remember." He stares at me. "But you are the Past Fate descendant, like your mother, daí? I saw your Helāni magic."

I chuckle. "Yeah, that came as a surprise to me too." I point at the fire and shoot my webbing over it. It catches flame instantly. "That, and seeing people's memories, and making them experience them is about all I can do."

"That's more than your mother was able to do."

I start fidgeting with the threads on my sleeves. "Tell me about her."

"She was bold. And brave. Like you."

Nkella smiles. I see him from the corner of my eye, and a butterfly lets loose in my stomach. Sehu continues, but he looks at Nkella now.

"She helped save you from the Empress. It took me a little bit, but I also know who you are." He looks at me. "I was raised in Danū."

"The king of Oleanu told me you were the late king's son..."

Sehu nods and looks at my necklace. "The Danū royal family took me in...but then the island was besieged and terrible things happened." He glances at Nkella somberly. His parents were murdered, and Nkella was kidnapped. "Take care of each other. No matter how terrible the world becomes, no matter how it turns on you. Always have each other."

"Always," Nkella says.

"After we awaken your father, please, take her out of here, my prince. The fate of the world depends on you, Soren. It depends on both of you."

Nkella and I glance at each other.

"I will do everything in my power to bring her safely home, Sehu. You have my word."

Sehu chuckles. "If she is anything like Diana, that won't be enough. But to try is all I ask."

I don't say anything. I wish I had known my mother the way he remembers her. Instead, I change the subject. "Do you think I will ever develop ouma like you?" I don't know why I ask; I already know the answer. Demitri told me that because I'm half human, I won't develop ouma if I haven't already.

Sehu laughs. "You didn't grow up with the Aō, but it could still be possible." My brows perk up. He rubs his chin. "It might require you to *lean into* the Aō. Learning with it, daí? It might take you sacrificing one power for the other as well. It's hard to tell."

Sacrifice my power for ouma? "That isn't something I'd considered."

"The Aō accepts any magic it can take into itself. But there is still a great divide between the two. It is not like the daekente"—he nods at Nkella—"or the mer-Ipani who are born with the ability to take a different shape. Helāni is from another world entirely, so there is still confusion over which can be dominant in a person. But this is my speculation, daí? Perhaps you can have both."

"And be ultra powerful." I laugh.

"Kh."

I stare at Nkella and laugh harder. Nkella's face grows serious. "You knew about daekente? No one I grew up with knew about it."

"Only because I knew your father. They tried to keep it secret from the Empress since before you were born; it's been a secret for generations. Sometimes it doesn't develop at all."

"I don't think my sister has it. I always thought it was a Helāni curse."

"Apparently, so did the Empress," I say.

Sehu quirks a brow. "I'm not so sure."

"Daí?"

"I don't think the devils hid it when the Helāni first arrived. Something scared them, and it was not only ouma."

I gasp. "You think she took credit for it?"

"To suppress it even further? Yes," Sehu says. "And also, to keep Ipani down."

A flash of crimson ignites Nkella's eyes. "When we go back to the surface, I will put an end to her. It will be a new Ipa when I'm finished with the Tower.

Sehu frowns. "You're both on the same hopeless mission I started with Diana. Be careful."

"This time, it will be different," Nkella says. "This time I am no longer afraid of who I might become, for I am in control of it."

The arena is a quiet contrast to my previous visit. There's no roaring audience or hoard of dead. I inhale a long breath as I gaze on the towering sandstone walls of the Colosseum-like building with Greek columns adorning the exterior. A minotaur stands in front of tall wooden doors with iron handles. He wears a bronze breastplate and holds a silver ax. "Why is it so quiet?"

"They only have one devil captured, so no fights," Sehu whispers back.

I suppose that means Nkella and his father are the only two devils in the Deep. Where are the rest of them?

We stealthily maneuver to a dead black palm tree near the far side of the stadium and out of sight from the entrance. Another minotaur turns the corner and stares out toward the sand dunes.

"They guards make their rounds every few minutes," Sehu whispers to us. "Keep an eye on them."

We watch quietly as the minotaur looks both ways before walking back.

"Now," Sehu says.

We run beside the wall to the next dead shrub and lay low.

"There's an entrance to the caves below the arena. I'm sure of it. It's where they would keep the fighters," he mutters as though trying to make sense of the design.

A minotaur emerges from the bottom of the wall, and I squint. I tap on Sehu's shoulder and point to it. "Over there. Is that minotaur coming from the sand or from a hole next to the wall?"

He squints, and his lips form a smile as the minotaur turns and descends what I assume is a set of stairs. "I believe it's a grotto. That must be the entrance."

I return the smile. "How do we get past the guard?"

Nkella peers intently at his hand, and his fist shifts into his devil shape—black pointy nails with metal armor along his knuckles.

I shake my head and bring his hand down. "You'll cause too much attention if you shift, I might as well use the World Card and attract all the undead.

"Koj, only my fist. Enough to knock him on his head."

"And I can distract him," Sehu says. "As soon as I do, get down to the grotto, Soren. It is more important for you to reach Nkura, than us."

I gulp. He's right. They can't bring him back to himself without me.

"But stay away from the shadows. There will be more guards there."

I nod and take a deep breath, bracing myself. There's a black palm halfway. While the minotaur is distracted, I can run to it and take cover until I get a chance to slide into the grotto. A few minutes pass, and a minotaur walks back up. This one's holding a club.

Sehu nods at us and walks toward the minotaur, waving his arms in the air and calling out to him in Ipani. The minotaur clutches his club, his gaze intent on Sehu. I prepare to run behind the dead black palm, but Nkella grabs my arm and tugs me to him. A breath escapes me, and he takes my face and kisses me deeply.

"Be careful, daí?"

I give him a sheepish grin. "We've handled worse."

He squeezes my hand and gives me a longing look before letting go. I make a dash for the palm tree. Sehu is trying to talk his way out of a fight, explaining how he's looking for an old village that used to be here. I smile; it's what I would have done. Nkella storms up to the minotaur, his fist the only part of him that's shifted. The minotaur doesn't even see him coming. My eyes widen as Nkella's wings spread open and he leaps toward the minotaur's face.

Now's my chance.

I sprint to the grotto, afraid the minotaur will spot me or accidentally stomp on me. The minotaur gets struck so hard, he crashes toward me. In a split-second decision, I slide past him, his body flying right over my arm and crashing against a metal gate. I almost fly down the sandstone steps.

I'm panting hard, and I dart a look at Nkella. Holy hell, he hit him hard. It doesn't matter that the minotaurs are fifteen feet tall and muscular. They're still no match for a devil.

Regaining my balance, I descend the stairway and keep my head low to avoid being seen by any guards that might walk by. I wait until Nkella and Sehu emerge behind me, and I exhale. Nkella holds a finger to his mouth as he walks past me and leads us to a narrow and steep walkway.

Metal gates block this entrance. The marching footsteps of another minotaur guarding the tunnel makes us pause. His back is turned to us, but it's only a matter of seconds before he turns around.

"What do we do?" I ask.

Nkella ushers us to take cover in the shadows against the wall while he inspects the lock. A roar comes from inside, and Nkella snaps his gaze to the tunnel. "My father is here." He turns to Sehu. "You were right."

"Then there's only one thing left to do," I say. I pull out the Ace of Swords. "I'm only going to use the World Card once. So when the guard turns around, I'm opening the gate and going in."

Nkella's eyes widen, but before he can protest, I take his face and kiss him.

"Trust me," I breathe into his lips. His eyes soften, and I know he really does trust me now more than ever. "Stay close behind me, because when I get the World Card ready, I'm shoving your father and taking all of us through the portal. The question is, where do we go? The moment I do this, not only will the dead be after us, so will the serpent."

"To the ship," Nkella says.

I nod. "Back to the ship."

The longsword shines its purple sheen as I pull it from its tether and stuff the card safely away.

The minotaur turns around and marches to his other post. I tap on the steel, and it rings a clashing echo down the dark tunnel. The minotaur pauses before turning back around and making a full run toward us.

I wait. Nkella yells at me, but I hold him back. I've done this more times than I can count, catching guards off guard inside fighting rings with the crew.

Just a little closer.

Dust rises around the minotaur as he sprints.

When I strike down on the lock, it opens immediately. The minotaur fixes its sight on me as he advances, and I start to run backward, making him chase me just far enough for me to duck and roll, positioning the sword under his armor as he falls over my head. He lands over me with a deafening thud, and a pool of blood forms on the ground underneath me. It's too dark to see the minotaur's face, but I don't take a chance and slam the sword into him two more times. His legs shake.

Sehu gasps behind me. I turn just in time to see the gleam in Nkella's eyes as he reaches down and takes the minotaur's head in his arms. The large horns scrape against the wall. In one tight squeeze, a crunch and a crack separates the minotaur's head from his body.

I bolt through the tunnel to find Nkura; sconces high up on the wall light my path. Nkella and Sehu follow close behind me. Dark open cells slow me down. I'm afraid a minotaur will step out of them. When I hear another roar, I quicken my step. Nkella glides past me and stops at the only closed cell. This door doesn't have a handle. Nkella shifts his arm to punch through the metal door. I jump back and exchange a glance with Sehu.

We search the tunnel for signs of more minotaurs when the ground rumbles. "They're coming," I say.

Nkella breaks through, a red light emanating from the inside as two minotaurs rush toward us. I whip out the World Card, already envisioning the ship and opening the portal as we all hold onto each other. Nkura grimaces as I grab his shoulders. It doesn't matter whether he remembers me or not. The portal opens, and just as we jump inside, a minotaur grabs my hair, pulling my neck back. I scream.

Nkella instantly shifts to his devil form, but I reach for him to keep him from doing anything stupid.

The portal closes, and the minotaur's hand falls flat on the ship's hardwood floor. Sehu reaches down and grabs it, wincing as he chucks it overboard. It lands with a splash.

"That was too close for comfort," I say. The ship sways in the still waters, crunching the stones of the rocky shoreline.

"How long until they find us?" Sehu pants. I shake my head but return to Nkura.

He winces as I touch his temples, but relaxes his shoulders, allowing me into his memories. I feel a tug as I find the most recent memory of us on the volcano. He grabs onto my presence, and I reel him up to the surface. His shift back to Ipani form is smoother this time, so I let go of him.

He blinks at me, and then looks around.

"We're safe for now, Father." Nkella walks up to him, and Nkura takes his son by the arm.

"Son." He pulls him closer and hugs him. "Let me look at you." He pulls away, and I can see the wetness in both their eyes. Nkura glances at me. "Engi."

I nod, speechless, as I stare at him. He has dark curly hair like Nkella, only shorter. He has a square jaw. His cheekbones are a bit rounder. "You'll want to practice shifting and taking control of your emotions so they can't trap you again."

"Father," Nkella says. "I don't think you're dead." His voice shakes. "We...were preserved by..."

"The curse," Nkura finishes.

Nkella shakes his head. "There's no curse. This is who we are."

Nkura raises his brows and smiles. "Yes, this is true."

"You knew?"

Nkura walks to the railing and leans against it, looking out toward the reddish hues of the sea. "Even though the Empress did not create us, some of us consider it a curse."

Nkella grows silent.

He grabs Nkella's shoulder and squeezes. "But it is also our pride."

"Come back with me," Nkella tells him.

Nkura smiles weakly, and a sigh escapes his lips. "I will not leave your mother. She's here somewhere, and I must find her."

Nkella purses his lips, then he nods in understanding.

"My son. Words cannot express how sorry I am for the hard life you must have endured. But I am beyond words at the man you have become." He looks at me, and reaches for my hand. I take it. "Take care of each other always. But you must leave now. Leave before you are fated to remain in the Deep for eternity." He looks back at Nkella, dropping my hand and placing it on Nkella's shoulder. "I will see you again. But not for a millennia, daí? Live long lives. Both of you."

A millennia.

I exchange a glance with Sehu, who stares at me. I've been feeling awkward. Nkella and I have had so much in common, and I hadn't even realized it. Here we both are, having found our fathers. And I've barely spoken a word to mine since last night. I walk over to him as Nkella and his father talk.

"There's still so much I want to ask you," I say.

"And we're running out of time. But I agree with my king." He looks toward Nkura. "I'll help you kill the serpent, but then you both must leave this place."

Nkura gapes at us. *"Kill the serpent?"*

The familiar cracking of bones sends a shiver down my spine. I glance toward the sound and walk over to the rail overlooking the black rocky shoreline in the red Danū sands. We all grow quiet, and Nkella and I glance at each other.

A skeletal hand reaches up out from the sand.

"Pull up the anchor," Nkella commands. He heads for the wheel.

A high-pitched squeal makes us turn. The serpent is swooshing down from the sky, headed straight for us.

27

I push Nkura out of the serpent's way just as Apeiron snaps his mouth shut, missing me by an inch. I swing my sword, grazing his scales, and his body coils back. He hisses at the blade; he must know this is powered with magic that can kill him.

The ship starts to reverse, and I steal a glance at Nkella who's doing the steering. Nkura and Sehu drop the anchor onto the deck, and I jump up on the rail, ready to take another swing at the serpent. Apeiron arches his giant head in attack position, ready to dodge me to strike Nkura.

"Nkura, get below deck!" I call to him. Sehu starts to push him that direction, but Nkura stands his ground.

"I will not leave you alone to fight," he says to all of us.

"You're not," I tell him. "We have a plan."

"No! He's here for you, my king." Sehu urges him to go down. Looking over his shoulder, he whispers to me. "What plan?"

I shrug. "Don't know yet." Sehu's eyes widen at me.

"Then let us flee!" Nkura shouts.

"Killing the serpent will release the tortured! And we're not letting him take you!"

Nkura pulls away from Sehu's grip. "It isn't worth it. Save yourselves."

"I can't do that," I say.

His gaze is intent on me, and then Nkella. "Then I must stay and fight."

He's just as hardheaded as Nkella.

Sehu and I exchange a worried glare, and I look toward Nkella who's let go of the wheel to raise a sail.

Apeiron whips his tail, trying to slink around me, but I slice at his neck. He squeals in pain, then recoils back in the air, creating distance between us.

A skeleton reaches for us from the branch of a dead tree. Sehu whacks it with his hammer as the ship pulls away.

"Apeiron's advantage is that he can fly," I say.

"I will keep him from leaving." Nkura shifts into devil form, and I jump back. Can he control it? Nkura's eyes glow crimson, and at first, he lets out an anguished yell, attracting the serpent.

"This is a bad idea," I point my sword toward Apeiron. "What's to keep the serpent from attacking him?"

Nkella shouts in our direction, and I dart my gaze to him. His eyes are blazing, wings are spread as he stares at his dad taking on Apeiron. "What is he doing?" he bellows.

"Helping," Sehu runs to grab the unraveling rope and set the sail. Nkella's hands are on the wheel as we continue to drift away from Danū.

Nkura jerks back in the air as Apeiron attacks him, missing him by a hair. My heart is in my throat as I aim my sword. I climb onto the rail, knowing I don't have the height or the balance to reach the serpent. Fire surges out of Nkura's mouth, and I almost lose my balance. I'd forgotten they could do that. The serpent strikes through the fire, and coils around Nkura.

No! I jump and land on the floorboards with the blade outstretched toward Apeiron, managing to slice his belly. Apeiron tightens his grip around Nkura and flies higher. I sprint up the steps where Nkella is and grab the wheel, shoving him to the side. "Your bow and arrows are in the room!"

Nkella's expression is unreadable, but I know he's afraid. Still, his gaze is determined as he moves away from me and runs inside the captain's quarters. A second later he flies out in his devil form, his bow and quiver in position. He ignites the tip of an arrow with his ouma fire and loosens it into the serpent.

This time, Apeiron catches flame, and releases his grip on Nkura. He plummets down to the ship but catches himself mid fall with his wings outspread.

Caught ablaze, the serpent shakes viciously. There's nothing that says ouma fire won't kill it, but from what I hear, only the sword can do that. If it were royal fire, however, that might do the trick. Apeiron dives into the red waters, and the entire ship jerks as steam rises from below.

Spinning the wheel to the left, we tilt too far to the side as I struggle to keep us steady. Apeiron's head rises, the fire gone out as he hits the ship. I lose my footing and grab the rail, my sword slipping from my grasp. Apeiron's tail whips at the ship, tilting the vessel sideways. I fall against the rail as water splashes over my head, plastering my hair against my skin.

Wiping the water from my eyes, I reach for the Ace of Swords on the hardwood floor. As I grab the hilt, a black boot steps on the blade and kicks it away. I arch my neck to stare at the large skeleton with dark, empty eye sockets glaring down at me. I gasp and spring to my feet.

An ignited arrow flies past me and lands in one of the eye sockets, the skeleton topples backward, and I kick it off the ship. All around us, the dead are rising from the waters, and the serpent is looming above, its eyes fixed on Nkella's father.

I grab the sword and walk back against his dad, shielding him from the serpent. "Come on, no-feet. It's now or never."

At once, the dead start to climb aboard. They're after me, but I'm not letting myself be taken before killing the serpent. If I don't kill him, he'll always be after Nkura.

Nkella and his father have shifted and are fighting the dead. Sehu is wielding his hammer. I have the sword trained on the serpent.

Apeiron ignores me and strikes at Nkura who's fighting the dead behind me. I strike at his neck, and blood spurts out, causing him to shriek in pain and whip toward me. He recoils, about to strike, but I hold my ground, not wanting him to get away. He snaps at me, and I swing my sword again, zooming my vision into him. Locking eyes and ignoring the fight around me. The dead come at me, but I dodge their grasps like I'm dancing with the snake.

Apeiron strikes at me, and I take a jumping slice forward, catching his face. He strikes me hard, this time grabbing me in his mouth. His teeth just grazing my body as I push at them. I'm trembling. My heart is lodged in my throat. There's no time to think.

The sword is still in my hand, but I'm losing my grip as Apeiron falls into the water with me in his mouth. I scream. I hear Nkella's agonizing cry as he reaches the rail, watching me plummet from the ship.

Apeiron drags me under, and the sword falls out of my hand as I struggle to regain my grip. I'm trying to pry his mouth open—to force him to release me. I gasp for air as I push at one of his fangs, kicking and screaming. He lets me go, only to wrap his body around mine, squeezing tight as he drags me deeper into the red waters of the Deep. It's cloudy down here, murky from the dead, skin, and blood. All the horrors of this world are trapped in the waters.

And now I'm going to die in them.

I failed.

The serpent won.

I guess the only saving grace is that Tetalla won't e able to use my powers. But he'll still have me in his castle. Dead and tortured.

My chest aches to burst open as water threatens to fill my lungs and my vision blurs. I keep pushing at his body, but it doesn't do any good.

The sword finds its way into my hand. My eyes blink open and a hand is gripped over mine. Long black hair covers the mysterious face, and he tightens his grip, twisting my hand, but I take the lead and do the rest. With all the strength I can muster, I twist the sword and plunge the blade into the serpent's body.

As Apeiron releases his hold, I stab him again, and twist the sword deeper into him. He moves furiously, trying to slither away, but I take another stab at him. Apeiron stops fighting and goes limp. His blood pools all around me. I'm on my last breath, so I have to let go and try to reach the surface.

The mystery man that had helped, puts his arms around my waist and pushes me up to the surface.

Our heads poke above water, and my eyes widen in disbelief. Long black hair is plastered against his skin. Black eyeliner runs down his face.

"AJ?"

AJ smiles. "Hey, Soren."

My throat struggles to swallow my heart. I stare at my best friend, whose bloodstained shirt starts to disappear. For a moment, the world feels fine again. Nkella and his father are alive. My father is here with me. And AJ is standing in front of me. A hot tear runs down my face, and I let him hug me tight.

"Let's get you back on the *Gambit*," AJ whispers into my hair. My legs are wobbly as I grab the ladder, and AJ helps me up. The air feels still.

All around us, the dead seem to have quieted. At first, I think it worked. I killed the serpent. The tortured are released. But then, I hear it.

The moans of the tortured fill the air, only they're growing fainter. They're moving farther away. All around us, the dead are taking their eyes off us. They're...leaving.

Movement of a small furry creature by Nkella's feet distracts me. Sapphire stares at me with her wide blue eyes. My lips part as I look from her to AJ who smiles down at her. Then she pops away again.

Nkella locks eyes with me as he slices the head off a bare skeleton that slams to the ground. His shoulders drop and relief washes over him. Nkura and Sehu shove the remaining bones off the ship.

Nkella stands before AJ, and I can't help the shuddering breaths wanting to come out of me. I grab onto my chest.

"Hi, Captain."

A reaper's screech pierces my ears.

This snaps me into motion. "The serpent's dead. It's time to go." Pulling out the World Card, I walk over to the wheel with AJ by my side. "They'll find us soon, but let's get out of here first." Glancing at the map, I aim the World Card in front of the ship. "To Ahan Doro."

We drop anchor by a grove of dead trees on the red sands opposite where we were. It won't be long until the reapers find me again, but this will give us enough time to say our goodbyes and for me and Nkella to drink from the Ace of Cups.

So far, the dead have left us alone, but the important ones who are still on this ship don't appear to have changed, from what I can tell. I'm not sure what we were expecting after I killed the serpent.

Did it work?

I step away from the wheel and lock eyes with Nkella who is standing at the foot of the steps. He'd been watching me steer his ship, passion in his eyes. *Later*, they tell me. I smirk at him and walk on down.

AJ stands by a cannon.

"Are you in any pain?" I ask him.

"Not physically."

"What does this mean?" I look at Sehu. "What did killing the serpent accomplish?"

"My spirit is whole. I can feel it," Sehu responds. "But I'm still here. There are parts of me that hurt."

"Yeah," AJ rubs his chest, looking down at his body, "My spirit doesn't feel split in two, like it did before. I think the pain is...normal. Emotional. I think you did it, Soren. We're released from the painful torture of being split in two, but...we're still tethered here."

Something is wrong. This should have worked. My brows furrow, and I start to pace. "Why did the dead stop fighting us? Where did they go?" My pulse quickens. The serpent guards the Deep. *Kill the serpent, release the spirits.* It made sense, what went wrong? "You shouldn't be stuck down here."

"I don't want to leave, Soren." AJ takes a few steps toward me. "Whatever *leaving* means for us, I don't want it. I'll make this my home."

I turn to Sehu and Nkura. "Can't he come back with us?"

Nkura shakes his head. "The dead cannot return. If they do, they go mad."

Memories of various spirits in the haunted forests and at sea flood me at once. An image of Soanalo resurfaces. Blinking in and out. Not making sense. Speaking in riddles. How much of that was eternal torment versus the wrath of an angry spirit?

I don't want that for AJ. I clench my chest with my fist, and he wraps his arms around me. A sob escapes my throat, and I cry into his shoulder. He holds me tight, and we stay like this for a little while longer.

"I tried to save you. I'm so sorry, AJ."

"Is Lāri okay?"

I shake my head. "No."

He pulls away from me. "Is she—"

"No, I mean she's fine. But she's not okay without you."

"Watch out for her for me, will you? She has the tendency to make rash decisions."

"I will."

"And Soren, I'm not done," he whispers. "I want to fight against the Empress. Pirates against the Tower." He leans his forehead against mine. "I'm sorry I died."

Nkella takes AJ by the shoulders. "You will always be a part of this crew. Daí?" AJ looks up at him. "Always."

AJ nods.

"I'm not giving up," I say. "There's gotta be a way to bring you back." My voice rises. "I'm going to find it, AJ. I will."

"Soren..." Nkella warns. I whip to face him.

"Don't. I can at least try. Let me at least try."

AJ pulls me in for another hug. "Make sure to give that hungry bunny of yours a nice juicy steak for me, for finding me."

I chuckle. "You bet I will." I squeeze him tighter. "I wanted to find Kae's wife, AJ." I whisper into his shoulder. "But I couldn't."

"I'll search for her," he says.

"And Soanalo," I say.

"Yes. Her too. Take care of yourself, Captain," he tells me, then he glances up at Nkella. "Both of you."

Regretfully, I let go of AJ. Nkella joins me to speak with Nkura.

"I'm sorry, Nkura," I say, "for not releasing the souls. I failed."

"Releasing my son from his binds to this world is enough. You have done us a great service," he tells me. "And when I find his mother, I will tell her of you."

I smile at him.

Nkella clears his throat. "This is it then."

"It is, my son. You must go."

"Before they come back for you," Sehu says to me, and I face him.

I swallow hard. "I just found you. There's so much I still want to ask you. I can't believe I have to leave you like this, here...in this place."

Sehu takes my hand. "You have your mother's spirit."

A tear runs down my cheek.

"Don't worry about us. Giving me back my memories has helped me immensely. I don't feel torture, daí? I feel at peace knowing you live."

A sob escapes my throat, and I shut my eyes.

"And don't worry about me either, my son," Nkura says. "I may choose to stay with your mother, but know that the Deep will be a safer place with me awake."

I open my eyes and stare at Nkura.

"I will watch over the dead of Danū. Help who I can. Put an end to the guards."

"You're going to take care of the underworld?" I ask.

"I will. That is the path I have chosen."

A reaper screeches from the distance.

"You need to go. Now," Sehu says.

I nod rapidly and give AJ another hug as Nkella drops the gangway.

We say our goodbyes one last time, and just before AJ leaves, he turns to me. "Tell Lāri I will always love her."

"I will."

28

After the gangway goes up, Nkella sails us out to the open waters, away from Danū. I walk over to where I've safely hidden the Ace of Cups Card. Nkella follows me inside just as I take out the canteen of water. He sits down on the bed beside me and watches as I pull the cup out from the card, a purple sheen flaring over it.

"Are you ready?" I ask.

A whisper of a smile plays on his lips, his eyes intent on me. "To be with you forever? I can't wait any longer."

My cheeks warm, and I glance down. His fingers run down my arms, trailing goosebumps in his wake. He takes my hands.

"You fought for me. You fought for my family and released my father. You never gave up. I will forever be in your debt, my aovate."

I caress his cheek. "No debt, Nkella. It's what we do for each other."

He closes his eyes, leaning into my touch.

"I almost can't believe I pulled it off." I huff a laugh. "Coming to a dimension of the afterlife, finding you, bringing you back...it all feels so surreal. Like a dream that I'm about to wake up from."

He lifts my hand and kisses it. "Do not doubt yourself, roé yani." Light of his flame. "You did it."

I chew on my cheek. "Not everything. I promised to help you release the tortured."

"You did help. You killed the serpent. My father and Sehu will take care of the spirits in the Deep. Until we kill the Empress, the tortured will not truly be released."

I nod.

"Let's leave this place." He takes the canteen and opens it, and I let go of him to fill the cup to the brim.

I take the first sip, and then he does. Cold, fresh water soothes the lining of my throat, and I can feel it revitalizing me from my chest all the way into my stomach.

When I open my eyes, Nkella is licking his lips. Neither of us have had anything to eat or drink in too long; he's gone much longer than me.

Nothing happens at first. But I'm sure the hunger and headache will catch up to me once the ship leaves the Deep. Next, I need to pour the remainder into the bottle by the wheel. Outside the window, the red hues of the Deep reflect on the water. Danū is farther in the distance as we sail to open sea toward Oleanu.

"Time to go," I say as I get up. He grabs me by the waist and pulls me to sit on his lap. He takes my lips and kisses me deeply.

"Let's get out of here," he agrees.

Out in the quarterdeck, I ready the portal. All I have left to do is add the water from the Cup to the ship. Nkella and I bump into each other as we both reach for the wheel.

"Oh." I snap my hand back from the wheel. "Sorry. You're my captain after all, aren't you?" I give him a lopsided smile.

But a wicked one crosses his face.

I shrug modestly, "I was only borrowing the title."

"Kh." He pushes me back, and forces my hands to take the wheel. His face presses against mine, and he whispers, "Watching you steer my ship is the most stimulating thing I have ever witnessed."

I bite my lip, his breath drawing out goosebumps on my neck.

His hand grabs my hair from behind and pulls, exposing my neck for him to bite. A moan escapes me as his hand wanders up my blouse.

The ship speeds up since we've enacted the potion, and Nkella spins me around, taking the wheel behind him. He kisses me deeply on the lips, then down to my neck.

His lips wander down my blouse, as he rips it open. My skin tingles all over as his kisses explore my sensitive skin.

His wings erupt from his back and wrap around us protectively. My mind explodes in a million directions, and I'm swept away in his taste. The feeling of him this close to me. Knowing that we're going home together. Never to leave each other's side.

I release a moan as I wrap my legs around his waist. Our clothes have already been undone.

He stares up at me, his eyes glowing and his fangs showing. His chest rises up and down, and the most mischievous grin sends a chill up my spine.

"How brave are you feeling, my neyuro?"

My eyes widen as he sinks down to my region. "What do you mea — Oh!" A moan rips from my throat as the fork of his devilish tongue takes my sensitive part in between it and rubs. A guttural sound escapes him as he tastes me, licking me up and down, building up my pleasure.

The ship tilts all the way to the side, and I don't know if I want to scream out of fear or from pleasure. I can't see from inside his wings, but somehow I don't care. I moan again, my entire body being filled with an intense sensation. He reaches up, without leaving what he's doing, and cups one of my breasts, squeezing me gently, then a little rougher.

My hand grabs at his hair. I arch back and now I can't hear myself moaning over the sound of the ship and the waves.

He lifts his head, and a delicious smile greets me. I stare down at him, my chest rising up and down.

"I am not finished with you yet, roé yani."

The look in his eye sends me falling fast.

"Remember the day you ran from me in Dempu Yuni?" he whispers.

"Uh huh."

"Running from me won't be an option anymore. I have you now, gembella. Forever and always."

I can't help the smirk reach my eyes. Even though he just called me his prisoner. In this form, I kinda like it...

Taking my hair from behind, he arches my neck and kisses me gently, pressing into me as he does. We both moan into each other's mouths as he stretches me wide.

The ship whirls, as we get transported from the Deep to living world. But we're spinning even faster as pleasure courses through every fiber of my body. Nkella has blocked any escape from me falling out with his wings, and his eyes glow a delicious crimson as he peers down at me while his waist thrusts deep into me.

Maybe one day we'll be in a bed like a normal couple. And not in a life-threatening situation.

My back arches against the wheel as he moves, faster and faster. Our moans filling our ears over the thrashing of the waves, and the spinning of the ship. We get lost in each other until my spirit is screaming and my body clenches, pleasure reaching me all over. Nkella kisses me softly, his body shaking as he finishes.

I take his bottom lip and bite it gently. "Take the wheel while I get cleaned up real quick." He smirks as I walk past him to the cabin.

I open the sink and let the dead water run for a few minutes until clear water comes out of the faucet. I splash water over my face and my body, taking a bit of a bird bath. The ship jerks forward, and I almost slam my face against the wall. We must be back already.

I can't wait to take a real bath. With Nkella. And do what we just did all over again.

To think soon we'll be in a real bed, probably in the castle for the first night before going back to our place at Dempu Yuni. For the time being, I forget about going see the Empress and the war that awaits us. I take the towel and dry off, slipping my clothes back on before heading back out to the quarterdeck.

Nkella's not at the wheel. Red hues still shimmer over the waters, and bodies hang from the surface. How are we still in the Deep?

My brows furrow as I walk down the steps to find Nkella with his sword pointed at a man whose back faces me. The man glances over his shoulder, a cruel and sadistic smirk on his face.

I take a deep breath and hold it as I walk down. "No," is all I can manage to say.

"My vicious one, it is so good to see you." He waves his hand, and Nkella's sword flies out of his grip, crashing against the floorboards. "You didn't think I would let you out of my abode without me finding you first, did you?"

"What do you want?" There's an edge to my voice.

His disgusting smile widens as he watches me walk around him to Nkella.

"That depends. How badly do you want your captain out of the Deep?"

"He drank from the Cup. Not even the serpent can keep him here. He can leave."

He shakes his index finger and makes a tsking sound with his tongue. "I say if he can leave. I am Death. I hold the contract. The serpent was only a guard." My lips part, and he guffaws. "It was comical watching you think that by killing the serpent, you would release the tortured. Kill the Empress, and the tortured will be freed, daí?" He shakes his head. "That much is obvious."

I swallow.

"She asked you what you wanted," Nkella demands. "Say it."

Tetalla glances at him and frowns. "Your fun is over," he says. Then he looks back at me. "You want him freed? Submit."

My breath leaves me. "No..."

"Daí?" Nkella's eyes widen. Panic is coursing through his features as he pieces things together.

Tetalla takes a few steps toward me, and Nkella moves in front of him in an attempt to block him. But this doesn't bother Death. He bypasses him and fixes his stare into my eyes so I have to look at him. "I will allow the prince to leave the Deep, if you, Soren, promise me your betrothal and submit to me. You will break your vows to him. And live with me in Danū as my wife."

The blood drains from my face.

Nkella's eyes flash red, and so do Tetalla's. He tilts his head at Nkella and smirks.

"You are a newborn devil and will lose against me." A menacing chuckle leaves his lips. "You couldn't command the royal flames, *prince*, because they answer only to *me*. Blood won't be enough. You are nothing. I am the king of Danū."

Nkella's face pales.

This fucking bastard.

"And if you accept my offer, vicious one, Nkella will be free to roam, I will not keep him in a dungeon, I swear it. You have my word."

My hands are shaking.

"No. She will never submit to you." Nkella rushes to me and takes my hands. "I will stay," he says between breaths. His eyes stare deeply into mine. Both our hearts are beating fast. He shuts his eyes tightly and opens them. "I will stay, and I'll wait for you." He caresses my cheek. "You are my aovate. Light of my flame. My princess."

My breath catches.

He'd stay here and wait an eternity for me if he had to. In the Deep. Escaping minotaurs and reapers. Living with the tortured. Away from me forever, until I die and come here?

"You have one minute to decide, Soren, or I will close the Deep, and you will be forced back by the Cups' water, and the prince will remain here forever."

My heart beats loudly in my chest, and reluctantly, with all the regret in the world, I let go of Nkella's hands. "I won't leave you here," I whisper.

Disbelief flashes across his face. "Do not do this. I don't want this." His voice turns harsh, and I shake. "You are my aovate, *not his*. I would rather wait an eternity here for you to come back to me than for you to submit to someone else."

"Nkella—I..." I shake my head. I want to tell him that I won't wait that long, but I can't find the words. A tear runs down my cheek. "I do love you," I whisper. My heart wants to erupt into a million pieces, after finally admitting it to him.

His features darken and his voice lowers into a growl. "You vowed."

"I'm sorry," I mouth. His eyes narrow with hatred and betrayal.

I turn to Tetalla. “I accept.”

THANK YOU

Thank you so much for reading *The Serpent's Deep!* I hope you enjoyed Soren's journey to the Deep as much as I loved writing it. Watch out for book four of *Chronicles of Tarotland*, coming out soon.

If you would like to receive updates on all my new releases, please join my mailing list at http://killianwolf.com/. You will also get access to my books at a discounted launch price when they first come out, along with an exclusive sneak peek or short story just for you.

GET IN TOUCH!

Come say hi in my Facebook Reader group. In there, every day is Halloween!

facebook.com/groups/killianwolf

Please feel free to get in touch with me.

Website: http://killianwolf.com/

facebook.com/killianwolfauthor

x.com/killian_wolf22

instagram.com/killian_wolf_author

pinterest.com/killianwolf22

goodreads.com/killianwolf

amazon.com/Killian-Wolf/e/B07WHFB8FW

bookbub.com/authors/killian-wolf

tiktok.com/@killian_wolf_author

patreon.com/killianwolfauthor

FREE BOOK

Scan to get this free book and sign up for my mailing list.

"Don't kill" is a no-brainer. But what if it's for a good reason?

My name is Harold and my family is cursed. When my aunt made the tough call to pull my mother from life support, she enacted the curse of the Frost Giants, freezing herself from the inside.

To save her, all I had to do was step through the portal, but one wrong move sent me flying off to Tarotland, a place where the tarot cards have come to life. The good news is I still have my runes. The bad news? Magicians are illegal here. Not to mention, I haven't exactly come into my powers yet. . . and I can't get the portal to reopen.

My salvation is a breathtaking native. She makes me act like a Fool, but she also told me about a sword that cuts through any doorway. Power doesn't come without sacrifice, though. With a mysterious predator out for blood, and my name on every wanted poster, who knows if we'll make it before my aunt breathes her final breath?

ACKNOWLEDGMENTS

WOW! I have to say that plot wise. This book was a brain teaser for me. I will be honest when I say that I almost threw the whole book out about five times! However, I'm glad I stuck to my guns and followed through because that climax between Soren and Nkella truly paid off after waiting for so long! (IFYKYK)

That being said, this book wouldn't be what it is without the help of some exceptional individuals.

A special thanks to Christian Thalman for continuing to work on this amazing language with me. I feel that the way the Ipani language has evolved has added a certain depth to the characters and their culture, making it so much more real. There is a little inside joke within these pages, where Soren thinks she's saying the right thing, but because the translation potion doesn't work fully well (it can't translate the full meaning of idioms), she says something quite literal that has the whole crew laughing. I couldn't do that without you, so thank you!

To my critique partner Christina, you have been my rock from the beginning to the end of this book. Thank you for constantly sanity-checking me, and for helping me develop the relationship between two characters when I knew what I wanted to say, but didn't know how to put into words — you helped me brainstorm. I always look forward to your hilarious and helpful comments, and cannot wait to work with you again on the next one — especially after another heart-wrenching ending. Seriously, thank you for believing in me and my books.

To Alice, your belief in me and my books has become my light at the end of the tunnel. If I ever feel like my work sucks, I think of how much you enjoy it, and it gets me through my writing. You're awesome, and I can't wait to continue working together!

Mom, you continue to inspire me. Thank you for always believing in me and my books. If not for you, I probably wouldn't have discovered the possibility of sneaking o# into other dimensions through books. And turning that power into writing.

To my husband, your patience and support mean more to me than you could ever know. I promise, one day this will all be worth it.

To Cali Ravenwing, words cannot express how thankful I am to have you as a reader. Your support has shined a light when I was feeling like quitting. Thank you for being my cheerleading and spreading the news about my books, and for your inspiration on a new special character, Sapphire. I hope that bunny makes her way to our world soon!

Lastly, a huge THANK YOU to my readers, especially the ones making it all the way here. I hope you enjoyed reading these characters as much as I loved writing them, and don't worry, there's more to come.

ABOUT THE AUTHOR

Killian Wolf is a Miami, Florida, native who enjoys pirates, rum, and skulls as much as she loves writing about dark magick and sorcerers. She holds a Bachelor of Arts degree in Cultural Anthropology and Sociology and a Master of Science in Environmental Archaeology and Palaeoeconomy.

Killian writes books about obtaining magickal powers and stepping into other dimensions. She lives in Florida with her husband, a tornado of a cat, and the most timid snake you'd ever meet. When she isn't writing, you might find her at an archaeological dig, rock climbing, or sipping on dark spiced rum while working on a painting.

GLOSSARY

IPANI VOCABULARY

á: Sound often used by natives of Sāgirang, used to represent a sound made in speech in a variety of situations, often used to ask for something to be repeated or explained or to elicit agreement.

Aō: [a.ˈo] world spirit

Āngaraeke: Yeti

Āngasoe: Minotaur

Aovate: (begisi aovate) [be.ˈɰi.si a.o.ˈva.te] soulmate, destined partner (lit. betrothed by the hand of the world spirit)

Bancha: [ˈbaɲ.ca] empty, free of, lacking, fool, idiot, stupid

Bayoa: turning light in the sky, northern lights/Nautilus

Daí: Sound often used by natives of Danū, used to represent a sound made in speech in a variety of situations, often used to ask for something to be repeated or explained or to elicit agreement.

Daekente: With horns

Diwe: Rabbit

Drakon: Ancient Greek dragon with a serpen- tine body. Can both swim and #y, and pop in and out of the Aō dimension.

Engi: Thankful

Garisi: drinkable potion, as opposed to explosive potion

gembella: [gem.'bel.la] from gembe, prisoner, inmate

Gichang: currency, money

gichang rīrō: money from Danu, pressed ruby gichachi: mark

guyuti: [gu.'ju.ti] shrivel-ear, derogatory term used to describe a human

Hn: A sound made by an Ipani when thinking out loud.

Helāni: Descendants of the Ancient Greeks who crossed the portal with the Moera

hū raku (raku): [hu: 'ɾa.ku] poison gas: poisonous breath

iá: [i.'a] hailing; hello, ahoy, greetings

Iéle: [i.'e.le] moon

Imboe: [im.boe] Ancient Greek-Ipani creole spoken in Ipa.

Indakepoa: [ˌin.da.ke.'poa̯] translation potion, liquorice

Ipani: [i.'pa.ni] of the World; the language of the World. Ipani (singular and plural) Ipononchi: [i.po.'noɲ.ci] cookie, pastry (lit.:little baked)

Pa chae: I love you

Kaehante: well prepared with a paddle (liter-al), or armed/prepared ($guratively).

Kaonī: Blcksmith

Kenjō: [keɲ.'ɟoː] (Open Sky)

Ko: Negative, soft no

Koj: [koej] No, none, no! don't!

Mei: Sound often used by natives of Oleanu, used to represent a sound made in speech in a variety of situations, often used to ask for something to be repeated or explained or to elicit agreement.

Mikiroro: Black palm tree, the Danū crest Moera: The Ancient Greek Fates

Mūhī: [ˌmu,ˈhi:] footprint [in the] sand Muse: [ˈmu.se] spider

Nangraku: [naŋ.ˈɾa.ku] poison tooth Neyuro: [ne.yuro] brave

Nkella: [ŋ.ˈkel.la] Hope, lifting, rising; name of Captain Nkella Mkiroro

Ouma: [ˈow.ma] magic; magical

Oumala: [ow.ˈma.la] mage, practitioner of magic, magic user

Rikorō: [ʻdik.oro] soul thief, plant

Rikwa: [ˈdik.wa] thief

Ruh: [ɾuo̯] wolf

saechi: peak berry, volcanic berry

Uoko yani: My viscous one

Tetalla: [te.ʼtal.la]: habitual dead-maker

Utwa: [ˈu.twa] scout, spy

PLACES

Ahan Doro: [a.ˌhan ˈdo.ɾo] «black forest»

Chong Alēla: [ˈcoŋ a.ˈle:.la] «ghost mist»

Danū: "Six suns." Farthest Southeastern Island. Currently called Pentacles, Danū by the rebels.

Dempu Yuni: trading post island

Dempu: foot; (i) standing, located; (i) river mouth;

Yuni: transparent, pure, clear

Ipa: [ˈee.pa] the global ocean, the World Naó: Greek Temple

Oe Nū: [ˌoe̯ˈnu:] «sacred water» (Ipani temple in Oleanu)

Oleanu: "Highwater" Island to the East.Currently called Wands, Oleanu by the rebels.

Pari Eitu: [ˌpa.ɾi ˈej.tu] «listening earth» (large ritual temple ruins)

Piupeki: "Steelrock" Island farthest to the North. Currently called Swords, Piupeki

by the rebels.

Ruta Helāni: Prefect's Tower

Rutavenye: "Cloudwall" The Floating island, location of The Tower

Uáo Siseli: Serpent's Deep

Upipurang: [ˌu.pi.pu.ˈɾaŋ] «Brokenhead» (castle ruins)

PHRASES

Ipani translations:

Roē yani: Light of my flame

Jalo kum a waoroang sa'y ā chie: "I caught them more than once."

Movi pa a l'le'v ekū pani, korū ko teteng ero en n'upite pamoe: "But you knew your brother, he never gave himself fully to anyone."

Movi chu a n'na'g e teng kunte yalo moé pamoe: "But it was the most I had ever seen him give."

Ko saora hevi: "The crotch does not testify."

www.ingramcontent.com/pod-product-compliance
Lightning Source LLC
Chambersburg PA
CBHW030535310726
48979CB00010B/1915/J

9781951140212